MY NAME IS LIGHT

MY NAME
IS LIGHT

ELSA OSORIO

TRANSLATED FROM THE SPANISH
BY CATHERINE JAGOE

BLOOMSBURY

Published by Bloomsbury, New York and London
Distributed to the trade by Holtzbrinck Publishers

Library of Congress Cataloging-in-Publication Data has been applied for.

ISBN 1-58234-182-6

First U.S. Edition 2003

1 3 5 7 9 10 8 6 4 2

Typeset by Hewer Text Ltd, Edinburgh
Printed in Great Britain by Clays Limited, St Ives plc

PROLOGUE
1998

L UZ, RAMIRO AND their son Juan landed at Barajas airport in
Madrid at seven o'clock on a sweltering Thursday morning. In the
taxi on their way to the hotel, Luz told them about the Plaza Mayor and all
those mysterious narrow backstreets with bars that stay open all hours and
haughty-looking women whose hands flutter like birds when they dance.
'You'll love the flamenco, Ramiro. I'll take you to *Retiro* Park, Juan.'

Maybe Luz wanted to convince them (or herself, momentarily) that
they were merely in Spain for a visit and not to support her in the quest
she had been swept up in ever since the idea first dawned on her, when
Juan was born. Because it was while she was in the clinic that the
suspicion had formed, and she had been unable to shake it off afterwards.
In between changing the baby's nappies and burping him and lulling him
to sleep, she had doggedly checked out facts and talked to people and
asked questions and poked around and investigated and ferreted things
out. And this is where it had led them. To Madrid.

That morning, while Juan and Ramiro were asleep, she had called
directory enquiries and got Carlos Squirru's number. So he was still alive,
he really did exist, and he was out there, in the same city as her. Her heart
started thudding as if it were about to escape. She dialled the number
from the phone box in the hotel. A woman's voice with a Spanish accent
said that they weren't there and to please leave a message after the beep.
Luz hung up quickly. She tried to put a face to that voice, but she
couldn't. Was that Carlos's wife? Would he have told her about his past?

She decided that she would put off calling him until the next day.
Ramiro and Juan deserved one peaceful day having fun and wandering

1

around, as she'd been promising them ever since they got there. She knew she ought to relax and take a break, but her anxiety kept resurfacing as they strolled through the city, laughing and playing with Juan. How would she broach the subject? She'd have to be brief and to the point. Carlos wouldn't refuse to meet her if she said she had a message from Liliana. She just had to find the right words. Ramiro offered to help, as he had done so many times ever since her search began.

'Let's talk it over tonight,' he said.

But she couldn't wait until then.

'Please try and understand, I want to get it over with, so I can stop wondering whether it's him or not, and what he's going to say to me. How he'll react.'

Ramiro just shrugged. This was Luz's thing, and it was up to her to decide how to deal with it.

Carlos answered the phone. 'Hello.' Luz was so nervous that she had to grip the receiver with both hands to stop herself from hanging up. Ramiro watched her from the doorway.

'I'd like to speak to Carlos Squirru, please.'

'Speaking.' His accent was so Spanish that Luz thought to herself that she'd been an idiot to get so worked up; it was perfectly possible there was a Spaniard with the same name. 'Who are you?'

The way he said it convinced her that she'd made a mistake and that he couldn't possibly be from Argentina, but she wasn't going to hang up until she was absolutely sure.

'My name is Luz, Luz Iturbe. You don't know me, and you may not be the Carlos Squirru I'm looking for. I got your phone number from directory enquiries in Madrid, but maybe the Carlos Squirru I'm after lives somewhere else – I'm not sure.'

She could kick herself for sounding so muddled. She'd have to begin again. She cleared her throat. The silence on the other end was not encouraging. Ramiro kept coming and going from Juan's room and she could hear a child crying down the other end of the line.

'Hang on a second,' Carlos said, and in the distance, 'Montse, can you see to the baby?'

'I'm sorry, I think I've made a mistake, I thought . . .'

'Are you from Argentina too?'

'Too,' he had said. 'Too!'

'Yes, are you? Because the Carlos Squirru I'm looking for is Argentinian.'

'Yes, I am, although I try and forget it.' He laughed. 'Tell me now,' he said flirtatiously, 'is this man you're looking for handsome, gifted and charming? If so, it must be me, unless it turns out to be one of the other five or six Squirrus scattered around Europe.'

Carlos was having fun, probably sensing Luz's awkwardness. She'd gone over what she would say to him so many times and yet now she couldn't remember any of it. He seemed friendly and pleasant, so why couldn't she get a single sentence out?

'I wanted to talk to you . . . about Liliana.'

After a long silence, he replied, in a harsh voice, 'Liliana who?'

'I don't know, I don't know her surname, you see – that's one of the reasons I want to talk to you. I spoke to Miriam López a few months ago and she gave me your name. Miriam . . .'

'Who?'

'Miriam López.'

'I don't know her.'

'No, I know that. She tried to find you in the phone book years ago. But she was looking under the wrong surname, she thought it began with "e", as in "Esquirru", with the "e" at the beginning. It was me who realised that Squirru began with "s".' None of this was brief or to the point or clear. She was ruining everything; she wished she could call Ramiro over to do the talking for her. 'Miriam told me that Carlos Squirru was Liliana's boyfriend about twenty years ago.' It had come out all wrong, but she'd said it and now he wasn't responding. She couldn't even hear him breathing. 'Did you have a girlfriend called Liliana?'

'Who are you?'

'I'm . . . My name is Luz. I've been looking everywhere for information on this recently, but I don't have all the facts. It's difficult to explain it to you over the phone. Could we meet?' The silence grew too long to bear. 'Liliana wanted to tell you something before she . . . Please, can't we see each other?'

'Do you know the Café Comercial?'

'No. But tell me where it is and I'll get there.'

'On the Glorieta de Bilbao. In an hour's time.'

'All right.' She felt a surge of mingled joy and fear. 'How will we recognise each other? I don't know what you look like. I'm blonde, I'll be wearing a green blouse . . . and I'll carry a book.'

'OK. Bye.'

Ramiro hugged her as she hung up. Luz pulled away from him in tears.

'I made such a mess of everything – did you hear? He never admitted he was Liliana's boyfriend, but if he agreed to see me he must be, don't you think?'

Ramiro said he would give Juan his lunch and wait for her there. 'Ring me if you need me.'

Luz got out of the taxi on the corner of the Glorieta de Bilbao. She asked some teenagers the way to the Café Comercial and crossed the road. She felt as if her feet were weightless, as if her whole body were floating and might come crashing down at any moment. The unbelievable dry heat of Madrid in July engulfed her as if it were trying to swallow her alive. 'Heatwave,' the taxi driver had said, and Luz thought it was the first time she had really appreciated the meaning of the word.

There were a lot of people sitting at tables outside the café. She realised she couldn't distinguish any of them: they were all just meaningless shapes. She stood and waited a while, clutching her book conspicuously in one hand. If Carlos was there, he would have come up to her by now. She'd be better off going in to get a cold drink, going back outside if he didn't show up soon.

The air-conditioned cool inside was an instant relief. Which of those men sitting alone could he be? She sat down and glanced around the café. That man at the next table was probably forty-something. But then, she didn't know how old Carlos was. The man was looking at her, but no, it couldn't be him, he wouldn't smile at her like that.

Luz ordered a Coke with a slice of lemon and kept her eyes fixed on the door. Carlos came up from behind and walked round to face her.

'Carlos?' Luz asked, wondering whether to shake his hand or not. He sat down opposite her, his only sign of assent, and her hand dropped to the table.

Neither of them seemed to want to begin. Carlos opened and closed his mouth at the same time as Luz. Their mirrored discomfort made them both smile.

'I really have no idea what this is all about. I don't know who you are, or who this Miriam is, or why you've been looking for me. You can't have known Liliana, you're too young.'

The waiter brought her Coke and Carlos ordered a whisky.

'She told Miriam López her name.'

'Was Miriam in the detention centre?'

'Not exactly.'

'Well, where then?'

'At her house. Liliana was in Miriam's house when she told her who she was.'

Luz saw something that was either desperation or impatience on Carlos's face. She was not going to make a fool of herself the way she had over the phone.

'Carlos, I'm going to tell you everything I know. I've been working on this for quite some time. It was difficult because I didn't know Liliana's surname. What was it?'

'Are you a journalist? Have you come to interview me? What do you want? Are you working on an article or a book? I haven't lived in Argentina for years and it doesn't mean anything to me any more, do you understand? Nothing.' An edge had come into his voice. 'Who gave you my name? Who is this Miriam you're talking about? And when was Liliana in her house? That's just not possible.'

Luz took a sip of her Coke, as if to give herself time before answering.

'I'm not a journalist. I've come to see you, not to interview you. I wanted to meet you. There are a lot of things I need to know, especially from you. Miriam López gave me your name, and I'll tell you who she is if you give me a chance.' Luz found herself responding in the same irritated tone. 'Just let me do the talking for now. You can say what you want later on, if you feel like it.' Her voice cracked and she tried to steady herself. 'And if you don't want to say anything, that's fine too. All right? I just want you to listen to me.'

The appearance of the waiter stopped her. Carlos took his time before replying.

'I'm sorry if I was rude. It's just the shock. Perhaps I'm trying to avoid the subject, or maybe I'm afraid of it. It's very painful for me, you know. Extremely painful.'

Carlos looked the other way and Luz realised for the first time not only that he was good-looking, but that she liked him. It was incredible the way he glanced aside like that – it was exactly what she did when she wanted to hide her feelings. But she couldn't allow herself to watch him and work out what he felt, and neither could she blurt out the one sentence which would instantly explain why she was there, the thing she wasn't even sure she dared say.

'Who was Miriam?'

'Miriam López met Liliana in rather bizarre circumstances – you might even call them tragic – in mid-November 1976.'

Luz wondered where to begin her story: with the baby born in the clinic in Paraná, or the other one in the hospital in Buenos Aires. Perhaps it would be best to begin at the beginning, with the strange and powerful alliance that had grown up between Miriam and Liliana. But she just told him things as they came into her head, without explaining why she knew so many details about both of them. The truth was, he knew very little, probably even less than Liliana had told Miriam. And nothing, of course, about Liliana's last days – Luz's first ones. If anyone could help her to fill in the blanks it was Carlos. But he was so taken aback by the story that unfolded that for the first hour he said virtually nothing, offering neither questions nor comments.

Eventually he asked if she wanted something else to drink, and signalled to the waiter. They both felt they needed a break, to slow down, steady their nerves.

'I'll have another Coke, please. You know, you sound so Spanish,' she said, uttering the first thing that came into her head, trying to make small talk. 'Your accent, the words you use.'

'Oh, my accent comes back when I talk to Argentinians. But I don't do that too often, thank goodness. I keep away from them. In fact, I hate Argentinians and Argentina.'

He didn't observe the anger that flared in Luz's eyes.

She looked at her watch.

'I need to make a phone call – I don't want Ramiro to get worried. He's my husband,' she added.

'You're married already?' Why did he sound so surprised? He didn't know the first thing about her.

'Yes, and I've got a son. He's called Juan and he's one and a half.'

Alone at the table, Carlos allowed himself to wonder about something that had been nagging at him for a while but which he had been unwilling or unable to take in at the time. It was when Luz slipped up, using the expression 'save me' instead of 'save her'. When he had said something derogatory about Miriam, Luz had reacted violently.

'That bitch, as you call her, risked her neck to save me.' She had stopped trying to be polite.

What if the words 'save me' had not been a mistake, or a reference to some other time when the woman had saved her? Carlos wondered. But Luz had glossed over it and carried on talking about Liliana and the baby girl. How could she know so much? And why couldn't he just come out and ask her?

He didn't want to betray his suspicions, and decided to put off asking her as long as he could. He would just let her tell it her own way. If what he suspected was true, that is – there might be another explanation.

When Luz came back, Carlos suggested that perhaps they should go and have dinner somewhere.

But neither of them was hungry. How could they leave without knowing the whole story?

'Please go on.'

Luz swallowed and continued, until at last, she wasn't sure how, she told him the truth.

Carlos never did ask his question, but when he took her hands in his and gazed at her with tears in his eyes, Luz knew for certain that he recognised her.

When they left the Café Comercial, Carlos had a sudden urge to put his arm round Luz's shoulders, but he didn't dare. His arm moved halfway involuntarily and then stopped in mid-air.

'May I?'

Luz gave a faint smile and nodded. They walked along together for ten minutes or so, commenting on the streets, still buzzing with life even at that time of night, and chatting about Madrid and the trip she'd taken after she left school. They tacitly agreed to avoid anything that would spoil the pleasure of just being able to walk side by side for the first time.

Carlos told her that he'd specialised as a paediatrician in Barcelona, where he married Montse, and that he had been living in Madrid for eight years. Luz said that she was still a long way from finishing her degree in architecture. 'I got behind when Juan was born, and then I got involved in . . . all this.'

An odd shyness stopped him hugging Luz when she used the words 'all this' to describe the enormous lengths she had gone to in order to find him.

At the door of the hotel, Carlos stood facing Luz and they looked at one another. Luz turned her head, as if she were suddenly intrigued by the English couple who were on their way in at that moment. Carlos took her face in his hands and turned it towards him.

'I didn't say this before, but you're very beautiful . . . and very brave.' Luz couldn't speak; she was on the verge of tears. 'What's going to happen now, Luz? Or is it Lili; I don't know what to call you.'

'Luz, I've always been called Luz. I like my name. It's difficult to say this to you, but it wasn't all bad – there's my name, for example, Luz. It means "light". I knew I had to shed light into all the dark corners of this story, to find out the truth. I couldn't stop – I didn't care about the risk I was running emotionally. I can only imagine how hard this conversation must have been on you, but it wasn't easy for me either. I didn't know how you'd react or whether I'd even find you . . . and I don't know what will happen to me if you leave now and I never see you again.'

'Ortiz.'

'What?'

'Her name was Liliana Ortiz. There's a lot I have to tell you, too.

Besides, there are some decisions we need to make together. Don't you think? The trials are going on right now in Madrid,' he said, suddenly animated. 'Do you think Miriam would agree to come and testify?'

Before Luz could answer, Carlos kissed her on the cheek, and then turned his other cheek towards her.

'The Spanish not the Argentinian way. They give two kisses here, not one. Go and get some rest. I'll ring you tomorrow.'

PART ONE
1976

ONE

TONIGHT I'M GOING to show Animal how pretty the room looks with the new wallpaper and all the stuff I bought. Will he be pissed off with me for spending all that money doing up the baby's room and not on what he told me? I don't think so. He's not as bad as all that, in spite of his name. He might act tough, but his heart's in the right place, otherwise he wouldn't have been able to understand what I'm going through, would he? He was the only one I could talk to about it, and he didn't laugh at me or anything, he understood. He said it made sense, it was human nature, and there was even a tear in his eye. Kindness goes a lot further with me than a wad of dollar bills and, even though you wouldn't know it at first, Animal's a kind man. A big softy. Otherwise why would he be doing everything he can to get me what I want?

'They used to call him Animal because of his strength,' Luz told Carlos. 'When they went out on a raid, they would ring the bell and if no one opened the door, they'd say, "Go on, Animal," and then he'd take a few steps back and charge at the door so hard he'd break it down.'

I say to him, 'Be careful, don't hurt me,' and he goes, 'You know there's no door I can't break down,' and that makes me laugh, and then he sticks it in a little bit, and I say, 'You animal,' but I'm giggling. I'm not letting him have his way with me just because he's strong – it's because I can tell that he loves me and he wants me. He starts breathing heavily. 'My princess, that's my princess, my pussy-cat, my pet, my missus.' My missus, he calls me as he strokes my bum and that turns me on – I'm a silly cow I know, but when he does that, there's not a door in my body that can stand up to him.

It's not just in bed he says it. The other day he introduced me as his fiancée to that skinny guy with the moustache. He really does want us to get married. I used to think there was no way I ever would, unless I won the lucky dip like Bibi and landed myself a man with loads and loads of money, a big businessman or a famous football player or a boxer, someone like that, so I could have a house with a pool and servants and a nice garden and cars and stuff, you name it. But there you go – a girl doesn't go winning the lottery every day, and for the moment this will do. He's not rich or famous but he's going to get me what I want. He can pull a few strings, even if he's not well off. He says he's been earning a bit more recently and in a few months' time, when whatever it is they're up to is over, he'll be rolling in it. In any case, if he gets me the baby, I'm better off being married. They don't give kids away to just anybody, you have to be a proper family; we'll have to get married and in church and everything. Although church weddings have always seemed a bit of a waste of time to me.

'Do you think I'll have to go to confession?' I asked him the other night. But I never even heard what he said, because I was wetting myself with laughter just picturing it. 'Can you imagine the priest's face when I tell him how many men I've slept with?'

He got a bit angry then, because he'd rather not think about that, he'd rather not acknowledge what I've done. I mean, look what I was doing when I met him. He's a bit of a thug, but he's a good, kind man is Animal. I've got everything all ready: the room and the baby clothes, I even bought some nursery rhymes on tape and I'm learning them off by heart, because he said it won't be long now until he brings the baby home. And he's going to be precious, or she is, maybe it'll be a girl, just like her mum. I hope she'll be less of a slut than me, I said to Animal, and he laughed at first, but then he stopped, and said I wasn't a slut or he wouldn't be marrying me. His wife's no slut, except in bed; of course in bed he wants me to be a bloody nymphomaniac, but none of that outside the bedroom. 'And don't go wiggling your arse like that, you're going to be Mrs Pitiotti soon.' He says it like I was going to be Lady Muck herself. And I pretend I'm thrilled to bits, because I want to keep him happy. Anyway, where am I going to go wiggling my arse now I don't go out any more? I'm not on the game any more: no fashion shows, no parties, no clients, no nothing.

'A call-girl! Liliana can't possibly have confided in a prostitute,' Carlos exclaimed.

'What's so terrible about that?' Luz replied indignantly. 'In any case, by the time Liliana met her, Miriam had given it up.'

Ever since he promised to bring me a baby, I just lie around day-dreaming, listening to music, watching TV and shopping. To tell you the truth, it's a bit boring, but I keep saying that everything's wonderful and that I really look forward to him coming home, and us having dinner together, and going out once in a while, whenever he can, because I want him to be happy with me and keep his promise. He says he's taking care of the baby's mother so she'll have a healthy pregnancy. He won't let them do anything to her because 'We're not making war on little kids.' He always says that.

I don't know what that girl did, he doesn't say, he just tells me she doesn't want the baby, and that anyway she can't keep it in prison. She must have got pregnant by accident. She's a pretty little thing apparently, sexy as anything. He gets this gleam in his eye when he talks about her. The other day I said to him, 'I hope you haven't been screwing her.'

'How can you say that when she's carrying your kid? How can you think a thing like that?'

Well of course, how can he screw her if she's eight months gone?

He sees to it that she gets good food, because apparently the food in there is really terrible.

'They used to give her special food and they didn't torture her like the others.'

'Don't you think it must have been torture just being there and knowing that all that care and special treatment was just so they could steal her child?' Carlos's voice was dark with hatred. 'They'd go and pick out a surrogate mother, as if it were a human breeding plant! It's horrific. Perverse.'

'Yes, it's terrible. But at least they didn't torture her physically, with the electric prod.'

The other day I made some nice croquettes for him to take to that girl. I feel sorry for her; when I think about her I feel bad. If she's so young, she can't have done anything too awful. What is she in prison for – has she killed somebody? 'Look,' I said to Animal, 'if I had the choice, right this minute, I wouldn't bat an eyelid, I'd kill that bastard of a sales rep

15

who raped me when I was fourteen. It's just, back then, it would never have occurred to me. Sometimes things happen that make you feel like murdering someone, and there are people out there who deserve it, like that man. If I could get my hands on him, I'd kill him, Animal, I swear I would. Did she kill someone who raped her? Because if she did, it's not her fault. If men had to go through something like that they'd have some idea what it feels like to be a woman.'

He says that's got nothing to do with it, that I haven't got a clue, there are these foreign ideas creeping in and destroying the country, this is a war, and they're going to bring back law and order and hunt down all those subversives and communists and murderers and terrorists one by one – he starts gritting his teeth as he says it and he looks scary as hell – until they've wiped out every last one of them. They're going to rid the country of that scum. But I still don't know what that girl did. When I catch him off guard, I'll get him talking – I'm an old hand at that, and sometimes he does let something slip, like when he said he can't understand how she got mixed up in all of this, because she's from a posh family, she went to private school. Maybe it was because of the bloke she was with.

'Her husband?'

'What do you mean, husband? You think that sort of girl gets married? No, they just shack up like animals.'

'We never got married. We were underground,' Carlos said.

For the first time since they'd started talking, Carlos had acknowledged that the story Luz was telling him was his own.

I didn't dare remind him that we'd shacked up together too, and that I'd lived with lots of different people in my time and so had he, because Animal's a bit funny that way, he gets carried away with what he's saying and then all of a sudden you'd think the two of us were just perfect, a lah-di-dah married couple who'd been together for ever, and that I was never on the game, and that he was never some snot-nosed kid scrimping and saving on his corporal's pay until his luck turned when the military took over and he started making some extra cash on the side. Now he's a sergeant. But he's still on the same piss-poor salary as before, I asked him about it. I used to earn more for a couple of parties than he does in a whole month, and I'm better off not telling him how much I got paid when . . . but he knows anyway, he knows perfectly well because he paid it once himself, that much and more. Annette used to charge them the earth to sleep with me. I wonder where he got the money from, on what he earns? From his savings, he told me. He paid an arm and a leg for that first date with me. I wonder if he's going with me because of the money? No, he can't be, otherwise he wouldn't have talked me into leaving the job. If he remembers how much it cost him that first time, he ought to feel like royalty whenever he sleeps with me. But no – he just takes it all for granted, because we love each other. As a matter of fact, he acts as if I struck it lucky when I met him, and not the other way round, which pisses me off a bit. After all, here he is living in my flat, something he never dreamed of doing. He tried to make me stay at his place at first, but there was no way I was going to live in that pigsty, so I said very nicely that since I was going to be home all day, I'd be better off with my things – my balcony to sunbathe on, my records, my mirrors, my ornaments and everything – and that moving would just be too much of a hassle.

'*Miriam was renting a flat in the Recoleta district, on Ayacucho Street. She'd paid a year and a half's rent in advance out of her savings, so as not to have to bother with the deposit. Apparently she was earning a lot at that time. She talked so much about that flat, I feel as if I know it. I once went up to the door, I don't know why, perhaps so I could visualise the place she'd talked about.*'

I'm always polite – I know how to treat men – but I'm not stupid enough to thinks it's natural for him to be living here, on the north side, sitting on fancy upholstered settees, in a place with silk curtains. I couldn't believe I was living here myself when I first moved in. At least that's something Annette did do for me, without knowing it. That bitch helped me in a way after all, because the first time I went to visit her, she promised she wouldn't rest until I had a place like hers.

'*Apparently the woman who set up the parties and the clients for her had a really elegant flat, full of fancy furniture and art works. She can remember all sorts of little details about it even now. Miriam admired her and wanted to copy everything she did.*'

I loved doing up the flat. I bought all the interior decorating magazines and got ideas and instructions out of them. I had ideas of my own as well, though – I know how to mix and match, I can make a place look nice, I always did have a knack that way. Sometimes I feel like shoving that in Animal's face, but I don't, I keep my mouth shut, I treat him nice. I have his glass of whisky waiting and get all dolled up just for him. Even if he is an animal, the poor bloke feels like a prince, and then he starts imagining we're God knows who. Something tells me that's a good thing and that it'll help me get what I want; I need him to go on believing that we deserve all this, like we inherited it all from Daddy, or we earned it the respectable way. He sits in the armchair by the lamp, and he says to me, 'The baby will do just fine with us, we'll bring it up to think the right way, to believe in law and order and clean living.'

I let him rattle on. What does it matter to me, so long as he brings me the baby? Why try and make him see sense, what's the point? He's better off believing he's a big shot and that he's going to be a good dad and a good husband. He can believe whatever he wants, just so long as he brings me the baby. And if that girl's stuck in prison and she doesn't want it, well it's better off with me, or rather with us, isn't it?

'What the fuck do you have to keep going on about her for?' says Animal.

'She didn't know what was going on, or what they were doing. She didn't understand. And he didn't give her any information whatsoever. Just a lot of fine words about duty and honour and serving the Fatherland. Animal thought he was "sort of like Saint Martin", according to Miriam, which gave me the shivers.'*

'What if she comes and asks for the baby when she gets out of jail?' I say. 'I've already told you, she doesn't want it,' says Animal crossly. 'But she might get out some time, mightn't she? If she's so young, at some point she'll have done her time and she'll be out.' And he says, laughing, 'No, no, don't you worry about that. After the delivery they'll do an interrogation and give her a transfer.'†

'Where to?'

'I said no more questions.'

---

* Saint Martin the Liberator, patron saint of Argentina. Saint Martin is also, coincidentally, the patron saint of butchers.
† To 'transfer', in the military slang of the dictatorship, meant to kill a prisoner secretly.

His face goes as hard as a rock sometimes, like it did that night when I asked him about the transfer. He grabbed the desk chair and smashed it against the wall. 'What did you have to go and do that for? You're a right animal, you are, that's an antique, it cost me a fortune.' And he goes, 'Why do you think they call me Animal? You should be happy I just smashed up a chair instead of you.' And I have to admit I just caved in, because Animal's a nice man but when he gets in that mood, he could make mincemeat out of me. I have to say, though, he doesn't stay that way for long. I went off into a corner and started to cry (if you act the poor little thing with men it always works), and he came up and hugged me from behind and started to rub my tits gently and talk in my ear. Said if I wanted the baby, not to ask him any more questions, it's under control, but if I keep getting on his nerves he's not going to bring me one. I'd be better off spending my time getting ready for the wedding, talking to the registry office and the church and everything because he can't right now, there's a lot going on at work, things are tricky at the moment. And then he went off into the bedroom and came back with a stack of money (I wouldn't have dreamed of asking him where he got it from, it's always best to act stupid with men) and gave it to me and said I should buy a wedding dress with it and start getting my trousseau together.

My trousseau! Animal's such an idiot sometimes. Like, what am I going to buy? A little white lacy number for the wedding night, like the one my cousin bought when she married that chap from the post office? I remember when she showed it to me, my aunt said, 'It'll be your turn soon, Miriam, any day now some nice boy will propose to you and you'll get married.' There was no way in hell I was going to marry some little nobody and stay in a godforsaken hole like Coronel Pringles. No, I had other plans, I wanted to be a model and become rich and famous. Getting married was something I was saving for later, when I got around to having a baby. That was one thing I knew I definitely did want: to have a baby. But later on, of course.

The same year that Noemí got married, I won a beauty contest. They said I was the prettiest girl there, and made me Queen of Coronel Pringles. Then came the photos, and the contest in Bahía Blanca where they named me a princess. I decided the only way I could live up to my dreams and make it big was if I moved to Buenos Aires. So then Oscar, who believed me, or pretended he did anyway, brought me here. I checked into modelling schools straight away and he said he would pay for my tuition and introduce me to his family. But then, what happened? I'd barely been here a month when like a fool I got pregnant. I couldn't have a kid then, it would have to be later on. Oscar paid for the abortion all right, but then he ran off and left me stuck in that filthy little hotel, bleeding like a pig.

'Later on,' that's what I always said. Until there wasn't a later any more. 'Never,' that's what the doctor at the Fernández Hospital said. I would never be able to have a baby. That was a lot later, of course. It's awful to think there is no later now, that I'm never, ever going to have one of my own. That's why I'll put up with whatever it takes from Animal, because he's going to get me a baby.

'No, of course that wasn't the first one, she'd had several abortions.'

The second time I got pregnant I decided it would have to be later on too. By that time I was working at Harry's. I was gorgeous-looking, all the men were gagging for me, you could see them practically drooling when I did my striptease, because I know how to move right, I know how to look at them and how to flaunt it. They were dying for me, not just because I'm good-looking but because I'm classy and I've got taste.

'She must have been a stunning woman – really, really attractive. She was tall and dark-haired. Her figure's still spectacular.'

'How old is she?'

'Forty-eight. Back then she must have been twenty-five or -six.'

It wasn't the job I'd been aiming for, mind. I knew that I wanted to be a model, and that I was just doing the club work to save money to pay for modelling school. If I did a class act, and I wore nice clothes, and came over really sophisticated, I was going to be a real knock-out. I was going to be a cover girl and model for all the big fashion shows in Buenos Aires and Europe and all over the world. And to do that, I needed to go to modelling school to learn how to walk and move and look sophisticated. But modelling school cost money and who was I going to get it from? Not my aunt, that was out of the question, she was hopping mad with me already because she always thought I should just marry a nice boy and stop giving myself airs and graces, and when she found out that I'd gone to Buenos Aires with that Oscar she hit the roof.

'What were you thinking, that he's going to marry you? He only wants one thing, to go to bed with you. He's got money, that boy; he's just using you.'

But I thought so what, I was using him too; even though I fancied him, I never had the slightest intention of marrying him. We were both sex-mad, that was all, and if he was using me for something, I was using him to get the hell out of that bloody place.

'Don't you realise,' my aunt said, 'that men like that never marry girls like you, especially if you've slept with them already? He's just taking advantage of you, you silly thing. Come back, Miriam, come back home.'

The silly cow actually thought I was a virgin, and that Oscar was my first, when actually he must have been like the fifth or sixth. I never told her what that bloke did to me that time, I thought she'd blame me for it and she'd throw me out or say, 'You're just like your mother.' I don't know what I was thinking, but I couldn't tell them about it. Anyway it was them that brought him to the house. My uncle invited him to dinner, they'd been at school together. He didn't make his move there, though, it was the next day, in the street, when he picked me up and took me to that piece of wasteland. God, when I think about it I could kill him. What a little fool I was, I was ashamed to tell anyone. I was ashamed of what he'd done to me! If it's a girl I'm going to tell her the moment she's old enough to understand that if a man grabs you and pushes you down and rips off your clothes, you kick him, you defend yourself, and if he sticks it in you anyway, you report him to the police, tell everybody about it. They're the bastards, not us.

The only explanation she could think of for a girl being held prisoner was that she must have tried to kill someone who had raped her. That was her world, the story of her life. At that point Miriam didn't have a clue what was going on. A lot of people didn't. Eduardo didn't either.'

'Because they didn't want to know.'

But I still had to pay for my tuition. I couldn't ask Aunt Nuncia for money and Oscar had gone and left me, just like she said he would. Then a girl at the hotel told me about this bar called Harry's, so I went to see them and they took me on, but I only did it to get some cash for modelling school. When I got pregnant I wanted to die. I was earning good money by that point, I had some savings, but I didn't want to touch them because I'd got everything set up to start the course in March, and pay the whole year in advance so I would only need to work to pay for the hotel, my food and my gear.

So then our Juli told me about about La Gorda, the fat lady; she said she wouldn't charge too much. The place made me feel a bit squeamish, it was so dirty, but Juli had recommended her and La Gorda seemed quite nice and hardly charged me anything.

I told them at the bar that I'd gone down with a bug that would clear up soon, but I went on bleeding for days and days. They said I couldn't miss any more work, but afterwards they took me back just the same, because I was so good at it, I always got them a full house and they weren't about to let me go just like that because of all the money I brought in.

Sometimes I'd agree to go out on a date with someone from the bar, but only if I fancied him, because I wasn't on the game then. The one who got me started on that was the old lady, Annette, the fucking cow. I felt bloody marvellous when I told her it was all over and she could go to hell. She really got to me, because I believed in her, I even admired her, I was that stupid. She used to say that I was lovely, I was perfect, I just needed to lose two or three pounds – that's what she said the day I met her – and that clothes looked fabulous on me because I had the right body. She always said I had the perfect body to model so-and-so's collection. It wasn't my idea, it was her, Annette, who took me out of modelling school before I'd finished the course. We were in the middle of a practice session and there she was, sitting watching us, with that smile of hers and her crossed legs, and that languid way of moving her hands that I tried so hard to copy. A bloody waste of time that was.

'That was absolutely marvellous, you were fantastic, you looked gorgeous.'

And I believed her – well I would have, wouldn't I? She set me up

22

with fashion shows and paid for the hairdresser and the gym and the make-up artist, the lot. She even got me a spot on TV. Me, Miriam López. So there, Aunty, you said I should stop giving myself airs, and now look, just you turn on the telly this afternoon and see what you see. Miriam on telly. Although Annette used to call me Patricia. She said Patricia sounded better, that Miriam was a bit, well . . . and she gazed off into space, as if she was looking for the right word, a word she couldn't quite put her finger on, a bit . . .

'A bit common,' said Inés, although come to think of it she probably wasn't called Inés at all, because they must have changed her name as well.

I was so angry I could have throttled her, but I didn't say anything because I didn't want to seem bad-mannered in front of Annette. If they thought I'd be better off as Patricia, what did I care? 'A big hand for Patricia,' and I'd turn on my heel and saunter back down the catwalk, I did that ever so well, my arms would swing lightly by my sides and the men couldn't keep their dirty eyes off me. Clothes used to hang on me like a dream, and I had learned how to walk, how to stop at just the right moment, how to look at them, not like at the strip club but getting the same effect anyway – I'm in my element doing that stuff. I've always been able to make men stare at me. It made me feel like royalty, as if I was in just the right place, on the right track. God, what a bloody fool I was!

I don't know how many fashion shows I did. Shows and clothes and photo shoots. Then one afternoon Annette invited me to her house for tea. She said there was something 'very important' she wanted to discuss with me. She said it in a whisper, and I spent hours wondering what it was and what to wear, and I even went to Joseph's to get my hair done just to go and see her.

The flat was on Alvear Avenue. The lift was carpeted and the landing was all done up. And when I went in, God, what a palace! That's when I got the bug for fancy upholstery and lamps and things. I thought to myself, I want to live like this, have a place like this, full of pictures and ornaments and rugs. And I said to her, 'I'd love to live in a flat like this.'

'You may very well be able to, Patricia. It'll take a few years' work. You just need to be efficient and discreet. If you're *clever*,' she said, stressing the word, as if she were letting me in on a big secret, 'you'll be able to have all this and more.'

Then she showed me the album with the swimsuit collection I'd modelled for, and stared at my pictures. I felt fabulous, incredibly sexy, because that's how she made me feel, and I thought all she said was true, that I could learn much more working for her than at modelling school, that she'd open all sorts of doors for me, all sorts of possibilities, and that I'd be able to have whatever I wanted.

I was annoyed that she'd invited Inés along as well, because I thought I was going alone.

Annette had shown those photos to a very important man, 'a big fish', and said I was lucky because he had chosen me. Inés and me.

'To model another collection?'

That set Inés off cackling like an old hen, ha ha ha, having a real laugh. 'What collection?' she said. 'Christian Dior?' What the fuck is she laughing at, I thought, she must be in on the joke. You see I was so thick or naïve or whatever that I really thought I'd been chosen for a big fashion show, that I'd be going off in a plane somewhere, I'd finally made it. In those two minutes no end of things went through my head. I imagined lots of foreigners clapping me, and women with cigarette holders and multi-millionaire husbands buying the outfits I was modelling.

'No,' Annette said, 'it's another job, not a fashion show.'

'Guess,' said Inés, who was obviously having me on.

I thought of advertising, of myself on telly or at the pictures, Miriam, or rather Patricia, coming out of the water in a designer bikini and sipping an iced drink.

'Advertising.'

'You're too cold, way too cold, think of something warmer, like, you know, hot,' said Inés.

I remember being afraid for a moment that Inés might know I'd worked as a stripper (I'd told Silvia and she promised to keep it a secret but perhaps she'd blabbed), and that she was going to try and make me look bad in front of Annette because she was jealous of me – I was of her too, I won't deny it. The old lady must have known about it anyway, because she said that I knew how to turn men on, I'd got experience, I'd learned something from working at Harry's, but this job involved going to a posh party and 'entertaining' people. I almost died.

'You mean strip? But I'm not doing that any more, I only did it to pay for my lessons.'

'No dear, that's not what I meant, you just have to be there, be nice to people, be charming, keep them amused.'

And anything beyond that, well, we'd see, but I had to be charming, discreet and really classy. Stripping, well, if I felt like it and I could do a good job, that would be all right. Stripping and anything else that might occur to me because she knew I was imaginative, I had charisma, and I'd managed to become quite sophisticated. And then she went on and on talking while I stared at her gorgeous flat and she said I would earn more money than at the fashion shows.

'But I want to go on doing fashion shows,' I said. 'That's what I studied for.'

'Of course you did, love. But this has got nothing to do with that. You'll still have your modelling career.'

Well, if it wasn't going to prevent me becoming a top model, and I was going to get more money into the bargain, why not – after all, it was Annette who was suggesting it.

So I went to the party. And there was the man who'd asked for me. 'You look beautiful, fantastic, they're going to love you.'

They were all really important people, the top brass, God, who'd have thought I'd end up meeting Animal there. He didn't do anything, didn't come up to me, just stared at me, with a hungry look in his eye as if he wanted to gobble me up – he still looks at me that way – and really and truly it made me melt but he never laid a finger on me. That's one thing I'll never understand. There he was, randy as can be, but he couldn't do a thing because he was with the officers and he was just an NCO, even though we were all crowded together knocking back the champagne. Why couldn't he just have gone ahead? I noticed him right from the start, perhaps because he never touched me, just undressed me with his eyes.

I started thinking about Animal. I saw him at other parties, a couple anyway, and he was always staring at me. By that time I knew his nickname. Once, when he came in, an old guy who was with me called him 'Animal' and started chatting to him. When he turned round, I asked why he'd called him an animal like that, in front of everybody, poor man.

'No, dear, that's his name, well, his nickname anyway, because he's so strong. He's a good chap, and very, very efficient.'

I seem to remember thinking, 'Well if he's so strong and efficient how come I can't do it with him, instead of this fat moron?' I took a good look at him, although he only stayed for a little while. He was talking to someone, but he kept on glancing my way.

After that party, things really took off. I made good money, loads of it, in a really short time. Annette kept encouraging me. She used to send me to a posh hairdresser's and buy outfits that were different from the ones for the collections, evening gowns for 'soirées' is what she said but soirée my arse, there I was with my tits half out, or else in wispy see-through things, I might as well have been in my birthday suit except I was a different colour. Not that I'm complaining, mind you. I have to admit I liked wearing the see-through stuff. I used to look at myself in the mirror before I went out and it gave me a real thrill. I'd moved by that point and I had a three-way mirror and I'd look at myself in that get-up, in that bright-red see-through outfit that looked as if it'd been sprayed on, showing everything but hiding it at the same time, and I used to run my hands slowly over my body, up and down, the way they all used to look at me, and I could feel myself, feel my skin all smooth and warm, underneath the sheer fabric. It was a weird feeling, as if I was getting off on myself. As if I turned myself on; that's it, I turned myself on, I really did, I loved touching myself, much more than when some bloke did it. I think that's why I was such a big success; I got them all going because I used to spend a long time beforehand turning myself on.

I can't remember now how I went from going to parties to being on the game and having my 'rendezvous' as Annette called them, but it didn't take long. Something really special always seemed to come up, someone who'd seen me at a party and who wanted to meet me, in private of course. When she said what they'd pay me, I almost passed out.

I said yes each time, but I was always on at her about the fashion shows and she'd go, 'All right,' and she'd get me a show now and then, but in the meantime, there was always another party and another phone call, always just one more. Someone who thought I was stunning and who'd like to see me that night. They were always very important people, real gentlemen all of them. She never gave me their names – maybe she didn't always know them herself.

'Animal set up some of those dates with Annette. Apparently the top brass trusted him. He used to settle the fee upfront beforehand – if that's what you call it,' and Luz laughed. 'That's how Animal got in. He said it was for the colonel, and that they should keep it a secret. He'd been mad about Miriam for months, he was really obsessed with her.'

'Lust.'

'I'd say that he was in love with her.'

But there seemed to be fewer and fewer fashion shows and more and more cocktail parties and clients. I started to wonder what the hell had happened to all my plans. By that point, being a model had become just a word clients would use: 'What a nice career you've got, being a model,' maybe because it turned them on thinking that they'd been to a party or gone to bed with a model, instead of a tart. But if they were paying for it, what was I? A tart, that's all.

So I decided to have a little talk with Annette and I invited her to tea at my house. It was around then that I bought all the stuff for the flat: curtains, sofas, carpets, pictures and a four-poster bed. Crazy, the money I spent on it all. I was the only one to see it, it was all for me, because I never, ever slept with a client there. I told Animal that, how he'd been the first, and the last. Because my flat was private, it was my home, my very own place, and I thought it was magic.

'How beautifully you've decorated it!' she said. 'You've got excellent taste!'

I think she really was surprised that this little nobody from the sticks, from Coronel Pringles, with the rather common name, had managed to do up a flat like that – not like hers of course, but not far off. I was feeling strong and I told her straight that I wasn't happy about working more on the other stuff than on the modelling.

27

What a coincidence, she had a surprise for me that I was going to really love. There was a big fashion show over in Uruguay, in Punta del Este, in less than a month, which could be a great opportunity for me because there would be people there who might sign me up and take me to Europe. I was thrilled to bits getting ready for the show; I never really admitted to myself that I was on the game.

Although I did say it to that bloke: 'I'm on the game.' Ugh, when I remember that it gives me the shivers.

'Let's play a little game,' he said, the bloody sadist.

He tied me to the bed with ropes he'd brought himself. I was giggling until he got out the gun, it froze my blood. 'That's enough,' I said, but he started rubbing it against my legs, going slowly up them, all the while saying all these dirty things. 'That's enough, please.' I thought he was going to blow me away when he stuck it into me, I completely lost it, I thought he was going to split me in two, blow me to bits. The guy seemed to be mixing me up with God knows who. 'I'll show you, you fucking little Montonera,'★ he said, with his finger on the trigger, 'I'm going to show you how they felt when that bomb of yours went off.'

'I'm just a tart,' I said, not loudly, trying to keep calm, 'I don't plant bombs, I'm here to give you a good time, that's all. I'm on the game, on the game.' Goodness knows what else I said – when I'm scared I say all sorts of things – but the bastard wouldn't take the gun out. He kept shoving that freezing barrel into me and all the while there I was talking like crazy out of my cunt. 'Annette said you were a gentleman, Major. I thought we were going to do all sorts of things tonight but I'm not going to be able to, with that thing in there.' I don't know how long he left it in there, for ever it seemed like to me, but eventually I managed to distract him and he untied me and I put the gun away myself. I never said anything more about it to him because I was so petrified I was practically shitting myself. I just carried right on and did my job. But afterwards I let Annette have a piece of my mind. I should have suspected something by that time.

'So what did he do to you? Nothing at all, in the end. He didn't hurt

★ The Montoneros were an armed Peronist group.

you. You know, men have their fantasies and if you're clever, you can always find a way to make them believe they're true.'

But she wasn't stupid. She realised I was livid and she let it go.

'Oh well, don't you worry, love, I won't give you any more assignments with him, I promise. Now, cheer up, it's not long till the show at Punta del Este.'

She went on and on about what a fantastic opportunity it was going to be until I didn't know if I was coming or going. That show was supposed to send me shooting off to my destiny like a rocket, I was hoping I'd get an exclusive contract to model for Yves Saint Laurent, or Christian Dior or some other big-name designer, and then I'd be able to give up the other stuff. I'd already bought everything I needed, and more by that time, and if the modelling business worked out, I'd be making good money. Then I'd settle down and get married so I could have a baby. I'd got it all worked out. And then *boom*, once again, I was late, and I got later and later. I practically went out of my mind. I did the test and it was positive. What was I going to do? I was due to try on the outfits for the show and that night I had a date with 'someone charming'. I told Annette I didn't feel well. I couldn't tell her. Getting pregnant wasn't smart, it wasn't what 'clever' girls did.

I had to get rid of it at once, but who could I ask? The models? I'd already learned it was better not to mention anything private to them, because they'd use everything they knew to screw you. My client that night wasn't from the military, and he was good-looking and even funny (he was a banker). But I could hardly turn round and say, 'Know of a good abortionist, do you?', now could I? There was just no way. I saw all sorts of important people, but I didn't know one single person I could talk to about what was happening. I was as lonely as a stray dog. I wondered about asking Frank, the bloke from the Claridge Hotel I'd gone out with and chatted to a couple of times, but I couldn't make up my mind. I didn't know him well enough; he might take it wrong.

That night I couldn't sleep. I looked all over for La Gorda's address. I went round there first thing in the morning and she basically butchered me. I wasn't trying to save money, it's just that I couldn't think what else to do. The show was in twenty days and I had to be in good shape. I told

Annette I couldn't go and try on the outfits and I wasn't going to be able to make the party that night. I felt terrible and I was losing pints of blood. 'It's my time of the month and it's very heavy,' I said. 'I'm not feeling well.'

'You haven't gone and done something silly now, have you?'

'What do you mean, silly?'

'Had an abortion.'

I swore blind I hadn't, but I wondered what I was going to say if it went on for ten days or two weeks. Periods don't last ten days. That same night I went to Fernández Hospital. I didn't think twice, it never occurred to me it's illegal to have an abortion and they could throw me in jail, or that Annette could find out, or anything; I just knew that if they didn't stop the bleeding I'd be gone. I'd lose every last drop of blood and I'd die. I was in the hospital one whole day and part of the next. The doctor was all right; he stopped the bleeding and didn't report me to the police, but he said, 'I'm sorry, but you'll never be able to have children.' Never again. I took it badly – I was devastated. As long as I could keep on putting it off, everything was all right. I'd always thought that I'd have a baby later on, I wasn't in any hurry, there were other things I wanted first, but when he said the word 'never', I became obsessed with it, I couldn't think of anything else.

When I told Annette I couldn't go to the try-outs because I was still unwell and I didn't want to get blood on the clothes, she threw a fit. She said that on Thursday I had to meet a client and she couldn't send anyone else because they'd made it very clear it had to be me, not any of the other girls. I had to look fantastic because it was someone really important.

By Thursday I was doing better. I was losing less blood, but I was feeling so miserable I'd no idea how I was going to pretend to be cheerful.

And who was waiting there, at the Claridge? Animal, that's who. He had paid Annette and told her it was for a colonel who couldn't give his name because he didn't officially use the agency's services, but who wanted me. If I couldn't go that day, then they'd have to pick another time, but his instructions were that it had to be me and nobody else. He really put himself on the line, telling a whopper like that. If they'd found out, they'd have hung him; and he's always been the type that does everything he's told. It took some guts on his part, I must say, he risked his neck pretending it was for someone else, someone important, and showing up himself instead.

There he was with his hair all slicked back, in a blue suit and an awful tie. He looked so, I dunno, the way he is, so clumsy and naff, staring at me the way he does, but admiringly, not as if he wanted to do it right away. When he poured the champagne and I looked at him, all on edge like a kid on his first date, I burst out laughing.

'Thank God it's you, Animal.'

He was surprised I knew his name. I said I'd seen him around, of course I remembered him, and I was really, really happy to see him. No sooner had I said that than I burst into tears; not just one or two, mind, I started bawling and sobbing my eyes out. God, how I cried – I was drooling, snivelling and hiccuping like anything. I've no idea what he made of it but he hugged me and rocked me and said, 'There, there, don't cry,' and I said, 'Please don't tell Annette, Animal.' And he asked me not to tell Annette it was him either, because if I did he was really going to be in for it. So we felt as if we were in it together. Maybe that's why I broke down and told him everything that was eating away at me: about the abortion, and what had happened at the hospital, and wanting to have a baby some day and now I never would, and he must think it was ridiculous, he'd laugh at a woman like me wanting to . . . No, no, he thought it was totally normal, it was just human nature that I wanted to be a mother, and he loved me, it wasn't just that he fancied me and he was crazy for me, he loved me because of what I'd just said, and who knows what else.

When he explained about how he'd had to pretend to be someone else, he didn't say it was because I was a high-class prostitute that only the top brass could use. No, he said that I was a real princess, the prettiest of them all, and that's why I belonged in the inner circle of the most important people in the country, and he didn't, not yet anyway. That's why I say he's no animal; being in an inner circle isn't the same thing as being a high-class prostitute, now is it? I went home with him that same night. And we started living together after a week.

31

When I told the old bag I was finished, I was leaving because I'd fallen in love, she asked me who my knight in shining armour was, but I wouldn't tell her because I didn't want to give Animal away. Even though I couldn't see why if he paid for it he didn't have just as much right as those others. But Annette said something that really got my goat. She said that I had a great career ahead of me and that I could have had whatever I wanted and that giving it all up for one man was a mistake, because she was convinced that I was going to become a top model. I forgot my promise to Animal.

'I'm going to marry Pitiotti.'

I can still see the rage in her eyes. 'He's a little nobody, a piddling little sergeant,' she said. 'How dare you? He tricked me, he's not allowed in, he's not an officer.' And she started threatening to report him to God knows who; we'd see where my little sergeant on a white horse ended up when she'd had her say. I forgot about speaking in a throaty whisper and that languid air of hers I'd been copying for months. I shoved my face up just a hair's breadth from hers and out came a voice I'd no idea I still had. 'Now you listen to me: if you breathe one word, Animal will come and smash this place to bits, he'll make mincemeat of you. They don't call him Animal for nothing, you know. You just forget about me and leave well alone.'

She pretended to calm down then. 'It's just it's such a pity; you had everything going for you. Oh well, what can you do, they come up from the dirt and they fall back down again.' And then, once I'd backed off and was getting ready to leave, she spewed out a boiling torrent of scorn and anger. 'A sergeant, how disgusting.' I turned to face her, with all the rage that had been building up inside me over the years, me, Miriam López, from that town in the sticks.

'And what's wrong with that? Do you think those precious officers of yours have got golden dicks and the NCOs' are just make-believe? Look, you stupid bitch, I used to admire you, but you know what, you're the worst of them all. You'd better watch out because with what I know . . . You wouldn't believe the things those VIPs with their golden dicks tell you, in those discreet little "rendezvous". I'll cause a huge scandal and your business will go down the fucking tubes.'

And with that I walked out. She won't lift a finger, I know, because there's no way she wants a scandal.

Tonight I'm going to show Animal the baby's room. With the money he gave me for my trousseau, I went and bought some lovely wallpaper covered in little bears, and a gorgeous cot, and a little quilt and sheets for it. I didn't want to show him until it was all ready, and as he never goes into that room he never caught on. I was afraid he'd blow his top, but when he sees how nice it's turned out, I bet he'll be as pleased as me.

'Animal was so tender and loving towards her that Miriam thought she was the one in control.'

I think he likes the idea of a baby; he's not just doing it for me. It's not just that he's so obsessed with fucking me that he gets mixed up and thinks he wants the same things I do; no, he'd like a kid too. Of course, there's no denying I'm good at getting my own way with men. He might scare the living daylights out of everyone else, but I've got him wrapped around my little finger, although I'm ever so clever and tactful about it. This is my home and I'm the one in charge here.

TWO

THINGS AREN'T TURNING out the way Eduardo had ima-
gined. Amalia's throaty, shrill voice hadn't been part of his mental
picture (he could never understand how such a low voice could sound so
much like the screech of a bird), and neither had Alfonso, who is
marching belligerently back and forth across the room. The way Eduardo
had imagined it when he talked about it with Mariana in their pre-natal
class, it would be just the two of them: Mariana in pain from the
contractions and him helping her, comforting her, holding her close and
encouraging her. And the doctor or the midwife coming in from time to
time to check on things.

Why do Mariana's parents have to be here? He doesn't know why he
is so tense, whether it's Mariana's labour pains, the imminent delivery or
the voices of his in-laws constantly intruding and giving their opinion,
prying him away from Mariana's side, as Amalia is doing right now by
sitting down in the chair he left a moment ago to get Mariana a glass of
water.

'Why don't they give her an injection and put her to sleep?' Alfonso
says loudly. 'Why has she got to suffer like this?'

Eduardo tries to reach past Amalia to stroke Mariana's shoulder, but he
can barely touch her. 'Just relax, love,' he tells her. 'Take a deep breath,
there you go. Now exhale.' Amalia gives him an irritated look, as if to
say, 'What is *he* doing here, and what *is* he babbling on about?'

Why can't he just tell them to go away and leave them alone? As soon
as Mariana went into labour, before she even called the midwife, she
woke her parents, and he couldn't very well stop them coming to the
clinic.

'*Alfonso and Amalia lived in Buenos Aires. They had gone to Entre Ríos to be*

35

with Mariana when she gave birth. They were staying at Eduardo and Mariana's, which made things more complicated.'

Mariana's pain goes right through him. It hurts in some ill-defined place in his body, and he plucks up the courage to ask Amalia to please get up, that's his chair, but like an idiot he has to justify himself: because they need to do what they learned in the pre-natal class for the contractions. Mariana reaches out to him and he squeezes her hand; she must want to be alone with him too. She moans again. He wants to say, 'Oh, sweetheart, my love, my pet,' but he feels inhibited by his in-laws' presence. Amalia remains seated on the chair, impassive. Eduardo can hardly push her off it, so he tries to get closer by squeezing past. He is in between the bed and the chair when he trips and falls, squashing Mariana.

'Eduardo, for goodness' sake, be careful. If you're in such a state, why don't you just go outside?'

And there goes Alfonso again. 'I don't understand why they let her suffer like this. I don't know what that doctor's thinking of.'

'Why don't the two of you just go outside?' says Amalia. 'This is no place for men. I'll stay here with Mariana.'

Eduardo stands paralysed opposite the bed, looking at Mariana, waiting for her to tell her parents to be quiet.

'You'd be better off waiting outside, Daddy, with Eduardo. You're just going to get all upset in here.'

So he has to go outside, he's got no choice, since Mariana herself . . . But when it's time, he'll be the one to go into the delivery ward with her, as they'd planned. He says so to Alfonso.

'Are you out of your mind? What for? You're not a doctor.'

'No, but I want to be there, to hold her and support her and see our child being born.'

He has to put up with more arguments from Alfonso: *he* was never there at the delivery, and his three daughters were all born just fine, and anyway, it's no place for a man.

As if Eduardo cared. The midwife goes into Mariana's room and he follows her, leaving Alfonso's command to stay where he is echoing in the hallway. God, if only this were over, if only they would take her to the delivery ward.

Amalia doesn't leave the room and Mariana doesn't ask her to. The midwife looks serious when she examines her. She goes out and comes back in with the doctor. Now they're taking her out. They'll never let Amalia and Alfonso into the delivery ward. Only Eduardo, of course.

Rushing down the corridors, into the lift, Mariana, darling, everything's going to be all right now.

They go into the delivery ward and Eduardo stands behind Mariana holding her head. She is in terrible pain. Eduardo can't work out what's going on. The doctor and the midwife keep on telling her to push, over and over again, and their voices are interspersed with Mariana's screams. The expression on Dr Murray's face is worrying. Everything starts happening very fast. Voices, tense faces, cries, and suddenly the doctor is ordering them to take her to the operating theatre.

'I'm sorry, Mr Iturbe, but you'll have to wait outside. The baby is in distress; it's in danger. We'll have to do a Caesarean and you can't be in the operating room.'

It could have happened any time of the day or night. Sergeant Pitiotti wasn't there twenty-four hours a day, needless to say. But as luck would have it (although perhaps it was not just simply luck) he was there when the decision was made to take Liliana to the hospital. He was the one in charge at the time. He wanted there to be doctors and nurses around while she was in labour, so that there wouldn't be any problems with the baby.

As soon as he got to work, before seven, the guard informed him that prisoner M35 had gone into labour, and that prisoner L23, who was a medical student, was monitoring the contractions.

'Teresa was at university at the same time as me,' Carlos explained. 'She'd seen Liliana with me a few times. We'd known each other ever since we were young. Her family was from Posadas, the same as mine, so when she got out, she contacted my father. It was pure coincidence Teresa was arrested, because she had nothing to do with us.'

'Us? Who do you mean?'

Carlos looked away.

'I just meant that Teresa wasn't involved in politics. She was over at a

37

neighbour's house when there was a raid and they grabbed her too. Her neighbour had been a shop steward, that was all she knew.'

He usually arrived later, around eight thirty. But that morning, he had woken earlier than usual, on edge for some reason, he didn't know why, perhaps because of that stupid kid he couldn't get a single name out of. He'd soon sort him out today. He looked at Miriam, who was fast asleep beside him, and that made him relax for a moment. He loved her so much. He kissed her gently and said quietly, not meaning to wake her up, 'I'm going to the office, love. I'll ring you later.'

'He used to call it "the office" when he talked to her, as if it were a bank or a solicitor's.'

He needed to get in early and take care of the problem so that when the head of the taskforce rang, he'd have something for him. On the other hand, perhaps it was some kind of intuition that had got him out of bed so early that day. Is there such a thing as father's intuition? Sergeant Pitiotti wondered, in shy excitement, when they told him the news. The image of Miriam and how delighted she was going to be when he took her the baby assuaged his hatred for the prisoner who wouldn't talk and his need to get information for the head of the taskforce by that afternoon.

When Sergeant Pitiotti came up to Liliana's tube-like cell, Teresa, who was not blindfolded, couldn't help giving a start.

'How long has she got to go?' Pitiotti asked Teresa.

'Not long now, her contractions are coming regularly. Will I be helping with the delivery?' Teresa asked, frightened and hopeful.

'No, I'll take the prisoner to the hospital myself.'

He ordered the guard to take off her leg-irons, but not the blindfold or the manacles.

Even though taking prisoners to the hospital wasn't part of his normal duties, nobody thought it strange, because everyone knew that Sergeant Pitiotti, alias Animal, had a special relationship with Liliana Ortiz, prisoner M35.

'He had a lot of power for someone who was only an NCO, probably because his methods of extracting information had made him Dufau's right-hand man. Dufau was the person in charge of the detention centre.'

Ever since he had interrogated her for the first time, months ago, Liliana had remained unscathed. He said he didn't want anyone to lay a finger on her, and that he'd see to her personally, but only after the birth, because 'we're not making war on little kids.' And although nobody understood (or asked) what Animal's reasons were – after all, she was not the only pregnant woman there – they treated her as if she belonged to him. The head of the taskforce had been quite explicit: no one was to touch Sergeant Pitiotti's prisoner.

People thought that maybe Animal fancied her, or that she reminded him of his mother, or that he'd got something in mind and was keeping her to take out of the camp and identify her accomplices for them. But they were only surmises in the minds of men who weren't much given to surmising, men who just followed orders – and the order was not to touch her. Nobody could have imagined that Sergeant Pitiotti was protecting the carrier of his own child. He saw to it personally that she was well fed, and that no one beat her up or interrogated her while he was away.

So no one thought anything of it when he drove the car himself that day. Liliana lay down in the back, burying her blindfolded face against the seat, as Pitiotti had told her to. Once they got to the hospital, he took off the blindfold before they got out of the car. The light almost blinded Liliana, who had been kept in the dark for months. When he told her she should keep her mouth shut and let him do the talking, she looked him in the eye for the first time. Despite the fact that she was blinking uncontrollably, there was an unmistakable flash of something that might have been hatred, or panic, or disgust, or pain in her eyes (Animal preferred to think it was pain). It was as if she had struck him with a lash of dazzling green.

'I said keep your mouth shut, you little cow,' yelled Animal, even though she had not said a word.

How dare she look at him that way, after all he'd done for her? In order to break the magnetic power of that gaze, to avoid what it contained, he thought of Miriam. She'd be so happy when he took her the baby. Miriam in the baby's room with the new wallpaper. Miriam fucking him, Miriam moaning with pleasure when he touched her, anything to distract himself from Liliana's eyes and her skin that seemed to burn with venom when he took her arm on the way from the car to the hospital lobby.

Perhaps it was the larger-than-life image of Miriam that Animal was evoking so desperately to ward off Liliana's hatred that made him register her as Miriam López, born in Coronel Pringles.

'He told Miriam that he'd done it on the spur of the moment. He hadn't planned it that way.'

He mustn't look at her again; mustn't be exposed to that gaze. 'Don't you dare breathe a word, or it'll be the worse for you,' he said in her ear, as Liliana walked towards the delivery room. But he couldn't prevent her from stopping, turning around and looking at him again with that concentrated hatred, distilled over long months. This time, there was no doubt in Sergeant Pitiotti's mind that it was hatred in her eyes.

He could go back to work, and do an interrogation to get rid of the tension that gaze had stirred up in him. But Miriam's baby was about to be born, and he wanted to be there, like a good husband and father.

When he noticed the public phone opposite the bench where he was sitting, he decided not to wait until that night, but to let Miriam know as soon as the baby was born.

He doesn't even have the consolation of being left alone to wait, because Amalia and Alfonso keep talking constantly: they let her go on too long on her own, all this rubbish about natural childbirth means they don't help her, and then when things go wrong, surprise surprise, they don't know what to do, where on earth did they get that doctor?

Mariana and Eduardo chose him. 'Why, what's wrong with him, Amalia?'

'Now, look here, Eduardo, I know you're upset, but don't you go taking that tone with me. How do you think I feel? I'm her mother, after all.'

He could kill her, knock her out with one blow. It's stupid, he knows, but he feels as if it's Amalia's fault that Mariana has to have a Caesarean; it was because she was there that Mariana couldn't concentrate on the contractions and things went wrong. And obviously Amalia thinks it's his fault for having chosen that particular doctor. Fortunately Alfonso takes her by the arm and draws her away.

'We're going to have a coffee downstairs, Eduardo. If Mariana comes out, let us know.'

Why has all this happened? Maybe his in-laws are right; maybe they did let her go on too long. Eduardo doesn't know who to be angry with: Amalia, or Alfonso for always ordering everybody else around, or Dr Murray and his team, or himself for being so obsessed with the idea of natural childbirth and now heaven knows what's happening to Mariana. Oh God, let everything be all right, they've been together for so long. Eduardo prays that Mariana will pull through, because if she doesn't he'll never forgive himself. She wasn't very enthusiastic about having a child; he was the one who had kept on about it. 'But I won't be able to go to Buenos Aires so often if I have a baby,' Mariana used to say.

When they got married, she agreed to go and live in the province of Entre Ríos, because that's where Eduardo's land was and he needed to be around to oversee things on the estate. But as time went on, he kept on finding her in tears in the mornings out of sheer homesickness, and she started going back to Buenos Aires constantly. 'They're my family . . . I love you, Eduardo, but I miss then all so much. Please understand, oh, go on, be nice, come and get me on Saturday and don't make a fuss.'

That was why he had wanted a child so much. It was selfish of him; he thought it would bring Mariana closer to him, make her grow up and separate from her family.

Down the hallway come the screeching bird and the marching steps. He doesn't know which irritates him more. But there's Dr Murray walking towards him. He hurries to meet him, and so do they. Murray, who is looking very serious, waves them aside and says he needs to speak to Eduardo in private.

It can't be true, he can't be hearing this. It can't be true they couldn't save the baby. 'Why? Everything was going all right.'

'Mariana is in a serious condition, but she'll recover. She's still under

41

anaesthetic at the moment. I'm so terribly sorry this has happened, Mr Iturbe.'

Murray is on the verge of tears, like himself. It seems clear to Eduardo that the doctor feels to blame. 'You can go in and see her, but only for a minute.'

Sergeant Pitiotti was strangely delighted when they told him the news. He had absorbed so much of Miriam's excitement that even he believed what he told her over the telephone.

'Congratulations, love! You had a baby girl five minutes ago. She weighs seven pounds three ounces and measures nineteen and three-quarter inches.'

The sergeant knew perfectly well that she hadn't really had a baby, but what he said wasn't just an emotional truth: the birth certificate corroborated it. It said that Miriam López was the mother of a baby girl born on 15 November 1976, at twelve fifteen, weight seven pounds three ounces, length nineteen and three-quarter inches.

'That birth certificate ended up in so many hands and confused all sorts of people.'

'A girl?' Carlos said, in surprise. 'Then it can't be Liliana. She had a boy who was stillborn. I know that from Teresa, the girl who took care of her when she was in labour. One of the guards told her that Liliana got an infection afterwards, went into a coma and died.'

It's Amalia who comes up with the idea. Hasn't her husband, Alfonso, told her that sometimes they give the subversives' babies to respectable families? After all, it's not the babies' fault who their parents are. Yes, of course Mariana could have another one, but it would be so hard for her, and in any case why should they be deprived of their first grandchild, after they've gone and announced it to everybody. Hadn't he told her that plenty of those babies aren't dark-skinned? No one will know it isn't Mariana's child. Of course, they'd have to make sure the mother wasn't a Jew or a half-breed. They can do it, and why shouldn't they; Alfonso deserves a few perks for having got this high in the service. Why should her daughter have to suffer a disappointment, why should a stupid

42

accident have to turn into a tragedy, if there are so many orphan babies out there? Maybe it's God's will. They'd be doing a good deed – Father Juan, her confessor, is bound to agree. Her instinct tells her (and feminine intuition is never wrong, as her husband knows from long experience) that the thing to do would be to get hold of one of the subversives' babies. Poor little things, having those murderers for parents. Of course they can do it, they can, he can't deny that. Alfonso's got a lot of power and Amalia wants him to prove it to her.

The word 'power' begins to work its way up Alfonso's body while Amalia goes on and on talking and arguing, the way she always does when she wants something. If he wants to, he can, his wife's right there. He's never seen it so clearly as in the last few months, while they've been cleansing the country. He is overcome by a sense of excitement, rather like the buzz he gets when he orders the transfers, except perhaps stronger. If he has power over death, why not also over life?

Alfonso's smile when he comes back from making the phone call proves that Amalia was right. What an incredible coincidence ('No, it's not a coincidence, it's the hand of God, it's God who's behind these things,' says Amalia); a little while ago they took a girl into the delivery room who is blonde, pretty and well educated. Animal, his right-hand man, brought her in. He doesn't know what she's had yet, a girl or a boy, but he's ordered Animal to wait for him to call back. Everything seems to be turning out beautifully. His wife's feminine intuition has worked once again.

'Now we've just got to stop that idiot Eduardo. The man's utterly pathetic. To think he's got such good prospects, and he owns land, and that Mariana loves him.'

Colonel Alfonso Dufau suggests it would be best if his wife stays out of it from here on. She should act as if she knows nothing. These things are best handled man to man.

Even though it was her idea, Amalia will let things go the way he says. She has always preferred working behind the scenes. That's her place, she knows, and she enjoys it. For years she has been plotting things that Alfonso carries out with great efficiency. It will be she who masterminds everything her son-in-law will say and do; she is so good at making things up. Her husband will make sure her scheme is carried out. There's no doubt that they complement one another extremely well. The perfect couple, as their friends are always saying.

Why did Colonel Dufau want to speak to him? He'd said to wait until he rang back. The colonel must have found out he'd taken her to the hospital. Maybe he'd be punished for overstepping the mark and leaving his assigned duties for several hours, just when they were in such a hurry to get results. Maybe his interest in Liliana, prisoner M35, would be interpreted as weakness on his part. Animal was supposed to be the toughest of them all. He was the one who got the most information, the one who used electric shocks most effectively and showed the most imagination in getting people to crack. Animal knew every ruse in the book. That's why he gave orders and had responsibilities way above his rank. And it was Dufau, the person in charge of the detention centre, who'd given the order for him to have carte blanche. The major who led their taskforce agreed, since he admired Pitiotti's efficiency. And even if he hadn't, it wouldn't have mattered: he couldn't disobey Dufau.

Sergeant Pitiotti was afraid of falling from the colonel's good graces and losing power. But he would think of something. Maybe if he confessed that he wanted the baby girl for himself, that would explain things. A sort of war trophy. They wouldn't be able to refuse it to someone as efficient as him.

What does he mean, 'Don't say anything to Mariana'? Alfonso's gone mad. What on earth is he talking about? Eduardo is dazed with pain. Couldn't they just leave him alone with his grief, is that too much to ask? He understands his father-in-law must be feeling bad, but he can't listen to him now, no matter how often Alfonso says that it's urgent and it can't wait until tomorrow; he goes on and on, but he's not making any sense. Luckily Amalia's gone quiet. She's watching them from a distance, pretending not to notice.

Alfonso's come up with a solution. All is not lost. 'Your wife's happiness is at stake,' he stresses, looking grim. 'I can turn this whole business into just an unfortunate accident that we can put behind us.

44

There's no need for Mariana to know. When she comes round, don't tell her the baby's died, or that she had a boy, because we don't know yet what it will be.'

What is he thinking of, that her dolly's broken and Daddy will buy her another one without her finding out?

'Pay attention, boy, there's no time to lose. Wait for me here. In five minutes I'll tell you what we're going to do.'

But the call wasn't about the information he should have got by now, or a dressing-down for going to the hospital when he wasn't supposed to. On the contrary, Colonel Dufau was delighted it was Animal, a man he trusted so much, who was in charge of the job, since it required absolute secrecy. He lowered his voice to a whisper, which was more powerful than bawling an order. 'The newborn is for me. Family matter, sergeant, personal, you understand.'

Nobody but Sergeant Pitiotti was to know. If anyone asked him at the centre what had happened, he was to say it had been a boy, but that it was stillborn. Was that clear? The colonel himself would go and pick up the baby, but in the meantime she was to stay at the hospital with her mother, under police guard. The prisoner mustn't be allowed to talk.

Those were Colonel Dufau's orders.

'Do you know if the baby is in good shape physically? Do you know the weight?'

'Affirmative, sir. Seven pounds three ounces and nineteen and three-quarter inches, sir.'

How efficient Animal was; he had such an excellent memory for detail.

'It's my job to remember details, sir.'

'Very good.' Dufau was proud of Sergeant Pitiotti.

How could he say that the reason he could remember so well was because it was supposed to be Miriam's baby? How could he refuse the colonel, and above all how was he going to tell him that the baby Dufau needed for personal reasons, family reasons, was the very one that Animal had promised Miriam, the one he'd already told her was on its way? She would have to wait for another one. Damn, he shouldn't have said anything to her. But he'd sort it out. He'd get her another. And to make sure that no one beat him to it, he'd speak directly to the colonel. After this, he wouldn't be able to say no.

'Eduardo, if they let you in and she's conscious, tell her she had a girl. And stop worrying. Let's just keep this whole thing to ourselves, as if nothing had happened. Not a word to anyone, mind. Now wipe your face, I don't want anyone seeing you in this state. Off you go and make the announcement: it's a girl.'

'Most likely Alfonso arranged the whole thing and made Eduardo go through with it. Alfonso was the sort of man it's difficult to disobey.'

'What kind of person would obey an order to steal someone else's baby?' Carlos retorted heatedly. *'Who was Eduardo, anyway? Another soldier? The sort that justify what they did by saying they couldn't disobey orders?'*

Alfonso's mad, Eduardo thinks. What does he mean, nothing's happened? Mariana is in intensive care and their son is dead. He struggles to understand what his father-in-law is saying to him: that he's just heard of a girl who doesn't want her baby, the sort who sleep around and get pregnant by accident.

'No, Eduardo wasn't in the military. And he didn't try and justify everything, either. I don't believe that Alfonso told him the truth about that baby. He must have made up some story, something about it belonging to a woman who didn't want it. In fact, I know he didn't tell him the truth. Not even when . . .' Luz looked down and fell silent for a moment. *'But that was afterwards, several years later.'*

'She's all yours. There'll just be a few papers to fill in and that's it. You can register her as if she'd been born here, and I'll get you the exact information – weight, length, and so on. The birth certificate is on its way. We should grease someone's palm here so that we get a certificate saying she was born in this clinic. We have to do whatever it takes. We need to move very quickly and efficiently. Mariana won't even realise; we can tell her that the baby needs special care, and so does she, until everything is all set up. And when she's ready to go home, I'll bring her the baby girl.'

'It's not a girl, Alfonso, it was a boy, and he's dead.'

'Be quiet!' He glances around, as if he's afraid someone had overheard Eduardo's senseless remark. His voice becomes threatening. 'Just forget that, Eduardo, right now, do you hear me? You had a baby girl, all right?' His voice becomes less sharp. 'She was born at the same time that Mariana went into the delivery room. What a stroke of luck, eh? God must be on our side.'

I run around frantically, checking myself in the mirror and doing my hair and putting on my make-up. I want to look my best for her, so she'll love me right away. I make up the cot with the embroidered sheets. A girl, a little girl.

'She was happy. She didn't know that the colonel was going to take away the baby she'd been promised.'

'Happy, was she?' Carlos said indignantly. 'What a bitch!'

'That bitch, as you call her, put her life on the line to save me.'

'What do you mean, to save you?'

Luz blinked, and carried on talking as if she hadn't heard Carlos's question.

With everything that's been going on, I haven't had time to think of a name for her. María Pía. Mónica. No, that's a model's name, no, definitely not. I'm so nervous. Animal didn't say if he was going to bring her today or not. I hope he does. But maybe it'll be tomorrow. There goes the phone.

'Yes, love, I'm so pleased, I can't wait till you both get here . . . What do you mean, it's all off? You said . . . Look, Animal, if you don't bring her to me tomorrow, or the next day at the latest, you'll have a lot to answer for.'

I don't care if he gets angry, I'm just not going to let him fucking mess me about like that. He can say what he likes, what do I care if the colonel wants her? He can get another one. We'll soon sort this out. I don't want any explanations, I want him to bring her here. Didn't he call me just a couple of hours ago to say I'd had a baby and what she weighed and how big she was? Didn't he? Well, if he's a wimp, that's not my problem. Who am I, I'd like to know, who does he think I am, the scum of the earth? Why else am I putting up with him, in my own home, so the first bastard who feels like it can balls everything up for me and say I can't have her? No, I won't stand for it.

In the last three days Eduardo has often thought that he must be as crazy as his father-in-law, if not more so.

47

'It's difficult to say how Eduardo went from thinking that his father-in-law was out of his mind to getting sucked into a vortex of feverish actions and lies. It was probably a combination of his own grief and confusion and Alfonso's domineering personality.'

They were both there when Eduardo was told he could go in. Alfonso said, 'Please, just do as I told you. If you tell Mariana the truth, you'll regret it for the rest of your life.'

'That threat, especially after such a terrible loss, threw Eduardo off balance.'

Already he's told the first lie. 'Yes, the baby's doing fine, she's lovely. She's in the special-care unit because she had a hard time with the labour.'

'That lie he told Mariana started him down a tunnel from which there was no escape.'

Any moment now, he'll say or do something that doesn't belong in the script his father-in-law has handed him, and he'll get found out. It's odd that people believe him, because he's such a bad actor. Not only did the woman at the clinic do what he asked, thanks to the money in the envelope (a little something that must have been three or four times what she made in a year); she completely swallowed the lie Amalia had come up with, that the daughter of one of Eduardo's farmworkers had just had a baby at a hospital in Buenos Aires and she was giving it up for adoption.

'I managed to trace the woman who worked at the clinic. It was hard, because she had retired. What she told me sent me off on the wrong track. I wasted my time searching for someone who didn't exist and got nowhere. She remembered having forged the birth certificate by copying one from some hospital, but she had no memory whatsoever of what the mother's name was. It was Eduardo's brother, Javier, who told me about Miriam López. He knew very well that Miriam wasn't the sixteen-year-old daughter of one of their farmhands, as the woman from the clinic had told me. But even so, if it hadn't been for his wife Laura, Javier would never have said anything to me.'

The woman from the clinic begged Javier, with tears in her eyes, please not to tell anybody that she was the one who had made out the birth certificate so Eduardo could register his daughter. She didn't want to jeopardise her position or create problems at work, even though at the time it had seemed the right thing to do, a good idea, seeing as how the mother didn't want it.

'She's only sixteen, you see,' Eduardo had improvised.

'How old is Miriam López, the baby's mother?' he asked Alfonso that afternoon.

Alfonso's reaction frightened him. His lips compressed into a grim line, his eyes grew steely with scorn, and his hand chopped down through the air, like a machete. Eduardo imagined his own head rolling on the clinic floor.

'He knew then that he was up to his neck in something it would be difficult to get out of unharmed.'

'Just forget you ever heard that name. Right now. It's completely irrelevant. And give me back the birth certificate. I gave it to you to get things done faster, not so you could go sniffing around.'

'Eduardo made a photocopy before he handed it back. Javier saw it years later.'

'I don't quite follow about the birth certificate. How did Eduardo come to have it?'

'It seems that Alfonso wanted the correct information, so he had the birth certificate sent over to Entre Ríos immediately, I don't know who by. I suppose it must have been Animal who sent it to him. Since time was of the essence, Alfonso gave it to Eduardo. I don't really know myself. But it's lucky he saw it, because otherwise he would never have known Miriam's name.'

They told Eduardo at the clinic that he also had to register the death of his son. They gave him the death certificate. Yet he had only handed in the false birth certificate to the registry office.

'Don't worry,' said Alfonso. 'I'll see to it that the death certificate is filed.'

Better not to ask what he'll do with it, or how. Everything is so insane. It would look odd if Eduardo registered a birth as well as a death, his father-in-law explained, and he agreed. Eduardo's family is very well known in Entre Ríos. His surname won't go unnoticed and it's better not to get people talking.

'But how did he end up being so deeply involved, if he was against it?'

'Javier says it was because of Alfonso's threat that something might happen to Mariana, and because Eduardo felt to blame for having chosen a doctor who mishandled things, and because he was in shock at losing the baby; all that caused him to simply cave in to Alfonso.'

'I don't understand how you can justify that bastard's behaviour. If he was capable of registering a baby that had been kidnapped from its mother under his own name, a baby who was just plain stolen, you can't say that . . .'

'Just hear me out, please, before you judge him like that,' Luz cut in sharply. 'Eduardo's mistake cost him dearly.'

So everything will be taken care of, the way it was when Mariana asked for the baby, and Murray and the nurses didn't give anything away.

Alfonso said he would talk to Murray to make sure he kept his mouth shut. He would sort him out. 'What's he going to do, the damn fool, after the mess he made?'

'No, please, don't worry, I'll talk to him.'

Alfonso smiles at last, it's incredible but he actually smiled. Eduardo feels somewhat relieved. He's not used to all this tension. In his family, things are very different; he can't handle being ordered around all the time. Alfonso claps an arm around his shoulders, as if they were good friends, and says, 'I'll get that psychiatrist who treated Mariana to write a letter saying that he advises against telling her the truth.'

'What psychiatrist? She's never said anything to me about seeing a psychiatrist.'

'Of course not, he doesn't exist. I'll write it myself.' His laugh boomed out, hearty and obscene. 'We've got to move fast, Eduardo, and efficiently.'

'Murray remembered the case well, because he went into a deep crisis about his career as a result. Afterwards, he moved to Buenos Aires, which is why he never ran into the Iturbes. He's retired and lives in Rosario nowadays. He said he was very unhappy when Eduardo asked him to lie to Mariana. He personally thought she should get some therapy, and said so. But he felt so guilty about mishandling the case and the baby dying that he agreed not to tell Mariana anything during those first two days. Later, when her condition worsened, he was taken off the case and replaced by a doctor Alfonso brought in from Buenos Aires. He had no idea about Eduardo's plans, he told me so many times, and he was staggered when I told him. He explained what his original mistake was, the one that led to the baby's death.'

He feels as if everything is unfolding in a dream, or rather a nightmare. He feels like a thief, an amateur crook who will be unmasked at any moment. But Alfonso and Amalia keep assuring him that everything will be just fine, and that they will have the baby home before Mariana comes out of the clinic.

When Eduardo's brother Javier gets there, he finds Eduardo hunched over with his head in his hands, as if it is too heavy.

'Javier realised at once that something was wrong. Eduardo was really suffering. He went to see him every day, even though Eduardo asked him not to.'

'What are you doing here? I thought I told all of you to wait until we got home.'

'What do you mean, what am I doing here? I've come to see you, to keep you company. What's wrong, Eduardo?'

Javier asks after the baby girl and Mariana. Eduardo explains, in a bit too much detail; he feels as if he's on thin ice when he talks about the baby. She's not in the nursery; he can't see her. Javier asks what's going on.

'Nothing's going on. I've got a headache. Please go away now, I want to be alone.'

As Eduardo watches Javier walk slowly away, he's aware he hasn't fooled him: Javier knows him too well. He wants to call him back and tell him everything, but he's afraid his brother will think the same as he does. He's a party to the crime now, he's registered her. He's gone too far to change his mind.

THREE

I T STARTED AS a fever that wouldn't go down and then the pain kept worsening, until finally it was confirmed that Mariana had contracted an infection in the operating theatre and developed septi-caemia. A few hours later, she fell into a coma.

'For two weeks, it was touch and go whether Mariana would pull through. That made things a lot more complicated for Alfonso, not to mention everyone else. It changed Animal and Miriam's lives for ever, and it was terrible for Eduardo. His father-in-law had forced him to go along with something he thought wrong and which led to lies, fraud and a guilty conscience. What began the night he learned that his wife was in a coma didn't end until just recently, many years later. And it turned out badly.'

That first night, Eduardo thinks to himself that if Mariana doesn't recover, he will have lost everything that matters. His in-laws will just have to take care of the baby they've foisted on him on their own. But how can he simply wash his hands of her – he's legally the father. It would never have occurred to him to adopt a daughter, why should he, they could always have more children of their own. 'Not any more,' Murray said, and the doctor Alfonso brought in from Buenos Aires agrees. Mariana won't be able to have children.

Amalia and Alfonso are euphoric. They congratulate one another on their brilliant idea, which came at exactly the right moment.

'Don't you see, Eduardo, that if you'd told her she can't have any more children now and that the baby was stillborn, it would have been the death of her. When Mariana gets better . . .'

'And what if she doesn't get better, what if she dies? Mariana's in a coma. How can you be so bright and cheery, Amalia?'

'Take me out of here, Alfonso. I can't listen to him being so negative. He doesn't deserve what God's given him.'

53

A shiver runs up his spine and grips him by the throat. He shakes his head as if to ward off the dreadful idea of Mariana dying. No, she'll get better. It's just that he's been sucked into some sort of vortex that makes all these black thoughts come up out of nowhere and feed on each other.

By the third day, Sergeant Pitiotti began to suspect that this business of the baby girl which was meant for Miriam, and the top-secret mission the colonel had entrusted him with, could make a real mess of his personal life and his career. He had to admit he hadn't handled things well. He didn't know now whether the idea of keeping the baby and the prisoner in his own home was really as brilliant as he'd thought at the time, or whether it was a dreadful mistake that could do him a lot of damage.

'Why did he take her home?' said Carlos, in surprise. 'It's extremely unusual. Ridiculous, in fact. Although all sorts of things happened during that period which were far worse than that, appalling things. This shouldn't surprise me.'

'Miriam said that Animal wanted to stay in the colonel's good books.'

Two things coincided: Miriam's threat and the colonel's request.

'If you don't bring her to me tonight, you're not setting foot in this house again,' Miriam had said over the phone.

And then there was the colonel asking him to find somewhere safe and discreet to keep the baby until his daughter was well enough to take care of her. Unfortunately, she was in a bad way.

That was when Animal learned that the baby was to be given to Dufau's daughter. They couldn't leave the child or the mother in the hospital for more than two days, and Dufau didn't want her sent back to the detention centre, 'for the baby's sake, of course'. Animal was well aware that wasn't the only reason. Dufau had taken every possible precaution to make sure no one would ever pin this case on him: he had asked Animal to spread a rumour in the detention centre that the prisoner had had a baby boy who was stillborn and that she was in a critical condition. Liliana's guards at the hospital were from the police force, not the army, and they had nothing to do with the detention centre Dufau directed. The only one who knew was Animal. Needless to say, that gave Animal some leverage.

'It was awkward, because they couldn't take the baby to Entre Ríos until

Mariana left the clinic. Nobody wanted to take responsibility for it. What if Mariana died . . .'

Maybe the daughter will die, Sergeant Pitiotti thought hopefully, and then Miriam can keep the baby. He didn't dare ask how serious her condition was. At least it gave him a chance to kill two birds with one stone: calm Miriam down and buy some time to persuade her to give up the baby, if they had to, and also score a few points with his superior. It would be best to keep the kid at home, but together with the mother so that Miriam didn't get too many ideas.

'My wife could take care of her, sir. She's discreet and she knows how to keep her mouth shut. She's as good as they come.'

It was the perfect moment to confide in the colonel to make sure that they got either that baby, with a bit of luck, or the next one that came along; it also gave him a good excuse to explain why he wasn't married. 'As a matter of fact,' he said, lowering his voice and looking down, 'we're not actually married yet.' He concocted a melodramatic tale: his girlfriend would love to have a baby, but that was no longer possible because of a botched operation. She was such a good person that she wouldn't marry him because she didn't want him to miss out on being a father. He'd had an idea, though, and he was requesting the colonel's authorisation to go ahead with it: how about offering her one of those poor little orphans that were due to be born?

'Of course, by saying that he gave Dufau the perfect solution. If his daughter died, he could donate the baby to his faithful Animal,' said Carlos bitterly. 'For them, those babies were just things, plunder.'

'But, don't forget, the child was already registered under his son-in-law's name. Mariana went into a coma after that. I don't know about Alfonso, but Amalia said she knew all along that Mariana would recover. I don't think Alfonso would have gone so far as to tell Animal he could have the baby if Mariana died. Who knows what he had in mind; the only thing I do know is that he kept phoning and asking after the baby during those few days, as if she were something that belonged to him.'

'Of course, the next baby will be for you. Are you sure your girlfriend will agree to guard the prisoner?'

'Positive, sir. She'll do a good job.'

'We'll have to post a guard at the door. We can't leave this all up to a woman. That wouldn't be wise.'

'Was she under guard while she was at the hospital?'

'Yes, there were police officers there. The same ones who were at Miriam's flat when Liliana arrived. Three of them.'

He had a few more days to talk Miriam into it and explain how good this could be for his career; he was bound to get promotion and a payrise. 'The next kid will be for you, Dufau promised me,' he told her. But he didn't want to build up her hopes too much about keeping this baby either. No, Miriam being the way she was, it was better not to tell her anything that wasn't one hundred per cent certain, because otherwise she'd make his life hell.

But that wasn't the worst of it, because in the end, regardless of what he said to her, she'd have to give the baby to the colonel and wait for the next one, like it or not. No, the worst thing was, he was putting his career on the line, because Miriam wasn't as discreet as an army wife should be and she'd already disobeyed his orders by talking to the prisoner. He had strictly forbidden her to, forbidden both of them in fact. But it was clear, from the kinds of questions Miriam was asking, that they had talked to each other. What had she done? What was going to happen to her? Where was her comrade? 'Her comrade,' that's what she'd said, and that meant she must have talked to Liliana, because Miriam would never say comrade, she'd say husband or boyfriend or fella. 'Comrade' was the sort of thing that fucking little cow would say, she must have been getting Miriam to talk, which was a stupid waste of time because Miriam didn't have a clue what was going on, he'd only talked in very general terms, saying that there was a war going on and that they were cleansing the country. Miriam didn't have the training to be an army wife, but she'd soon learn.

On the third day, Animal decided that since time was short the best thing would be to threaten her, put the fear of God into her. He'd have to tell her that what she was doing wasn't just hurting him, but herself too, because he wouldn't marry her or bring her the next baby. I don't understand women at all, thought Animal when he saw Miriam's reaction. She's been dreaming about that baby for months, and now that Dufau's promised her the next one, she acts as if she couldn't care less.

'If you carry on behaving like a spoilt, thoughtless brat, you're going to ruin everything: my career, our child, our wedding, the lot.' Miriam turns her back and walks towards the bedroom. He has to make her react somehow. He yells, 'I'm bloody well going to kick you out on your ear if you say one more word to the prisoner.'

'You? Kick me out of my own home? You must be out of your tiny mind. I'm the one that'll be kicking you out. It's my flat.'

His urge to strike her was so intense it frightened him. He lunged at her and then pulled himself up short; just a fraction of a second more and he'd have knocked her to kingdom come. He changed tactics just as he was raising his arm and crushed her in a brutal embrace instead.

'Where's the baby?' Eduardo asks Alfonso. 'She can't be at the hospital any more. Shouldn't we be taking her home now?'

'She's in safekeeping.'

'Where?'

'Don't ask so many questions, Eduardo; the baby's just fine. As I said, I'll make sure she's taken care of until Mariana can come home. Everything's going according to plan.'

'I'm not allowed to know where she is, or who's got her, but she's legally registered as my daughter, remember, Alfonso?'

'She's in the best possible place. The mother is looking after her. Breast milk is best for babies for the first few days, and she'll breastfeed her until Mariana is well enough to take over.'

'But I thought the mother wanted to give her away?'

'She does, but she agreed to take care of her for a few days. It's the least she could do, isn't it? You'll be taking care of her for the rest of her life.'

Something viscous and rotten-smelling seems to flood the corridor where Eduardo stands talking to Alfonso.

'Can I at least go and see the baby, get to know her?'

'Absolutely not. Don't be stupid. Now stop worrying. Everything is under control. It's better for everyone concerned if you don't meet.'

What an animal; he's left my face black and blue. Why did I have to go and open my big mouth? That's what always happens when I try and keep quiet: I end up saying worse things, like last night. But if I tell him to go to hell now, what will happen to the two of them?

Lili's been here in the flat for a week now, and I love her more than I've ever loved anyone in my whole life. Touching her lovely soft skin gives me a lump in my throat, it feels just like a roll fresh out of the oven. Lili's the sweetest baby in the world.

'Who's the sweetest baby in the world?' I say to her. Animal's forbidden me to talk to the mother, but not to the baby. 'Lili, Lili.'

I call her Lili because I didn't know what to call her, so on the first day I asked the mother what her name was and she said Liliana. I told Animal I called her that because of something they used to sing when I was a kid about someone called Lili.

He said not to talk to her but I did anyway, especially the first few days, until he threatened me. The girl doesn't want to talk and I had to really work to get her to open up. It didn't look to me like she didn't want the baby, the way Animal said. I never told her I was planning to keep Lili because it seemed so awful. It was like saying to her, 'She's going to be mine, not yours, so there.' Horrible.

The truth is, I felt sorry for her the minute I saw her. They brought her in wearing handcuffs, all filthy. Her hair was in rat-tails and you couldn't tell what colour it was. She was wearing a sort of black mask because she's not allowed to see anything. She says it's like being walled up. She's been wearing it for months. When I lifted it, she covered her eyes, as if the light hurt her. But since she couldn't see with it on, she hadn't a clue how to get her nipple in the baby's mouth and the poor little thing was crying with hunger. It's tricky at first, and Lili wasn't latching on right or else she didn't know how to suck properly, so now I helped her. I put her on one breast first, watch the time, then switch her to the other one. I feel almost like I'm feeding her too. Then I burp her and sing 'Manuelita' or 'La Reina Batata' to her. I learned them off that record of nursery rhymes by María Elena Walsh.

I talked Animal into letting me take the handcuffs off her that first night.

'If you think I'm going to be up and down all night fetching the baby for her every time she's hungry, or she cries, or she needs changing, you've got another think coming,' I said.

Although that's not why I did it – I actually love picking Lili up. I just thought it was creepy, her breastfeeding with handcuffs on; she can't even cuddle the baby. In the end he agreed, because I gave him a good piece of my mind. 'I may be doing you a big favour, but I'm not your slave,' I said. 'Anyway, the door's always kept locked. You don't have to go overboard.'

At least he agreed to take the handcuffs off that first night, but he said that whenever she went to the toilet I should always put them back on and go with her. The next day, as soon as Animal had gone, I took her to the bathroom, without the handcuffs, because I wanted her to have a shower. I gave her soap and shampoo and conditioner and I told her not to get out of the water until she was all nice and clean.

'She can't be with the baby like that, all filthy,' I told Animal, because he realised what I'd done. 'Besides, she stank to high heaven and I don't want the house smelling like that.'

I told Animal a lie: I said I'd put her in the bath in handcuffs and that I'd washed her hair myself.

While she was in the bathroom, I picked out some old clothes of mine that might fit her; two or three blouses to try on, and a pair of cotton shorts. She's much smaller than me, but having just had a baby she's still got a bit of a belly. She spent ages in the bathroom. I could hear the water running and I got scared that she might do something stupid; Animal said she's very dangerous. So I went in, and there she was in the shower still.

'OK, out you get now, or you'll get waterlogged. Here's a towel. I'm leaving you some clothes to see if they fit.'

When she peeked around the shower curtain, I could hardly believe my eyes. What a transformation. She's got gorgeous hair, sort of light blonde and shiny. Even her face had changed under the shower. She seemed softer. It wasn't that she was smiling exactly, but almost.

I thought it must have been ages since she'd looked at herself in the mirror so I left her alone so she could see herself all nice and clean and pretty and try on my clothes without being rushed. I put the blindfold back on her before we left the bathroom.

At the beginning I would put it back on every time she finished breastfeeding or having a shower, but now, when I'm sure Animal isn't going to get back at any minute, I leave it off. I hate seeing that black thing covering her face. She used to look at me as if she hated my guts those first few days, but not any more. Now she even smiles at me when I bring her the baby. Or maybe she's smiling at her child.

That first morning, when I took off her blindfold in the bedroom, she stared at me and then gazed round the room at the baby-bear wallpaper and the cot. I realised she might suspect that it had been done up like that for her baby, but she never breathed a word. Right away I started feeling guilty, and that was even before she said what she said later on. So I did the first thing that came into my mind, and told her a whopping lie: that we'd done up the room because my sister was having a baby and she was going to come and live with us. 'Do you like the wallpaper? Aren't the little bears sweet? We don't know if it'll be a boy or a girl, you see.'

Eventually she plucked up courage to ask me some questions.

'Who are you? What am I here for? Why did they bring me here?'

I told her my boyfriend had asked me to take care of them for a few days until they took her back to prison, seeing how much I liked babies. 'And yours is just gorgeous. Isn't she gorgeous? Look at her little feet, her tiny little toes; I could just gobble them up.'

Then she said softly but sternly that I must know they weren't taking her to a prison, they were going to kill her, like all the other women, and take her daughter.

'You're going to keep her, aren't you?'

Liliana has sparkling green eyes, they're sort of mesmerising, and she stared at me with so much hatred I thought she was going to knock me over.

'No, of course I'm not.'

She made me feel like a real shit, because I almost did steal the baby from her, or Animal would have for me.

'Miriam didn't want the baby or any other baby by that point. She told me that the moment she saw Liliana with her daughter, she realised how horrific it all was.'

She said she couldn't understand why she was being held in the flat and why they'd taken her to the hospital. 'Where else would you have a baby?' I said. 'Anywhere,' she said, 'like that girl who was screaming for help for hours, until finally they put her on the kitchen table, with a male nurse who did nothing but yell at her, and guards standing around saying obscene things, and that's where she had it. A baby boy. But they took it away and two days later they took her away too.'

On the third day, when she kept saying that they were going to kill her and what would become of her daughter, I promised her that I wouldn't let anything happen to the baby. And I hugged her, because she was crying her eyes out and hugging her seemed the most natural thing to do, because I felt so sorry for her. At first she flinched away, as if she was trying to protect herself, but then she let go. And then, while she was in my arms, she asked me in a low voice if I knew anything about her comrade, where he was, or whether they'd killed him.

'No, at first she didn't give his name, she just asked for her comrade. She only used your name the last day she was in the flat.'

When I asked Animal he went crazy, completely berserk. He smashed all the plates on the top shelf of the dresser and called me every name under the sun, so I don't dare bring the subject up again. He must have said something to her, because she hasn't talked to me since then. And I haven't tried to talk to her either. We just look at one another and something sort of happens when we do, or else we watch each other looking at Lili and playing with her.

Yesterday, when I took off the blindfold, I showed her how much better Lili's taking the breast now, she's feeding really well, and she opened her mouth as if she was dying to ask me something but was too terrified. I moved closer to her and even though there was no one there I whispered, 'What is it? I'm not allowed to talk to you either, but no one's going to find out.'

She asked me again about her comrade, did I know if he'd been killed or what had happened to him, because he wasn't being held where she was. She said he must have fallen, they must have killed him by now, and she couldn't understand why she was still alive because all the people who were seized with her were dead by now. He wasn't there when they came for her, but in all these months she's never, ever seen or heard anything from him. Apparently even though they don't let you talk in there, somebody always manages to say a word or two from time to time.

'One of my neighbours warned me. He waylaid me on the street when I was on my way home, just a few blocks from the house. According to poor Ramón, they'd taken Liliana and they were waiting for me, heavily armed.'

Carlos fell silent. Luz wanted to ask him all sorts of things: what did he do then, how did he survive, how could he abandon Liliana like that? But she'd already decided not to deluge him with questions. She would just let him say whatever he felt like, and she'd tell him as much of the story as she knew.

She spoke so quietly and so fast that the words came tumbling out of her mouth and I couldn't understand her. Apparently she wanted to let him know she'd had the baby, which was natural enough, I thought.

'Are you sure he's in prison too?'

At that moment we heard the sound of the key in the front door. I whipped the blindfold back on her and started singing 'Manuelita'.

Animal was going to have to listen to me this time, I thought. Were they really killing them? Those pigs. Why? What have they done? Why are they being held? I didn't know how to bring it up – after he got so angry the second night I don't dare mention it. The truth is, I'm getting more and more scared of Animal. I can't even pluck up the courage to ask him what's going on with the colonel. He said he'd be coming here when his daughter gets out of the clinic, but Lili's been here for a week and he hasn't said a word about when they'll be fetching her. Last night I behaved as if nothing had happened, gave him his dinner and some wine, but I never found the right moment to bring it up.

Later on, the usual thing happened. Whenever we fuck, he lies around afterwards as if he'd just stuffed himself. I did it so many times without feeling like it, for work, that I don't know why this was so hard, but it was different. It's different fucking a bloke because he's paying you to than because you want something out of him. Maybe, too, it was hard because I used to like it with Animal sometimes, when I thought he loved me or I loved him, but doing it like this seemed disgusting and unnatural.

'She started to feel repelled by Animal. And that revulsion turned into a terrible hatred. The only reason she didn't throw him out was because she thought he might still be able to do something to stop the baby ending up in Dufau's hands and save Liliana. She couldn't believe they were really going to kill her.'

But all the same, I pretended I was dying for it and that I'd had an amazing orgasm and I told him he was a fantastic lover and then I waited, not too long because otherwise he nods off, and I asked him. I was careful. 'Now don't get angry with me,' I said softly, 'but I want to ask you something. It's really none of my business, I know, but since I'm with her all day every day, I'd just like to know if they're going to kill her.'

He didn't like me saying that one bit, but he told me not to worry, that she'd just be sent back to prison. And I'd been trying so hard to be good and keep my mouth shut that I blew my top.

'So why can't she keep the baby, she'd be better off with her mother in jail than with that fucking bastard of a colonel.'

He was livid and he gave me such a clout I can still see his fingermarks on my face. Its completely black and blue. I'm going to show Liliana as soon as the baby wakes up.

No, it would be better to show her beforehand, while the baby's asleep. I don't want Lili getting upset.

'Javier and Eduardo weren't just brothers, they were close friends. Javier thought it was normal for Eduardo to be feeling low, given Mariana's condition, but he couldn't understand why his brother didn't want to see him, why he reacted the way he did whenever he asked about the baby, and why he kept sending him away and asking to be left alone.'

'No, I won't go away. Not until you tell me what's going on, Eduardo. Why are you talking to me like this? I know something's wrong, but you won't tell me what. Is it something to do with the baby? Is she ill? Why can't I see her? Just trust me, Eduardo, please. I'm here to help you. Don't tell me to go away again.'

'Look, I'm sorry, Javier. I've not been myself the last few days, partly because of Mariana, partly because of my in-laws. They're just so controlling. They won't leave me alone and they keep coming up with weird ideas all the time; they make me do whatever they feel like and I'm such a bloody wimp that I can't stand up to them. I was a mess and I wasn't thinking straight and Alfonso's so strong-willed it's hard to resist him. And now I'm at my wits' end. I feel as if I'm going out of my mind.'

Javier can't make sense of Eduardo's confused babbling. He can't work out what Eduardo meant by 'weird ideas', and Eduardo only gets more distressed when he presses him.

'Javier knew Eduardo was being pressured by his in-laws, but not what he'd done. Eduardo didn't tell him until many years later.'

Eduardo asks him to please, please be quiet now, not to ask any more questions. It's true something's wrong, but he can't talk about it and he doesn't want to lie to him, not to him, because he always knows. Eduardo breaks down in tears and Javier puts his arm around him and comforts him, the way he used to when they were little. They've always had a lot of respect for one another, and he will respect Eduardo's silence.

'Liliana, wake up. See this great big bruise? That's what he gave me for asking about you. Just think if I'd asked about your comrade, I'd never live to tell the tale. If I haven't bloody well thrown him out by now it's for Lili's and your sake. He's a punter who moved in with me, and this is my place, not his. I'm going to play along with him for now because he's jumpy about all this, but as soon as you two have gone, I'm going to tell him to piss off.'

'What do you mean, we're going? When? And what about my baby? What are they going to do with my baby? Tell me the truth. You're going to keep her, aren't you? That's why the room's all done up like this.'

'I already told you that's not true. The room's for my nephew.'

There's no way in hell I can tell her about the colonel, the shit would really hit the fan then. I tell her I haven't a clue why they brought her here, that Animal doesn't tell me anything, and when she starts crying I say maybe it's so she'll be more comfortable these first few days. I can't tell if she's laughing or crying, it's both, yes, she's laughing and crying at the same time, as if she's gone mad. I don't know what to say. She looks at me and those green eyes of hers are like daggers.

'You're lying to me. You're going to keep her,' she says. 'That's why you've done up this room. And where did you get the clothes Lili's wearing? Are they for your nephew too? Why are you putting them on Lili, why?'

Now she's sobbing as if her heart would break. I feel angry and sorry for her all at once, and she goes on and on, although now she's not shouting at me.

'Promise me you'll tell her who I am, that I'm her mother. And that they killed me because . . .'

'That's enough now, Liliana. I'm not going to keep her. Colonel Dufau is going to give her to his daughter.'

'Miriam didn't want to tell her, but apparently she lost it because Liliana asked her if she . . . to tell me if . . .'

Luz broke off and wiped her eyes furiously. 'I'm sorry, this is painful.'

She cries and cries and says, 'Dufau, Dufau,' like a broken record.

'Don't cry, Liliana. There's nothing I can do. I'll ask Animal again not to give her to him, but he's such a bloody wimp, he always obeys orders. I don't know if there's anything I can do, I really don't. Don't cry. I'll come and visit you in prison, I'll bring you food.'

'Let me go, please, let me escape.'

'Are you mad? Are you trying to get me killed? And anyway, how could I, there's always a police guard outside the door, they change them every eight hours but there's always someone. They're watching me the whole time.'

I tell her if she doesn't stop crying, her milk will dry up and she won't be able to feed Lili properly. Babies need peace and quiet. But the truth is I'm at the end of my tether. There's a great big lump in my throat and I can't take any more.

I put the blindfold back on her so she won't see the tears running down my face and I start patting Lili's back and lay my cheek on her fuzzy little head until I start to calm down.

'Manuelita vivía en Pehuajó, pero un día se marchó.' Singing nursery rhymes always helps me to calm down.

'I like the way you sing. What's your name?'

'Miriam.'

'Sing me some more, Miriam. There's something I want to say to you,' she says in a murmur. 'I don't know why you're living with Animal, but . . .'

What can I say? 'I don't know, I fancied him. He used to be gentle and kind.'

I start singing again, '*Manuelita vivía en Pehuajó,*' and she goes, 'Gentle? Kind?'

She's so amazed I feel ashamed. I'd better not answer. '*Pero un día se marchó. Nadie supo bien por qué, a París ella se fue.*'

'But you're not like them, otherwise you wouldn't be taking such good care of my daughter. Please, let me escape. There was always a risk I'd be killed, we knew that all along, but now that Lili's here, how can I let those monsters steal her and keep her for themselves? You love Lili, you gave her her name. Do you think the people who murdered her parents should be allowed to keep her? Please, let me escape. Dufau is the worst of them all, he's the one in charge. I've never seen him, I was always blindfolded, but sometimes they would bring us out, when there were "visitors". And I know it was Dufau who talked to me. He asked who my parents were, what school I went to. "How did a nice girl like you get mixed up with that scum? You're so pretty and well educated you could be my daughter." He actually said that to me – "You could be my daughter." And now he's going to give Lili to his daughter!'

She cries and cries and I carry on singing 'Manuelita' while I put Lili back in her cot, shut the door, and double-lock it.

No, I don't want those arseholes to get her. Because if that bastard really does want to steal her, then anybody who takes care of Lili for him is a right shit. A shit like I almost was, without realising. I had no idea it was like this. Can it be true, what Liliana told me? That they're going to kill her? That they kill them like that? That they make the other girls give birth right there in prison?

I don't want to hear this. I'm going to try and stop her talking to me any more. Animal says they're all killers. They must have done something to be in jail. But all the same, it's hard to believe, and besides Liliana loves her baby. It doesn't matter what she did. If she loves her, why should I get her?

Sergeant Pitiotti informed the colonel that everything was going fine. The baby was getting bigger, his wife was carrying out her role efficiently, and everything was under control. The doctor had been and had said that the baby was gaining weight normally, and that she had no health problems. Needless to say, Animal did not tell the colonel that things were under control only thanks to a good beating.

Dufau gave no hint as to when this mission would end. Sergeant Pitiotti wished it would be over as soon as possible and that the colonel's daughter would either die or get better once and for all, because he didn't want this tension with Miriam to go on any longer, what with the way she'd been looking at him lately. Because even though Miriam had been putting on a brave face and had stopped talking about keeping the baby, he could tell she wasn't the same as before. She even went so far as to ask him why they didn't leave the baby in jail, with her mother. Before, when she was busy getting everything ready, she would never have said anything like that. It was as if she loved the baby more than him. It was all that fucking baby's fault. If only they'd get things over with and take it away for good, he could make a fresh start with Miriam. He'd win her over, he promised himself. He didn't want to lose her.

I'd told myself I wasn't going to talk to her any more, or rather that I wasn't going to let her talk to me, because I'd rather not know. I'd only end up letting something slip to Animal and then I'd be in for it. But then, I don't know how it happened, we were changing Lili together, and all of a sudden Lili's cord dropped off and I was so thrilled that I don't know what came over me. I went to the kitchen and opened a bottle of white wine so Liliana and I could celebrate, because now the cord's off, Lili's little tummy is so sweet, all pink and soft.

Lili is such a love. Every day she does something new. That funny face she used to pull at first has turned into a proper smile now. And she's got lovely bright eyes, green eyes; they're getting greener every day. It's as if she can see you now. I think she recognises me. Every time she does something new I'm so proud; that's why I forgot about not talking to Liliana or letting her talk to me. We were just so happy, and after we'd had a bit to drink we started laughing at anything and saying all sorts of silly things, toasting her green eyes, her tiny little feet, and her smile. We kept on coming up with new things and chink, bottoms up, let's have another glass.

'I can't see Liliana drinking wine and toasting things with Animal's girlfriend. That can't be right. Who told you that? Miriam?'

'Yes. What is it you don't understand? Things were desperate for those poor women, but they let themselves go for a bit and tried to celebrate as best they could. Miriam told me that for both of them, the baby represented life itself.' Luz made no attempt to hide her emotion. 'I think that experience was very important, crucial even, in cementing the alliance between the two.'

Maybe too it's because I can't stand seeing the pain in Liliana's face, and because I don't know how the hell to get out of this, my hands are totally tied, I'm scared to death of Animal and I keep thinking they're going to take Lili away, that I'm not going to see her again, and what will happen to Liliana. I just felt like living for that moment and being happy, both of us.

We must be completely barmy, giggling away as if we were at some great big cocktail party, with the pigs there outside the door, in the mess we're in, as if we were clueless. Liliana has flopped on to the bed, laughing her head off. It's all my fault. I put my finger to my lips and signal her to shut up.

'Now let's drink to you,' said Liliana slowly.

'And to you,' I said.

Then she stops laughing, that light goes on in her eyes and she says something that knocks me for six. 'Miriam, let me escape.'

I put the blindfold back on; that's my way of telling her enough is enough, but really it's so she can't see me, because she's driving me mad. The baby starts crying and I pick her up and start singing 'Los Tres Alpinos' to her. I don't know why the words came back to me – maybe because Aunt Nuncia used to sing it. 'Eran tres alpinos que venían de la guerra, ahití, ahitá, rataplán.'

'Don't stop, Miriam,' Liliana says.

'Que venían de la guerra,' I sing, louder still because Liliana has started talking. 'Look at the state my ankles are in. That's because of the leg-irons. I spent months like that.' Eran tres alpinos que venían de la guerra, ahití, ahitá, vataplán. This is a war, Animal always says, and Liliana keeps talking about being kept blindfolded and chained and filthy dirty, and the horrible smells, el más chiquitito traía un ramo de flores, ahití, ahitá, rataplán, and she's telling me all this stuff: what they do to them in the operating room, that's what they call it where they torture them, and she says it's Animal who does it, himself, personally, although not to her, she never could understand why not when he did it to all the others, I know why all right, because he was taking care of Lili for me! *La hija del rey que estaba en la ventana ahití ahitá rataplán, que estaba en la ventana,* louder, louder, I don't want to hear this but I don't tell her to shut up, I just sing louder so Lili can't hear about when they came and took her mother away, what they stole from her, she was lying on the floor and they kicked her, and she put her hands up to protect her belly where Lili was growing, *oh bello alpino dame el ramo de flores oh bello alpino dame el ramo de flores ahití ahitá rataplán,* this can't be true, oh my God, it can't be true, she was naked and Animal started feeling her up, so you're pregnant are you, you little bitch, and all that stuff he did to her, I'm trying to hide behind the nursery rhyme, I don't want her to stop any more, I want her to keep on spewing up all that stuff I'd no idea about, that's bottled up inside her, get it all out, all of it, even if it turns my stomach, and makes me sick, and splashes all over me, and covers me in horrible stinking stuff, I just want Liliana to feel better. Lili's in my arms, and I say in her ear, 'Listen to me and not her, *te lo daré si te casás conmigo,*' but why why, why are they doing this to them, they turned the radio up to drown the screams but it didn't stop those blood-curdling shrieks climbing up the walls of her cell, just as I'm trying to cover up these blood-curdling words, *te lo daré si te casás conmigo, ahití, ahitá, rataplán,* but why, why, between the *ahitá* and the *rataplán,* because we wanted social justice, and I'm singing louder and louder, *buen día señor rey me caso con su hija,* because we wanted a just society, God knows how the rest of this song goes, but I've got to keep going, *dame el ramo de flores,* singing loudly as if I really wanted the princess to marry the fusilier, crying as I sing, crying away when she says, 'I just can't bear thinking that they're going to kill me and that my little girl, my Lili, your Lili, Miriam, because you love her too, will end up with those murderers who are going to steal her from me and take away her identity so she won't know who her real parents were.'

I put down the baby, who's fast asleep, knocked out by that deafening version of 'Los Tres Alpinos' mixed in with the horrific things Liliana's been whispering.

Liliana has fallen silent. I run out, lock the door, throw myself down on the bed and cry my eyes out. I hate Animal, I hate him, and I hate myself too. How could I be so selfish, such a shit. I've got to do something. I've got to save Lili and Liliana.

'When Javier found his brother over the moon because Mariana had come out of her coma and was recovering fast, he decided to confront him. Why couldn't he see the baby, and what exactly had his in-laws been up to? What had he done? Afterwards he was sorry he'd said anything, because Eduardo's good humour vanished instantly.'

Eduardo's eyes cloud over, and he stares at the wall.

'There's nothing wrong with the baby. They're taking care of her, that's all. You'll see her soon enough at home, Javier. In a few days, two or three at the most.'

I don't know where to start after what happened yesterday. But I can't behave as if she'd never said anything. I tell her I had no idea this was going on, that I couldn't even imagine what it must have been like. 'Please believe me, I've got nothing to do with it, I'm really shattered, he was always so loving with me and he's always going on about how they're going to free the country from foreign ideologies and what have you, but not this.'

'Let's escape, Miriam. I know where I could hide.'

'Look, Liliana, if you keep on going on at me and saying horrible things like yesterday, I'm going to have to blindfold you. Don't talk to me unless it's about Lili. I can't do anything, he'll kill me. You put the fear of God into me yesterday with all that stuff you told me. You don't want the same thing to happen to me, do you? You got yourself mixed up in this because you wanted social justice, that's what you said, but I don't buy that crap, do you hear me? I think it's all a load of garbage and I've no intention of dying for something you believe in and I don't.'

'You're right, Miriam.'

I lay the baby down on top of her: Lili loves going to sleep on her tummy. I watch them fall asleep as I sing 'Manuelita'. They're so sweet, both of them. It's horrible they're going to take her daughter away

70

from her like that, it's inhumane. I don't know what on earth I was thinking of before, that maybe because she was in jail she didn't want her, I don't know, I was just thinking of myself, and that brute Animal made me think everything was all right, what a fucking bastard. Is it really true they do those things to them? Could Liliana have been exaggerating? I've got to do something to save Lili and Liliana. But I don't know what.

The main thing is not to let on to Animal that I know anything. He mustn't suspect I know who he is and what he does. If I can, I've got to try and get hold of some information that might help us.

When Sergeant Pitiotti stopped at the florist's and picked out a dozen roses he was convinced he was doing the right thing. He wasn't just doing it because he knew it was dangerous to be violent with Miriam, because after all she was a bird and she might take it badly and mess up the mission. It was also because he really did want to make things up with her, because he loved her as he had never loved any other woman. He'd always dreamed of having a bird like that. Dead sexy, a real peach, and good-natured too.

The mission was winding up. The next baby was earmarked for him. He'd given the necessary orders so the prisoner would be well fed and no one would touch her. And soon he'd be able to give the baby to Miriam, although she never said anything about it these days. That fucking baby had even made her forget her dreams.

Sergeant Pitiotti's career was very important to him, but so was having a good woman at his side. He told her he was sorry, that he'd been very worked up, things were too tense at work, and what she'd said had pushed him over the edge but he'd been thinking it was only logical what happened, because she had started feeling sorry for them. 'You're so naïve and good-hearted there's no way you could imagine what a fucking little murderer like her is capable of, even if she does look harmless.'

'Miriam was determined to stay calm and controlled, not to give herself away. She wanted to make the most of the fact that things were going smoothly to winkle some information out of him.'

'Thanks so much for saying sorry, Animal. I've felt awful all day because of what happened. It's just that I'm here all day long so I've got fond of the baby and it's going to be hard for me when they take her away. The sooner they go, the better. When are they coming to get them?'

'Either tomorrow night or the day after. He's going to come by himself, now that his daughter is better. It'll be a good chance for me to introduce you. He promised that the very next baby that's born is for us. Probably next week.'

' "Tomorrow night or the day after." Those words kept echoing in Miriam's mind as she handed the baby to Liliana.'

Of course he's happy, he's delighted Mariana has recovered. 'So why the long face?' How can he tell her? He's terrified she'll ask about the baby. Deceiving everybody else was hard enough, but deceiving Mariana like this, having to tell her that yes, the baby is beautiful, and that she's at home, waiting for them, that Amalia's taking care of her – it's ridiculous. How can the baby be at home, and her here, without ever having seen the child? Mariana's going to ask him to bring her along and then what's he going to say? But Mariana believes everything Alfonso says and his explanation must be a convincing one because she doesn't ask anything. He feels like a fraud.

In another day or two, I'll never see Lili again. I won't be able to stroke her lovely soft skin or look at her dimples or her little hands or her tiny fingers gripping mine. And I'll never see Liliana again either. I've got to do something, but I don't know what. What if instead of buying pepper I buy poison and kill Animal? No, I can't, and besides how would I get out of here afterwards? The guards are outside the door. I'm going to tell Liliana. She'll think of something. She's a revolutionary. I put the roast in the oven and go to her room.

'What are you doing?' Animal asks.

'I'm going to give her the baby, it's time for her feed.'

'She can manage by herself, she's not wearing shackles or handcuffs.'

I smile, and give him a kiss – ugh. 'I'll be back in a second, love, I just want to go and take a peek at the baby and then we can have a cuddle. Why don't you lie down for a bit until lunch is ready?'

'Hurry up and get back here – I want to fuck you.'

Animal goes into the bedroom. Thank God, he can't hear me from there.

I go in and lock the door. I don't take off Liliana's blindfold. I lean up close and whisper, 'They're coming for you both tomorrow or the day after. Don't say anything because he's here. I'm going to keep Animal occupied. Think of something, because I can't.' Lili has started bawling, as if she knows what's up, and her cries cover what I have to say. 'Something so all three of us can get away.'

'She was afraid, not so much of Animal, but of her own words, of what she had said, of what might happen to her, of how things were turning out in a way she'd never thought possible but didn't want to stop. Just think about who Miriam was and the kind of life she'd led, and bear in mind that just a few days earlier she had wanted that child for herself. She told me that at that moment she remembered Animal telling her Liliana was a murderer. What if she helped Liliana escape and then Liliana killed her? she thought. Then Liliana's hand took hers and Miriam jumped and almost cried out. Liliana raised Miriam's hand to her mouth and kissed it. She felt Liliana's tears falling on to her hand.'

How could he say she's a murderer? Anyway, if Liliana doesn't kill me, Animal will. I whisper in her ear, 'Think of a place for us to hide, and how we can get out of here without being killed.'

'I need information,' Liliana murmurs. 'Where we are, who lives underneath, the layout of the flat, everything you know.'

I go out and lock the door.

FOUR

WHEN ANIMAL WOKE up, I pretended I was still asleep, even though I'd been wide awake all night. Lili woke up I don't know how many times, as if she knew what was going on. I went in once, on tiptoe, because Animal hates me going into the 'cell' (as he calls it) at night, and under cover of Lili's crying I gave Liliana the information she wanted: where the flat is; how there are two flats on every floor and a staircase through the door on the landing outside; and how there's a guard posted downstairs that changes every eight hours. Whenever I go out or he wants to have a coffee or go to the toilet he comes into the flat. At night, when Animal's here, there's another guard too.

'We won't do it while Animal's here,' she said quickly.

She's terrified of him. I'm scared of him too, but not the way she is. He can be such a big softy with me that I have a hard time imagining he could kill me. Of course he would, though, and very, very slowly too – that's what he enjoys.

I left the room quickly, not just because I was afraid Animal would catch me talking to her, but because I didn't want her to make me scared, otherwise I wouldn't be able to go on. I couldn't help thinking about what he would do: he'd take me to the detention centre and make me lie naked on that bed Liliana talked about and he'd tie me up. I covered my eyes, the way I do when I'm watching a horror film, but it was no use, because the images were inside my head, not outside like at the pictures. I saw myself being tortured like Liliana described while I was singing 'Los Tres Alpinos' and my body writhing with pain with that electric thing on my nipples and my gums and up my . . . oh God, stop, that's enough. I can't bear to think about it any more.

I went into the room a little while ago and the two of them were sleeping so soundly I felt bad waking them. When I see them fast asleep like that, all sweet and helpless, I start to feel that I can't let this horrible business go on any longer, I have to put a stop to it. Then I see myself again, screaming, strapped down on that bed, and Animal with that look he gets when he's turned on, jabbing that electric thing all over my body. What's happening to me? Why can't I stop thinking about it?

Lili's woken up, what a love, she's saved me. She brings me luck, she's going to bring us all luck, I know it. I mustn't think about what could happen to me. I've just got to do it.

'Miriam went into Liliana's room many times that day. In just a few hours, the two of them got to know each other better than many people do in a lifetime.'

Liliana can't understand why I want to escape with her, she thinks it's pointless for me to take the risk, that it'll just set Animal on to us. She says that last night she started thinking about how we could do it and she decided she would leave me tied up and handcuffed on the bed, so that Animal will think she made me help her.

'Oh, right. You think he'll believe that? Animal's no fool. You're locked in. How on earth could you make me do anything? I'm not a wimp, and you're a lot smaller than me. You wouldn't dare try and take me on, and if you did, I'd win – look, I'm much bigger and stronger than you.'

I burst out laughing from sheer nerves. And what does she say to calm me down?

'You've got a big knife in the kitchen?'

'Yes. Why?'

'You've got to work it so that when Animal rings up, you say something that will explain your having the knife in your hand. What time does he usually phone?'

'On and off during the day. Why the knife?'

'Because afterwards you can tell him that the baby cried and you weren't thinking and you went into the room with the knife and closed the door and then I grabbed the knife and held it to your throat and made you do whatever I wanted.'

Just thinking about it scares me sick. I refused to say yes; I want to be able to escape with them. There's no way I'm staying behind. It doesn't matter whether Animal thinks she made me or not, if they escaped when I was supposed to be guarding them and he can't give the baby to his colonel it's going to mess up his career and there's no way he'd forgive me. I don't think he'd kill me, but he'd definitely beat me up bad. Oh God, I don't want to think about it. In any case, what would I do, how would I ever get him out of here? How would I tell him, after I've gone on at him for months about a baby, that I don't want one, not from a fucking murderer. I'd be sure to let something slip some time, however careful I was. I don't think I'd always manage to worm my way out of things the way I did that night with that sadistic bastard of a major who tied me up and stuck a gun up me. There's no way I could pull it off, because I hate Animal much more than that pig. I hardly knew him and Animal disgusts me much more than he did. To think I ended up, I won't say loving him, but at least being touched because he loved me and he was so kind and gentle. Gentle! He's a torturer. Life's too short to go on being such fool. That's what I said to Liliana a little while ago and she laughed.

'You're not a fool, you just made a mistake, that's all.'

I told her about how when I met him I was on the game, and the lengths he went to to sleep with me, and about how I thought he was sweet. It was lucky I pulled myself up short in time, because I got so carried away I almost told her about the abortion and she would have put two and two together and worked out what a cow I'd been.

It's funny, what happened; I usually don't like telling people anything about my life, and the few times I have, they've gone and done the dirty on me. But this situation with Liliana is so weird I feel like telling her everything, as if she were a close friend, the sister I never had. There's something about her that I trust. Maybe I just felt like talking because it was the last chance I'd ever have to tell my life story if they kill me. I felt a bit awkward, because she just watched me and didn't say a word, so I asked her to tell me something about her life. It was like I wanted us to be even. I felt as if I'd taken off all my clothes and she hadn't. But before she'd even opened her mouth, I got frightened that she'd go on about the detention centre again and I'd start seeing horrible things.

'It's got to be something nice, not like that stuff you told me about the other day, please, or I'll end up having nightmares. Tell me about your boyfriend, your comrade. Do you love each other very much?'

It was like a light had been switched on; her smile lit up everything. She's so pretty when she smiles and laughs. I don't know how she can, with what's going on. But this morning, she laughed quite a lot. She was in a very good mood.

'I'm just glad we're going to escape,' she said, when I finally persuaded her to talk. And she laughed again, so happily that seeing her that way made me look forward to it too.

In the end she told me that her boyfriend's name is Carlos Squirru and she asked me, if something happens to her, if they kill her, to try and find out what happened to him. If by any chance he's still alive, I'm to tell him that Lili was born and who has her.

'Liliana gave her a phone number and a name so she could try and find out about Carlos.'

'What was the name?'

'It's one I still remember. Franco.'

'Oh.' A bitter smile came over his face, and he flicked his hand as if to swat away a fly.

'Do you know him?'

'Yes, but I'd prefer to forget. He cracked, or rather they broke him. He was a collaborator. By the time I found out, I was in Spain; for me that was a turning point. It opened a chasm between me and everything I'd believed in until then. He was one of the top people in the organisation – and a friend. He was the first person I saw after they took Liliana. I was desperate that night.' Carlos fell silent, lost in his memories, which he obviously didn't want to share with Luz. Finally he roused himself. 'So what happened? Did she ever ring that number?'

'No, never. When Miriam tried to write it down, Liliana told her to memorise it, because she didn't know what was going to happen and it could be dangerous; you never wrote down names or phone numbers. It was part of their discipline. Miriam didn't want to imagine anything happening to Liliana, and besides she was never one for discipline, she didn't understand, unlike Liliana. She did remember the name, but she forgot the number. And she couldn't remember your name properly either; she wasn't sure she'd got it right.'

'I asked you for something nice, and you talk about how they're going

78

to kill you. If they kill you and we're together, most likely they'll get me too.'

'You never know,' she said. 'Animal's in love with you. And when a woman's got influence with the powers that be . . .'

I got cross and told her to stop taking the piss; I'd gone and told her about my life and all she could do was show off and make fun of me. She said she was sorry, but when she's nervous she has a hard time being serious. She told me about a night when there were screams of terror coming from what they called the operating room. The screams seemed to be climbing up the walls of her cell, ricocheting off her, ripping into her, and in order not to listen she started telling jokes with another girl who was in her cell for a few days, and they kept on talking and laughing louder and louder until a guard came in and started beating them up and calling them names.

'He threw us on the ground and he didn't trample on me, but he did her. He kicked the hell out of her. Sofi was screaming and he . . .'

'You can't stop talking about that stuff, can you! I don't want to hear about it, Liliana, please. Hasn't anything nice ever happened to you?'

'Lots,' she said. 'When I was a little girl, I liked riding my bike. I used to go out with Dad, very early in the morning. It was so much fun,' and she smiled faintly. 'Poor Dad! I didn't mean to hurt him. He never understood why I got involved in politics, he couldn't . . . He died, last year, from a heart attack, after I'd moved out of the house.'

'I asked you for something nice, Liliana.'

'When I met Carlos, the first time we made love, it was just so wonderful.'

Carlos was the first and only man she'd slept with. I couldn't believe it. A girl with her looks could have had all the men she wanted.

'They spent hours and hours talking. Eleven hours, Miriam said. They didn't just plan the escape; they talked about all sorts of things. I think what happened between them that day changed Miriam's life for ever. Despite the enormous differences between them, they shared a bond that went very deep: their love for Lili.'

'I'm only twenty-two,' she said, almost apologetically. 'And we loved each other very, very much.' She nearly broke down in tears. She's pretty certain that they killed her boyfriend when they caught him.

'It's better that way,' she said, 'because in the centre they kill you little by little, they degrade you, they wear you down, they make you feel dirty. They kill you over and over again. And if you're pregnant, well, if I hadn't been, I would be dead by now. Now I know why they only used the prod on my legs – they were trying to make sure the pregnancy went OK because they wanted my child to be healthy to give to Dufau's daughter. He chose me, the dirty bastard, the murderer. And it was Animal who came to me and . . .'

'All right, that's enough, Liliana,' I interrupted, because I didn't know what to do when she said that.

If she only knew that Lili was saved for me, not for that other woman! I have to get Liliana and the baby out of here, it's the least I can do, even if it means putting my life on the line. Even thinking of what I was going to do before makes me sick.

We still don't know if Dufau is coming today or tomorrow. I've got to wait until Animal phones.

Now she's working out how we can escape. I gave her the times when the guards change and what little I know about them. They're always the same men. The one who's on from twelve till eight is quite nice and he fancies me like mad. His name is Pilón, Corporal Pilón. The other day he was in the kitchen making *mate*★ and I came in and bent down to get a cake out of the oven. When I turned round, he was pouring hot water just about everywhere except into the pot. I was wearing a miniskirt and he must have seen everything, but I didn't realise until I saw his face.

'What's the matter with you, corporal?' I said as I took the kettle out of his hand. 'You're flooding my kitchen.'

'I beg your pardon, miss,' he answered, looking incredibly sheepish.

I hate them, but right then I found him funny. Anyway, I'm like that, what can you do? When a bloke looks at me as if he's dying for it, I love it. I was tempted to come on to him a bit, there's no way he'll say anything to Animal, he's terrified of him. And if he does tell him, all the better. Sod Animal. So I get up close to him and he starts panting like a dog. When I'm just an inch away from him, I say, in that husky voice I

★ A kind of tea, popular in South America.

80

learned from Annette, 'Now you just watch where you're pouring that water, corporal, instead of watching something else, however much you like the look of it. Or do you want me to tell my husband?'

I went out laughing to myself. Later on, he knocked at the door again wanting to go to the toilet, so I let him in. I'd gone and changed, and I went on the attack again. 'Look at me, dressed like a nun, so I don't distract you, corporal.'

'I didn't mean no disrespect, miss. I was just looking. Please don't say anything to Sergeant Pitiotti.'

'Don't worry, honeybun.' I copied that word from Inés; men love it, I don't know why. 'I was just pulling your leg. Of course I'm not going to tell him.' I leaned against the bathroom door as he was going in, so I was pretty close. 'But don't look at me that way – you make me nervous.' I eyed him as if I couldn't wait, and licked my lips slowly with the tip of my tongue, the way he must have wanted to lick me all over.

The man practically threw himself at me, he came at me and then stopped dead, as if he'd been pulled up short on a leash. I walked off quickly and made sure I wasn't around when he came out of the bathroom. He must be shitting himself thinking about what will happen if he fucks me and Animal finds out. Since then we've been looking at each other, flirting, but he never crosses the line.

Afterwards I started wondering why I'd done that. Perhaps because I hate Animal: I want them all to think, even to say that his girlfriend's dead sexy but he can't be any good because if he was I wouldn't be making eyes at every bloke who looked my way. Just thinking about it made me feel pleased. After what Liliana told me, I hate them so much that leaving Pilón all wound up and randy feels good. But it must be because I feel like fooling around too. I'm out of practice these days, I've been shut up here all day for months now, going out of my mind, not knowing what to do with myself. I won't deny that I like the idea of that bloke thinking about me all the time, the way Animal used to, and not being able to do anything about it because I'm his sergeant's girl. That's why sometimes when Pilón's around I wear miniskirts or skin-tight jeans and a cropped T-shirt. I get changed, of course, before Animal comes home.

If Animal ever did get to hear of it, I'd just swear blind nothing ever happened (that's what you have to do with men). I even imagined the conversation we'd have if Animal ever happened to say anything: 'So what, didn't you ever do the same thing, you never got the hots for your boss's girlfriend? You're not going to take it out on the poor kid, are you, it's normal, isn't it? I was never aware of anything. I don't even know what this Pilón looks like, I've never noticed him.'

But nothing happened. I'm just thinking about it because I like the thought of Animal suffering, looking like a prick, as if he couldn't get it up and his girlfriend's sleeping around. Sometimes I wish I could go a little further and actually do it with someone. Mrs Pitiotti, as he calls me, doing it with some little corporal. But I'm sticking to glances and the odd display of my charms. Pilón's just dying for me, I've got him wrapped around my little finger.

I've just had a great idea. To think Liliana's beating her brains out trying to work out what to do to get past the guard, when really it's a breeze. I'm going to tell her.

'But why not? Why do you keep on saying no? I've come up with the perfect plan. It's a lot less complicated than that stuff with the knife. I take Pilón to my bedroom and knock something over as I go past your room, the vase on the table, say, so you'll know we've gone in. I leave your room unlocked, you wait ten minutes or so and then leave. After fifteen minutes I tell him I'm going to the bathroom, ask him to wait, and I make quite sure he isn't done by then, because otherwise men forget you right then and there, they go back to being their usual disgusting selves, don't want to know any more; no, I'll leave him bollock-naked on the bed waiting for his sugar plum. Why are you giving me that accusing look? You look like my Aunt Nuncia from back home, the same prissy face, like I've got no shame. Men are like that, Liliana. Take my word for it, I've been in this game a long time. As long as they're feeling randy, they'll put up with anything, but the moment they're done . . . So anyway, I leave him there, waiting, and go and pick up my clothes from the bathroom, quickly get dressed, slip out and meet you on the corner of Ayacucho and Posadas. Oh, and I'll leave him locked up so it takes him a while to get out. Not everyone's as quick as Animal at breaking down a door. Stop shaking your head like that. I hand it to you on a plate and you won't even look at it.'

'You're going to go to bed with that bastard and let him put his filthy hands on you? How can you even think of doing it with someone like that, a murderer? I know who Pilón is, I saw him at the hospital. I've gone through some horrific things and I've met a lot of Pilóns along the way. Like the one who shoved us to the ground and kicked us. "Not this one," he said to the other bloke, and picked me up, but they left Sofi black and blue and covered in burns from the electric prod. Or the other Pilón, the one who brought us some cider and then while we were drinking it knocked the glasses out of our hands and starting screaming at us and beating us. They're sadists and monsters. Miriam, you can't stoop that low.'

'Christ, What's the problem, Liliana? I'm not doing it because I like him. It's so we can get away. To beat the enemy. Come on, don't be so bloody stupid.'

'I don't like it. And I've got a plan you haven't even listened to, you're so excited about yours.'

'You really are incredible, Liliana. What is it you don't like? Me going to bed with that bloke? I don't give a damn about that, I've done it tons of times to make money. But there are lives at stake now, Lili's and yours and mine. You're bloody pathetic sometimes. What difference does a quick fuck make? Don't give me that look – you're pissing me off. And anyway, I told you I'm not going to sleep with him, so calm down, I'm going to break off just at the right moment, I'll tell him I've got to go and put my diaphragm in, and while I'm getting dressed I'll shout, "Hang on a minute, love, I can't find it." Then I'll get dressed. You slip out before me and wait for me at the corner. That's it. All we have to do is get the timing right.'

'I don't know why Liliana refused point-blank to go along with Miriam's plan,' said Luz. 'Under the circumstances, I'd have thought . . .'

'Oh, I can totally understand it. She was like all of us, we were very strict about things like that. Which is why it seemed so odd she would have confided in a prostitute. We despised bourgeois morality and its double standard.'

'If you were so strict and so pure,' said Luz scornfully, 'maybe you should have realised that those weren't exactly the best circumstances to have a child in.'

'We wanted one.'

'If you were such hardened revolutionaries, how come you never wondered whether you had the right to expose a child to being kidnapped, like you were, and having its identity stolen? Children weren't given the chance to decide whether they wanted to run that risk for the sake of their beliefs, the way their parents were. You just imposed that choice on them.' Resentment smouldered in Luz's eyes. 'Was that part of your revolutionary morals or was it just sheer selfishness?'

'When I used the word morality, Luz, I meant . . . We didn't know; how could we have imagined that . . .'

'The thing is,' Luz interrupted, 'that one of those children could say today: it was the military regime that made me disappear, but it was my own parents who exposed me to the nightmare of disappearing – and surviving.'

'Your plan isn't just immoral, it's full of holes. First of all: what if the guy doesn't go into the bedroom with you, or he refuses? You can imagine how terrified he is of Animal; he won't hop into bed with his wife just like that.'

'Oh, Liliana, either you're being thick, or you're underestimating me. Look at me. Do you honestly think a bloke's going to be able to turn me down? I'm telling you, as sure as my name's Miriam López, or Patricia as they used to call me, there's no way he'll say no. I know exactly what to do, and besides, I've had him eating out of my hand for days now. He looks as if he's about to come every time he lays eyes on me. Don't give me that look again, Liliana. I thought you were a revolutionary, not a nun. So tell me the other flaw in my plan. You can forget the first one.'

'If you leave him shut up in the bedroom, and he doesn't get out, Animal's obviously going to find out that it was you who let us escape. On the other hand, with my plan . . .'

'If we get away, what does that matter? What the fuck do I care what Animal thinks?'

'With my plan, you're in the clear. Animal might suspect something, but he won't have a shred of evidence that you're to blame. Who gave me the key to my room and locked the guard in? You did. If he catches you, he'll kill you. I can't let you do this, I can't let you humiliate yourself by letting a murderer touch you. I won't stand for that kind of violence. I don't care what you've done in the past, you're not doing it now. I don't want to hear another word. Listen to my plan. You come into my room with a kitchen knife because you weren't thinking and didn't realise it was dangerous.'

'I know, I've already thought it through. When Animal phones, I tell him that I'm in the kitchen cutting up meat for a stew. I could quite easily have answered the phone with the knife in my hand. And then I say, "I've got to go, the baby's crying." He's going to think that I went into your room with the knife. See, now you like it. You know, I'm good at planning, even if I'm not a revolutionary.'

'They spent the whole day coming up with ideas, but they were all so different! Miriam wanted to show Liliana that she too could come up with something that would work; she wanted Liliana to respect her. She cared a lot about what Liliana thought of her, and did all she could to hide the fact that she had wanted her daughter. Liliana believed her, probably because she was in Miriam's own flat. It was a crazy situation. I think it was a good thing Liliana didn't know, because otherwise their relationship would never have gone so far.'

'OK. But first we have to wait for Pilón to go into the kitchen or the bathroom. What time does he usually come in? Animal will never call at the same time, that would be too much to ask for.'

'Oh God, that's easy. I can get him in here whenever I want. I'll just go and invite him in for some *mate*. It won't matter if Animal doesn't ring while Pilón's there; he's not going to be sitting there with a stopwatch counting the minutes.'

'All right then, we'll work out the details later. You come into the room with the knife, I hold it to your throat, I make you open the door and we go down the hallway, you first and me behind, very slowly. If he comes out of the kitchen, I threaten to cut your throat if he doesn't throw down his gun. Then I pull it towards me with my foot and make you pick it up.'

'You mean you're going to take his gun as well? No way, I don't like this.'

'I've got to disarm him. We lock the front door to give ourselves some time and we leave. Leave the key in the door for now. What time does the replacement show up exactly?'

'At eight, or quarter to. But I don't like this. What happens if you get nervous and cut my throat? And the idea of you taking the gun off him is even worse. What if they come after us? Are you going to start shooting with the baby there? Do you even know how to use a gun?'

'Of course.'

'I'd never have thought it. Oh yes, and who's going to hold Lili if you've got me by the throat?'

'You are. They must all know how much you love Lili, it's logical you wouldn't just drop her.'

'But think of that poor little thing with all those guns and knives. I just don't get you. You think me going to bed with Pilón is violent and yet this madness with weapons you've dreamed up isn't? Can't you come up with something less violent? If you do it my way, Lili just leaves with you and she doesn't have to be exposed like that. It might affect her later on. I read in a book that children understand a lot more than people think, even at a very young age.'

Oh God, what am I saying, she's going to suspect something, why would I buy a book about babies? 'I read it in a magazine, at the dentist's.'

Luckily Liliana is too busy working out her plan to notice. I go out quickly before I put my foot in it again. I tell her to think about it and decide which plan is better and that I'll be back in a little while, so she should get a move on. It's already three in the afternoon. If they decide to come for her today, we're almost out of time. But I don't think it's very likely it'll be today because Animal hasn't said anything to me about it. It would be better to do it tomorrow morning or lunchtime. We'd have more time and maybe more information to go on.

My voice sounds normal when I ask Animal if he knows yet when Dufau is coming, and before he answers I'm already giving explanations: I want the house to look nice for the colonel, and I want to look my best too, I don't want to be caught by surprise looking a mess. 'Let me know ahead of time.'

'He's coming tonight, probably late. He hasn't confirmed exactly when yet.'

Today, oh no, not today, we're not going to have time. I remember the line about the knife, but now it doesn't sound convincing. 'I'm going to make stew with some steak I bought yesterday. I'm going to cut it up.'

Animal must be wondering what the hell I'm on about. I was supposed to say it as I was about to go into the room.

I try and mend matters as best I can. 'What do you think, love, just in case the colonel stays for dinner?'

He says, 'Negative,' and I almost swear at him, even though I'm used to him saying 'negative' instead of 'no'. The stupid prat! He must think it sounds good because it's an army word. 'Negative what?' I ask, practically hysterical. He says the colonel will only be coming round for a few minutes to pick them up and that I shouldn't cook anything, because he has to work afterwards.

But I want to make beef stew, I say, and who's he to tell me I can't. He's going to get suspicious, why am I acting so pig-headed, I'm such an idiot, I'm ruining everything. I change the subject quickly. 'What should I wear? What do you think I should wear tonight?' It seems to work, luckily, because he says I'll look gorgeous no matter what and I should just wear something simple. He'll choose my clothes for me when he gets back.

'What time?' I'm trembling, I hope to God he doesn't decide to come home early.

He says he thinks between eight and half past. If there's any change, he'll ring and let me know.

Miriam got very nervous. If they were going to do it, there wasn't a moment to lose. She went and told Liliana to hurry up, it was too late to tell Animal that she had the knife and was cutting up the meat, and it was better to go ahead with the other plan: to use Pilón.

Liliana is studying the layout of the flat so she can work out our movements, barefoot so her footsteps won't be heard. She insists on using the knife. She says it's best if Pilón is in the kitchen. If he asks to go to the toilet, I've got to wait for him to come out and then offer to make him some *mate* in the kitchen and have him sit with his back to the door. I've got to think of an excuse to have the knife in my hand, like having the meat out on the kitchen counter, and then Liliana will make sure Lili cries, or I can pretend that it's time for her feed and rush off to her room without putting down the knife first. I don't like it. And the business with the gun is even worse. What happens if Pilón won't give it up, what's she going to do, cut my throat?

'*They argued a lot. Miriam kept refusing; she didn't want to follow Liliana's plan. The weapons frightened her. Liliana was losing patience.*'

'You want everything your way. But you can't escape without me. So you'd better do as I say.'

'*Time was running out and they couldn't see eye to eye. It was almost seven o'clock when they agreed that the important thing was to escape and that they would use whichever plan seemed best as events unfolded. Liliana said she'd be willing to adopt Miriam's plan, and Miriam agreed to do the stuff with the knife, if she had to. They thought that maybe they could combine the two plans. Liliana wanted to take another look at the flat to check the location of the bathroom where Miriam was going to get changed, and whether you could hear her leave from Miriam's bedroom, in case the baby started crying just as they walked out.*'

'It doesn't matter, Liliana, I'll talk in his ear the whole time, I'll make sure he's not thinking of anything but me while we're in the room so you can escape. He won't hear a thing.'

'*But Liliana wanted to check it out. Just then Lili started crying and Liliana shut herself in Miriam's room and asked her to walk out of the other room with the baby to see if the plan would work. If you could hear the baby, they'd have to scrap it. At that very moment, the doorbell rang. Both of them ran out into the hall and bumped into one another. Lili cried even louder at the commotion. It was ten past seven, they hadn't worked out the details, and there was Pilón at the door. "Don't forget about the knife," said Liliana, when Miriam left her room. "And don't you forget that if you hear the vase being knocked over, you're to wait five minutes and then leave," said Miriam. She opened the door for Pilón with a dazzling smile. He asked if he could go to the toilet.*'

'Wasn't that where Miriam was going to get changed?'

'*No, there were two bathrooms. He went to the other one, near the living room.*'

'Yes, of course, come on in.'

In all the rush, I forgot to get changed. I wanted to open the door wearing my black miniskirt with the bright-pink top – clothes always help. Too bad, there's no time now. I'll just have to undo the top buttons on my blouse. I'll get the meat out of the fridge and dump it on the counter. Shit, the knife. Where's the kitchen knife? But I don't need a knife, do I, we're going with the other plan. Liliana told me not to forget, she'll be pissed off. Oh, here it is, but I can't take him to bed with a knife in my hand. I'll take it with me when we go outside. I'll leave it in my bathroom, oh yes, and the clothes too, because when I go to the bathroom I'm going to be in the nude and if I'm carrying my clothes, he'll realise something's up. I open the cupboard to look for some clothes. Oh, please don't let him come out of the bathroom now, I hope he gets the runs really badly and stays in there for hours. What shall I wear to run away in? Oh, I'm terrible. What does it matter what I wear? I just need a pair of jeans and a blouse. And money. Shit, there goes the bathroom door! I haven't got time to find my purse. Or the house keys. I hurry and catch him just as he's leaving the flat. I look at my watch; it's twenty past seven.

'Can I get you a quick drink, Pilón?' I say, with the kind of smile that makes blokes melt.

'No thank you, miss, I don't drink on duty.'

'Well, a *mate*, then. Come and keep me company for a while. I'm so lonely.'

Now here he is, sitting right where Liliana said. But what good is that, I've got to get him out of here somehow. Oh God, I'm so nervous, please don't let it show, I can't remember her plan properly. We talked for so long everything's all mixed up. I drop the kettle on the floor, oh well, maybe he'll think I'm nervous because I want him to fuck me. I bend down, lose my balance and trip over, and of course he has to come to the rescue. Good, this will save time. He takes my hand and leans over to put his arm around my waist. I put my arm around his neck. Pilón's panting so hard as he pulls me up that I almost keel over, I'm so edgy. Now I'm up. How do I keep things going? I'm so jittery I don't know what to do. There's no time for subtlety. I lean against him, my lips open and wet, and the man can't control himself any more, he shoves me up against the counter and bites my mouth, ouch, he's so rough, he's going to leave marks, my back on the cold marble and him all hot and hard, now he's unbuttoned my jeans and yanked down the zip and he's pawing away at me down there with one hand and sticking the other one in madly from behind. Now his mouth is on my neck, sliding down, will you look at Pilón for Christ's sake, I'd never have thought he could be so desperate and passionate. It's all kind of exciting, being frightened about the escape plan, the way his hands are ripping off my clothes, Animal being due in a little while. What if he came in right now? I'd like him to see me like this, sprawled out in the kitchen, my body sliding across the counter and this bloke's mouth inching greedily down over my tits. He bites one of my nipples as if he were drunk, and then the other, and starts licking my belly, oh God, oh God, I'm getting turned on, this can't happen, Liliana's waiting, poor thing, she can't know what's going on. How long is it since he came in? I hope Liliana doesn't do something stupid and walk out now, why did I leave her room unlocked? No, she's going to wait for a signal from me. Will she remember about the vase being knocked over? He pulls my knickers down with his teeth and licks me and my hand reaches for his dick, yes, that's how I want you, nice and hard, oh God, I can't believe I'm feeling this, count on me to mess things up, how the hell can I feel like doing it now, just when I have to escape, but maybe that's why, it must be the nerves, my cunt is swelling and his mouth is open and wet, eating my hair, his tongue going into me. This bloke is one of them. One of them! I can see myself, sliding off the kitchen counter, touching him, and then I remember what Liliana told me, and my hand jumps away from his prick in a movement I try to cover up, and now all of a sudden I've come out in a cold sweat, and it feels like his filthy saliva is contaminating my body, degrading me. I grab him by the hair, stifling the urge to yank out handfuls of it and spit at him and insult him, but he goes on thrusting his hand in and out and pawing my tits and I say softly, 'Come on, let's go to bed,' and I give him a little push and take him by the hand, that hand that must have beaten so many people, and I suddenly find myself looking at his feet as he follows me, meek as a lamb, and I think about Liliana's cell-mate's feet, and her body all covered in burns and bruises from the electric prod and this pervert's feet or someone else's like him, and I hurry as if I was gagging for it but in fact I just want to get it over and done with. It's not just because of the way I feel about Animal; this is something more, something else, I've started to hate all of them, including the one who raped me. Now I understand

90

why Liliana said she didn't want me to degrade myself; but I'm almost done now, in a little while I'm going to escape and then it's goodbye and good riddance to you, Pilón, you bastard, and Animal and all the rest of those fucking murderers. I'm going away with Lili and Liliana, I don't know where yet but it's got to be better than this, and Annette and the strip club and that piece of wasteland. Here I am, scared to death, and Pilón stops me in the hall and pushes me up against the wall; he must like doing it all over the place, in the kitchen and the hall, everywhere except in bed. Oh God, just when time's almost up he turns out to be a weirdo! What happens if he decides he wants it in the bathroom and he follows me in when I give him the line about the diaphragm? No, I'm going to have to lock him in, I'll work out a way. I'll take his hand here and lead him into the bedroom. How's Liliana going to know when the five minutes are up if I don't knock something over in the hallway like I said? Did we say five minutes or ten? I've forgotten, oh no, I've forgotten how long we said and I forgot to knock over the vase. Well, I'll just have to knock it over on my way to the bathroom and I'll wait in there a bit longer. But my bathroom's on the other side of the flat. That's OK, though, he's got no idea what the layout of the place is. I'll go and knock it over and then go straight to the bathroom, I know it's not what we planned but . . . Pilón peels off all the rest of my clothes and his as well. I get him into bed and all of a sudden he starts up as if he'd been struck by lightning, his eyes all wide and bloodshot with fear and lust. 'What about your husband? What time does he get back?' Oh God, if I lose him now I'm done for. Good thing I didn't make the noise with the vase, just imagine if Liliana had come out and they'd run into each other; she didn't think of that. I've got to prevent it somehow, I've got to stop him taking off. I can do it, I'm a genius, I already solved the problems with the vase and the keys.

'He's not going to come back now, he's not due for another hour or more, but just in case, you wait here and I'll go and lock the door and leave the key in the inside lock, that way if he does show up, he'll have to ring the bell and we'll have time to get dressed.'

He makes a face that I don't like one bit. He's cooling off, I can tell, but I'm not going to let him. I play with his thing with one hand and feel around frantically with the other on the bedside table for the damn house keys, they're not there, yes, yes, here they are and the bloke's got a massive hard-on; I'm clever, as Annette would say, I really am, I'd better work on it a bit more though, so there's no time for him to go limp before I get back. It's the best way to handle him: keep him primed.

'I'll just go and lock the front door. I'll be back in a second. You just lie here and wait.'

I look at him as if I was dying of impatience. Filthy thing – if he touches my body one more time I'll throw up, although I'm going to have to put up with him a bit longer. Now at last I go and knock over the vase on the table at the end of the hallway that leads to Liliana's room. The baby's not crying, luckily, and I put the keys in the front door; that way they'll be there when we make our escape. I run back to the bedroom and shut the door. The bloke's naked in bed, with a dazzling smile on his brown face; he wants me so much I almost feel touched, but I'm not going to let myself because he's a bastard, one of them. Liliana must be leaving the room now. I throw myself down next to him and say slowly, 'God, I want you so much; I've been dying to fuck you.' I say anything I can think of, just so he won't hear anything outside the door. How will I know when it's time? Should I count to twenty? He's got his great paw on my arse, his skin's all rough and he's trembling. He keeps on pinching me and I giggle and complain; the pinches are getting harder and they're frightening me. What if he starts torturing me?

'Oh God, I'm such a fool, I forgot to put my diaphragm in. You've got me so excited I can't think straight.' The bloke looks as if he could kill me, you can tell he wants to do it this very minute. 'I'm sorry, but if I get pregnant there'll be hell to pay, because Animal . . .'

I wag my finger from side to side, disapprovingly, and then let it dangle as if to say, 'His doesn't work any more, he can't get it up.' I love the thought of Pilón going and telling all the others that Animal's impotent even though his girlfriend's a bit of all right; and me being some place far away, free at last. I crouch down and start going down on him as if I wanted him so much I can't help myself, when what I really feel is intense disgust, so strong it makes me nauseous; but the important thing is to get him nice and fired up so he'll wait for me. The man's not going to move from here until he's fucked me, until he's well and truly screwed every hole he can find in me, hah, but you won't be able to, you bastard, because by the time it starts to shrink I'll be out of here.

I hurry off to the bathroom. Liliana must have left by now, I hope to God she has, I haven't heard a sound, either from the baby or her, although it wasn't as if I would have heard much with that bloke panting in my ear like a dog, and all the crap I was making up for him. I get dressed. What a shame I couldn't look for my purse. With all the things I've forgotten or mixed up, the only way the plan will still work and we'll get away is if Lili brings us luck. If I'd ever tried to rob a bank I'd be in jail by now for sure, I just don't have the discipline. That word discipline is Liliana's. Now I'm zipping up my jeans and where oh where am I going to put the knife if I haven't got a bag? I slide it in under my jeans and cover it with my blouse. It's not too noticeable. But what do we need the knife for anyway, once we've escaped? Liliana said not to forget it, though. The key is in the door and I slip out, close the door behind me and lock and bolt it. Pilón, Pilón, you're the best, you haven't stirred. Miriam's not going to be alone any more!

I made it. I take the stairs down two floors and press the lift button on the fifth floor. Liliana and her complicated plans. I run into our next-door neighbour on the way out, we hadn't planned for that – oh, yes, Liliana did, but I don't remember now what she told me. Hopefully the woman will forget she saw me and that I was alone. Will Animal ask all the neighbours when he finds out? He wouldn't care about making me look a fool. He never did get used to living in a classy flat. Oh, well, what do I care, so long as I never have to see any of them again? Liliana said not to run; no, I'll just keep on going cool and collected to the corner, as if nothing is wrong. What's Pilón going to tell him, that he was in bed with me? I don't think so. I hope Animal finds him in bed, that way he'll know I did the dirty on him twice over; Liliana and the other girls he's tortured will be glad. I'm almost at the corner. My stomach knots up; I'm scared to death. What happens if Animal comes right now? What if Liliana isn't there? Or if I've worked out the time wrong and she hasn't left the house yet? I've got no idea how long it was after I knocked over the vase. It seemed a long time to me, but who's to say, what with him making me feel sick and everything else that was going on, I had no way of telling. What if I left her locked up and she came out just as the bloke walked out stark naked? They're not there. Liliana and Lili aren't there! I look around, trying to seem bored and casual. Yes, there they are, over on the other side. It's them, thank God for that! I shout and wave. Liliana gives me a furious look and nods at something with her head. What? What am I supposed to do? Now she's leaning against the wall and facing away, as if I weren't there. I go up to her.

'The knife,' she says, and keeps glancing around as she hands me the baby.

She signals to me. What does she want? Oh, yes, I have to pass it to her under cover of Lili. She hides it up her sleeve. She walks behind me, right up close.

'What are you doing, Liliana? Are you out of your mind? You've gone mad.'

'Don't turn around.'

'*For the life of her, Miriam couldn't understand what Liliana was doing.*'

'But there's nobody here! Are you crazy? Stop acting the fool, Liliana. You're not planning to pull out that knife here, are you? I'm holding the baby, people will think we're behaving funny.'

We walk one block down Posadas. It seems endless. I tell Liliana we can't take a taxi because I don't have any money. She doesn't answer. I carry on walking and she says, 'Let's cross over.' I don't understand why we've got to go to the plaza, perhaps it's to get away from the street. She must think they might come looking for us. Pilón must have realised by now, but how can he know where we are? We walk across the place. I ask her where we're going, and she doesn't answer. Well, perhaps it is better I don't talk to her, she must know where we're going and how we're going to do it without paying. Maybe someone can lend her money when we get there.

We're in the middle of the plaza, walking across it. Animal! My heart lurches and jumps out of my body.

'*When Miriam saw him pointing the gun at them; the only thing she could think of to say was, "Don't shoot!" And then she felt the chill of the knife at her throat.*'

94

How did he get here? Now I understand about the knife, it's so I don't get the blame. But having the knife there scares me. Oh God, please don't let her get nervous and cut me.

'Drop the knife or I'll shoot!' That's the voice of the eight o'clock guard; they're both there.

'No, don't, I'm in the way!' I shout, and shrink back against Liliana so they'll realise that if they shoot at her they'll kill me. 'Tell him not to fire,' I beg Animal. His eyes are gleaming with a crazy light, one I'd never seen, before, and they're boring into me. That brooding hatred isn't for Liliana, it's for me.

'Everything happened so fast, she told me, that she didn't really know who did what, whether it was Animal or the other bloke. Someone gave Miriam a shove and she stumbled. Immediately a shot ran out and Liliana was on the ground. They'd hit her in the leg. Miriam didn't think at all. She threw herself down on Liliana, shielding her; perhaps she thought they wouldn't shoot if she covered her and the baby with her own body.' Luz's voice was as taut as a string stretched to breaking point. 'Liliana gave me a kiss and said to Miriam, "Save her, and tell her about . . ." and she repeated your name and her own. She must have known that . . .' The tears Luz was fighting back were on the verge of overflowing in front of everyone, at that table in the Café Comercial. 'Then Animal grabbed Miriam by the arm and marched her off.'

I try and fight but Animal drags me away. Lili, in my arms, starts to cry at all the shouting. She must realise, poor little thing.

'Then she heard the shots. Animal yelled, "Don't look," but she looked anyway, and saw Liliana there . . . dead.'

The couple at the next table wondered what could be the matter with that girl with tears streaming down her face. A single glance at her was enough to bring a lump to the throat. The man with her — her father, a friend, maybe a former lover — laid his hand on hers and gazed at her with infinite tenderness. He too looked as if he were about to cry.

They sat there in silence for a long time. Luz had her head bowed. When she looked up and saw Carlos watching her, red-eyed, she had no doubt that he now knew and believed that she was the baby she had been talking about. His daughter.

'They killed her. Those bastards, they killed her. She was just a kid.' He pulls me close, his filthy breath staining my skin. 'Oh, Miriam, you're so good, you feel sorry for her, and a few minutes ago she was going to kill you. Don't worry, sweetheart, it's all over.'

Does he believe me? He can't. He's faking it. There's something in his voice that tells me he's lying. That 'you're so good' sounded more like 'you fucking bitch'. I can't say anything to him anyway because I'm crying my heart out. I just keep walking. 'Save her,' Liliana said. I'm not going to let them take her away. But now what do I do, I can't escape. There must be some reason why he's coming with me, otherwise he would have stayed behind with them.

'What are they going to do with Liliana?' I ask.

'They'll take care of things. Just forget it, it's all over now.'

I walk back the way we came, clutching Lili, who's screaming her head off.

'Make her shut up.'

'She must be hungry,' I answer. 'We'll have to buy some baby milk or something, now that she hasn't got her mother.' I choke on my tears. I feel as if I'm going to die of grief and despair, as if it were me who'd been left motherless. 'Go and buy something to feed her.'

Yes, and then we'll run away, as soon as he turns his back.

'There's some at home, I already bought it the other day, the kind the doctor said. Now stop crying, Miriam, it's all over.'

Oh, Lili, Lili, the monster won't go away. But we'll work something out, I promise you. I'm not going to let those nasty men get you. I'm going to save you, like your mummy asked me to.

FIVE

ROM THE OTHER side of the room, Eduardo watches Dr
Jáuregui talking to Mariana. 'There's no need to worry, you're
doing very well; tomorrow you'll be able to go home. Make sure you
sleep well tonight; get all the rest you can, because after tomorrow, for
the next twenty-four or -five years, you won't get much.' He gives a
braying laugh. 'You never stop losing sleep over them, even after they
grow up, you know.'

Jáuregui knows perfectly well that Mariana had a stillborn son.
Eduardo is amazed how naturally the man can lie. He can't do it himself.
Every time someone mentions the baby, he's terrified he'll slip up
somehow and people will realise he's faking it.

He can't stand this new doctor, but he didn't dare put his foot down
when Alfonso asked Jáuregui to take over the case. Although he believes
Murray made a mistake in not realising the need for a Caesarean in time,
he's sure that the infection Mariana caught in the operating theatre
wasn't his fault. But when Eduardo hinted as much, his in-laws pounced
on him. He was to blame and he would have to pay the price: from now
on, they would make all the decisions and they would correct his
mistakes. Another doctor would nurse Mariana back to health and
the baby would be replaced with a different one.

If it dies, you get a new one, it's as simple as that. He feels a wave of
indignation colouring his skin, while the doctor goes on talking to Mariana
about the baby with complete spontaneity. 'Yes, of course I've seen her. I've
spoken to the paediatrician in charge. Everything's going fine. She's
beautiful baby. Of course, with parents like hers, she was bound to be.'

What will the baby look like? What if she doesn't look anything like
either of them? Won't Mariana get suspicious? If she realises he's

deceived her, she'll never forgive him. Would he, if Mariana tried to pass off someone else's baby as his own? Of course not. Perhaps he'll tell her in a few days, he reassures himself, as the doctor shakes his hand and gives him a friendly pat on the back.

How can he be so friendly, knowing what he knows?

Animal's given me some cans of formula and two bottles so I can get Lili's feeds ready. I wonder why the doctor who came to see her the other day didn't give me the instructions himself – I was there when he examined her. Instead, he told Animal afterwards. Why did he do that? I suppose he didn't have the guts to say to me, 'Look, when they kill Liliana, this is what you have to give the baby.' It was all planned ahead of time. I couldn't stop myself saying that to Animal and he was really nasty about it. 'You escaping wasn't part of the plan, though,' he says, and gives me this piercing stare, his eyes boring into me like rusty needles. It made me think he knew I was responsible, and that he hated me for it. But he corrected himself straight away. 'And neither was her threatening to cut your throat in the plaza – we had to kill her. The plan was that the baby would be handed over to Colonel Dufau today, and that's just what's going to happen.'

I knew from the threatening look he gave me and the way he banged his fist on the table that Animal hadn't fallen for what I'd told him; he knows, or suspects, that it's my fault things turned out the way they did, so I'd better not try anything else or he'll squash me like a fly.

'Do you understand, Miriam?'

I just nodded. He was keeping all his hate bottled up for some reason, but it was like it was streaming out anyway. He kept mopping his skin with a handkerchief.

'Christ, it's so fucking hot,' he said, and went into the bedroom, I suppose because it was getting hard for him to stay calm and not scream at me and beat me up like he wanted to.

Why is he pretending like this? Maybe so there won't be a scene before his stupid bloody colonel shows up. He wouldn't want to admit to Dufau that his girlfriend nearly wrecked everything. That would make him look bad. It would ruin his career.

As we were walking back to the house, he tried to pull the wool over my eyes, going on about how I'd been the victim, and he even said how scared he'd been when Pilón told him the prisoner had got away and taken me hostage. He told me exactly how they found us so fast – because he's very efficient and he'd never let anything happen to me. But it's clear that he knows perfectly well that I ran away with them, even though he's pretending not to. I wonder if he knows about me and Pilón too? Because if he's lying to me about the other stuff, he could easily have lied to me about that. Maybe he found Pilón naked in bed, and he's not telling me because he's planning a slow, horrible torture, something he's dreamed up specially for me, a sadist's delight, and he wants to catch me unawares.

'Here's your bottle, sweetheart, don't cry. Here you are.'

Lili pulls away from the teat of the bottle and wails. She opens her mouth, desperately searching for her mother's breast. I stuff the horrible rubber thing back in and she spits it out again.

'My search began when I touched the teat of a baby's bottle Mariana gave me when Juan was born. It's odd; I believe – no, I know – that day left its mark on me, in my memory, or my body.'

I hold her close, so she'll feel my warmth, the way Liliana used to when she breastfed her, and at last she takes the bottle. She must be starving.

'There you go, Lili, drink your milk up, even if it's not as nice as your mummy's. She's not here any more, my lamb; you're going to have to drink this instead.'

I've started shivering and Lili's going to notice. She spits out the teat and cries and then latches on again. Now I'm walking around the kitchen singing 'Manuelita' to her. I remember Liliana, the way she used to smile when I sang to Lili. If I hadn't run away with her, perhaps she'd still be alive. But for how long? They were bound to kill her, and they would have tortured her first. They kill you again and again in there, Liliana told me. She's better off having died only once.

I bet Animal gave the order to kill her beforehand, because out there he didn't say a thing, the others stayed where they were and he came with me. Animal killed Liliana, even if he wasn't holding the gun.

After the colonel's gone, he'll kill me. Although of course he'll do it some other way. How, though? I don't want to think about those things Liliana talked about.

I peek around the kitchen door. I can see the bedroom door from here and Animal's in there. What if I leave now that Lili's having her bottle and isn't crying? Yes, it's now or never.

I flatten myself against the wall, so he can't see me, my stomach's in a knot, a bubble of fear dances madly round my body. 'No, don't spit out the teat, keep going a bit longer, sweetheart, hang on, we're almost there.' I'm a couple of feet from the front door when I hear the sound of the lift stopping. I can't risk the neighbours seeing me. I wait there until I hear the door of the other flat closing. Now we can make a break for it. But no, there's our doorbell, and I hear Animal's footsteps. I run to the door and open it as if it was a perfectly ordinary, natural thing to do, the lady of the house opening her front door. It's Pilón!

'Is your husband in?' He doesn't seem angry at me so much as frightened. He keeps shaking his head as if he's trying to tell me something, but I don't know what it is. Not to say anything about what we got up to maybe?

Here comes Animal.

'Off you go, Miriam.'

I go into Lili's room, trying to imagine what they're talking about. Animal must be furious with me.

I put Lili up on my shoulder and pat her back, hugging her close, feeling her smooth, warm, baby skin. My tears wet her head and she jerks backwards, with more strength than she's shown until now. May you be strong, Lili, as strong as can be, so you can survive those monsters if I can't save you.

'What's wrong? You seem preoccupied.'

'Oh, nothing.' There's nothing wrong with him. What right has he to get angry with other people after what he's done?

'You don't like the doctor, do you? You're not very nice to him.'

Of course he likes him. There goes another lie, he can't stop now. How can he tell her he doesn't like the doctor because the man doesn't seem to disapprove of his behaviour? He would so like to be able to confide in Mariana, to ask her forgiveness for having lied, to talk everything over. Does Mariana want this baby girl her father's got from

God knows where? Is she willing to accept someone else's child as her own? Because if she is, there's no problem, but even if she isn't, it's already too late. He himself has taken control of her destiny and registered the baby as Luz Iturbe, daughter of Mariana Dufau and Eduardo Iturbe. Alfonso has already left for Buenos Aires to fetch her. Everyone keeps saying it's for Mariana's sake. Eduardo doesn't know what to do. He hugs her and tells her that he loves her so much and that he was petrified when she was so ill.

'It's over now, Eduardo, cheer up. Tomorrow we'll be home with our daughter. She must be so sweet. Does she look like you? Did you lay out the red carpet for her when she came in the door or did you forget?' Mariana laughs.

Now Eduardo remembers the evening when Mariana asked him to roll out a red carpet when they came home for the first time with their child, to give it a princely welcome. She still lived a kind of fairy-tale existence, and Eduardo had planned on making her wish come true. He had fun buying a roll of red carpet and imagining the scene. Mariana was bound to have forgotten what she'd said by the time she came home from the clinic. How she would laugh when she saw the red carpet and heard the music he'd bought at the record shop. He'd spent a long time in there, looking for the right piece. He'd asked Willy, the shop assistant, for help, since he'd known him for years. 'I need some music like the stuff they play in the palace scenes in those Romy Schneider films from the fifties.' Mariana had often talked about *Sissi* and *Sissi the Empress*, which had enthralled her as a teenager. He told Willy about the surprise he was planning. They found a record of trumpet fanfares which made them split their sides. There'd be a trumpet fanfare and a red carpet for his child's triumphant entrance.

How much time had gone by since then? Three weeks, just three weeks. What a world of difference between his life now, trapped in dark tunnels, and that chat with Willy and the fun he had had hiding the roll of carpet in the garage where Mariana wouldn't find it.

Eduardo nuzzles Mariana's neck, searching for the smell that will bring back the innocence of those times, the fooling around, the optimism, the laughter and the love they used to share. He buries his face in Mariana's warm skin to seek refuge for a moment from the creeping weight of deceit that has entwined itself around his life.

There won't be a trumpet fanfare, or a red carpet, or laughter. Alfonso will sneak the baby into the house in the middle of the night. Amalia will be waiting for him.

How can he hug Mariana and say that he loves her more than ever and at the same time conceal something as fundamental as the fact that her daughter is not really hers?

'Mummy told me she thought Luz's eyes were blue or green. Which are they?'

'I don't know, I couldn't really tell.'

How can he tell her he's never even seen the baby, that Amalia must have said the first thing that came into her mind because she hasn't seen her either? How can his mother-in-law lie so easily? And how can he keep coming up with these excuses?

'It takes babies' eyes a while before they turn their real colour. Your mother can't really know.'

Now he's acting like a criminal and covering things up. Is that how he wants to live, continually churning out lies and excuses? No, of course not. He's got to pluck up the courage to tell Mariana the truth.

Eduardo meant to tell Mariana, but he was always afraid of her reaction. The thing with lying is that when you tell one lie you end up having to tell another to back it up, and then another and another and you end up trapped in a web you can't escape. Some people can lie their whole lives and never bat an eyelid, but to Eduardo it didn't come naturally.'

She can't talk much now, she wants to rest like the doctor ordered, tomorrow's a big day and she wants to feel her best so that she can look after the baby.

'You're my sweetheart and I know you love your darling one. Will you snuggle up quietly and stroke me while I go to sleep?'

Mariana kisses him on the lips, pats his head and dutifully shuts her eyes.

Corporal Pilón informed him that his orders had been carried out to the letter and that everything had gone smoothly. The car was parked where he'd said. They had scared off the onlookers in the plaza by pointing their guns at them, and then they'd stowed the corpse in the boot of the army Ford Falcon* as discreetly as possible.

Sergeant Pitiotti had thought initially that maybe they should issue a press release about the incident in the plaza, saying that a female subversive had been fatally shot, so as to avoid any witnesses getting suspicious. But he soon ruled that out; it wouldn't be a good idea to run the risk of the family asking for the body and then doing an autopsy. Although there wouldn't have been any problem because they'd blown her belly to bits, so no one would ever realise she'd just had a child. He'd given the order ahead of time, just in case. But there was really no need. He decided not to take the body to the detention centre either, in case anyone saw it and started talking. He remembered that the colonel had been quite explicit about keeping the whole affair under wraps as much as possible. Dufau didn't want anyone except Animal and the three police officers who'd been on guard to know about the situation; he didn't want anyone to know that prisoner M35 had given birth to a baby girl who would become his granddaughter. Animal had covered his tracks at the centre a few days ago by saying the prisoner had gone into a coma and died.

Sergeant Pitiotti was very careful about his lies: it was always a good idea to repeat the same thing to everybody. You couldn't stop rumours getting out at the centre, and if one of the prisoners found out about Liliana (there were always guards who talked more than they should) it was better if there was only one version of events circulating.

'That's why I was so struck when you told me about the statement by the girl who helped Liliana in labour, because the story about Liliana having a stillborn son and being in intensive care and going into a coma came from a guard. It happened to Mariana, not Liliana. They must have concocted it on purpose.'

'Various witnesses who managed to get out all said the same thing.'

'Did anyone try to corroborate it at the hospital?' The reproach in Luz's voice was unmistakable. 'Did anyone try and check the name of the hospital where all this supposedly happened?'

* The Argentinian armed forces used green Ford Falcons with no number plates for clandestine operations during the dirty war. They became a symbol of the repression.

Carlos looked stricken. '*I heard that story from Teresa. When she got out, she told my father, in February 1977. I believed it. I just had to live with the pain and also the relief of knowing Liliana had died like that, and not from torture.*'

It was better to wait for the colonel's orders before going ahead. Sergeant Pitiotti knew he could trust the two guards to kill the fugitive, so he asked them to leave the body in the boot of the car and park it somewhere quiet. He would go and get it later on and carry out the colonel's instructions. He was sure Dufau would be pleased with his plan, but he needed to check with him first.

Once he had carried out his orders, Corporal Pilón came to ask permission to leave. Sergeant Pitiotti had the impression Pilón was hiding something, maybe because of the way he avoided his eyes when speaking to him. He'd thought the same thing when he found him in the flat, but there was no time to lose then. His version of events was rather confused, too.

'*When Animal tried to open the door to the flat, he found that it was double-locked and bolted too. He rang the bell impatiently. The few minutes it took him to get past the locked and bolted door must have given Pilón time to finish getting dressed and make it to the living room. Animal told Miriam, as they were walking back to the flat from the plaza, that the moment he walked in, Pilón informed him that the prisoner had escaped while he was in the toilet, and that his wife was gone too. He said that everything had happened very fast and he hadn't heard a sound. He had only realised when he tried to open the front door and found himself locked in. Then he had put two and two together and rushed around checking the flat, or so he said to justify why he'd just come into the living room via the bedroom hallway when Animal ran into him. Miriam remembers Animal telling her several times on the way home that Pilón seemed very edgy. And she thought: well he would be, wouldn't he?*'

Did Pilón by any chance suspect, as he himself did, that Miriam had gone along of her own free will and not because she was threatened with a knife? He couldn't allow him to harbour that kind of suspicion, or risk him being careless enough to voice it. He felt like asking him to go through the sequence of events again, but he was afraid Pilón would start contradicting himself and he wouldn't be able to let it pass. The best thing was to swear him to silence and issue a blanket threat.

'Before you go, Corporal Pilón, I'd like to point out that your behaviour doesn't fit the facts. You talk about what happened as if it were just an accident, instead of your responsibility. You were on guard in the flat when the prisoner escaped. Not only that, but you put my wife's life in danger. Do you realise how serious that is, corporal?'

Before Pilón could say a word, Animal raised a hand to cut him off. However, given the satisfactory outcome thanks to his rapid response, and the fact that all this had happened in his own home, it would be best if Pilón refrained from commenting on what had happened. If he did, he would be disciplined. Very harshly.

Pilón knew full well what Animal was capable of doing. Whatever he suspected or knew, he would keep it to himself.

Sergeant Pitiotti told Pilón to expect a phone call, because he might ring him that night about a secret mission. He couldn't go into any more details until the time came.

Corporal Pilón saluted and left the room.

I lie her down on the changing-table, undress her and wipe her down with a cotton cloth. There's a lump in my throat. I look at Lili. I can't believe how much I love her. She smiles at me, as if she knows what I'm feeling. It only lasts a second but it makes me so happy, the lump in my throat dissolves. Now she waves her little legs, she's pleased to be naked and clean and here with me. She loves me back, I'm sure of it, it shows. She's calmed down and her eyes are wide open. They're green, light green. I won't put her nappy back on right away; she can just enjoy being naked for a bit.

'You see, Lili, you're so sweet and lovely that you make me forget about those nasty men.'

She gives me that little smile that lights everything up. If only I could just concentrate on her warm skin, and how much we love each other, and forget all that horrible stuff on the other side of the door. What if I just lock him out? We can stay here.

There's no point, though: Animal would just knock the door down. The thought of him has ruined all my happy feelings.

I look down at her again and get the nappy ready. 'Up with that little bottie, that's it, Lili, good girl.' I put on her nappy and kiss her plump little arms, her tiny hands and her cheeks. The door bursts open.

'Hurry up and get her ready, Dufau will be here for her in a bit.' He looks me up and down, glaring.

'What's wrong?' I ask, trying to shake off the fear that grips me. 'Why are you looking at me like that?'

'Nothing, I'm just looking at what you're wearing. I thought you wanted to look smart. Leave the kid here and go and get changed.'

I've got to do something, right away, but what, I wonder, as I put on her vest.

'Come on, get a move on.'

'I don't feel like getting changed or putting on any make-up, I just want to be with Lili.' My eyes must have gone red, the way they do when I feel like crying.

He comes over and grips my arm. 'Do as I say, Miriam.' Seeing his filthy paw so close to Lili's sweet pink skin makes me feel like throwing up. I shake him off. 'Let go, I'm going to put her in her cot.'

Lili is crying and Animal frowns impatiently.

'It would be better if I could get her to sleep before he comes,' I say.

'Go on, off you go, I'll stay with her.'

I'm not going to leave her with that murderer, but I can't think of an excuse the way I used to. I could give him a kiss and say, 'Oh go on, let me stay,' but I can't, I hate him so much. I've never, ever hated anyone this much.

'I'll take her with me while I'm getting ready, so she won't bother you if she cries.' Without waiting for his reply, I walk off with the baby in my arms.

On my way to the bedroom, it occurs to me that maybe there's still a chance I could escape, if I can fool Animal.

'Miriam kept hoping to escape with me until the very last moment, but Animal knew something was up, even if he wasn't positive, and he never let her out of his sight.'

I'd barely laid the baby down on the bed when Animal came in and sat down beside her. Lili starts crying, out of disgust I suppose; kids understand a lot more than you'd think. I'm just about to pick her

106

up when Animal stands in my way and stops me. 'Go and get changed now.'

It's an order I know I can't ignore.

'What are you doing here? You're making me nervous, and the baby as well, look at her, she's crying her head off.'

'I thought you wanted me to tell you what to wear when Dufau comes? That's what you said on the phone anyway.'

I turn round and open the cupboard so he won't realise how much I want to hit him, to kill him. I savour the thought of raking him with my nails and hitting him and kicking him in the balls. What a sadist, he just wants to spoil this time I have with Lili.

I get out a pair of trousers and a blouse. I don't want to get changed here, with him giving me filthy looks, but it'll be worse if I go into the bathroom and leave Lili alone with the man who killed her mother. Oh God, I'm going to cry again. I turn round so he can't see me and change as fast as I can. He's got a cynical smile on his face when I go over to pick up Lili.

'You look very nice, but put some make-up on. You've been crying and it shows.'

I pick up the baby. 'So what? Am I supposed to be all smiles after what happened today?' The hatred in his eyes has died down for a moment and I try my luck. 'I've been threatened with a knife, I've watched Liliana being killed, and I'm never going to see Lili again.'

He snatches the baby. I don't want to grab her back, I'm afraid he'll hurt her. He tosses her down on the bed and turns to me. For a moment, I think he's going to hit me. His arm reaches out as I'm running for the bathroom; he grabs me by the waist and yanks me back. His steely arm is squashing my stomach and bruising my skin. Animal pulls me close. I can feel the length of his body against mine, polluting me, stifling me. He's getting hard. 'If only you weren't so beautiful, Miriam, such a great lay.'

He's started to breathe quicker, his other hand is squeezing my tits to death. If I don't do something, I'm going to faint with disgust.

'Let me go, I need to put my make-up on,' I say, and I push him away, but he won't let go.

'Now you behave yourself, Miriam, and don't go doing anything silly.' His breath poisons my ear. 'You're so pretty, it would be a shame if you came to a bad end.' He loosens his grip on my arm but still holds on. 'I want to be proud of you when I introduce you to the colonel. Do you understand?'

At last he lets go of me and I go into the bathroom. As I do my face, I try to work out what Animal's plans are. Will he kill me when the colonel leaves? He doesn't seem to want to report me. I bet he's planning to kill me gradually, the way Liliana described. After all, she knows him better than I do. Even if he doesn't torture me with electric shocks or whatever, it'll be bad enough if he stays here, raping me with his personality and his hands and his revolting body, killing me one bit at a time.

When Alfonso Dufau arrived at the main entrance of the block of flats on Ayacucho Street and rang the buzzer, he was quite surprised that Animal and his wife lived there. He'd had the address written down for several days, but hadn't paid attention to it. The flat must be hers. So Animal must have managed to land himself a rich woman. He couldn't help smiling indulgently. He was a bright fellow, Pitiotti, not just a yob – that's why he had entrusted him with so much responsibility for some time. But the truth is, he was still surprised. Who would have thought the sergeant would be living in a ritzy place like this?

Colonel Alfonso Dufau congratulated himself on deciding to send the baby there and confiding in Animal. He wouldn't have liked his granddaughter to spend her first few days in a pigsty. Who was the woman? he wondered. How did Animal seduce her? Perhaps he'd lied to her, and said he was an officer. Animal was very keen on power, something Dufau appreciated. He thought very highly of that young man. He would promote him as soon as possible. As the lift stopped on the seventh floor, he promised himself that he would praise Animal's wife to the skies, even if she was as ugly as sin.

He had been surprised enough that Animal lived where he did, but when he saw Miriam, he could not believe his eyes. This ravishing woman was Animal's wife?

'Wasn't she afraid he would recognise her? Wasn't she an escort at those parties of theirs?'

'Animal must have known Dufau hadn't seen her before. Alfonso probably didn't use call-girls or go to those parties. If you remember, when he asked for that first date with Miriam, he pretended it was for Dufau. Miriam hadn't met him.'

It would have been remarkable enough if he'd landed some old bag with money so as to get on in the world, but this stunning brunette! Dufau only had to look at her to feel a surge of desire he hadn't felt for a long time, so intense he could hardly speak. 'Pleased to meet you, ma'am.'

However, that wasn't the only surprise Colonel Dufau was in for that night. Sergeant Pitiotti asked her to leave the room and get the baby ready because he wanted to talk to the colonel in private. He spoke with an innate authority that seemed strange when you saw them together – he was so ordinary, and she was so extraordinarily beautiful.

The sergeant told him briefly what had happened that afternoon, altering the details to make Miriam look good (in his version it was she who had shoved the prisoner over when she saw Animal, so that they could shoot her and get his granddaughter out of danger). He had acted quickly and efficiently and everything had been taken care of. He thought that, even though there were witnesses, it would be better not to report it as a shoot-out, since he understood this case was to be kept as quiet as possible. The prisoner's corpse was still in the boot of the car, pending further instructions. He had an idea about what to do with it, but he wanted to check with the colonel first.

Sergeant Pitiotti had done the right thing; the colonel certainly didn't want people talking about the case. He must make sure the police officers involved didn't say anything either, even though they weren't anything to do with the detention centre.

The body had to be disposed of as soon as possible, without raising any suspicion. As he'd already said, he didn't want anyone to know that his granddaughter was the child of one of those women. It's not the children's fault, but all the same, he'd prefer it that way. This wasn't an order, just a request, a personal favour – but perhaps Sergeant Pitiotti could get rid of the corpse without attracting too much attention.

That was just what Sergeant Pitiotti had been going to suggest. He'd already worked out how to do it. He would use the corporal who had been on duty at the time.

'He won't talk, you can be sure of that.'

Dufau shook his head.

'I'd prefer you to be the only one involved. Is that possible, sergeant?'

'Of course, sir.'

Although actually it spoilt Animal's plans a bit. He didn't want to leave the house tonight for the time this job would take, but he agreed to it. He didn't think it would really matter. He'd made things quite clear to Miriam: 'You're so pretty, it would be a shame if you came to a bad end.'

Eduardo gets up and goes out into the hall to light a cigarette. He gave up smoking four years ago, but ever since he begged a cigarette from the woman at the clinic who wrote out the false birth certificate, he can't stop himself. He feels as if the smoke is defiling him and it's somehow pleasurable to feel tainted with nicotine and tar, anything apart from his own lies and deceptions. He's not just deceiving Mariana, after all. What will he tell this baby, when she's older? He'll have to lie to her too. This is the painful thought that's dragged him out of bed and into the passage-way. Before he was merely scared and apprehensive about the baby, but now that he's getting closer to meeting her, now that she's become a reality that he will have to face tomorrow, he feels ashamed when he thinks of her. If he doesn't dare say anything to Mariana, he will have to lie to Luz too.

What kind of father will he be, if he deceives his child from the very first day? He inhales the smoke and feels unclean. At least he could try and find out who her mother is. And then one day – he doesn't know when, but he and Mariana will pick the time – he'll tell Luz.

'Even though he tried hard to find out who the mother was, he never told me. Never.' Luz fell silent suddenly and looked away, as if her thoughts had carried her to some other place she didn't want to discuss with Carlos. At last she murmured, almost as if she were talking to herself, 'There was no record in the National Genetic Data Bank, either . . .'

'The what?'

'Oh, nothing.' She looked at Carlos. 'The Data Bank was officially created in 1987, although people had been working on it for many years by that point. 1987, Carlos,' she emphasised, reproachfully. 'Hundreds of relatives of the disappeared deposited blood samples there to help establish the identity of missing kids. I had the blood test done and they checked in the Data Bank but there was nothing – no blood samples related to mine. No one searched for me.'

What was smouldering in those green eyes, burning into him? Carlos wondered. Hatred? No, but a feeling as powerful as hate, that Carlos could sense but couldn't name. He couldn't elude that green whiplash, the way Animal, twenty-two years earlier, couldn't shrug off Liliana's gaze from the back seat of the Ford Falcon. Carlos stared back in silence for what felt like a very long time, and the fire in Luz's eyes never faded.

He stood up suddenly and thumped his fist on the table. Luz flinched and stood up too. She opened her mouth to say something, but it never came out. Perhaps she was trying to ask him not to be angry, to understand her resentment. Carlos sat down again and laid his hand on her arm, pulling her back down. He shook his head as if to say, don't worry, I'm not going to walk out.

'They told me it was a boy and that it was stillborn. I told you that already. But what hurt most was that they had taken Liliana away from me. I'd never feel the warmth of her skin again, or hear her laugh, or enjoy her enthusiasm and energy for getting things done, to struggle, to change the world. I believed our baby was dead, I never questioned that . . . I don't know how to explain it. I was sad, of course, but how could I mourn your death in comparison to the appalling loss of Liliana?'

Luz seemed to soften, but only for a moment.

'But Carlos, I wasn't dead. I was and am alive.'

Lili, my love, you'll never forgive me if I hand you over to those bad men. But what can I do, Animal's threatened me. If I live to tell the tale, one day I'll come and rescue you. If I die, there's no hope. Lili dear, I want you to know how much I love you. What you've given me in these last few days, and your mother too, your poor mother, nobody's ever given me anything like that. Lili, remember this – I'm telling you in case Animal kills me: your mother was called Liliana, and she was a wonderful person. And your dad's name was Carlos. They were killed because they wanted a just society. And remember me too, the way I used to sing 'Manuelita' to you and I'd say:

'"Who's the cutest baby in the world? Lili, Lili." That's the last thing Miriam said to me.' Luz's voice broke. 'Then Animal called her, and she wiped away her tears but of course it was obvious she was upset. She didn't want to cry in front of Alfonso. She wanted to attract as little attention as possible, because that very night she started planning one of her many rescue schemes and needless to say she didn't want Dufau to notice her too much or he'd remember her later. When she went into the living room, he looked at her, according to Miriam, "with that disgusting expression men have when they fancy you". He stared at her and not at the baby. Miriam felt so much hatred and fear and pain that she burst into tears on the spot, even though the last thing she wanted was to show how much it hurt her to be separated from me, but she couldn't stop herself. She was shaking; the only thing she could think of to say was that she was sorry, but that she'd been through a lot that day.'

'There's no need to apologise. It's understandable that you're upset, given everything that's happened.'

I'm sitting there with Lili in my arms, but I just can't make myself give her to him.

'Congratulations on being so brave! You really kept a cool head.'

Animal reaches out to take Lili, he knows I can't give her up, or show it either, and we have a little tug of war.

'Miriam's grown fond of the little thing, you see, this is hard for her.' He tries to justify himself in front of the colonel, as if I were something that belonged to him which wasn't working properly, as if I needed oiling. In the end Animal gets her away from me and I break down and start sobbing out loud.

Animal looks at me angrily and that monster, Dufau, instead of taking the baby, puts a hand on my shoulder.

'Don't take it so hard, you'll have your own any day now.'

My tears dry up instantly, since that's the quickest way to get his filthy paw off my shoulder, and he removes his hand. I keep my head down. I don't want to watch Animal handing her over to him. Luckily, Lili's asleep. Thank goodness she can't see these scum passing her from one to the other. Animal must have given her to him because he comes over and

112

says in a voice that's meant to sound loving but has a definite edge to it, 'Say goodbye to the colonel, dear, he's leaving now. I'll be back soon.'

I stand up. I'm not really alive, this is a dream, a horrible nightmare. The monster is carrying her awkwardly and staring at her, but as soon as I get up, he stops looking at Lili and gazes insolently at me.

'Thank you again for everything.'

I don't know whether they say anything else, I feel numb, I can't cry. The door has shut. I can't move.

Sergeant Pitiotti accompanied Colonel Dufau out to the car and helped him put the baby into the carrycot. He also stowed the bag he had asked Miriam to pack with some spare baby clothes, two bottles and an assortment of dummies that he'd bought himself. On the way from the flat to the car they crossed the plaza where the prisoner was shot.

'Your fiancée is a very brave woman. Hurry up and marry her, sergeant, that's an order.' They both laughed. 'I bet you've never been given a more welcome order, now have you?'

They talked about how pretty the baby was and how lucky they'd been that everything had worked out so well.

'I'll be back soon,' he said. Maybe he's only going out to the car with him. When he gets back, he'll kill me. I don't know exactly what his plan is but I can't risk waiting around, trying to second-guess him. I'm leaving right now. Got my purse, with all the money I have in it. My keys. I go down three flights by the stairs and then take the lift. Oh God, please don't let Animal be down there. Liliana, love, help me if you're watching. He's not there. Thank goodness, there's a taxi.

'Take Libertador, it's quicker,' I tell the driver.

SIX

WHEN I TOLD the taxi driver to take Libertador, I wasn't sure where to go. Where was Liliana headed? Where could I go? To the Claridge, why not? So here I am, in one of those suites I used so many times for work. I was planning to go and register like an ordinary guest – after all, I can afford it, I'm paying. But I never had to. The moment I walked in, I ran into that nice man Frank at reception.

'Patricia! What a surprise, I thought you'd given up work – and I was glad.'

Miriam got to know Frank when she was working, since she usually met her clients at the Claridge. Once, they got chatting and he suggested they meet up later. They went out a few times for lunch and to the cinema. Frank's father was American and his mother was Argentinian, so he was bilingual. He wanted to work in the hotel business. He was interested in Miriam's life, even though she never told him very much. She liked him.

'Were they ever lovers?'

'No, just friends. She had fantasised about sleeping with him, but Frank never suggested it.'

He asked which suite I'd been given, because the agency hadn't said anything to him. I put him right. 'I don't work for Annette any more, or anybody else for that matter, I'm here as a guest. I'd like to register, and by the way, Frank, my name's not Patricia, it's Miriam. So you can just write that down in the book, all right?' I said, rummaging through my bag for my ID card.

Frank shook his head. 'How many nights is madam planning on staying?' he said with a straight face, getting out the key and handing it to me. He pointed to my handbag and asked, 'Shall I have your luggage sent up, or can you manage yourself? Number 603 is free. I trust you'll find it satisfactory.'

I smiled at him and hurried off to the lift, before the other receptionist came back to the desk, that old bloke who gives me the creeps. It was nice of Frank to let me have the room for free.

Now that I think about it, it's a good thing he didn't register me. What if Animal decides to search the hotels and asks for me here, the place we first met, the time that . . . I'd rather not think about it. To think I was happy when I saw it was Animal.

Oh God, the phone's ringing. What if Frank did register me after all? No, he can't have, I only said my name was Miriam, he doesn't have the surname. But what if Animal asks for all the Miriams in the hotel?

I pick up the receiver but I don't say hello, just in case.

'Patricia?' Frank says on the other end. 'It's me. Can I come up? I need to talk to you.'

'Yes, of course, but I'm very tired.'

I wonder what he wants – to screw me? Is there anyone left in this world who'll do you a good turn just for the sake of it? One day, when we were having a drink, I said to his face, 'Don't you want to sleep with me?' I couldn't work out how he could fancy me and not give anything away. He gave me that peculiar smile of his and said, 'I can't afford it, you must charge a lot and I don't have much money.'

'I can give you a discount, if you like,' I said, 'I'd be doing it on my own time and not for the agency.'

I was just kidding, pulling his leg, because he never chatted me up, and I remember I fancied him that day. It had been a while since I'd done it because I felt like it, for my own sake and not for work. And I liked Frank. He was nice. Of course I wasn't really thinking of charging him, but I never got around to saying so because no sooner had I opened my mouth than he snapped, 'No, actually I wouldn't dream of paying for you, I'd never pay to sleep with you, I'm not interested.' And that made me angry.

We're talking about that time now, about how I was only pulling his leg, but I'd been hurt because he turned me down so rudely, as if he didn't find me attractive.

'You misunderstood me, Patricia. I just didn't want you to do it for work. I was fond of you. I cared about you, obviously. Of course I wanted you, but I would have liked you to make love to me because you wanted me. I don't go for hookers, I'm different from other men like that.'

'Oh, you idiot, I'd have gone to bed with you for the hell of it, because I fancied you too. I was only kidding about the discount.'

Frank smacks his forehead. 'I can't afford to go on acting dumb, life's too short.'

That makes me laugh. 'That's just what I said to my friend yesterday,' I said.

A friend, yes, Liliana really was my friend, my only friend, and now she's dead, and the colonel's got her baby. Animal must have got home by now and he'll be doing his nut because I've run away. He'll be looking for me, maybe at this very moment. I'm gripped by panic. 'You didn't register me, did you, Frank? I told you my real name was Miriam. Who knows that I'm here?'

'No, of course I didn't register you. The old man's gone out for a while and I gave you this suite because it's free. There was a cancellation. But tomorrow you'll have to . . .'

'Oh, thank goodness! When I got here it never occurred to me, but he might think of looking for me here.'

Frank moves closer. 'What's wrong, Patricia? You're trembling. Who's after you? Who are you afraid of?'

I don't answer, but I realise I can't hide my panic. I let Frank hug me. I rest my head on his shoulder and start crying my eyes out. 'Oh, Frank, I was so wrong, terribly wrong.'

'You're crying as if someone you love had died.'

Of course someone's died. I just go on bawling. I'm making his shoulder all wet. He strokes my head and says nothing. Poor Frank – how could he possibly understand? I just want him to comfort me. I collapse on the bed and he looks at me. I can tell what he's thinking by the expression on his face. I think to myself that it was stupid of me to bring the subject up, and I really should make myself clear. Perhaps I overdo it a bit. 'Oh, Frank, love, please don't get any ideas, you don't know what I've been through the last few days.' That makes him cross. 'I've got no intention of trying anything, stop making things up,' but I go on crying, I know that sort of look.

'If I'm looking at you it's because I find you attractive, but I'm not going to do anything in the state you're in, crying like that, I'm not an animal.'

Frank doesn't know it, but the word *animal* brings on a shock of fear that starts in my toes and goes right through me. Fear and disgust, a deep, deep disgust. It makes me shiver. 'Don't use that word.'

'All I meant was, I'm not such an animal that I would . . .'

'I know what you said, it's the word *animal* I can't stand, I've been living with this bloke, you see. I was even thinking of marrying him. He was called Animal, that was his nickname, and I went to live with him, as if it was the most natural thing in the world. Animal's too good a name for him, though. He was a murderer, a bloody sadist.'

Frank says he doesn't understand how I got involved with someone like that. 'Because I thought he loved me and understood me. I swear, I thought he was kind, but guess what he is: a torturer.'

'Which one is he? We know all the army guys here.'

'No, this one only came once, you don't know him.'

He asks what happened. I shouldn't tell him, but I do. I explain how I was in terrible shape because I'd just had an abortion when I met Animal, and he . . . No, I just can't say he promised me a baby. 'He was kind to me, but I didn't know that actually he was sick, I didn't find out until later on . . . and after that all kinds of things happened.'

How's he ever going to understand me when I start saying things and stop halfway? I don't really want him to understand anyway, I just need to talk. I'm at my wits' end and I need to get things off my chest and there's something about Frank's face that makes me feel safe. I don't tell him what's happened, though. I just say that I've run away and now Animal's out to kill me.

Frank hugs me and tells me not to be afraid, just let him know what's up and he'll help me. 'Was he one of your clients? Is he in the army? Has he been to your house before?'

'He's in my flat. He moved in with me.' Then I remember the furniture and all the upholstery. I should do something about getting that stuff back. 'Frank, would you be able to go over to my place with a van and pick everything up? I can't go myself.'

'But if he's living at your place, you should just tell him to leave, say everything's over, and that's it. If you want, I can pretend to be your new boyfriend so he doesn't hit you.'

'Oh Frank, you were right, you know, life's too short for dumb ideas. If the two of us go there, he'll kill us, it's as simple as that. Why do you think he's called Animal? I let him down big time, and not just in the relationship. I've mucked up his career, and he's an army man. By now, he'll know for sure it was me that did it, and he'll be out to kill me, even though he's mad about me.'

Frank says nothing, but he must sense how desperate I am. I feel as if I'm falling into a black hole. Liliana riddled with bullets in the plaza, and no more Lili ever again, with her lovely soft skin . . . He gently pushes my hair off my face and strokes my head, as if trying to put out the bonfire of horrible images inside me.

'I have to go to sleep now, I'm shattered. I can't think straight until I get some rest.'

Frank tucks me in, kisses me on the cheek, turns out the light and leaves.

'Even though Frank couldn't make head or tail of Miriam's garbled story, it was obvious she was in danger. If the guy was that much of a threat, it wasn't a good idea for her to stay at the hotel. After all, it was, or had been, where she used to work. So he woke her up at seven the next morning, gave her his address and the keys to his flat and asked her to wait there for him and not move.'

He says no one will notice me at this time of day. 'Why don't you write down the address for me, instead of making me repeat it over and over? You're like Liliana, Frank, hung up on discipline.' What am I saying this to him for, he doesn't even know who Liliana is.

'Frank didn't want Miriam to have his address on her in case Animal found her. It was just common sense, not discipline. His neighbour had disappeared, he *told Miriam later on, just because his name was in the address book of some guy who was supposedly a Montonero. He couldn't see his friend Patricia, the call-girl, as a subversive, but if she was having problems with someone in the military, it was no time to run risks. That's also why he refused to go with her or to be at the reception desk when she left the hotel. His shift was over anyway.'*

Frank says that if anyone sees me on the way out, I should just smile, but not say anything about him giving me the suite. It turns out that was the right thing to do, because the doorman recognises me right away, but he just smiles at me and asks if I need a taxi, and I smile back. 'No thanks, I'm going to walk.' You've got to have every last detail worked out, Liliana used to say. I don't know who was on reception, I deliberately didn't look. Although I don't think Animal will come to the Claridge today, I'm making too much of this. Poor Frank hasn't got a clue what's going on. I must have really put the wind up him last night because today he was even more nervous than me, and that just made me more scared than ever.

Frank didn't drop in on his parents as planned. He went straight home and sat on the steps waiting for Miriam. He had been so nervous he had accidentally given her his only set of keys. The first thing Miriam asked him, when they went in, was to go to her flat and see if he could spot Animal leaving. 'He usually goes to work at half seven or eight.' Frank didn't understand why she was asking, but he said he would do it as long as she promised to stay in the flat.

He got out at the corner of Ayacucho and Alvear and walked slowly towards Posadas. It wasn't hard to spot Animal. He was standing outside the building, looking up and down the street, as if it was hard for him to leave. There was something on his face that was not rage, as Miriam had predicted, but pain. The man's rugged, harsh features bore the marks of deep suffering. There was no one guarding the door and Frank was sure Animal had not seen him. He followed him as far as the car park on the next block. Animal never once looked back.

Now he was going to bed to get some sleep. She should stay in his room and he would use the other one. Miriam went up to him and gave him a kiss. 'Bless you, Frank, you're a sweetheart. Look, I'm sorry I wasn't in the mood yesterday, but if you like, we could do it now.'

'No, Patricia, I'm the one who needs some sleep this time.'

Thank goodness he said no, because the truth is I really didn't feel up to it. I've got to decide what to do next. I can't stand the thought of Animal staying in my house with my things, but there's no way I can throw him out, because he'll kill me. The best thing would be to go and see the landlord and try and get out of the lease. That way he can be the one to throw Animal out, if he hasn't already left.

Frank won't mind moving my things for me.

'*She phoned up the landlord. She said she was moving to Italy that week, or the next, and that she'd return the key. The landlord agreed, because there were still three months to go on the lease and Miriam had paid the rent in advance.*'

How am I going to go about finding the baby when I don't even know her name? She must have Dufau's son-in-law's surname. There must be a phone book in this place somewhere. Yes, here it is. I look up Dufau's number.

'*Judging from the accent of the maid who answered the phone, she was from the provinces too, from Corrientes, and that encouraged Miriam to say she was a childhood friend of the Dufaus' daughter and that she would like her phone number.*'

'Which one? There are three of them,' she said.

I had no idea there was more than one daughter. I don't even know the daughter's name. I don't answer, because I don't know what to say, but the Corrientes woman is chatty and gives me some clues. 'Were you a friend of the twins?' Yes, I say, trying to sound convincing. 'They'll be back around six this evening.' If they live with Dufau it can't be them, but now I can't say, 'Oh, no, I went to school with the other daughter.'

'*She said she'd call later on or some other day, but she gave up the idea after discussing it with Frank, especially after what happened later in Coronel Pringles. It could have been very dangerous. It was around then, she told me, that she looked for your surname in the phone book, trying to find a lead. Although, as I said, she spelt it with an "e" at the beginning.*'

'She didn't try too hard,' said Carlos, rather scornfully.

'No, she thought you were dead.'

'You couldn't go and get my stuff for me today or tomorrow, could you?' I ask Frank when he wakes up.

'Are you crazy? What if Animal shows up?'

'If you go while he's at work, you won't run into him. I don't think he'll have changed the locks; he'll still be waiting for me to come back, the bloody fool.' Frank says we'll have to think about it. I bet I can persuade him.

Sergeant Pitiotti couldn't get any information out of the prisoner. He was absent-minded and full of anguish. Would she be there when he got home? He rang several times that day. She wouldn't just walk off like that and leave him behind in her flat. And anyway she'd left all her clothes there. Miriam would be back. He was sure of it.

The baby cries constantly and Mariana is worn out. Eduardo tells her to try and get some rest; he'll stay up with Luz until she goes to sleep. He takes the bottle with him and walks around rocking the child until she gradually calms down. He goes out into the garden. It's a warm night. He tries giving her the bottle and this time she takes it. The silence is a blessed relief. He looks at Luz, his daughter. Does she feel like his daughter? Yes, but she isn't. He sits down on a bench, some way from the house. 'Now that nobody's listening, I'm going to tell you. I need to tell you, Luz, my sweet, I don't want to lie to you.'

He tells her the truth, soundlessly, promising that he'll explain it all when she's older and that he'll find out everything she wants to know. Now, at last, he feels relieved and plants a kiss on her downy head before putting her back in her cot.

For several days, Sergeant Pitiotti clutched at straws, as lovers do. Maybe Miriam would come and see him to ask him to leave and then he'd convince her to stay. She wouldn't just leave without trying to get her furniture back. Miriam was crazy about her furniture and vases and rugs, something he'd never understood. One of these days she'd come back and as soon as he brought her the next baby, she'd get over it. Come to mention it, in the three days since Miriam had left he'd forgotten to go and see the prisoner who was about to give birth.

'How long has she got?' he asked Teresa, the girl who'd monitored Liliana's labour.

'I don't know exactly, but I could examine her,' she offered.

She had never done a gynaecological examination in her life, but it was better for her to do it than that beast of a male nurse. Teresa put her fingers in the woman's vagina and pretended to be calculating something, and then she palpated the woman's stomach. 'It's still quite high up, and she hasn't dilated. I'd say ten days to two weeks, maybe.'

When Animal had gone, Teresa whispered in the woman's ear that she had no idea whether what she'd said was true or not, but she thought it was better to string them along like this. 'That way they'll take you to the hospital, like Liliana. It's always safer, and who knows, there might be a chance of letting your family know.'

'Yes, that would be better,' said the prisoner, and she smiled wanly under her blindfold.

'Teresa told me,' said Carlos, 'that not long after she found out about Liliana's death, they also took away another girl who was earmarked for Animal, when she went into labour. But it wasn't Animal who took her.'

'Where? To a hospital? Maybe it was the same one they took Liliana to.'

'I don't know, Teresa didn't say, perhaps she didn't know. The girl never came back, and they never heard anything more about her, unlike Liliana.'

'Couldn't you find out any more than that? Didn't you check whether anyone had testified about that girl at the trial of the Juntas? You might have found a clue that would have led you to Liliana and me. I looked at every single statement by anyone called Liliana or Carlos . . .'

Carlos puts his hand on hers.

'I already told you that I thought our baby was stillborn, I found that out long before the Juntas' trial.' Carlos straightened up in his chair. He looked at Luz. It was his turn to talk now. 'I was in Paraguay, hiding on a farm on the other side of the river from Posadas, where my family lived. My brother-in-law helped me escape. We crossed the river by boat, at night. It was dangerous for me to stay there,

but I refused to leave, even after my sister got me a false passport. I couldn't do anything, but it meant I was closer to Liliana. I was still hoping that she might show up. I told Nora, Liliana's mother, that she'd been kidnapped, and she got a lawyer to issue a habeas corpus and mobilised as many people as she could. But nothing came of it. As always, they said that Liliana was nowhere to be found.'

'So my grandmother's name is Nora?' Luz interrupted, her eyes bright. 'Is she still alive?'

'Yes. My parents were in contact with her, but, of course, they didn't know where I was. I moved around a lot, but I always stayed in the area. I was desperate being stuck in Paraguay, unable to do a thing, all those months. I kept calling to see if there was any news, and my sister and brother-in-law would beg me to leave. They managed to get out of Argentina themselves in December. In February 1977, my father told me what Teresa had told him. Then I did finally go to Spain.'

'What about your parents? Are they still alive?'

'My father is. Mum died in 1980. I never saw her again.'

Frank helped her with everything, even though during the week she stayed at his house she didn't tell him the whole story, just bits of it. She didn't tell him about Liliana until the afternoon after the furniture had been put into storage, when he gave her Animal's letters.

'When Frank went in, half an hour before the removal men came, he found a series of letters and notes spread around the flat. Animal must have left them there in case she came back to get her things when he wasn't there.'

'So they moved Miriam's things, in spite of everything? What on earth for?'

'Miriam made such a fuss about it that Frank agreed to go there in person to get her stuff. The storage space was rented in Frank's name. I don't really understand why Miriam was so hung up on the things in that flat. It must have had something to do with how much she'd invested in the place emotionally — it was a dream come true for her. And it was a way of telling Animal: it's over. It seems incredible, but he hadn't done anything up till then, even though more than a week had gone by.'

Miriam read the letters out loud, cursing. 'Miriam, next week our child will be here, wait for me.' 'I have to talk to you, don't do

124

anything silly.' 'I love you. I adore you.' There was another long, revoltingly cloying letter in which he talked about when they'd met, and the plans they'd made, and how happy they'd been until the colonel's baby messed everything up. 'She's Liliana's, not Dufau's, you bloody murderer.' It wasn't his fault, he was only doing his duty. 'Doing his duty, the bastard.'

Frank had only just heard the whole story about how Miriam had run away with Liliana and Lili, and how Liliana had died and the colonel had taken Lili, and how Miriam escaped by herself.

'Didn't Animal look for her?'

'He called Annette, to see if she'd started working for her again. I think it was the same day, but obviously it was before he found out that the only thing left in the flat were his clothes. Frank carried out Miriam's instructions to the letter.'

When Frank got to the hotel the next day, he was asked if by any chance he'd seen Patricia lately, which alarmed him a great deal. If Animal was looking for her already, how would he react when he found the flat empty?

'No, I haven't seen her for ages.'

But the doorman had seen her walk out of there one morning, about nine or ten days ago. Hadn't he been on the desk the night before?

'I don't know. What day was it the doorman saw her leave? I told you, it's been months since I saw Patricia.' He would have liked to ask more, but it was better to change the subject fast and not seem interested, so as not to arouse suspicion.

When Sergeant Pitiotti walked in and found the flat empty except for his clothes, all he could do was kick and pound the walls impotently, until at last he collapsed on the bare floor and lay there until the next day. In the morning, he asked the concierge and his neighbours if they'd seen the removal van. They had, but no one remembered the name of the company, or knew where the things had been taken. Sergeant Pitiotti didn't want to make too much of a fuss about it. He didn't enjoy playing the part of the jilted lover.

'The only thing Miriam knows is that when the landlord arrived, there was no sign of Animal left in the flat. He must have taken his clothes away that same day.

He didn't want to attract attention by making enquiries. I know he didn't launch an official search for her.'

'*It would have been hard for him to admit that his girlfriend had given him the push. I wonder what he told Dufau?'*

That very afternoon, after an incredibly humiliating chat with the colonel, Animal regained all his efficiency for extracting information.

As soon as the prisoner arrived, they handed her over to him, and he remembered Dufau saying, 'When are you going to name the day, sergeant?' He punched her hard because she was refusing to get undressed, and they strapped her hands and feet to the pallet. He'd had to tell him that he'd had a falling out with his fiancée. But it would all blow over. Bound to.

Although Sergeant Pitiotti (who was considered an expert) had explained several times that it was best to apply the electric prod to the long muscles like the forearm and the legs first – you find the pain threshold, but don't cross it, because then they go numb and won't talk – that afternoon he seemed to forget all his expertise and went right from the legs to the vagina. 'She was really upset by what happened the other day, sir, she's the sensitive type, but she'll get over it.' He brings it down once, 15,000 volts at thirty milliamps. Miriam would soon get over it.

'Now start talking, you fucking little Montonera bitch.'

Those first three hours were vital, as Animal was well aware, and he always gave it everything he'd got during that time, using every ounce of imagination he possessed to make sure they squealed as soon as possible. By the time three hours were up, word would be out and the cell would be disbanded, and it would be harder to get them.

That day Animal wanted to do his job as efficiently as he could to banish the image of himself looking pathetic in front of Dufau, saying his fiancée had gone to see her family, that he'd be going to visit her and they'd make it up. Then, as the electrodes were searing the prisoner's nipples, he wondered whether she could possibly be in Coronel Pringles, when he was looking for her at Annette's? As soon as he had a day's leave, on Sunday, he'd go there. 'Make sure you write down everything the prisoner says, quickly, before they disband the cell.' He would need help, but he didn't want anyone to know about this operation – after all, it was his girlfriend he was looking for, not a subversive. Pilón? Yes, he'd call Pilón. He knew he'd keep his mouth shut.

Sergeant Pitiotti still had time to find her and talk her into coming home.

When Laura and Javier went to visit them, Amalia was still there. 'To help Mariana, the first few days are always so hard. And the baby cries so much. But isn't she pretty?'

'Yes, who does she look like?'

It's always the same, Laura thinks to herself, having been through this experience when her son was born. Everyone thinks the baby looks like someone in their own family. So she was surprised when Amalia, of all people, said she looked just like Eduardo, rather than Mariana or herself. 'Don't you think, Javier?'

'Yes, maybe, although when they're so tiny, I can never tell.'

His mother says he's right. 'She's got a bit of Eduardo in her,' and to be magnanimous she adds, 'although she's got Mariana's eyes.'

Why does she think they're alike? Laura wonders. Mariana's eyes are brown and this baby's eyes are clearly green.

'Your mother will say anything to be polite,' she said to Javier on the way out, 'but Amalia was behaving really strangely. Why did she insist the baby looked like Eduardo? And did you see how furious he was when she said that?'

'I thought Eduardo was looking fine. He seemed happy.'

'Yes, but not when Amalia was going on about how they look alike; he gave her quite a glare. There's something weird going on, Javier.'

Nonsense, she was imagining it. 'No, I'm not! You said yourself something was up when the baby was born. Why wasn't anyone allowed to see her at the clinic?'

'I did say that, it's true, but now she's here, she's fine, and Eduardo seems OK. Maybe he is a bit tense, you're right, but perhaps he's just tired, which is perfectly understandable. Having a baby changes your life. I felt the same way at first when Facundo was born.'

No, it wasn't the same, Laura couldn't say why, but there was something going on she didn't like, something fishy. But she realised she'd better stop talking about it because her comments were obviously bothering Javier. Anyway, perhaps he was right, she disliked Eduardo's in-laws so much that everything they did seemed sinister.

I ask Frank not to go to the other bedroom, to stay with me instead.

'Why? Are you frightened?' he asks.

'Yes,' I answer, although he seems more scared than I am. 'But that's not why. I want to sleep with you. Don't you fancy me?'

He says of course he fancies me, but he's not a client. He's tried to be a good friend. And that's what he is. 'But what's wrong with being friends and making love?' Frank grins. 'All right then, if you're going to take it like that, I won't push you. I just want to sleep with you, and I mean just sleep. I swear I won't lay a finger on you,' I joke.

We lie down on his bed. I'm the one who moves in closer. 'Know what? I just want to snuggle up to you and rest.' He hugs me and I don't totally believe him when he says he doesn't want to. One thing leads to another.

'We'll only go as far as you want,' I say to reassure him.

He kisses me softly and slips my nightie off gently and his mouth inches across my shoulders and down my breasts. I tell him that I love him, that I want him to make love to me. It's not that I'm grateful and I want to give him something, it's because . . . He kisses me on the lips to shut me up.

He's right: bodies talk better than words. I can feel how much I want him and how much he loves me, and we just let it happen. We both want it so much, and all this tenderness and love and passion comes flooding out and when I finally reach the top with Frank, I'm so high, all my defences come tumbling down and my eyes fill with tears. I like these tears, they're different from the way I usually cry. I'm happy and sad at the same time, not just because of what happened, but because I won't see Frank again. I don't want him to realise this, though, so I nestle up against him and wait for him to go to sleep. It damn well would have to be this way, just when it starts feeling right! I never realised it could mean so much and now I can't stick around to enjoy it.

I made up my mind today, when he told me what happened at the

Claridge. Maybe that's why I insisted on us sleeping together – to say goodbye. I don't want to put him in any more danger. Any day now, someone is going to find out that I'm hiding here and he'll be out of a job. And it's not safe for me either. Tomorrow, when Frank leaves for work, I'm going to Coronel Pringles. Animal won't think of looking for me there. He called Annette, so he must think I'm going back on the game. And if I was, I wouldn't go back to the country.

As I watch Frank sleeping, I go over what to say in the letter I'm going to leave him in the morning.

Two days after Miriam left his house, the old man asked Frank about her again. 'Why, what's up with Patricia?' he asked, staring at his book and trying to feign indifference. The old man said he didn't know, but he'd had a call from the agency a few days ago, and then that afternoon some bloke had shown up asking about her. He wasn't in uniform, but he was obviously army. He'd even threatened him – said he'd pay for it if he was hiding anything, that he'd be back the next day, and he'd better have something more concrete by then, like who she was with and where she was.

It must be Animal, thought Frank, and he tried to disguise his unease with a joke. 'Maybe it was some randy bloke who's desperate to track her down, now she's stopped working.'

If Animal had reached the point of searching for her openly, he could easily go to Coronel Pringles. He had to find some way to warn Miriam.

Aunt Nuncia could scarcely believe it was me standing there. She hadn't heard from me for years.

'Have you come back for good?' she asked, looking at my huge suitcase.

'No, I've just come to see you both for a few days. But I can go to the hotel, if that would be easier.'

'No, of course not, stay with us.'

So here I am, in the same old room I used to share with Noemí, who's just had her third kid. She couldn't understand why I went all weepy when I saw my little nephew for the first time.

'I never knew you liked babies so much.'

'Of course I like babies,' I said, and there were tears in my eyes as I remembered Lili.

Noemí said she was happy everything had turned out so well for me. 'You've got a great career and plenty of money, but it's a shame you haven't got any kids, seeing as you're so fond of them. You should get married and settle down.'

'Yes,' I said, 'I will some day, but I've got to travel a lot right now, I've got my modelling career to think of.' I told her they'd given me a contract in Italy and that I'd probably go and work in France after that.

Get married, have a baby: it's as if I was in a time warp. That's just what my aunt used to say to me before. Maybe that's why, when I went back to her house for a *mate* and she started asking me about my life and whether I had a boyfriend, I pretended I did. I made up one who was just like Frank, blond, kind, good-hearted, hard-working, with a lovely smile!

'Oh, Miriam, it's so nice to see you in love.'

The more my aunt got into the story, the more I started believing it myself. I began really wanting to ring Frank.

'Why don't you marry him, then?'

'No, I can't right now, I've got some big contracts in Europe, but maybe when I get back.'

Back from what I don't know; I have no idea where I'm going next. I can't hang around here for ever, and I can't go back to Buenos Aires with Animal looking for me. Oh, Frank, what am I going to do? I can't even ask you for help.

I go to the bar for a bit. It's exactly the same. El Gordo, the fat barman, is still there, and he says something that tickles me: 'It's Queen Miriam!' I'd forgotten that I was once the beauty queen of Coronel Pringles, but they haven't. I order a whisky and tell him the same thing I told Noemí: about the contracts I've got in Europe, how successful I've been, and how I wanted to see my family before I go.

But even though I'm happy they all recognise me and that they're all so nice to me, nothing gets rid of the awful feeling whenever I think of

Lili with those murderers, Liliana dead and Frank . . . I told him we'd never see each other again.

I'm going to ring him right now. I ask El Gordo to let me use the phone.

'It was lucky she had that sudden impulse to ring Frank, because he ordered her to get out immediately. He told her the situation was extremely dangerous and that he was afraid Animal might go looking for her there. That saved her. She must have passed Animal and Pilón going the other way, because they ransacked her aunt's house the very next day.'

It wasn't hard to track her down. El Gordo at the bar said she was staying at her aunt's house. Needless to say, Animal didn't believe Aunt Nuncia when she said that Miriam had left that very morning. He shoved her aside and searched the house from top to bottom, throwing things all over the place. It was Pilón who held a gun to her head to get her to say where her daughter lived. 'What do you want to know for? I've already told you Miriam's not here, she's gone to Italy.'

There was no sign of her at Noemí's either. Animal went crazy in the baby's room, smashed it to bits, and if Pilón hadn't intervened and got the baby off him and handed it back to its mother, Animal would have hurled it to the floor the moment it cried.

Noemí didn't know any more than her mother: just that Miriam had left that morning, without even saying goodbye. 'She was always ungrateful, Miriam was. I was never that fond of her.' And now they'd gone and smashed everything up and it was all Miriam's fault.

Corporal Pilón didn't think Miriam was hiding in the town. It was probably true that she'd left that morning. 'Anyway, sergeant, it's not a good idea to go on kicking up a fuss here. You said yourself it was supposed to be top secret. If we stay, people might get suspicious, and it's a personal thing, right, there aren't any subversives involved, your wife's not a subversive, is she?'

Sergeant Pitiotti didn't answer. He got into the car and set off back to Buenos Aires. He spent the first thirty miles mulling over the phrase in his mind. What exactly did he mean? What did Pilón know? Did he think that the prisoner's escape was . . . He pulled over on to the hard shoulder and braked violently.

'Now you're going to give me the real version of what happened on the seventh of December.'

He noticed Corporal Pilón's lip tremble. He claimed not to know what he meant. 'So why did you insinuate that my wife was a subversive?' Pilón said he hadn't meant to, he didn't know anything about it. But Animal's menacing air was too much for him and so he said, 'That woman you're looking for, I don't think she's a subversive, I just think she doesn't deserve you.' Sergeant Pitiotti ordered him to explain himself.

Well, sometimes, she'd come on to him. What did he mean? In his own home! But of course, he'd always pretended not to notice, he respected Sergeant Pitiotti a lot. 'And it is really awkward, sir, to have to say this.'

Pitiotti started the car again and they drove the rest of the way in silence. He would almost have rather Pilón had said she'd helped the prisoner than this. He could have questioned him further, but there was a lump in his throat. He didn't really want to humiliate himself by hearing the details from Pilón. He'd get them from Miriam, because he was determined to find her now, and when he did, he'd make her pay for humiliating him. He'd do all the stuff he liked best, with all the cruelty he could muster, as slowly as possible. He was going to enjoy Miriam's pain almost as much as he'd enjoyed making love to her.

'I shouldn't need to remind you, corporal, that this mission never took place, and neither did the one in my house,' he told Pilón.

Here I am, in the hotel where Frank and I are registered as Mr and Mrs Harrison. Frank had to leave right away, we had hardly any time, but we did it anyway and it was lovely. He's asked me not to go out and not to talk to anyone until he gets back. He's gone out to run some errands: 'Don't you worry, I'll take care of everything so we can get you out of danger.'

I walk round and round the room. I feel like ringing Dufau's house to see if I can find out anything about the baby and maybe get the daughter's phone number. I wonder what her name is. But I'm too scared and anyway Frank will get cross. When I told him how I was planning to kidnap Lili he said I was completely out of my mind.

There's room service here, they've left a menu. I'm feeling hungry, so I ring and ask them to bring me up a hamburger and an orange juice. 'This is Mrs Harrison,' I say, 'in room 328.'

Mrs Harrison! I laugh out loud when I hang up. I don't know how I can be so happy, with my friend dead, the only friend I've ever had, and little Lili in the hands of those pigs who kidnapped her. Plus Animal's looking for me and this time he's really got it in for me, there's no doubt about that. But right now I'm happy even though I have to give up something I've only just discovered: how wonderful it is to make love with a friend – or whatever – an equal, someone who's really supportive, even though he's so different from me, even though he doesn't like tarts and he thinks I'm called Patricia. Even with all that's going on, I'm having fun playing at who I'd like to be for a while – Mrs Harrison. It's not to make Aunty happy, it's because it would be nice to be married to someone who's willing to put his life on the line for me. Right now I'm having a good time pretending to be Mrs Harrison. Why do I need an excuse to be happy for a bit? Even though I'm up to my ears in stuff that should make me want to slit my wrists, the fact is I'm having a good time. That's just the way I am.

Maybe that's why I ring my aunt: I want to say I'm sorry for rushing off like that, with only a note, and to let her know I'm with my boyfriend and that I'm happy.

Then she tells me what they did. What had I done? Why were they after me? Please tell her the truth. I don't know what to say. 'I have no idea,' I say at first, but I know I have to make up a reason big enough to fit what's happened. 'I bet they were hitmen working for this guy who wanted to marry me, he's rich, but horrible, and I said I wouldn't marry him, because like I told you, I'm in love with someone else.'

'Yes, that's right,' she says, sounding a little softer. 'What's he called, your boyfriend?'

'Bobby,' I say on the spur of the moment; thank goodness I didn't give her any other name. I tell her not to worry; tomorrow I'm leaving for

133

Italy but I'll write. And I'll send them some money before I go to make up for some of the stuff they smashed.

When Miriam told him, Frank was relieved he'd got his friend to agree to take her across the river. 'You're off to Uruguay tomorrow, in Charlie's speedboat.'

'Frank had friends with money, because he'd gone to Lincoln College. He had a scholarship, of course, because his parents didn't have a penny, but he was American. He still saw one of his friends, who had a boat and who used to go over to Carmelo, in Uruguay, where there was less police control. Frank asked him if he could take a woman over there, so that he could meet up with her later in Montevideo. The friend didn't ask too many questions. He must have thought it was an affair of some kind, because Frank hinted as much, and so he agreed.' Luz laughed.

'What are you laughing about?' Carlos asked.

'I just remembered something Miriam said when she told me the story: "When he laid eyes on me and saw what a looker I was, he must have felt proud of Frank. He tried hard not to grope me, his hands were all over the place." Since she knew what Frank had hinted to him, she made up a long story about how she'd split up with her husband because she'd fallen in love with Frank, but her divorce hadn't come through yet and the husband was suspicious, so they used to meet up in Uruguay so that he wouldn't see them together.'

'I don't want to leave tomorrow. I know I'm petrified, but who's going to find me here? If I have to go, then come with me.'

After what she'd just told him, how could she not realise how much danger she was in? 'If you won't go, I'll take you there myself. Although, of course, it's not a good idea for us to be seen together.'

No, he was right, Miriam said; she didn't want him to put himself out any more than he already had for her. 'I don't want you killed because of me.'

She agreed with Frank's plan. It was best if they weren't seen leaving the country together, that way nobody would associate the two of them. 'Because I know where you live and that could be dangerous if they get me.'

'It wasn't to protect herself, but to protect Frank that Miriam decided not to ring with her address in Uruguay.'

'And she never called, even after everything he'd done to help her?'

'No, she decided she had to make a complete break; she knew he would insist on seeing her and she didn't want him to get into trouble, because she loved him and wanted to save him. Frank didn't see it that way, though, obviously. After a while, he got a job in the States and went to live there. He ran into her, years later, in Punta del Este, on Gorlero Street. He'd gone there on holiday with his family. And so, that winter, he took two months off and went back to Uruguay, just to see her. But that was much later, in the winter of 1983.'

'And what about Lili?'

'Lili.' Luz smiled and paused for a second. She said the next word slowly, as if it were the result of a conscious decision. 'Luz grew up with her new parents. She suffered from what Mariana used to call congenital angst from time to time, but she was happy too . . . until 1983. And now I think I'd better order a glass of wine, before I start telling you everything that happened that year.'

PART TWO
1983

SEVEN

LAURA'S BIRTHDAY PARTY was going fine until Carola Luccini started talking about her friends who disappeared. Dinner was over and the guests had broken up into groups.

'Those kids weren't involved in anything.'

'How do you know?' Mariana interrupted insolently.

'Because I knew them really well. I've known them ever since they were little. Our mothers were friends. The girl taught at a private school, she was never mixed up in anything. And what could her brother possibly have done? He was only seventeen when he was seized.'

'When what?' asked Mariana. 'I don't understand.'

Eduardo noticed Alberto Luccini signalling to his wife.

'When he was kidnapped. It was all a mistake, but they were never seen again. Their mother's in a terrible state. She's written letters, got the lawyers to issue writs for habeas corpus, and they've met with army and navy officials and bishops, the police and the Church. No one knows anything. It's as if the earth had opened up and swallowed them alive. Most likely they've been killed.'

'If they were arrested, there must be some reason. How would you know? The fact that you've known them since you were young doesn't mean a thing. They could have changed. They may very well have been nice, well-brought up kids, but the communists could have brainwashed them into joining the guerrillas. Their mother must be the sort who has no idea what her children are up to, she probably hadn't the foggiest idea, and now she's crying over spilt milk. She should have kept a tighter rein on them before.'

Eduardo and Alberto both tried to change the subject but Eduardo's 'Can I get you both a drink?' and Alberto's 'Now, now, girls, lighten up a bit' merely ricocheted off the walls of the tense bubble that had formed around them.

Carola lost her temper. What did Mariana know about it, she hadn't even met them. They were super kids and good Catholics, and their mother was absolutely devoted to them. Mariana shouldn't talk like that – she wouldn't stand for it. 'I'd like to know how you think a kid who's only just turned seventeen can possibly have done anything that bad?'

Eduardo laid his hand on Mariana's arm and looked at her, mutely beseeching her to be quiet, because he could feel an explosion mounting in her as Carola was speaking. Not only did he dislike unpleasant scenes; they were in his brother's home and it was his wife Laura's birthday. He would have given anything to be able to stop this argument, but it seemed to have its own momentum. Mariana was as furious as Carola, if not more so.

'Oh, really? Have you forgotten about that fifteen-year-old girl who made friends with the police chief's daughter and got into their house and set off a bomb? She was a murderer at fifteen. So how can you tell me your little friend couldn't have done anything because he was seventeen?'

'I've told you, he didn't do anything.' Carola looked as if she were about to hit her. 'They took his life and nobody ever told his parents why. You said he was arrested: all right then, where is he, I'd like to know? Just tell me, because his family's completely in the dark. How would you like it if something like that happened to your daughter?'

'It would never happen to me. I'm going to bring her up properly.'

Alberto tried to stop her, but Carola had already sprung to her feet. Pointing her finger at Mariana, she shouted, 'You don't have a clue what you're talking about, Mariana. People have been disappearing here for years for no reason, and they don't just kidnap them, they steal all their possessions, and make them . . .'

'So what?' Mariana interrupted. 'Are people supposed to sit back and do nothing? You don't seem to care about the fact that bombs are going off and businessmen are being kidnapped, and that we're all in danger. I assume that means you agree with them.'

If Alberto had not intervened to pull Carola aside for a moment and steer her towards the table, talking to her along the way, who knows how things would have ended.

'Why are you getting so worked up?' Eduardo asked Mariana. 'Don't you realise she's talking about some kids she was really fond of, who'd been friends of hers since childhood?'

'Oh, shut up, Eduardo, you don't know what you're talking about. You're just too nice and naïve, or else stupid.'

He could not answer back because Carola and Alberto were coming towards them, drinks in hand. Carola's face was still red with emotion and her eyes were wet and bloodshot, but her voice was calm and controlled as she said to Mariana, 'I'm so sorry, I think I got a bit carried away just now. It's just that I really loved those kids. Of course I don't want people setting off bombs, or anything like that. We,' and she gestured to her husband, 'are totally against the guerrillas.'

After seven years away, Buenos Aires seemed utterly unreal to Dolores. The streets and the trees and the places all seemed the same, and yet somehow totally different.

'Running into Dolores again had a big effect on Eduardo's life. It was her story that made him realise he couldn't keep avoiding things. Dolores's sister-in-law was pregnant when she disappeared.'

'Who was Dolores?' asked Carlos.

'Dolores was the niece of one of the Iturbes' neighbours. She and her brother Pablo lived in Buenos Aires and they used to spend some of the summer months in Entre Ríos on her uncle's farm. She was much younger than Eduardo. When you're young, a few years matter a lot more, and perhaps their relationship was doomed as a result. Javier told me that Eduardo was very much in love with Dolores when he was younger, and that he spent hours writing to her. But then life intervened: they stopped going to Entre Ríos, Eduardo went off to university at Rosario, they stopped seeing one another and presumably forgot about each other. Twelve years later, during the winter of 1983, they ran into each other by chance in Buenos Aires. Dolores had just come back to Argentina after seven years in exile. Not to live; she was planning to stay in France. She had come to get in touch with the Abuelas de Plaza de Mayo* about a missing child.'

* The Grandmothers of the Plaza de Mayo, a non-governmental organisation devoted to finding the children and unborn infants who disappeared along with their parents during the dirty war of 1976–83.

141

The taxi glides down Libertador in a drizzling rain. It had been raining too the day Pablo took Dolores out for a ride in the brand-new car their parents had just given him for his eighteenth birthday. They went hurtling down Libertador, breathless with laughter. Dolores can still hear and feel that laughter, as real as it was back then. But then screams of pain start filtering in. She doesn't know if those screams come from the outside world, where Pablo no longer exists, or from inside her, because their sound is burnt into her mind for ever, even though she heard them for only one night.

Luz brought Mariana her exercise book so that she could look at her homework, but Mariana barely glanced at it.

'Very nice, dear,' she said, and shut the book.

'No, Mummy, you've got to look at all of it. There's more on the next page. I did a drawing.'

She flipped through the pages quickly and then rang for Carmen. It was late – time for Luz to have her bath. 'No, not yet, please.' Luz wanted to play with her new Lego, and build houses with her mother.

Mariana found Luz's persistence whenever she wanted something very irritating. 'Oh, go on, Mummy, please, please, say yes.' It also irritated her when Carmen didn't come as soon as she rang. She got up and shouted from the doorway, 'Carmen, go and give Luz a bath and get her into her pyjamas.'

It wasn't really Luz or Carmen's fault that she was in a bad mood, she realised; the real reason was the row she'd had with Eduardo after Laura's birthday party yesterday. Mariana felt Eduardo hadn't understood what Carola Luccini had said, or why she herself had reacted the way she did. She tried to continue the argument after they left, but Eduardo changed the subject, and then he was so sweet to her that she stopped being angry and they fell asleep in one another's arms after making love.

Eduardo always managed to disarm her by being affectionate and she ended up not really speaking her mind. This time, though, she wasn't going to let him get away with it. When he got back from Buenos Aires she'd have it out with him. Carola deserved what she'd said to her, even though they were at their in-laws'. She'd do the same thing again if anyone dared to defend a subversive to her face. Eduardo could let other people think and believe whatever they wanted, without ever pointing out that they were wrong, but she couldn't. His laid-back attitude exasperated her, but it was very difficult to confront him about it. He had a way of distracting her from arguments and turning it all into a game and then caressing her that she found irresistible. She couldn't let this one pass, though, because any day now it might come up in front of Luz, and they were responsible for her upbringing so they had to be clear about their values. Eduardo was so naïve; he had no idea what was going on in Argentina. That explained why he could feel sorry for people like Carola instead of wondering why she was defending a couple of subversives so vehemently. Carola might easily be a closet communist.

So when Eduardo telephoned to say that he wouldn't be home until the next day because his last meeting was running late, Mariana asked him to come back that night because she needed to talk to him.

Dolores glances to her right and is surprised to see the Dandy. After all these years, and everything that's happened, the bar's still there, as if nothing had changed. Without thinking, she tells the taxi driver to stop, pays him and gets out. She makes her way through the chairs and tables under the awning outside the bar and goes inside. It seems crazy that the Dandy is still here, the same as always, when her brother isn't.

All those years in France have formed a thin skin around her wound, but ever since coming back to Buenos Aires, the pain has returned, unavoidable, staring her in the face. She can touch it, smell it, feel it twisting in her body. It is a pain that will not let her be, that demands action and revenge and reparation. And the only reparation possible, she thinks to herself, is to move heaven and earth to find her little niece or nephew – if he or she survived, that is.

She sits down at a table next to the window and orders a *café con leche* and a piece of toast. She gazes round the bar. Memories start surfacing, one after the other: herself in uniform, meeting up with Pablo and his friends at the school gates; telling Pablo she was 'really, truly' in love with Eduardo, and if they didn't let her go to Entre Ríos that summer, she would run away from home; having beers and sandwiches with friends after going to parties or the cinema; Pablo, looking serious and euphoric, telling her he'd joined the party.

When Pablo arranged to meet her in the Dandy that time, Dolores was not surprised, because ever since she was thirteen and he was fifteen they had got in the habit of sharing their secrets there instead of at home, as if they couldn't talk with their parents around. By then they no longer saw as much of each other as before. Pablo had started university and had a different schedule as well as new friends, so he spent a lot of time out of the house. Little by little, he had grown apart from Dolores and her crowd. So she'd been really pleased when he suggested they meet up at the Dandy that Saturday evening.

It wasn't that he didn't love her as much as before, Pablo explained, or that he found going out and talking to his little sister boring, as she had said reproachfully; it was just that his life had changed because he'd come to see some fundamental things about society that he hadn't been aware of before. He talked to her about the class struggle and the injustice of the bourgeois system. According to him, he had joined the only movement that was capable of organising and leading the masses in the right direction. He had decided to join the Revolutionary Workers' Party. He was full of pride as he told her this. For the first time, he felt useful, as if he was helping to make history.

The word *revolution* made his eyes shine; he rolled it around his tongue like a delicious sweet or an intoxicating liquor.

He wanted to share this with her, he said, because she was his best friend and his little sister and he loved her. Besides, the party had decided it was safer if some of the members' parents knew they had joined. Since he didn't think it was feasible to tell their parents for the time being, he had decided to let her in on it. 'But don't tell Mum or Dad, please.'

'No, they wouldn't understand. They were very upset when you told them you didn't want the car they'd bought you, and that you were ashamed of owning one at your age when there were people who didn't have enough to eat,' Dolores said reproachfully. 'You shouldn't have hurt their feelings like that.'

Pablo asked her to think about what she was saying and not to get hung up on the personal level; to try and look at things in terms of the class struggle. 'Thinking about things on an individual level makes them seem obscure and confusing, but looking at the world from an objective, historical viewpoint takes us into the heart of the masses, into their joys and sufferings, their perspective. It shows us the real struggle.'

How long was it between that meeting and the next one Dolores asked him for, as their mother sobbed and their father ranted in the background, the day Pablo announced he was leaving home? Six months? A year? Until then, she had kept his secret, as he asked her to, not just from her family, but also from her friends. Pablo had given her a copy of the journal *Nuevo Hombre* to read, but Dolores had told him she didn't want to get mixed up in politics, and he got angry. 'Take off your blindfold, Dolores. Don't you remember that tango line about how bad it is to be blind by choice?'

They didn't fight over it, but their day-to-day lives were so different that they were drifting further and further apart.

That evening, as they talked in the Dandy, he told her that he was going to live with Mirta, his comrade, in a working-class neighbourhood. He said he was going to join the proletariat. 'Join the proletariat? What on earth do you mean? Are you going to become a worker? Really? Pablo, you're mad. Why?' He explained, but Dolores found it difficult to understand him. She was furious. 'Why do you have to do everything this way, always going to extremes? Can't you communicate with "the masses" without having to dress like them?'

Even though by that point Dolores was beginning to use the jargon she was picking up at university, she still could not understand Pablo's decision. He told her he didn't hold it against her: it was the fault of her upbringing, and all those well-intentioned but ignorant people she must be listening to, because neither the Montoneros nor the Maoists, nobody but the Revolutionary Workers' Party was equipped for the struggle. It was time she woke up and realised what was going on around her.

'You can't avoid the terrible need out there by playing around with academic abstractions, Dolores. You've got to march with the masses and share their path, to victory or defeat. Those are the only two options in the revolutionary struggle.'

145

But a long time went by before the letters Pablo wrote while under-cover began to give her a clearer sense of the passion that was now driving his life. For he did believe in life; Pablo was not the suicidal type. Their father had been terribly wrong on that score, and she herself had made the same mistake. 'You're wrong, Dolores. It's not that I don't care about my life. We're fighting for life, but for us it means something very different from the bourgeois system. We're struggling for life in a broader and simpler sense, a life of dignity for all, by means of collective action,' Pablo had written. He sounded happy, full of enthusiasm, and sure of the way.

Eduardo decides to go and have a drink at the Dandy before his business meeting with Urrutia. Lord knows when they'll be finished. He's none too happy about having to drive home late at night in this weather, but Mariana asked him not to stay in Buenos Aires because she has something important to say to him, and he just couldn't bring himself to say no. Her bad mood probably has to do with the incident last night at Laura's birthday party.

Maybe it would have been better not to argue with her, but it's too late now. Deep down, he was indignant that she was so crass and insensitive during the row with Carola.

Why was Mariana so hard on her? She didn't even know Carola's friends. When you listen to her talking like that, lecturing rather than giving her opinion, without knowing the first thing about the situation, you can't help hearing her parents. The same certainty, as if the world belonged to them, and their role in life was to tell everyone the way things should be.

'An Old Smuggler on the rocks, please.'

Eduardo glances at the woman who is sitting by the window. He's got a feeling he knows her.

Dolores? It can't be. Her face looks very different, although she must have changed after all these years. Now she's turned her head away, and he can't see her. He heard, years ago, that Dolores and Pablo had moved to Europe. He gets up, intending to go over and say hello, but what if it isn't Dolores? He sits back down again and then he notices the pain on her face. Is she crying? Yes, she's wiping away tears. Now you're sure it's

146

Dolores. It's as if you could still feel the soft, cool flesh of the peaches you picked off the trees during the torrid afternoons in Entre Ríos. From time to time, when you bite into a peach, you flash back to the uncontrollable desire you used to feel for her.

Eduardo sips his whisky. If he goes over to say hello at once, he'll embarrass her.

What can have happened to her? The suffering on her face has obliterated the dazzling smile she had at fifteen. She was just fifteen that summer in Entre Ríos. Fifteen! And Eduardo, who at twenty-two had slept with four or five women already – a track record which he considered highly impressive at the time – thought of himself as mature, an older man. A dirty old man, you called yourself. You were convinced the relationship would never work out, but no other girl had ever disturbed you as much as Dolores. Everything you did together – talking, laughing, playing, lying in the sun, horse riding, swimming in the river – took on a special fascination.

You forbade yourself to go beyond flirting with her, not just because of her age but because you were afraid of the intensity of your desire. Getting any closer might be like diving into a lake of pleasure that you wouldn't be able to get out of until you'd possessed her. Night and day, you were overcome by fantasies of touching and kissing her, feeling her warm breasts straining against your skin, sinking your teeth into the peach and feeling your body enter hers. But in the end it was Dolores who took the initiative – when she climbed trees to pick peaches, or ran down to the river to go swimming, or avoided the others so as to be able to meet you alone.

Eduardo remembers, all these years later, how moved he was by the seductive pose she struck the first time they kissed. She must have copied it from a Hollywood film. She turned her head towards him with her lips half open and her eyes closed. Your lips had scarcely touched hers when your arms closed hungrily round that warm, young, firm-fleshed body. It was hard to stop, and the next afternoon it was even harder. You used to meet at the river. Your hand now knew the curve of her breasts and your lips had explored her neck and shoulders. It was on the third afternoon, just as your hand was travelling slowly but surely up her thighs, that her mother appeared.

He was more shocked by Dolores's reaction than by her mother screaming and accusing him of who knows what (although he does vaguely remember that he agreed with her). As Eduardo was getting up and straightening his clothes, Dolores said, 'It wasn't his fault, why are you shouting at him? It was me that asked him. What's wrong with that? We love each other, like Dad and you. Why are you so furious? You should be happy, like I am.'

'Go home this minute,' was all her mother said.

You stood there lamely, not knowing what to say.

'I'm so happy,' Dolores shouted, as she walked away. 'It was lovely, Eduardo, thank you.'

'This mustn't happen again, Eduardo,' said Dolores's mother grimly. 'You're a grown man and Dolores is just a girl.' You assured her it wouldn't, but you couldn't stop wanting Dolores. You sent each other letters that had to be burned, promising to love one another till death and to elope if her parents insisted on intervening. You fantasised about going all the way with her. But she didn't come back the next summer, and time did the rest.

When Dolores finally saw the little place Pablo and Mirta had moved to out in San Justo, she felt less worried. Actually seeing where Pablo lived allowed her to let go of the bleak scenarios she'd been envisaging. He was living there, like that, because he'd chosen to. He was happy, she told herself, and that was what mattered. She wasn't there to antagonise him, but to share as much as possible; Pablo had been living away from home for more than four months. Unfortunately, however, things didn't turn out the way she intended. Dolores had started studying humanities at university and was attracted by the Argentine University Leftist Federation. Although she hadn't yet joined the Communist Revolutionary Party, she believed she was moving closer to Pablo. He took it upon himself to destroy that notion with more ammunition than Dolores would have liked. Suddenly they got caught up in a ridiculous argument which Dolores eventually stopped by reminding him that she was there to see him, so they could have a nice time together, and instead they'd spent hours talking about Soviet imperialism and Mao and Perón and

148

Santucho, and the true revolutionary course, which wasn't what she'd gone to visit him for. 'I miss you a lot, you silly thing, so just lay off me. I promise I won't join a party without asking you, I'll take my time. Now tell me how you're doing, and what life is life for you these days.' He replied that he was happy because he'd proved that it was not only possible to join the proletariat, it was actually good for you. The people there were really supportive and Mirta was working in a textile factory. The party was gaining the trust of the masses.

Pablo's revolutionary zeal frightened Dolores, but she stuck to her resolve and did not contradict him. She wanted to keep in touch with him, and she was afraid that if she said anything Pablo might treat her the same way as their parents, whom he hadn't seen for months. His mother cried every day.

'Yes, I'll ring Mum, I promise,' Pablo said, to reassure her.

They arranged to meet again the following Sunday. Dolores would bring fresh pasta and Mirta would make the tomato sauce. 'She makes a fantastic *marinara*,' Pablo had said, with as much pride as if he were talking about the growth of the party.

A few days later he called to ask if they could meet at the bar at Retiro station. He'd been within a hair's breadth of being caught. A neighbour stopped him on the street corner and told him that they'd gone to his house, so he escaped. Luckily, Mirta was at the party school that week, so she was safe too. They smashed everything up, and scrawled three As on the walls.★ They would have to go underground.

Until then, Dolores had not understood the meaning of that word. Pablo started using another name and she never knew where they were living. She would get short phone calls, fear thudding behind every syllable, and letters which she tore open impatiently. They would meet in out-of-the-way places, feigning indifference, sometimes walking one behind the other, as if they were complete strangers, until Pablo decided that there was no danger and they could talk.

Dolores told her parents. She couldn't bear to see them suffering, feeling abandoned and unloved, when he really did care about them. Didn't he?

★ Argentine Anti-Communist Alliance, a right-wing paramilitary group that carried out attacks and killings before the coup.

'Of course I do, Dolores. I don't mean to hurt their feelings. It's ultimately the system that's to blame for the way they've reacted.'

Pablo agreed she could tell their parents he was in hiding, that it was better they knew, so they'd be ready in case he fell; he knew he was facing serious risks.

Dolores recalls listening in terror to the news about the disastrous rebel attack on the arsenal at Monte Chingolo, the day before Christmas Eve 1975. She and her parents paced wordlessly back and forth next to the telephone. Please let him call, let him be all right, let him not be one of the ones who got shot in Monte Chingolo. It was her father who won the race when it rang. 'Pablo's all right,' he told them, 'he had to hang up. He says to wish you happy Christmas.' And with that, he went to his room, looking as if he'd aged ten years.

Pablo had been underground for some time when the military coup took place in March 1976.

Her mother went with her to Morón to meet Pablo. Dolores had lectured her about not arguing with him. She was just to go and visit him, give him a kiss, say whatever she had to say and that was it. But her mother was so petrified about what might happen to Pablo that she tried to beg him to leave the country. She said they could get him out; they'd made a few discreet enquiries. A friend of Dad's would take them to Entre Ríos in his biplane, she told Dolores on the train. When they met Pablo and Mirta that Sunday afternoon, she laid out the rest of her carefully constructed plan in a pizzeria reeking of burned cheese and oil, knitting all the loose ends the way she used to knit their jumpers when they were children. She never stopped talking. 'You can go to Entre Ríos, then Dad's friend will take you to Brazil, and there . . .'

Pablo cut her off by opening Mirta's jacket. 'Look, Mum.'

She will never forget Pablo's smile, the proud look in his eyes. 'That's your grandchild in there, Mum, growing away.'

'She was seven months pregnant when she was captured.'

Dolores can't remember who was the first to react, her or her mother. So Mirta was pregnant? 'Yes, although to look at her you'd never know, she's so small you'd think she'd just swallowed a peach stone.' Even more reason to get away, now. How could they have a child in those

150

conditions, always moving around like that? But Pablo was adamant. No, they couldn't go – he was in charge of a lot of people and he wasn't going to leave them in the lurch at a time like this. He might have promised to think it over to keep the two of them quiet. It wasn't safe to be seen together any longer. Dolores had to hold her mother by the arm and drag her away. On the way back she talked to her non-stop so she wouldn't break down and give in to her anguish and fear. What had they done wrong for things to turn out like this, for their son to be so thoughtless? 'Persuade him, Dolores, please. When he rings, try and make him see he has to get out of the country as soon as possible; he'll listen to you. Promise me, love, promise me you'll talk him into it.'

From Pablo's next letter, it seemed unlikely that Dolores would be able to convince him. They couldn't see one another until he sent word. It was a difficult time; a lot of comrades had fallen, but he was safe.

Dolores planned it carefully. She persuaded herself that if she just had one chance to talk to Pablo, she could change his mind. She went through his arguments one by one, and his possible replies, and what she would say back. She had a plan, a perfect escape plan, if only he wouldn't let himself be killed. She asked her parents not to answer the telephone, since she was the only one who could phrase it so that Pablo wouldn't refuse to meet. She didn't care if she had to lie to him, she would do whatever it took. And she managed it.

Dolores feels a jagged spoon churning up her stomach as she re-members. If only she hadn't insisted on meeting him, perhaps . . . If only she hadn't told Mónica . . .

'She had told her friend that Pablo had agreed to meet her that Monday at seven, but not where.'

She had never thought to connect what she'd said to Mónica with the arrest. She had wondered again and again why they had caught them there of all places, how they knew that Pablo would be there. They must have followed her from her house, and when they saw them together . . . There were eight or ten of them and everything happened very fast. They pulled hoods over their heads and took them away.

'Dolores didn't even remember having told Mónica about it, until Mónica *confessed to her three years later, when they met by chance in Madrid. Mónica was her best friend.'*

But nothing lasts under torture: neither friendship, nor affection, nor loyalty – nothing.

'More than twenty years had gone by when I met Dolores and she was still torturing herself for her carelessness. She felt responsible for Pablo's capture.'

'You met Dolores?'

'Yes, a few months ago, through Delia, one of the Abuelas.'

'Why does Dolores feel responsible?'

'Because when she met her friend Mónica in Madrid, Mónica told her, in despair, that she'd been tortured and that she'd told them Dolores was going to meet her brother.'

Mónica had been quite clear about it that night when they got drunk together: no, Dolores had never said where they were going to meet, just that they were going to. She told them because she couldn't stand the agony of the electric prod on her nipples any longer. She didn't know anything about anyone, not a thing; she was just what they called a 'window-shopper'. Who knows why they took her in; perhaps because she was seeing that bloke who was a Montonero, or maybe just by mistake, like so many other people. She would have told them whatever they wanted, anything to stop that agonising pain, but she knew nothing. The only person she knew of who was really involved was Pablo, Dolores's brother, and so when she remembered that Dolores was going to meet him . . . 'Will you ever be able to forgive me, Dolores?' She'd forgiven Mónica, but she had never been able to forgive herself. She cannot.

'Dolores?' That man's warm smile strikes an odd note that doesn't fit her thoughts at all. 'Do you remember me? Or am I too old?'

Dolores barely nods, without saying a word. She may know him, she thinks, but the ghosts that have haunted her ever since she walked into the Dandy are thronging her memory, preventing her from placing the compassionate gaze of this person opposite her.

'You know, you once wrote that I was the man of your life, and that life with me would be one long celebration, and now you don't even recognise me.'

The torrid afternoons of Entre Ríos, the fizzy excitement of being fifteen and wild at heart sweep in like a breath of fresh air.

'Eduardo! Oh, Eduardo, it's so great to see you!'

'When is Daddy coming home?' Luz asked.

'Late, you'll be asleep by then. You'll see him tomorrow.'

'Well, you tell me a story then.'

'I have a very clear memory of Dad telling me stories before I went to sleep.' Carlos *was only too aware of the tenderness in Luz's voice when she talked about Eduardo. 'I was always asking him for one about a girl from outer space with the same name as me, Luz, who used to have these amazing adventures. Dad made them up every night; he was a brilliant storyteller. I can still remember some of them.'*

Carlos forbade himself to tell Luz what he was feeling at that moment. He couldn't put his finger on exactly what the emotion was, but he knew that it was illogical and perhaps unkind. What right did he have to ask Luz to stop calling that man 'Dad' when he'd only met her a few hours ago? What right did he have to spoil her happy memories of a childhood he hadn't been able to share? Was it Luz's fault that she so loved the man who had stolen her?

It was strange how Luz's voice and even her expression seemed to become more childlike as she told Carlos one of the stories about Luz the space alien. He could only try and imagine the little girl of five or six inside the woman before him, the child he would never know. He knew he had to fight that feeling, let go of his resentment, forget the circumstances and the hatreds, and try and float off in the atmosphere Luz was creating. They had to share the story as best they could, even though it was too late, and even though it was someone else's story since he had never been able to tell her stories himself. Luz must need this, otherwise why would she be digressing to tell him a fairy tale when there were so many things he didn't know?

Carlos was able to laugh with Luz at the end of the story. Yes, it was brilliant, and she told it very well.

Mariana preferred to read stories to her, rather than make them up. She was tired and cross, but she read to Luz because she wanted her to fall fast asleep as soon as possible. She couldn't face another of Luz's bad nights: those green eyes of hers would go as big as plates and glitter

153

feverishly, and she would give shrieks of terror, as if she were being murdered.

'She's having nightmares,' the paediatrician had said.

What can she be dreaming about? She's so young, thought Mariana in desperation. She didn't know what to do to calm her down; sometimes she started crying as hard as Luz. Then Eduardo would pick up the child and get her to relax, showing a patience that Mariana had to admit she didn't possess.

Luz had been asleep for a while when Eduardo rang to say that unfortunately he wouldn't make it back that night. The meeting was still going on and they'd had to postpone the rest of the agenda until the next day. He would set out for Entre Ríos tomorrow lunchtime.

What Eduardo told Mariana is not totally untrue: he does have a meeting with Urrutia tomorrow. But it is also true that it was he who proposed they postpone the rest of their business until the following morning, with the excuse that they still had various things to discuss. The first thing he did was to ring Dolores and invite her to dinner.

'Sure, why not?' she said.

She did not seem surprised that Eduardo was calling her the same night, rather than the next time he was in Buenos Aires, as he had said he would. She had no idea when she would be there again; she had just come to sort out some paperwork, but her plan was to go back as soon as possible to France, where she had been living for the last six years. He rang her on impulse; the idea just came to him while he was in the meeting.

Dolores seemed in bad shape. But that's not the only reason, don't kid yourself, the truth is you want to see her, to be with her, don't pretend that you just want to comfort her. Maybe you'll never have another chance. That's why you were so evasive with Mariana.

Could you ever tell Mariana what happened to Dolores? She'd react even worse than she did with Carola, because Pablo was obviously in some leftist organisation. For Mariana those kind of people were the baddies, as simple as that; she had no sympathy for them. Isn't that why when Dolores asked who you'd married, you just said a girl from Buenos

Aires? You may have referred to Mariana by name, but you took good care not to mention Dufau. You'd be ashamed to have to tell Dolores your father-in-law is in the military after what she told you. She hates the military. With good reason. Wouldn't you, if Javier and Laura had disappeared?

You think back to the incident last night and realise what it was that bothered you most. Why did Carola feel the need to apologise to Mariana for everything she'd said? Why was it so important that Mariana didn't think they agreed with the guerrillas? For one reason only: because Mariana is Dufau's daughter and Luccini must be afraid of her. When you asked Mariana in the car why she couldn't just let people think and feel what they wanted, she hit the roof: was that how he was going to bring up Luz, telling her that everyone is free to think what they want? What if she turns into a guerrilla or a drug addict? And then she started ranting on as usual about the baddies, whom she portrays as a blend of drug addicts–guerrillas–homosexuals, while on the other side are the goodies, like Daddy, for example. Sometimes you find Mariana's childishness funny, but in this area it sickens you. You're going to have to talk to her, you can't leave things the way they are. She's the one who can't see what's been going on in the country over the last few years. Look at Dolores – she told you she was never involved in politics, but they arrested her anyway.

'It's a miracle I got away. I could be dead,' Dolores says to him over dinner.

'But you weren't a guerrilla, they wouldn't have killed you.'

Dolores gives him a loving but disgusted look and wonders how she can possibly be telling all this to someone who can say such a thing. But it's too late, she's said it now. She should probably get it into her head that she's back in Buenos Aires, and that Eduardo isn't like the people she's talked to in Europe, the exiles. This is what it means to be an Argentinian in 1983, even though they're shifting to a democratic government here. However, she can't help herself.

'No, I wasn't involved in politics. But that's irrelevant. Do you think that's why they let me go?' She paused for a moment and then went back

155

on the attack, more angrily than before. 'Or do you think that people who were involved in politics or who had different ideas from you deserved to get mangled and humiliated and killed or broken by psychologically forcing them into some agonising betrayal? Come on, tell me.'

She knows Eduardo didn't mean to hurt her. If he had, he wouldn't be sitting there with his hand on hers, quietly, looking at her so fondly, even though he's frightened. She shouldn't judge everything in black and white; there are shades of grey. Maybe it's not his fault he doesn't know anything about all this. She shouldn't assume that people who don't think exactly the same as her are just like those bastards. Her parents, for example. It was so hard for them to understand. 'No, they won't kill them. Mirta's pregnant, the Argentinian army wouldn't mistreat a pregnant woman,' her father used to say, with a conviction based on an era utterly different from those savage times. He just couldn't understand it. He endured so many hours waiting in corridors for former close acquaintances, only to be fobbed off with refusals or replies riddled with falsehood. How many habeas corpus writs and useless applications had they filled in, and how much sheer pain and impotence had they had to endure to reach the point of saying what her mother had whispered feverishly to her that very afternoon, 'Those bastards, those murderers, they must have given the baby away.' Yes, there are shades of grey.

'I'm sorry, I didn't mean to hurt your feelings,' Eduardo said. 'Maybe there's a lot I don't know. Nobody close to me went through anything like that. But I don't want you to assume that I think it's OK for them to kill or torture people, or that anyone deserves that. I want you to know how terribly sorry I am about Pablo – I know how much you've suffered.'

'It's me who should be apologising. I'm not feeling well. I shouldn't have shouted at you like that. I have so much hate inside me. What you said made me think you were on the other side. Which isn't fair – who knows what I'd think if all this hadn't happened to me, if I hadn't been there that night . . .'

Dolores stops abruptly. She looks at Eduardo, who is listening so attentively, drinking in everything she says just like he used to, when he was the grown-up and she was the kid. She thinks how funny it is that now she's the adult and he's the naïve little boy.

Calm down, calm down, I'm here to have a good time, to relax, Dolores says to herself. I'm supposed to be remembering how nice it was when this man sitting there made my body feel so alive. I ought to be totally happy and excited; I should try and relive what life was like before the horror came, even if it's only for a little while. But she can't seem to find the phrase that will take them back to those peach-scented after-noons. Eduardo, who is still struggling with what Dolores said earlier, is trying to defend himself.

'I just mean, I don't know, I thought if you weren't involved, they let you go. But I don't know what I'm talking about . . .'

'I was released because the bloke who was in charge at that moment felt like it. He could have changed his mind and then I'd be dead. "Get the hell out of here. Next time we'll kill you, you Bolshevik whore," that's what he said.'

'She was only in there one night. They let her go the next day. But her brother stayed there; she heard him screaming as they tortured him.'

Stop, stop now, you wanted to relax, take your mind off all that. Eduardo's not one of them, or he wouldn't be trying to apologise and opening up to accept what you say. Later on there'll be time to explain; for now she's got to get out of those dark corridors. There's sun outside, right here, opposite her, in the warmth of Eduardo's eyes, in their adolescent love.

Dolores tries to smile. It's as if she had stretched out a hand, and Eduardo quickly takes it.

'Tell me about it, I want to know.'

'No, please, let's not talk about it now, I need to take a break from all that.'

'Dolores, if there's anything I can do to help, just tell me.'

'Yes, there is: help me remember those afternoons in Entre Ríos and the way we were back then.' Just that, just conjuring up the blurry image of the two of them by the banks of the river, has changed the expression on her face. 'Do you know I was madly in love with you? I must have seemed ridiculous to you, I was just a kid. And the letters I used to write!

I used to read Neruda's *Twenty Love Poems and a Song of Desperation* and I'd lock myself up to write to you. I used to copy out lines from Neruda. You must have thought it was hilarious . . .'

For the first time since they've met, Eduardo hears Dolores's infectious laugh.

'I was head over heels in love with you too, I really was.'

Dolores says she doesn't believe him; he must be exaggerating. 'Whenever I remember you, I think how you must have laughed over my letters, with that funny mixture of Amalia, Corín Tellado and Neruda.'

No, he never laughed, he found them very moving, they went to his head.

'I probably shouldn't tell you everything that went through my mind . . . or rather my body, when I read your letters.' And now it's Dolores's turn to rediscover Eduardo's laugh.

Dolores says she doesn't mind where they go, it's up to him to choose a place where they can carry on talking after the restaurant.

You'd like to say to her: 'Let's go to my hotel.' It lasts only a second, as you're helping her into her coat, just a second, but you're dazed, almost as much as you used to be, by the intensity – and the bad timing – of your attraction to her. Perhaps that's why you hurriedly say the name of the first bar you can think of that's nearby.

But the conversation is not about hot afternoons full of peaches and desire and passionate letters.

Eduardo really wants to know what happened; it's not just that Dolores can't stay away from the topic. You press her for more, you guide her, you suffer for her, and so, once they're in the bar, Dolores tells you the whole story: the three As scrawled on the wall in Pablo's house, the hoods, the kicks and the screams, those terrible screams she heard that night, about the torture and the robbery, about how Mirta was kidnapped when she was seven months pregnant. Dolores was out of the country by then, because as soon as they let her go, she left, first for Brazil, following her parents' plan for Pablo that he would never use, and then on to France. She told him about her contacts with human rights organisations in Europe and what her plans were in Buenos Aires: to get in touch with the Abuelas, the group that was searching for the babies that disappeared in the detention centres; to talk to people; to try and get her parents to rise above their pain and get involved with the organisation.

What country, what world have you been living in while all this was going on, all these things Dolores is telling you?

'Until Dolores told him about her brother and about her sister-in-law's baby, he had never suspected that Luz might be a detainee's child.'

'That's impossible. I don't know why you're determined to believe Eduardo didn't know. Maybe because you loved him so much and . . .'

'No, that's not true,' Luz cut in sharply. 'I'm telling you that until then he didn't know that they stole children from the people they kidnapped. I knew about it, because I'd heard about some of the cases, one involving twins and some other ones too, but even so, it never occurred to me that I might be one of them.'

'Why should it? They never told you that you weren't their daughter. Did they?'

'No. But I often suspected that I wasn't Mum's, because of the things she used to say when I did something she didn't like: she'd go on about my genes, saying there was something I'd inherited, that I had a devil inside me, a dark side, and all sorts of stupid things like that. And then I used to remember what Miriam said to me when she came to get me that time from school; I remembered about that for years, even though I was very young at the time.'

'Miriam? What did Miriam say to you? When?'

'I'm not going to tell you that part yet, you'll only get mixed up. I just mean that until my son was born, it never occurred to me that I might be one of the babies who were born in captivity. It was a crazy idea; it just came to me out of the blue, but if I hadn't got obsessed with it, you and I wouldn't be here in Madrid, talking.'

'But why did you start thinking that way, if nobody said anything to you?'

'Just let me tell you things in the order they happened. As I was saying, Eduardo started to suspect something only after he talked to Dolores, not before. I really believe that. Everything he did from that point proves that he took a lot of risks – terrible risks – in order to get to the truth.'

'So what happened? Did he ever find out?' Carlos can't help the sarcasm in his voice. 'Or did he just forget to tell you all those years? How can you defend someone who stole your identity like that?'

Luz's furious look was more eloquent than the retort she was obviously biting
back. Carlos told himself once again that he should try and hide how he felt when
he saw how much Luz loved the man. It wasn't sensible or helpful to reveal his
feelings about it. She stayed silent for what seemed like an eternity, and when she
finally spoke, her words came out slowly, as if it were tremendously hard for her to
go on talking, and she was having to force herself.

'I would prefer it if you listened more and stopped being so judgmental.'

It is very late when Eduardo takes Dolores back to her parents' home.
He says he will ring her if he's in Buenos Aires in the near future.

'Yes, of course I had a good time, it's lovely to see you.'

Dolores has no idea how much worse she has made him feel, but he is
obviously letting something show, otherwise she wouldn't be saying this:
'I'm sorry, I didn't mean to make you feel bad. No, really; I would have
liked us just to have a good time reminiscing about Entre Ríos instead of
me dumping all that shit on you – I couldn't help it.'

'Don't worry. You're right, I am feeling bad, but it's not your fault.
Really, it's not. I'm glad you could trust me, and that you told me all
those things. I had no idea about all this, believe me.'

He gives her a kiss. 'Good luck, Dolores.'

'Next time it'll be your turn to tell me your life story. OK?' says
Dolores as she turns to go.

EIGHT

AFTER SHE CAUGHT sight of them that summer at the seaside in Punta del Este, Miriam couldn't shake off the idea. She had decided a while ago that her plan to kidnap Lili and bring her up so she could tell her the truth was insane. Nevertheless, when she saw Dufau walking by holding hands with a little girl who could only be Lili, Miriam's heart started pounding so fast that she realised at once that her dream of rescuing the child was as strong as the day she handed her over.

'During those seven years, she kept telling herself that it was a crazy idea, far too risky, but at the same time she never missed an opportunity to take one more step forward. Just in case, she told herself. And so, before leaving Buenos Aires, she made a phone call and found out that there were three Dufau sisters: the eldest girl and the twins, who lived with their parents. Once she got to Uruguay, she started saving up so that if she ever managed to rescue me, we could leave the country together. She kept planning almost unconsciously, telling herself she'd never do it and at the same time perfecting all the details. In the meantime, things were changing in Argentina. By the time she started focusing on the idea again and decided to go ahead with it, the Falklands War had been fought and lost. Things were different. The transition to democracy was under way. Perhaps she didn't even need to be in exile.'

'Miriam wasn't exactly an exile,' said Carlos scornfully. 'If she was, she wouldn't have gone to Uruguay. The Uruguayan military co-operated with the Argentines.'

'Yes, she was, because she couldn't go back to her country. She knew Animal would kill her. Don't you think that after what she'd been through, she would have been as scared as any of you? What makes someone an exile? Being involved in politics?' Carlos shrugged and did not answer. 'As a matter of fact, she was very frightened. She knew she couldn't do anything to help me, and yet she came up

with a scheme for getting us passports about four years after moving to Uruguay,
which shows she never completely gave up the idea. At a disco in Punta del Este
she got in touch with a man who forged documents and found out how much he
charged and how he did it. She pretended it was for a friend who was a battered
woman and wanted to run away with her daughter. Although she had supposedly
given up, she was continually fine-tuning the plan so it would be all set to go, if she
ever got the chance.'

She could think of nothing else. The night before, when she and
Frank were having dinner together and he was telling her about his life in
the States, describing his house, garden and job, she broke in to say, 'Do
you think Animal is still looking for me? I've been gone for seven years.'

'I don't know. Why? Do you want to leave Uruguay?'

She didn't know whether she did or not, she was just thinking about it.
She had a decent, steady job, no more nasty shocks, she was making good
money, and she could even take July off, like last year. A whole month
with no demands: no shows, no dates, no nothing. A whole month just
for her. A proper rest.

'Do you ever think of travelling?' asked Frank.

Miriam sensed the hopefulness in Frank's eyes. Maybe he'd got
something in mind that he hadn't told her about yet. All he'd said
was that he'd come to see her, and she had corrected him. 'Oh go on
now, stop exaggerating, you must have come to see your mother too,
and your friends, and to travel around Uruguay a bit. 'You're not going
to spend your whole holiday just visiting me.' Frank had smiled faintly.

No, she replied, she'd never had any interest in travelling. Only when
she'd wanted to be a model and star on catwalks all over the world. She'd
given up dreaming about that a long time ago . . . and some other things
as well. She said those last words meaningfully, so that Frank would get
the message that even though it had been lovely, it was over and done
with now.

She was glad she had run into him on the street that summer so she
could explain that the reason she had never called him all those years was
because she wanted to prevent him from getting into any more trouble.
Frank didn't seem very convinced. But the night they spent together at
Miriam's flat cured him of his resentment. She told him to come and see

her again, if he was ever back in South America, but she never imagined he'd return just a few months later.

'In any case, it was lucky I came to see you this month, when we're both on holiday,' said Frank, with a trace of bitter irony, 'because otherwise you'd never have time to see me.'

'What did she do in Uruguay? Did she carry on working as a prostitute?'

'At first she just worked at a cabaret in Carrasco as a topless dancer. It was very hard for her to say yes to the first date, she said, but after that . . . well, as Miriam put it, what did she have to lose? Nothing, and it was all she knew how to do. The owner of the cabaret put her in touch with a call-girl agency in Punta del Este, where she spent the summers. She earned a lot of money. So yes, Miriam carried on being a prostitute until she went back to Argentina, when she came to kidnap me. After that, her life . . .'

'She tried to kidnap you?' Carlos sat up, impressed. 'That woman's certainly got balls!'

Luz smiled, amused by the expression. Clearly, Miriam had stopped being despicable in Carlos's eyes; he no longer thought that Liliana could not possibly have confided in her. And Luz was happy about that, because she liked Miriam – loved her even.

'Why are you thinking of leaving Uruguay when everything's going so well for you? Are you getting tired of living here?'

Miriam smiled. Frank could not disguise how much he disliked her lifestyle, but she pretended not to notice, and merely said it wasn't that she was getting tired of it, but she was thirty-two now, and even though work was going well at the moment, it wouldn't last much longer. Besides, she'd got other things in mind. That's why she'd taken a month off, to think things over. 'Oh yes,' said Frank, intrigued, 'such as?' His eyes lit up again and he leaned forward attentively in his chair to listen, in a way which suggested that maybe he really had come just to see her, to propose something there was no way she could accept. No, she had other plans: she had to rescue Lili.

'I can help you think things through,' Frank suggested enthusiastically. 'Help you come up with ideas.'

'No, you can't,' Miriam laughed. 'My plans are top secret,' and she tried to disguise her seriousness by joking.

What would Frank say if she told him her plan was to kidnap Lili and run away with her somewhere where nobody could find them? He'd be bound to think she was mad.

Why had she asked him about Animal? Frank wanted to know. He couldn't believe she was thinking of going back to Argentina. He would only ever go back there for visits, nothing more than that. He could never live in Buenos Aires again.

'I might go back. I don't think it's so dangerous now. Animal must have forgotten about me. Anyway, now the military are on their way out, I don't think I'd be in too much danger.'

'I'm not so sure. I don't believe that guy can possibly have forgotten you. Not after what you did to him. Besides, you're not easy to forget. I never did.'

She didn't want him to go on in that vein, getting his hopes up for nothing. If she hadn't seen the family on the beach that summer, maybe she would have been more receptive to his unspoken but obvious invitation. But now she had only one thing on her mind: kidnapping Lili, and she was certainly not going to tell Frank about it.

She preferred him to think it was something else: she told him she was setting up a business somewhere, either in Buenos Aires or the provinces. She was going to be in charge of a night club, let other girls do the work. A madam, that's it, and they both laughed, even though Frank obviously didn't find it funny.

Later on, watching him lay his clothes on the chair in her room, she thought it would be better not to look at him, or make room for him in her bed, because Lili might just melt away. His warm hand slid under the blouse she was still wearing. She shouldn't let him go on, she didn't want to lose sight of the image of herself driving away with Lili, but Frank caressed her thighs with such passion that her body surrendered to the heat and elation of desire. Although she loved making love with him, she felt the need to pull away and turn her back on him in bed so as not to dissolve into that sense of wellbeing. She had to rescue Lili.

'Miriam.' No, she didn't want to listen, she didn't want him to say it, but he did anyway. 'Why don't you come and live with me? We could just see how it goes.'

'Don't be silly,' she said, with a laugh. 'What on earth would I do with you, so far away? Anyway, I've already told you, I've got plans.'

She mustn't let him change her mind or make her lose sight of her true goal, no matter how much she likes being with him (which she has to admit she does). She'd been making progress; she was more prepared now. When she saw Lili and Dufau on the beach that day, she said to herself that she couldn't just grab her and run off there and then – there was no hope of that – but it wasn't a bad idea to get as much information together as possible, just in case she ever summoned the nerve to do it. So she followed them casually and lay down on her stomach in the sand near the group they were with. She didn't even know what they'd christened Lili, or what her surname was, or where they lived.

'So how did she go about finding out your name and address?' Carlos asked.

'In the summer of '83, we went to Punta del Este. We'd been invited by some family friends of the Dufaus, the Venturas.' Luz continued as if talking to herself. 'That's when I first met Daniel. I'd forgotten all about it. He was with his wife and children, they hadn't separated at that point.'

Luz fell silent for a long time. There was something dark and brooding about her that Carlos could not fathom.

'What's wrong?'

'Nothing, it's beside the point. I started thinking about that summer and I got sidetracked – Daniel Ventura became very important in my life later on. When Miriam saw Alfonso with me, walking along the beach, he didn't recognise her. Our family always went to the same beach and Miriam managed to get quite near and eavesdrop on our conversations. One day, she walked into the sea right next to where I was swimming, and another time, when I was playing by myself next to the water, she helped me build a sandcastle, but when Alfonso came up she walked away, because she couldn't risk him recognising her. I got very emotional when she told me how she spent hours watching me back then. It's strange to think that although I had no idea who she was, she loved me so much and so much of her waking life was spent thinking about me. By listening in to the conversations on the beach she found out that their names were Mariana and Eduardo Iturbe, that they lived in Paraná, in the province of Entre Ríos, and that he owned land there. Afterwards, when she'd made up her mind to do it, everything became easier: she already had the surname and the city, so it wasn't difficult to get hold of the address.'

Perhaps because she liked being with him so much that she was afraid he would distract her from her goal, Miriam asked Frank to leave rather than spend the night. They'd see each other another day, definitely, she promised.

It's possible that Frank actually precipitated Miriam's plans, without meaning to, because that very night, after he left, she decided not to fritter away any more time researching the details: she would do it that month. First she would go to Buenos Aires and then to Entre Ríos. She'd find the best means of getting Lili away. If anyone found her out, she'd leave the country. And if she managed to get Lili, she'd take her too and go as far away as possible.

The next day she met the forger to arrange for a passport for herself and the little girl. She had to come up with a story to explain why she was using her own photo, although he didn't seem to care too much about her motives, as long as she paid him what he'd asked, and more. According to him, getting a passport photo for the little girl from the photo she'd taken on the beach was going to be quite a challenge, but a few dollars would help him get over the technical difficulties.

She saw Frank a few more times, always fighting her attraction to him but giving in anyway. She told him she had to go on a business trip, but that she'd be stopping in Buenos Aires on the way, and they could meet there.

Eduardo drives back to Entre Ríos feeling shaken. The things that Dolores said have made a deep impression on him, but if he had to choose which bit of their conversation hit home the most, it was the fact that her sister-in-law had been pregnant, and that they'd never heard any news of the baby. They didn't even know whether it had been born or not.

That one remark was enough to pierce the thick walls around a dormant memory. It was like suddenly getting sucked into a whirlpool which pulled you down so that no matter how you struggled, you were dragged in deeper and deeper. What if Luz was the baby Dolores was looking for?

Eduardo asked what month and year her sister-in-law had disappeared in, torn between wanting and not wanting to know the answer, because if the dates did happen to coincide . . .

Dolores wasn't sure exactly, but the baby must have been born in July. What a relief! So it definitely wasn't Luz. Luz was born in November.

But why does it matter that she wasn't Dolores's sister-in-law's child? She could perfectly well be someone else's in the same situation. It had never occurred to you before; you didn't know they could be so twisted.

But did you really try hard enough to find out? You just swallowed what Alfonso said about her mother: that she was one of those girls who sleep around and get pregnant, and that it was better for everybody if they didn't know.

It is true that in all these years Eduardo has never brought up the subject of where Luz came from with Alfonso.

But now, as you drive very fast down the road, you are once more overcome by the sheer volume of suspicious things, the weight of lies and guilt. You immerse yourself once again in that night at the clinic: you suspected then that it wouldn't be easy to get rid of that dreadful sense of mental and physical unease. There were times, early in the baby's life, when you felt it only occasionally, but it was incredibly intense. Later on, you surrendered to happiness, to the pleasure your daughter gave you every day. You just enjoyed being with her and Mariana. But now, after what Dolores has told you, that unease is growing. You allow it to take root in your body and mind, letting yourself experience it as you somehow know you deserve to, reliving the way you felt that first night when Mariana was deep in a coma.

Perhaps if Mariana had asked, as Eduardo feared at first that she would, why Luz was so fair-haired and why she had green eyes when both of them were dark-haired and dark-eyed, he wouldn't be obsessing about it now. But for seven years Mariana has never had the slightest suspicion that Luz is not her daughter. And everyone went along with it so automatically that you stopped questioning yourself years ago, as if you'd forgotten too.

You tried hard to forget. You love her so much, you feel as if she's so much a part of you, that it's hard to remember she's not your own flesh and blood.

As soon as Eduardo arrived, Mariana said she had to talk to him right away. But he wanted to have a cup of tea and play with Luz for a while.

Couldn't it wait until after dinner? Was it that urgent? Luz started showing him her exercise book. 'Look at the drawing I did, Daddy.' And without waiting for Mariana's reply, he looked at the book and talked as if nothing were wrong, as if his wife weren't waiting for him. 'It's wonderful! You did a lovely job.'

Sometimes Mariana thought that Eduardo loved Luz more than her. How could he go on talking to the child and showing her the box of crayons he'd brought her, when he knew perfectly well she had something to discuss? She'd told him so every time he rang.

'I'm waiting, Eduardo,' she said, her impatience palpable.

Eduardo's resentful glance told her that not only was he oblivious to the fact that he was being rude, but that he had no intention of getting up. He simply went on discussing the crayons and the drawings and asking Luz about her day at school, as if Mariana didn't exist.

'Since your daughter is so important to you, you'd better come and talk to me this minute. I'll be waiting in the bedroom.' She had not raised her voice, but the effect was the same.

'From that moment on, they started fighting, sometimes about issues that were obviously political, and other times about silly little things, but their rows were always ultimately about politics. Eduardo told his brother about some of those fights. Javier and Laura started seeing him much more often than before. Javier realised how profoundly what Dolores had said had affected Eduardo. Before, he had never paid much attention to what Mariana said, just tried to keep the peace.'

When Eduardo came into the bedroom, he didn't even ask her what was wrong, why she had spoken to him like that. He just said that she seemed annoyed he was playing with Luz, that she wasn't to speak to him that way in front of Luz ever again.

She'd done it because she cared about her daughter, she was worried about the sort of upbringing Luz was going to get from him. Because what happened the other day, when he was so stupid about Luccini's wife, showed he was in cloud cuckoo land, he'd said all sorts of ridiculous things. 'Well, I suppose it's understandable, you're clueless about this country, you've no idea what's going on.' In any case, it had made her think they should agree on what they were going to tell Luz, in case subjects like that came up in front of her. They couldn't be so irresponsible about their own daughter, they had to take a clear stand and not give her the impression that anything goes, she had to know right from wrong.

Perhaps because Mariana was used to Eduardo always being nice to her and trying to smooth things over when she lost her temper, she was quite shocked by the tone and forcefulness of his response: it was she who didn't have a clue what had been going on in the country all these years, not him, and he wasn't going to let her dictate what he could say to Luz, or anyone else. If she wanted to believe everything her father told her, well fine, but he knew for a fact that the armed forces were committing atrocities and there was no way he could support her on this, as a matter of principle.

Mariana couldn't believe it: what was wrong with Eduardo? This was much worse than the other night; he was clearly defending the subversives. And the way he was speaking to her was unusual. Her first thought was that he had gone mad, but she never had a chance to fire off the cutting remark on the tip of her tongue, because after giving her that load of nonsense Eduardo said, 'I'm going to see Luz. If you come in, make sure you put on a different face and don't use that tone of voice.'

You can't help it. You watch her drawing and looking up and asking, 'Do you like it, Daddy?', and you feel you've got no right to that 'Daddy', or to the kiss she gives you when you tell her it's lovely.

He doesn't want to think about Dolores's sister-in-law right now, or who they might have stolen Luz from, or who really deserved that 'Daddy' and that kiss. He can't know for sure that's what happened, anyway. He's just deeply disturbed about what he discovered last night and his sense of guilt is out of all proportion. Maybe the mother really was someone who didn't want her baby, he tries to tell himself.

Weren't you being unfair just now, being so hard on Mariana? What are you blaming her for? It's not her fault about Luz, she doesn't even know about it.

Just as Eduardo is thinking of going to the bedroom to make amends,

Mariana stalks past on her way to the kitchen and doesn't even look at him. Eduardo goes up to her and gives her a kiss. 'Truce?'

Mariana stares at him stony-faced, doesn't answer and walks away. He decides he should talk to her when they've both calmed down a bit, try and make her understand. It would be best not to mention Alfonso.

But the calm conversation Eduardo was hoping they would have spins out of control. Mariana thinks the way he talked to her that afternoon was insulting. At first she thought he was just being ridiculous, but now she's sure someone's brainwashed him. He's just so gullible.

'It's you who's gullible.'

After that, you can't help yourself. It's as if the words just come pouring out and you can't control them. 'Things aren't the way you think they are, Mariana. People have been kidnapped and tortured who weren't involved in politics at all. Even the ones who were, do you really think it's right to kidnap and torture and kill them, without any sort of a trial?' You don't know what else you say; Mariana just stares at you, wide-eyed and stunned. The things that have been happening in this country are so very painful to you. All that stuff you shut your eyes to so obstinately.

Eduardo misinterprets Mariana's silence and consternation and goes on talking, trying to share his pain with his wife, hoping to open her eyes to a reality she hadn't seen either, until Mariana interrupts abruptly, 'Where on earth did you get all that rubbish from? Who told you all those lies? You've been with someone in Buenos Aires who's brainwashed you. You never said such dreadful things before. Did you see someone in Buenos Aires? Who was it? Tell me the truth.'

'Of course I never mentioned meeting Dolores.'

'Why not? Do you think Mariana would have been upset? Does she know you used to be in love with Dolores?' Javier asks.

'Yes, I told her years ago. But that's not why I didn't tell her. I realised that Mariana can't take anything in, she won't let herself know anything; I couldn't make her understand how I felt. If I'd told her everything Dolores told me, she would have just written it off completely. In her mind, Dolores and Pablo are on the other side. She'd be furious if she found out that I'd had gone and had dinner with someone she would call a subversive, one of the enemy, and that I'd felt shocked and sorry for what happened to her. She would see it as a betrayal, of the country and her and most of all of that swine of a father of hers.'

Javier had never liked Alfonso, but he was struck by the intense hatred his brother seemed to feel towards the man now. It wasn't like Eduardo to be vindictive. What had Dufau done to him? Javier said he had always suspected that something had happened he didn't know about.

'Do you know when I realised? When Luz was born, in the clinic – you were so furious.'

Eduardo didn't want to talk about that now. He had just wanted to tell him what Dolores had said, because he was very upset by it. Javier agreed it was horrific, although he wasn't as surprised as Eduardo, since he was aware of other things that had happened. What he didn't understand was why it was weighing on him so much. 'Is it because you think your father-in-law is directly connected with the repression? Because if that's the case, Eduardo, there's no need to go overboard. You only married his daughter. You can't take responsibility for everything he's done, although I can see it must be difficult to talk about it with Mariana, given how mad she is about her father.'

But there seemed to be something more, because otherwise Eduardo wouldn't be feeling so upset. There was something he wasn't letting on.

'When Eduardo began to wake up . . .'

'Wake up?'

'I mean, to realise, or suspect, that I could have been a detainee's daughter, he approached his brother Javier. Javier told me how upset Eduardo was, and that's why I keep telling you you're wrong, Carlos. He didn't tell Javier the whole story until a few days later, after the thing with Miriam happened.'

The day before her trip to Entre Ríos, Miriam went out to dinner with Frank and spent the night at his hotel in Buenos Aires. She was very frightened, but she said nothing to him. He seemed to sense that something was up and that she was in need of loving care, even though she was so independent, because the crazy Yankee, as Miriam liked to call him, showed her how much he loved her. That night she fell asleep in his arms and even enjoyed listening to him talk about his plans for them in the States: they would live together in a house with a garden, and she wouldn't have to work, there was no need, although of course he wasn't insisting on anything – if she wanted to go on with her lifestyle she could, he was just asking her to take a break for a while, to let herself be loved and made love to slowly for a bit, to be taken care of and spoiled. For that one night Miriam enjoyed listening to him; it was just what she needed.

'If things don't work out here, I'll come and stay with you. You can keep me safe and sound in your house until they forget about me.'

All of a sudden she felt a shiver run up her spine: what if they find out and put me in jail . . . or worse, what if they kill me and the colonel tells Animal and they . . . ? No, she refused to think of Liliana that night. She was frightened enough as it was.

Frank blinked and sat up in bed. What was she up to? What did she mean she was going to have to hide if 'things didn't work out'?

Poor Frank, he was worrying about her again, just like the first time he'd had to help her out.

'Don't worry, I just meant the thing I'm trying to set up in Entre Ríos with my partner. It looks like it should work out pretty well. But you never know who you'll end up with . . .' A slight but unmistakable tremor in her lip made it hard for her to continue.

'In Entre Ríos? You never mentioned that. Who lives in Entre Ríos? Dufau's daughter?' Miriam examined her nails, as if she wasn't listening. Frank took her by the chin and made her look at him. 'Miriam, are you crazy enough to be still thinking about that? You know what I'm talking about.' Miriam looked at him blankly, trying desperately not to give anything away. 'That crazy idea of stealing the kid back from the colonel.'

She was so afraid that she was tempted to tell him all about it and ask him to help her get Lili back, but she just snuggled up closer and asked him to talk to her about his house in the States and how he was going to love her and take care of her if she was crazy enough to go out there.

Laura wondered over dinner what Javier was so worried about; he seemed distant and serious, and barely answered when the children asked him something. She waited for them to go to bed before questioning him.

'Eduardo's not doing too well.'

What was wrong with him? Well, he was very shaken up because he'd just found out about the kidnappings and the torture. 'It's taken him long enough, thanks to that wife of his, that bloody colonel's daughter,' Laura was about to say, but restrained herself because Javier didn't like her to be rude about his brother's wife. 'She's a nice girl and Eduardo loves her.'

'Yes, she's nice, but she's pretty unbearable. She worships Daddy and her politics are horrendous.' Alberto Luccini had told her about the business with Carola at her birthday party, and she'd been glad not to see it because it would have spoilt everything.

Laura, who is very cautious, never brings up anything to do with the repression in front of Mariana. A few years earlier, when her friend Enrique disappeared and La Negra and her son had to hide in her house until they could escape, Laura had been a wreck. Mariana had asked her what was wrong, commenting that she looked terrible, but she would never have dreamed of telling her the truth. She fed her a white lie, that her best friend was going to live abroad and she didn't know if she'd ever see her again. And Mariana had asked, 'Why is she leaving?' How was she supposed to say to her sister-in-law, the daughter of a colonel, 'She's going because they've taken her husband, she barely escaped herself and if she doesn't leave the country, they'll kill her'?

Without thinking twice, Laura said, 'Because her husband has been offered a job in Europe.'

'Oh, I see, so she's going with him.' That was something Mariana could easily accept. She was always going on about how good she was to agree to live in Entre Ríos, so far from her family. If her friend's husband had been offered a contract abroad, then of course she had to go. 'A death contract, carried out by your father, among other people,' Laura would have liked to retort.

For the first time, Laura understood why it was hard for her to be with Mariana: because she could only ever make small talk with her. How are the twins, do they have boyfriends yet? Or sharing recipes, talking about their tennis game, anything to keep up the patter, and if Mariana started

173

talking about her father Laura would say the first thing that came into her head and leave. 'Yes, she's a nice person, and she can be fun. As long as she doesn't start on about the enemies of the Fatherland, she can even be quite sweet.' Laura was surprised that Eduardo had found out what was going on, because whenever she saw him he seemed to be completely immersed in Mariana's world. Then Javier told her that Eduardo had run into a woman he had once been very much in love with, called Dolores. Laura laughed and said, 'Ooh, I hope they have an affair, it'd do him good.' Javier smiled. 'Got sex on the brain, haven't you?' and he tapped Laura's head.

'And here too,' Laura replied.

They collapse on the bed and start giggling and fooling around, and for a while Javier's preoccupied expression disappears and his face reverts to normal, the face Laura likes so much. She thinks to herself that even though Eduardo and Mariana seem to love each other so much, they can't be as close as Javier and she are. But when Javier tells her about Dolores and her brother Pablo – a wonderful bloke, he remembered him clearly – Laura stops laughing and says she's glad that Eduardo was upset by the story, however he'd come to hear of it. She was really fond of her brother-in-law; she thought he was a good person, even if a bit weak, and it bothered her that he seemed so blind. She kept asking what it was that had affected him so much about what Dolores said, and how much Javier knew about his father-in-law. 'It might be that Eduardo knows more than he's saying; you know, Javier, it must have been hard for him to tell you. Eduardo's a very respectful sort of person and Dufau is his wife's father.'

'But Eduardo is incredibly critical of him to me. He really hates his guts, and he's not the type to be like that usually.'

Then Laura had an idea. 'What if Luz isn't their daughter? What if her parents were disappeared?'

'Are you mad? You saw Mariana pregnant, didn't you? Why on earth would they do something like that?'

'There was something strange going on when Luz was born,' Laura continues. 'Nobody was allowed to see her and Eduardo was incredibly upset, you told me so yourself.' There was no stopping her now. 'And later on too, don't you remember the way Amalia kept on insisting Luz looked like Eduardo? It was really weird – Luz doesn't look like any of them. Maybe their baby died and their father-in-law stole another one.'

Javier hit the roof. He told her she was crazy and that he refused to listen to her any more, it wasn't funny. His brother would never, ever get involved in something that despicable, did she understand? Luz was their daughter and if Laura said anything like that again he would be really angry. 'I'm sorry,' Laura said, 'I was being stupid, I get carried away sometimes. Don't be cross. I do love you, you know, and I'm fond of Eduardo too.'

Laura slept badly that night, worrying that she'd said something really awful without meaning to. Javier turned his back on her in bed and she could hardly pluck up courage to reach over and touch him. He didn't respond.

Miriam took a room in a hotel in the centre of Paraná. It was easy enough to get hold of Eduardo Iturbe's address in the phone book. The first few days, she spent hours in the little café on the corner of the block where he lived, gazing out the window. From there, she could see the Iturbes' house easily and she watched them coming and going. But from where she sat, she had no idea where they were going to. She would need a car. Luckily, she had learned to drive in Uruguay; the owner of the Carrasco Cabaret had told her you couldn't get by without a car in Punta del Este.

'*Although she spent years planning how to get the documents and money to live abroad, oddly enough she never planned how she was going to get me away. She thought it would just come to her once she got there, depending on the circumstances. She came up with a few mad ideas which she had to rule out because they were way too complicated and risky.*'

'*Like what?*'

'*Like going to work at the house as a maid. It would have been a huge risk because she could have been recognised almost immediately. It was crazy.*'

If they took her on as a cook or a maid or whatever at the Iturbes', she would be on the spot and would find an opportunity to kidnap Lili, she thought to herself in the café.

She asked the lady in the nearest shop how to go about getting work as a domestic.

'You need references. Have you got any?' the woman said, appraising her.

Her suspicious look made Miriam realise something she hadn't thought of. Did she seen like someone trying to get a job as a maid? Of course not; something gave away the fact that she was from another class. She laughed at herself: another way of life, she should have said, not another class. Would people guess her 'profession', despite the fact that she'd dressed down in jeans, a blazer and low heels, with just a touch of make-up, and pulled her hair back?

'She was scared that the old lady in the shop would get suspicious and so she made up a story.'

No, she didn't have any references because she hadn't worked as a maid before. Her husband was a bank clerk in Buenos Aires, and she used to be a receptionist, but she gave that up when their daughter was born. Her husband had left her for another woman, without a penny to her name, and she felt ashamed in front of her family and friends . . . She wanted to forget the past altogether, so she had come to Entre Ríos, where there'd be nothing to remind her of how badly she'd been hurt.

The woman's expression had changed completely and her tone of voice altered when she asked, 'And is your little girl with you or did you leave her in Buenos Aires?' She'd lost her, said Miriam, looking down as if she were about to cry, which she was.

'Miriam felt as if she'd lost a daughter: Liliana's daughter.'

The woman came out from behind the counter. Poor lamb, she would help her out, she'd give her a reference herself. 'So he left you after you lost your baby? What a terrible thing to do.'

The woman might be able to get her a job, but why did it have to be at the Iturbes'? Miriam said that she wasn't sure, she'd have to think about it, maybe she'd look for a job as a receptionist, although of course she'd have to find a place to live.

Back in the café she decided she'd hire a car to follow them around. She already knew that Lili left the house at eight thirty, in the Iturbes' car, and that she usually got back at five, with a girl in maid's uniform.

'So what did she do in the end?'

'She hired a car and followed them. That's how she found out where the school and the English teacher's house were. Then she hung around at the school gate for days.'

During the first week Miriam spent watching the children leave school, the maid who came to pick Lili up was late twice. Miriam would wait for her to be late again and go up to Lili. That was her plan.

'She was insane! What could she possibly have said to make you go with her? What would have happened if the maid had shown up as the two of you were leaving?'

The first time Miriam approached the child, she said, 'Do you remember me? We made a sandcastle together in Punta del Este.'

'Oh, yes,' Lili answered, although she didn't seem to recognise her. 'What's your name?'

'Miriam.'

She was going to suggest they go and get an ice-cream when she saw the maid coming round the corner. 'Bye-bye, pet.' And she walked casually off in the other direction. She was sure she hadn't aroused any suspicions, although maybe she'd been careless, telling Lili her name.

It isn't the first time that Dolores has found the image of Eduardo cropping up in her mind; since they ran into each other again, it keeps reappearing at all sorts of odd moments. But it seems inappropriate to be thinking of him now, on her way back from a meeting with the Abuelas. Maybe she is allowing herself this little indulgence, this connection to life, because the meeting has left her feeling hopeful. It would be nice to make love with him now they are both grown up, to be able to feel the way they used to for a while. It seems odd to Dolores to be thinking this way, because she doesn't recall being attracted to him the other day. Or maybe she was, but only in her memories of another time, long ago. When he rang to ask her to dinner, the very same evening they met, that small happiness leapt up again, the way it used to all those years ago, whenever she opened his letters.

But then again, she hasn't come to Buenos Aires to get involved. If that's what she wants, she should admit it. She touches her knee and there's Eduardo again, his smile, his hands. If she really wants something like this to happen, a quick fling, if she needs it for some mysterious reason she doesn't want to analyse, the best thing would be to find someone she doesn't know, someone she can't talk to about all that's happened. Because even if Eduardo was hoping for a one-night stand with an old flame, if that's why he'd called so soon, she had quenched any desire he might have had by letting all that horror come between them. All the burning acid she had vomited up on him had done for him. Eduardo had been in really bad shape when they said goodbye.

The conversation with Javier, and his own feelings every time he looks at Luz nowadays, make it difficult for Eduardo to put up with Mariana's sulkiness and resentment about their argument.

He pretends he's working in his study to avoid another row with her. Lately they've been fighting over the slightest little thing. It's obvious that it's not what you say to Mariana that causes the rows, so much as all you cannot say.

Eduardo doesn't know what's happening to him. He needs to talk it over with someone. But who? Dolores? No, you don't even have the guts to bring it up with Javier; how would you dare tell Dolores?

But you have to know, you have to know more, you desperately need to.

What if you spoke to Alfonso and asked him straight out what you don't dare even think to yourself? Is Luz the daughter of prisoners who disappeared?

Eduardo panics at the mere thought of Alfonso's reaction if he told him what he suspects. Alfonso would threaten and insult him, and he'd make it even harder for him to discover the truth. It would be better to find out some other way before you confront him. You ought to have more to go on, then you'd feel more confident. What if you called Dolores? You could listen to her, you wouldn't have to tell her your story.

Maybe it would do her good to go out for a while, take her mind off things, Dolores thinks. And then, out of the blue, she pictures Eduardo.

She stretches out on the bed in her room, the same room she had seven years ago. Her mother has left it exactly as it was, as if she'd just gone away for a short holiday and not into exile, with no idea of when or even if she would be able to return. She was exhausted from her long day, first the meeting with the Abuelas and then talking to her parents.

Susana, her mother, had got very excited when Dolores had mentioned her meeting with the Abuelas that afternoon, especially when she passed on what they'd told her about the blood tests. She kept on asking for more and more details about the American organisation that was helping the Abuelas. The blood tests had been developed to the point where they could be used to identify both missing children and their biological parents. The system was there in principle, but it would take time, of course. Family members could now give a blood sample to a special databank to verify relationships.

'The compatibility studies were carried out in the Immunology Department at Durand Hospital, which had all the right equipment. It's one of life's little ironies, because it was the ex-mayor, Cacciatore, who was in cahoots with the Junta, who had the centre built as a sort of gift to his own doctor, who was very interested in kidney transplants. And then it was used to prove the blood relationships and the identity of those kids.'

There's a feverish glitter in her mother's eyes. 'How wonderful.' That way they'd be able to prove that Pablo and Mirta's child belonged to them because it had their blood and not that of the people who stole her. Would they get custody then? Of course, or else Mirta's parents, they'd have to agree which. Just putting it into words seemed to bring it within the bounds of possibility. Susana started planning which room the child would have if it came to stay with them: 'Pablo's, or yours, what do you think, Dolores?'

Her mother was getting too carried away. Maybe it hadn't been such a good idea to share her enthusiasm after talking to the Abuelas. Her father was obviously worried too. He said he would co-operate and give a blood sample, if the project went ahead, but he wasn't expecting miracles.

'Don't get your mother's hopes up for nothing, Dolores. How do we know what happened? Maybe the baby was never even born. Maybe those scum killed Mirta while she was still pregnant.'

179

How much time had gone by since him telling her that such a thing could never happen, that the Argentinian Army would never touch a pregnant woman? Centuries of waiting in the halls of horror for his former friends, being inwardly poisoned by impotence and despair. Dolores went over and stroked his head.

'I know, Dad. We've just got to do what we can, carry on fighting. I didn't say we'd find the baby, just that we should keep on looking.'

Julio shook his head. No, she wasn't to build up false hopes. Dolores doesn't live there, he's the one who's with Susana every day.

'Dolores is right, he who seeks shall find, Julio. We mustn't lose hope. Now that we're going to get a democratic government, things will change. They'll definitely go after them. I feel hopeful about finding our grandchild.'

Dolores offered to arrange a meeting with Mirta's mother. It would be easier for Dolores to talk to her than her parents. They were so different that it would be tricky for them to come to any kind of an understanding. No, Susana said, she wanted to invite Mirta's mother over for tea, it was better to fight together; maybe she could even convince her to join the Abuelas.

If only you could see her now, Pablo, trying to fit all the pieces together, she won't let anything stand in the way of her hope. She keeps on cheering Dad up, making plans to get your child back, clumsy, foolish plans, but they've both grown and changed so very, very much.

'Dolores, it's Eduardo on the phone.'

If only he'd come back to Buenos Aires, Dolores finds herself thinking, surprised, as she goes to pick up the receiver. But Eduardo doesn't suggest it, he just asks how things are going, and whether he can do anything for her. He says he'd like to say thank you for the talk they had, she has no idea how important it's been for him. What does that tremor in his voice mean? She doesn't know, but it hits a nerve somewhere deep down in her body. Spontaneously, she says, 'Why don't you come and see me? I'm staying a few days more.'

Even before he replies, she's wishing she hadn't said anything. Why complicate things? Does she have room for this?

'Yes, I'll be coming any day now. I'll let you know.'

Why did he hang up so quickly, and why did he ring at that time of night?

She doesn't have time to work out why Eduardo is behaving like this, because Susana knocks on her bedroom door, wearing an expression that Dolores hasn't seen for so long she'd forgotten it. 'You looked so happy when you went to pick up the phone. Who's the young man?' A friend from before or someone she's met recently? Does she like him?

Poor Mum, thinks Dolores, I've set her off again. Today's been too much for her. But I suppose that's what being a mother is all about: getting excited because your daughter's fallen in love. Take a deep breath.

'No, Mum, it was Eduardo, remember him? The boy from Entre Ríos, the one you hated. I bumped into him the other day and we chatted for a while.'

'But he's married, isn't he?' Her brother had told her he'd got married . . . Now there is fear in her eyes. The little breeze has been stifled, the enemy's lying in wait. 'He married an officer's daughter. Pepe told me. You be careful, Dolores, don't tell him anything.'

The happy atmosphere has been destroyed. If only she could have told her that yes, she'd met a young man, as her mother puts it, a young man she likes. If only they could talk about love and all those other things that no one remembers these days. The only thing left is fear; it's taken over.

'Don't get worked up about it, Mum, I don't expect I'll see him again.'

That might explain Eduardo's reaction. Maybe she opened his eyes. Can he have been that blind? The phone rings.

'It's Eduardo again.' Susana gives her a strange look. 'It's late. Why is he calling at this time of night?'

He'd be there the next day. Yes, he wanted to talk to her. At five o'clock, OK? At the Dandy, yes.

'Are you going to see him again? Do be careful, Dolores.'

Why is she so frightened? Who is Eduardo's father-in-law, what is she hiding? Susana says she'll ask her brother; all she knows is that he met the Dufaus at Eduardo's wedding and he told the Iturbes that Dolores and Pablo had gone to live in Europe because he was afraid to tell them the truth.

'I'll ring him and ask.'

'No, it doesn't matter, Mum.'

The next day, before Dolores meets Eduardo, Susana tells her that the father-in-law's name is Alfonso Dufau. 'He's the head of some regiment or other and he was heavily involved in the repression. Don't go and meet him. What if he's trying to find something out about you?'

No, she's got a feeling it's something else.

NINE

ALTHOUGH SHE'D BEEN uncertain after talking to her mother, after half an hour with Eduardo, Dolores is convinced she wasn't wrong about him. Eduardo isn't lying; he has no hidden agenda. Apparently what she told him the night they met upset him deeply and he wants to know more: whether the human rights organisations have lists of the disappeared; who handles cases of missing children and how they go about it; and how long the Abuelas have been working. His questions come tumbling out one after another. How did they find out that Pablo and his wife had been killed? Were they told officially, or did it come from someone who got out of the detention centre? How many secret detention centres were there and who ran them? Eduardo has been asking himself all these things and more since talking to Dolores, and he needs to know, even if it's painful for her.

'I'm asking you as a personal favour. I can't stay in the dark, or blind, or whatever you want to call it, any longer.'

'No, Eduardo, the other day we talked about me and my life; now it's your turn. I want to know everything. Tell me about your wife and your daughter and your life in Entre Ríos.'

There's nothing much to tell, he says lamely, and reels off some trivialities. He doesn't mention his father-in-law.

'Mariana who? What's your wife's surname?'

Yes, this time there's no doubt about it. Dolores has hit the mark.

'Dufau.' The word comes out almost inaudible, muffled by shame.

The silence between them lengthens, laden with unspoken words. Finally, Dolores decides it's better not to beat around the bush.

'Isn't he one of them? An army officer?'

He nods.

Then he rebounds from silence to nervous loquaciousness. 'That's why, Dolores. Or maybe it's because of other things I couldn't or wouldn't see, out there in my protective bubble with my wife and daughter and the farm and our friends. I never realised what was going on. As for my father-in-law, well, as you can imagine, he doesn't go around talking about what he does. Mariana idolises him. She thinks he's a hero – or a saint.'

Dolores can tell how much Eduardo hates Dufau. His resentment goes deeper than mere irritation at the way his wife admires him.

'The other day I would have liked to tell Mariana what I was feeling, but I couldn't say I'd been with you or what you'd told me, given how she feels about her father. I tried, but it's impossible.'

So that's it, thinks Dolores, that's why he's come looking for me. Eduardo is silent, inscrutable. Eventually he says something that smells musty from being bottled up so long.

'Although it's not her fault. It's all my fault.'

What is? Dolores doesn't know, and doesn't ask. Guilt looms heavily over Eduardo, stifling him and gnawing at his words.

'Actually, there is something I would like to tell you, something that happened years ago, but I can't. It's something . . . It's a family thing; it's private.'

She wonders what's tormenting him, but she thinks it wiser not to ask. He'll tell her in good time, no doubt. Eduardo is suffering, badly, and she is overwhelmed with a tenderness towards him that is stronger than her wish to know what's causing his pain. She feels like holding him close and comforting him, even letting him cry on her shoulder, if he feels like it. But he can't just start crying right there in the Dandy.

'Let's go somewhere quieter,' she suggests.

'Where?' Eduardo asks, as he signals for the bill.

Dolores shrugs her shoulders and smiles. 'We'll think of somewhere.'

You walk right in through the open door of her smile, which is still there, unscathed, and you start driving down Libertador, knowing it's better not to talk. You turn off and head north. Any lingering doubts you felt disappear when Dolores rests her hand on your neck and you feel its assenting warmth. After you've parked opposite the lake at the woods in Palermo, you decide you ought to say something to justify your behaviour, even though she's asked no questions.

'I'm really in trouble, Dolores, but I can't tell you why.'

Her only response is to place a warm hand on your cheek. You dive into her open arms, which are probably only meant to comfort you. You kiss her ear and nuzzle the side of her neck. That simple movement and the slight tremor that runs through her are enough to make that old, sharp desire for her come rushing back with the breathtaking speed of happiness. Your hand reaches greedily under her clothes for her skin and all you can feel now is this extravagant desire which has instantly healed all the wounds life has dealt you. But all of a sudden she pulls back, straightens her clothes and gazes out of the car window. You ask yourself what you were thinking of, how you let yourself get so carried away by her well-meaning attempt at comfort.

Dolores says softly to you, 'Eduardo,' and then stops, still looking away. You try and come up with some kind of apology, but you can't form a sentence. 'Dolores, I . . .' She looks at you and giggles, probably because you're so uncomfortable.

'Eduardo, let's go somewhere more private. We don't want my mother walking in on us again.'

And she bursts out laughing. Turn the key in the ignition, quick, don't lose this moment. You are aware of your hand on the gear-stick by her knee and she lays her hand on yours in a way that says it doesn't matter that neither of you meant this to happen. There's no need to explain, her body and yours are calling one another. This is life, right here, right now.

Frank had rung the day before to ask if he could come and see her, saying his vacation was almost over and he had to go back to the States in a few days. Miriam said that she was still very busy, but she would let him know if she could take some time off so they could get together.

How many days had Miriam been hanging around at the school gates? Ten? Twelve? That afternoon she told herself she was in luck. Her heart was pounding the way it had seven years earlier, when she left Corporal Pilón behind in bed and locked the front door. Luz had been waiting outside the gate for five minutes and the maid still hadn't shown up. Luz's schoolfriend had just left. It was now or never.

'Hello, sweetheart, how are you?'

'Very well, thank you. How are you?'

'Would you like an ice-cream?'

'She spent hours wondering whether to offer me an ice-cream or some sweets, or whether to tell me she had something to show me in the car – anything just to get me to walk the few yards so she could whisk me away before they arrived. She had parked on the other side of the plaza. Her plan was pretty basic.'

She was amazed how easy it was. Luz looked towards the corner and said, 'Will you bring it to me or shall we cross over? Carmen is always late.'

'Why don't you come with me? We'll be back in a second.'

'No, I don't remember. I do remember what she said afterwards, when Mum showed up. But the fact that I don't remember . . .'

'You call her Mum?'

'I mean Mariana. I've called her Mum all my life.' Luz looked away. 'It's a word you only come to appreciate with time. I bet you don't remember when you first realised that your mother was your mother? For me the word Mum always meant Mariana. She was the person I'd called Mum ever since I started connecting that sound with a person.'

Luz fell silent, as if it was hard to go on.

'I won't interrupt again, I'm sorry. I just can't help being angry and resentful. But this is no time for that. Please, go on. So it was Mariana who came to fetch you, not the maid?'

It was ten past five when Mariana left her friend's house. Why on earth had she told Carmen not to pick Luz up? She had called home but there was no answer and Eduardo was in Buenos Aires. She walked the three blocks to the school as fast as she could. She couldn't see Luz at the gate and for some reason – it must have been God's doing, she told her mother later – she looked across and there was Luz, with her back turned, holding a woman's hand, crossing the plaza. She assumed it must be some other mother who was taking Luz home to call from there. She didn't know why, but she felt uneasy. She started walking after them quickly, almost running. 'Thank goodness I moved fast, because if I hadn't she would have got away, Mummy, I swear. Daddy and Eduardo can say what they like; I know that woman was trying to kidnap Luz.'

When she saw the little girl walk round the car, she knew for certain that it was Luz. Was she going to get in? Who was that woman?

'Luz!' she screamed, although she was still quite some way off.

'Mummy!' Luz called back, smiling.

Then the woman looked up at Mariana and waved. She said something to Luz and got quickly into the car.

'What did she say to you?'

'That's not your mummy.'

'Who is that woman, where were you going?' Mariana is so over-wrought that she grabs Luz by the arm and shakes her. The lady had asked her if she wanted an ice-cream. 'You mustn't just go off with someone like that, are you mad? What did she say to you? Why did she rush off like that?'

'At the time I didn't tell Mum what Miriam said; I guess I was scared to because she was so worked up. But when she eventually found out she went on about it so much I couldn't possibly have forgotten it. She always held it against me, as if it was something I'd said myself. For years, whenever we had a fight, she'd accuse me of "going off at the drop of a hat with some crazy woman who said I wasn't your mother". By going on about it she made the incident stick in my mind. When I was a teenager, I sometimes thought I couldn't possibly be Mariana's daughter, and then the memory would surface again.'

'So you thought you weren't her daughter?'

'Yes and no. It was the sort of fantasy all teenagers have when they're at loggerheads with their parents. I'd remember that woman at the school gates and wonder what she meant. I've come to believe that when you live with something you don't know, you can somehow sense it as a lurking presence, although of course I worked that out much later, after I started looking. For a long time I felt constantly on edge . . . a kind of nebulous angst that wasn't caused by anything real, it just came and went, as if it were part of my personality.'

Luz told her that the woman had said she would buy her an ice-cream, and that when Mariana arrived, she just drove away. Yes, she'd seen her before, she thought, at the school gates.

Mariana waited impatiently for Eduardo to call from Buenos Aires. She had already told Amalia and Alfonso what had happened. Alfonso said there was no reason anyone would want to kidnap Luz. When she spoke to Eduardo, he also told her not to worry, it would turn out to be nothing, but his voice betrayed his anxiety. 'What do you mean, someone tried to kidnap her?' Mariana explained over the phone that Luz's version of events was contradictory. 'First she said she knew her, then that she didn't. She also said the woman didn't say anything to her, but I saw her say something before she drove off, although Luz insists she didn't.' Eduardo told her not to keep asking Luz about it, just to read her a story and talk about something else; she must be frightened.

'No, not at all, she was quite calm, waltzing off with a total stranger. She's a bright little thing but she certainly didn't act it. You've got to confront her about it, Eduardo.'

'Don't worry, I'll talk to her tomorrow.'

'You've got to come home right away.'

'I can't come today, I'm sorry; I've got meetings scheduled tomorrow. I'll head back as soon as I'm done.'

Eduardo and Dolores made love with such intensity that everything around them seemed to disappear. It was as if they had been waiting years for that moment. Afterwards, they made plans for the evening ahead: they would have dinner and go for a walk around the port, and then they'd fall asleep in each other's arms.

Eduardo said there was a phone call he absolutely had to make. Dolores decided to go and have a shower, so he could talk in private.

When Dolores comes out of the bathroom, she realises that the atmosphere has been shattered. The expression on Eduardo's face is totally different, although he attempts a wan smile. Is he feeling guilty about his wife because of what's just happened? Dolores thinks it would be better just to make some excuse and leave, so as not to prolong a situation that might cause problems for both of them. All she'd been trying to do was comfort him because he was in pain for some obscure reason. The rest had just happened somehow, but it had been so intense that she hadn't wanted to stop. But now she'd rather not stay here; she doesn't think it's a good idea. They would be better off meeting up again another time, because she'd completely forgotten that she was supposed to be having dinner with her parents and some friends. Eduardo barely nods, as if he can hardly speak. He seems completely different from the person who caressed her so urgently a short while ago, reinventing her body again and again, planning a night of non-stop pleasure.

'Eduardo, I have no idea what's wrong, but you know I'll always be here for you,' she says, before leaving.

'I know.' Eduardo hugs her tenderly. 'Thank you, Dolores.'

She closes the door, thinking perhaps she should have said something that would have helped him open up and talk to her. She feels something clench in her stomach. It's fear. Yes, it's stupid, but she's afraid for him.

'Dolores told me that even before she knew what was going on, she could tell he was in danger. Maybe because she . . . I think Dolores was in love with Eduardo, although she never said so and of course I didn't ask. They must have been extremely close. She never said a single thing about her relationship with him, but the way she talked about him, her silences, the things she was clearly not saying, and her expression whenever she talked about him to me, even years later, pretty much convinced me that he was someone very special for her. Talking to her a few months ago was very important for me, because it made me see Eduardo in a new light, something I hadn't been able to do until then.'

What on earth was up? Had she been wrong to allow herself to be swept off her feet by passion instead of letting him talk? No, it had happened because it was meant to be. But maybe she should have . . . That's enough, thinks Dolores as she gets into a taxi. She's offered Eduardo her support and he'll work out what to do next. What if he doesn't call, though? There's that sense of oppression and danger again. She mustn't let herself give in to anxiety after the marvellous evening they've spent together. She sinks back in the seat, feeling the heat of lovemaking throughout her body, and feels grateful to be alive. She remembers that afternoon in Entre Ríos, when her mother was so furious, and she'd shouted to him, 'Thank you, it was lovely.' Deep down, even after everything she's been through, she still loves life.

Miriam kept wondering whether Dufau's daughter would have suspected anything. She had waved at her and thought she even remembered giving her a smile before she got into the car and drove off. Would that have been enough? What had Lili said? Would she have understood the phrase. 'That's not your mummy'? Lili had stood looking at her for a fraction of a second, as if she had heard a noise, and after that Miriam saw nothing more; she was driving away as fast as she could.

'She wasn't planning to say it. She said it just came out. Maybe she was afraid it would be the last time she saw me, so her promise to Liliana . . .'

'Was she going to tell you about Liliana, or was she just planning to run away with you?'

'Of course she was going to tell me, I've already said so several times. She never forgot what Liliana said to her in the plaza while Miriam tried to shield her with her own body.' Luz's voice broke. 'Carlos, Miriam really did want to save me. Why else would she have done what she did and been crazy enough to say that to me, and then put herself at risk again? Because she did. She waited a few days and then she went back to the school gates. She hid behind a tree and waited for a chance to go up to me again. Even though she was scared, she was also hoping that nobody would have found out she'd offered to buy me an ice-cream.'

Mariana can't stop talking about the woman who tried to kidnap Luz. 'Why else would she have tried to get her into the car? What was she doing there? She's not one of the other mothers.'

'How do you know that?'

'I asked Luz all sorts of questions, but she just says that she offered to buy her an ice-cream. She won't talk about whether she would have got into the car, even though I've been asking her all day. It's as if you don't care about any of this.' Mariana is furious with Eduardo: her father would definitely have handled things differently.

Eduardo has to make a superhuman effort not to say what he's

190

thinking about Alfonso. He doesn't want to start another row with her because who knows where it might end.

He asks her to let him talk to Luz by himself. Mariana's obviously so tense and angry that Luz must be frightened she'll get told off no matter what she says.

But Eduardo's already talked to Luz, he asked her the same thing himself, didn't he? Yes, but Mariana was always there.

In fact, he has been worrying about the incident ever since Mariana first told him what had happened.

'He was worried despite the fact that I didn't tell him Miriam's name or what she'd said to me until a few days later.'

'How did he react when you told him?' Carlos asked. 'He must have completely panicked.'

'I don't remember. I was seven. I only know about this from Javier and his wife Laura.'

The news worried you because you have a guilty conscience. If you stole Luz, then someone else could steal her from you.

Afterwards he told himself that Mariana's tone of voice had made it seem worse than it was, and that of course it would turn out to have a logical explanation. She could have been the mother of one of Luz's schoolfriends. Maybe there was another little girl in the car that Mariana hadn't noticed. How on earth is Luz going to say anything if Mariana gets so worked up every time she discusses it? He will try and get some more out of her. 'Please, Mariana, just leave me alone with Luz.'

Eduardo goes to the room where Luz is playing with her Lego and sits down on the floor. He takes his time working round to the subject of the lady and the car, mentioning it casually between one piece of Lego and another, as if it weren't important. Luz just repeats what she's already said many times.

'Weren't you afraid to go off with someone you didn't know at all?'

'But I did know her, I'd seen her before.' She fits a piece of Lego on top of another. 'Does this go here, Daddy?'

Eduardo connects the piece. 'At the school gates?'

You let out your breath. So it must have been another mother and not what you imagined.

'I don't know, I've never seen her daughter.'

'But does she go to the same school as you?'

'I don't know. I don't know her. Give me that blue one, Daddy.' So how come she's seen her there? Why? 'I don't know.' Luz can only remember that the lady told her a couple of times that she was very pretty. She seemed a nice lady, the sort that likes being with little girls, not like her friend's mummy who can't stand kids.

'Did she say anything else to you?'

'No.' She carries on staring at the Lego. 'Oh, yes, she said she'd helped me make a sandcastle in Punta del Este.'

You don't like the sound of that one bit. Could it be someone who's been following you all for some time, someone from the Abuelas maybe? There's a spider creeping up your spine. An iron fist grips your throat.

Could someone have reported them? You try and gain a breathing space. 'So is she a friend of the Venturas?' Luz doesn't know, she doesn't remember much, yes, she thinks that the lady helped her make a sandcastle once. Her name is . . .

'What? What's her name?' You try and mask the anxiety behind your question, so that Luz won't notice how afraid you are.

But Luz doesn't remember and Eduardo realises that, if he carries on pressuring her like Mariana, she will clam up. He reassures her that she was right to talk to the lady and it was OK to say yes to the ice-cream if she was nice, but not to get into the car with her. 'Unless of course you knew her . . .'

It was better not to press the point. Luz has started breaking up the Lego. She's on edge; he can tell from her face that she's not happy. It would be better just to build this thing or read her a story. Leave it for another day.

Mariana is very anxious. 'So, did she say anything more?'

'She said she'd seen her before at the school gates.'

'And she wouldn't say a word to me, apart from on the first day, but after that she claimed she couldn't remember.'

Mariana is just rushing off to confront Luz when Eduardo grabs her by the arm. 'How are you going to get her to tell you anything if you yell at her all the time? Luz is frightened of you.'

'Don't be ridiculous. What else did she say?'

You mustn't say anything to Mariana about Punta del Este. The most important thing is to get her to calm down. 'That the woman told her she was pretty and that she seemed like a nice lady. You shouldn't get so angry with her. What child would turn down an ice-cream, especially from someone they like?'

Mariana says she can't stand the fact that he thinks everything is just fine. 'Is this how you're planning to bring Luz up? To go off with anyone she wants, so long as they're nice?'

No, but that's all he could find out for now. 'Don't worry, if she'd seen her before, maybe she's somebody's mother.'

'Whose? So she told you that too, when I must have asked her a hundred times and she wouldn't say a word.' She says she's got the feeling she doesn't even know this child. 'Look, if this goes on any longer, I'm going to Buenos Aires to talk to Daddy so he'll send someone to find out who that woman is.'

The last thing she really wants is to know that, thinks Eduardo.

You realise now you're convinced that Luz's parents disappeared. You've known ever since Dolores talked to you. Maybe that's why she is so crucial in your life; that would explain your attraction to her, the way loving her seems so essential. She opened your eyes and now you're afraid that this person looking for Luz might be one of those women trying to find their grandchildren. You should ask Dolores more.

Mariana starts yelling and taunting him: her father would have found out everything by now. But how can she be stupid enough to think that her father is God – doesn't she know what he does? 'He kills and tortures people and steals their children.'

'What are you saying? You're out of your mind!' Mariana's features are distorted with rage.

'Well, maybe not him personally but he gives the orders.'

Eduardo doesn't have a clue about fighting for the Fatherland, like Alfonso.

You can't contain yourself. 'So fighting for the Fatherland means decreeing whether people live or die and giving the detainees' children away and stealing their identity?'

Luckily Mariana interrupts him with a resounding slap that shuts him up. Thank goodness, because otherwise God knows where this might have led – to telling her about Luz? Why did you have to shout at Mariana like that? She has no idea; you've deceived her about it all these years. You go up in an effort to give her a hug and say you're sorry, but she's crying on the bed and pushes you away.

Eduardo decides not to go on trying to hug her or talk to her. He is distraught and terrified of losing control again.

He leaves the room and goes into the kitchen. Luz is in there with Carmen; she's had her bath already and is in her nightdress, about to have supper.

'Would you like me to sit here and eat with you?'

'Aren't you going to have supper with Mummy later on?'

'Yes, but I can eat twice. You know how much I like food.'

She doesn't tell him anything then; it's not until later on, when he's tucking her in and getting ready to read her a story, that she says, 'Miriam. I think that lady who said she'd buy me an ice-cream was called Miriam.'

Your heart skips a beat. Wasn't the mother's name Miriam? Where did you put the photocopy of the birth certificate? In your desk at the office. You haven't looked at it for years. Only that one time, when Mariana was still in the clinic.

'And did this Miriam talk to you at all? Mummy said that she saw her say something to you. Was it about Punta del Este?'

His question obviously makes her uncomfortable because she turns over in bed and avoids his eyes. The lady just asked if she wanted an ice-cream, she's already told him loads of times, and said she was pretty. 'Will you tell me a story, Daddy?'

You'd like to tell her the story of a man who's desperate because he's lied to everyone – including his wife and his daughter, or rather the daughter of heaven knows who. But of course you can't do that. You have a sudden memory of a nanny you once had when you were little who said that you weren't your parents' son, but a chimney sweep's. For some reason, you didn't tell your parents until much later, when they sacked her for something or other, you can't remember what any more. Without knowing why, you tell Luz that once upon a time there was a little boy who was a bit naughty, and that the nasty woman who looked after him . . .

'Who, his mummy?'

'No, a nurse. One day she pointed to a man in the street who was all dirty and dressed in black and said that if the little boy carried on being so naughty she would send him away with the chimney sweep, because that was who his real father was. She said he didn't belong to his mummy and daddy.'

What the hell are you saying this for, you must be nuts, what about the bunnies and the squirrels and the fairy grottoes and the Martian that Luz loves hearing about?

'That's what the ice-cream lady said to me,' Luz says, opening her eyes a crack and squeezing his hand hard. 'That Mummy isn't my mummy.' She shuts her eyes. 'Go on with the story.'

So that's why she said nothing earlier, because she was afraid. He has to take that fear away from Luz. His childhood fear had been groundless, but hers . . . He quickly makes up an ending that will reassure her.

'In the end the little boy was so worried that one day he went up to the chimney sweep and asked him. And the man laughed and said that he had four sons and he wasn't one of them.'

'So the bad lady made it all up?'

Now would be a good time to say that the lady who offered her the ice-cream was a nasty person and that she was only pretending, but he can't, or won't. Better stick to the story.

'Yes, and the little boy and the chimney sweep became friends and they told his mummy and daddy and they sent the bad lady . . .'

'Is she a bad lady, then, Daddy? Was she trying to kidnap me, like Mummy said?'

'Maybe you misunderstood her, and she didn't really say that.'

'What?'

'That Mummy isn't . . .' You can't even finish the sentence. 'You must have misunderstood her. Maybe she said, "Is that your mummy?" because she didn't know her.'

Luz smiles and closes her eyes and Eduardo carries on, in a low voice, trying to lull her to sleep: they sent the bad lady in the story away and the little boy wasn't afraid any more and everyone was pleased and they all lived happily ever after.

He tells Mariana that Luz hasn't said anything new, and that night he tries to fondle her, but she shrugs him off, showing that she's still very angry. He is relieved when she turns out the bedside light, as if to say that nothing else will happen that night: no more accusations, or love, or hate.

He can't stop thinking about what Luz has said to him, and about the document he has, the photocopy of the birth certificate.

The next day, he unearths it in the third drawer of the desk. Miriam López.

The mother! You are alarmed, and at the same time so delighted you want to jump for joy. So they didn't steal her from anyone. And on a crazy impulse you dial Dolores's number. It's got nothing to do with her but you ring anyway, because now you can. You were feeling bad the other day, but it turns out there was no reason to – she wasn't stolen from her mother, just abandoned. The mother's alive, it's her name on the birth certificate. Of course, he's not going to tell Dolores any of that. But he could. The other day was fantastic, he can still feel it in his body. Making love is even better now than when they were young, because now Dolores brings him something more, not only incredible pleasure, but also access to pain and the truth. She's opened his eyes and made him strong. She makes him feel like a man, not some poor fool.

Dolores is completely taken back by this rambling speech of Eduardo's – she can tell something has happened, but she can't work out what. It makes her happy, too; somewhere deep down in her body there's a little prickling sensation that makes her feel dizzy.

'Why don't you come to Buenos Aires so we can see each other again? I'm leaving next week.'

'All right then. Let's meet tomorrow, at six. At the Dandy.'

Tomorrow she'll ask him what's going on, Dolores promises herself. There's this sense of physical joy, but also that something's up, although she's not sure what. She's got to get Eduardo to tell her what it is. It will do him good.

And what about her? What is she feeling? She doesn't know. She can't put it into words. In any case, in a few days' time she'll be going back to France. She's set things in motion here in Buenos Aires, and this thing with Eduardo won't go anywhere – although maybe . . . What was it he said – that she'd opened his eyes? The fact is, she's happy to see him again. The pull between them feels powerful and inevitable and she might as well just give in to it.

Eduardo tells Mariana he has to go to Buenos Aires the next day, but that if she's worried, to go and pick Luz up herself, and be sure to be there on time. Starting on Wednesday, he'll collect her from school every day so Mariana can relax. In the meantime he'll try to find out as much as he can about this woman.

'*He had already decided to look for Miriam, although it wasn't until a few days later, after he'd talked to Javier, that he worked out how to go about it.*'

'It's high time you did something. I rang Daddy today and asked him if he could take a day or two off to help me, because you seem to be incapable of finding out who that woman is and what she wants.'

If Mariana doesn't stop goading you by holding her father up as an example, you're going to blurt it out, you won't be able to stop yourself. You almost did the other day.

'Mariana, please don't sing your father's praises in front of me again. I'm serious, I can't stand him.'

Can this harpy whose face is full of rage and loathing possibly be your Mariana? There's so little left of her in this woman who's screaming at you. She has become ugly, because hatred has hardened her features. 'You're just jealous because Daddy knows how to take care of me and you don't – I've never felt safe with you.'

Eduardo forces himself not to answer back. He can't, he mustn't. He goes to his study and starts planning how to confront Miriam, if she shows up again. It's important not to scare her off, so they can talk.

She's simply a mother who abandoned her baby and has had a change of heart. The idea is a relief, however problematic it's going to be for you, because it's not what you were thinking, that other, horrific thing, the thing you're so afraid of. The thing that happened to Dolores's sister-in-law.

Although she had told herself over and over again that it was crazy to feel like this, Dolores couldn't help waking up with a sudden rush of joy that kept resurfacing throughout the day.

Of course Eduardo wasn't the only reason. Her mother had been elated at lunchtime. Who would ever have guessed, Pablo, that Mum would be this brave – that she'd have the guts to stand up to Dad's scepticism and join the Abuelas de Plaza de Mayo? You always used to say she's never done anything but obey all her life. But she never stops talking about those wonderful women who've been fighting since '77 and everything they've managed to do these last few years, despite being threatened and persecuted. Susana had gone on and on about the conference on the 'signs of grandparentage' in New York. Now the blood relationship could actually be proved. And Pablo, even though you thought that Mum's bourgeois prejudices made her look down on your girlfriend because her family was working class, these days she's trying to convince Mirta's mother that a lot of pregnant women survived being tortured and delivered their babies full-term, so the two of them should work in tandem, because together with other women they'll be able to make a lot more headway. She's sure they'll find their grandchild, she says she knows it in her heart. Mirta's mother has lost all hope; she knows her two children are dead, it's too painful for her.

'If Pablo could see you, he'd be so proud of you, Mum, and I am too. Don't worry about Dad. He may not be as strong as you now, but he'll understand one day.'

'You talk to your father, Dolores – try to make him see he should stop telling me to stay away from the Abuelas. I don't want any more arguments. Your poor father. It's not that he's weak, it's just that he's burned out, after everything that's happened, all those bishops and generals turning out to be bastards and turning their backs on him and deceiving him.'

She'll tell Eduardo about it, Dolores thinks, but not tonight. She says to her mother that she's got to meet some friends. But Susana is not deceived.

'You be careful, Dolores – I told you that Eduardo's father-in-law is . . .'

'Don't worry, Mum. I know what I'm doing.'

TEN

FRANK WOULD BE coming to see her on Saturday. Miriam promised she'd ring him beforehand, in case she changed her mind and left for Buenos Aires. That crazy idea kept popping into her head. What if she got Frank to agree and the three of them ran away together? No, it was out of the question; if she managed to get Lili, she'd have to make up some excuse not to see him. She'd call him from the airport so there wouldn't be the slightest chance of meeting up, even for a minute. She couldn't risk his life again. Somehow she had to rescue Lili quickly. She couldn't stand the waiting any longer.

Miriam was sitting in the car when she saw Lili coming out of school. She recognised her smile and the way she skipped along. Maybe this would be her lucky break and they'd be late coming to fetch her. She had parked opposite, so that if they were, she could easily get out of the car. I don't know how I'm going to do this, Liliana, but I promise you I'll get her out of here and tell her the truth. I'll take her a long way away, somewhere they'll never find us.

She was just getting out of the car, with her heart pounding, when Lili ran over to the grey Peugeot. Miriam got back in her car fast. She was sure no one had seen her.

They are at the Dandy, but so far they have barely said a word to one another. Dolores asks what the painful realisation is that Eduardo mentioned over the phone.

'Does it have anything to do with what I told you the other night?'

Eduardo doesn't answer. How can he tell her what's wrong? If he says anything at all, it'll set off an avalanche that he won't be able to stop and she'll end up hating him. Dolores doesn't persist, she just lays her

201

hand on top of Eduardo's. 'So much pain,' is all she says. And then, 'Shall we go?'

When you get to the hotel you make love to her slowly and passionately, as if by touching and licking and drinking in that solid, firm body, you could connect with life itself, with the truth. It is strange to find that your hands already know their way around the maze of pleasure, as if your bodies had spent years exploring one another, searching for new sensations. The two of you have the kind of intense connection that only comes with time; you progress seamlessly from tenderness to passion. You kiss the nape of her neck. She snuggles into the hollow of your body as if it had been designed for her to rest in.

Dolores is talking to him now as if they had somehow magically spent a lifetime together. She talks as if she were his wife and best friend about everything she's gone through during the last few days: about her struggle and the achievements of the Abuelas de Plaza de Mayo, about how much her mother has changed, and about hope.

Eduardo asks questions. 'How do they go about looking for the children? How do they know who has them?' Dolores tells him about the reports that people file with the Abuelas (sometimes they are anonymous and sometimes the informants give their names) about women who were never pregnant who suddenly showed up with babies. The Abuelas go to the places where they've been told the thieves live, in the hope of seeing their grandchildren.

Could Miriam be one of those women? It might be just a coincidence that her name is the same as the one on the birth certificate. Unlikely, though, because Mariana was pregnant, there was no reason to suspect her. Why would someone be following them? Maybe a nurse from the clinic who knew your son was stillborn had said something; maybe even the one who filled out the false birth certificate. As Dolores goes on telling you how the Abuelas work, you're nauseated by all the fraud. You're even deceiving her; that question you just asked made it sound as if you were interested in her life, when really it's about your own.

'I'm such a shit,' you say.

She asks why you say that, please tell her, she knows there's something eating away at you, she sensed you were in pain in the Dandy. But how can you possibly tell her? How's she going to feel having just made love to someone who's no better than a baby snatcher, like the ones she's trying to find?

Eduardo says nothing. He shuts his eyes. Dolores strokes him, trying to comfort and soothe him. You don't deserve her, and you don't deserve Luz's smile either, or the way she loves you. You tell Dolores so: 'I'm not worth loving.'

'But why, why do you say that?' Dolores leans over and kisses him and says of course he's worth it, she knows, she can tell. Eduardo hugs her. You wish you could let go of the sob you are choking back. It's been years since you cried, ever since that day in the clinic when your brother Javier put his arm around your shoulder.

If only you could tell her. But what will she think of you? Although it might turn out that Miriam's alive and that she's the mother . . . But you can't know that for certain. So you apologise, you're really sorry, but it's something you can't tell her about. It's not just her you should be apologising to, but your wife and daughter too.

'Why, why?' Dolores pleads for an answer, not just with words but with her whole body, the body he has just made love to, that he loves so much.

'Mariana had a Caesarean. Her parents were there right from the start.' Bit by bit, he tells her what happened, stammering and muddling things up.

Dolores recoils and sits bolt upright on the edge of the bed. You're frightened by the grim look on her face and the glitter in her eyes, which are very wide. He repeats what he has just said about Miriam, about her having the same name as on the birth certificate. 'So if it's her who went to the school, it's not one of those cases.' But it's as if Dolores isn't interested in what he's said about Miriam. She's wearing Eduardo's shirt, which she grabbed at some point and buttoned up, tensely, as he talked on and on.

'It seems it took Eduardo quite a while to tell Dolores. And when he did, she felt absolutely dreadful at first. You have to bear in mind what had happened to her and why she had gone to Buenos Aires. She was on the other side of the story Eduardo had told her.'

She hasn't interrupted once; just looks at you. She's very tense. Let her hate you then: you deserve it.

'No, I don't hate you. I'm just very . . .'

She doesn't dare come out with it, but you can imagine what she's thinking. Her eyes dart frantically around the room before coming back to rest on Eduardo. There is a determination in them that shakes him.

'You can't leave things like this, Eduardo; you've got to find out. You have to ask your father-in-law to tell you the truth about where that baby came from.' Her voice has risen almost to a shout, and she makes an obvious attempt to control herself. 'Get hold of that woman when she goes to the school gates, or wherever she is. Make her tell you if she's the mother or not. And tell your wife. How could you lie to her all these years?'

Dolores keeps on at you relentlessly, asking you all the questions you've asked yourself so many times: why did you let them, why didn't you ask more questions about where she'd come from, why all those years of silence, of turning a blind eye? You don't care that you're stammering, that you don't have an answer, that you can't justify yourself. You want to be seen, for once, as the naked, soiled thing you are, and let Dolores judge you.

'*Afterwards Dolores came to understand what Eduardo had been through. When we met, she told me over and over again that he tried to find out the truth; not at first, but when I was seven, and that she pressured him to do so. "I was very hard on him, but I think that was what he needed from me," she said, and you could tell she felt very deeply about it. That, among other things, made me think that Dolores really loved Eduardo, otherwise she would have reacted differently when he told her about me. She could have reported him, for example.*'

'*She didn't report it? Why on earth not?*'

'*She just didn't. It was her mother, Susana Collado, who brought it up when . . . But let me go on with the story.*'

At the end of their long conversation, Dolores was merciless but incredibly gentle with him at the same time. 'If you're right and Miriam isn't one of the disappeared, well, so much the better, but then why didn't she just give the baby up for adoption? And what are you going to do if you find out that Luz's parents were disappeared? You won't be able to live with it. Do you realise what all this means for Luz? She's been deprived of her identity, her own and her parents' history, and treated as if she were just a thing. You said so yourself when you were talking about your father-in-law; I remember the way you put it made an impression on me. "What does he think, oh, her doll's broken, I'll get her another one so she won't cry?" She was just another object of plunder as far as they were concerned.'

'That's enough, stop.' You bury your head under the pillow and give way to the sobs you've been choking back for years. Dolores lies down next to you and strokes your head.

She's crying too: for Eduardo, for herself, for Pablo and Mirta, and for their child who is God knows where, with God knows who. You'd managed to convince yourself that Luz wasn't stolen at birth, but now that doubt returns, like a skulking rat, gnawing at your throat and body. What are you going to do if you find out Luz was born to one of the disappeared? You don't know.

'First of all, I've got to find out the truth, and I promise I will, Dolores.'

'What you did was very wrong, Edurado, terribly wrong, but you've changed now and you can't let matters carry the way they were.'

Eduardo knows she's right. He can't go on denying things any longer. Dolores says gently that she can look into it; he should show her the copy of the birth certificate, she knows where they took the women. 'Although I'm surprised there was a birth certificate.'

'No, please don't say anything to anybody. I'll find out myself.'

It's late when Eduardo takes her home. Dolores is quiet. Eduardo can't think of anything to say either. He gives her a kiss.

'Ring me as soon as you find out anything,' she says. 'I can help you.'

Dolores turns to go inside and then swings round. She runs back to Eduardo and throws her arms around him. They embrace one another.

She knows, and yet she's hugging you. You feel comforted for a moment, forgiven. And strong.

'Eduardo, I love you. I trust you.'

'I'll get to the bottom of this, whatever it takes.'

Eduardo waits at the corner, rather than at the school gate. He doesn't have a plan. He doesn't know what Miriam looks like, and there are lots of mothers waiting. All of a sudden he loses sight of Luz and breaks into a run. What if the woman walks off with her in that mêlée of mothers and children? What if Luz disappears?

If Luz disappears. Disappears. The word bludgeons your brain as you run, elbowing your way through the crowd. Luz is one of the disappeared too, just like her parents. Who would she have been, what would she be called, if your father-in-law and his cronies hadn't condemned her by stealing her from her mother and erasing her identity? But don't be so easy on yourself. Who was Alfonso Dufau's accomplice, who disappeared her by giving her his own surname? And whose idea was it to call her Luz – 'light' – as if to block out the shadows?

'It was Eduardo's idea to call me Luz. Whenever Mariana complained about my black moods, she always used to say, "You know, it's funny you're called Luz." Apparently they'd been thinking of several names, and Luz was one of them, but Mariana was ill when I was registered, so in the end it was Eduardo's decision. Mum always said she didn't like my name because it "didn't suit me at all".'

Eduardo hugs Luz effusively, as if he hadn't seen her for years. She is overjoyed to see him. Daddy's actually come to pick her up from school!

When he drops Luz off at home, Eduardo tells Mariana he has to go straight back to the office. They will talk that night, but he hasn't seen the woman again.

'That particular day Miriam didn't go to the school gate.'

After Frank rang, Miriam flopped down on the bed and let herself daydream about taking refuge in his arms and going to live in that house of his with the garden and letting him spoil her and take care of her. She pictured herself as a little girl being rocked by Frank. For who had ever rocked her? Miriam had no memory of her mother, who had walked out when she was only two. Presumably the reason her mother had left her to be brought up by her aunt was because she didn't love her. She'd probably never held her. Years of weariness suddenly descended upon Miriam. What if she lost everything she had dreamed of, for nothing? If she didn't manage to get Lili she'd be lucky to end up in jail, or worse, in Animal's hands, and no one would make love to her slowly or take care of her ever again.

She sat up on the bed. She couldn't afford to carry on feeling sorry for herself; it was paralysing her. She couldn't be weak, there was no time for that. It wasn't too late. She still had a chance to get Lili away. She would tell her how she'd come to know her mother; she wouldn't try and fool Lili the way she had Liliana. She'd tell her the whole truth.

'And she did. She didn't try to lie or justify herself to me.'

They would find somewhere to live, and who knows, maybe when there was a democratic government she could look into it and find out who Lili's family was. Perhaps she could track down a grandmother or an uncle. She didn't think she'd find the father, Liliana's comrade; they must have killed him too.

Luz smiled, although there was a nasty edge to it. 'But you weren't dead, you were alive,' she said venomously. 'And you weren't exactly looking for me like Miriam was, despite what you think of her.'

This time Carlos didn't try to make excuses about what he'd thought or what he'd been told. He submitted to the aggression in her strained smile and stony face. Luz obviously needed to do this and he would just have to let her.

Miriam was just thinking that she was out of luck because the grey Peugeot had come again instead of the maid with the lace apron. She felt more secure about the maid because she knew she'd never seen her, whereas both Mariana and Lili had. Except that Lili didn't know she was Lili, she thought she was Luz, and that she was their daughter. Maybe Lili would point her out and say, 'That's the lady who tried to get me to go in her car,' or, 'That's the lady who said that you weren't my mummy.' And then they'd arrest her, and then . . .

Images of what Liliana had told her came crowding in. She switched on the television – anything to take her mind off those horrific scenes – and tried not to think.

The time to pick the children up from school came and went.

Luz fell silent for a while. Her face looked drawn. She had reached a dark passage in Eduardo and Mariana's life.

'That night Mariana found out that I wasn't her daughter. She never knew or suspected anything until then.'

'It must have been very hard for her,' Carlos said. 'After all, she was lied to as well. It's not as if she was aware.'

There was something sharp in her answer, the cutting blade of an old grievance. 'Yes, they deceived her, but she didn't care. She never protested, perhaps because she would have done the same thing herself.'

For the first time, Carlos realised the degree of conflict Luz felt about the woman she called both Mariana and Mum, whom she must have loved and perhaps still did love, even though she was so critical of her. After all, Mariana had been a mother to her for many years.

Luz is already in bed when they start arguing. Why hasn't Eduardo managed to find anything out? She bets he never even tried. Yes he did; he'd even waited for Luz without her seeing, like a spy. 'But no one went up to her, I promise you.'

Mariana shakes her head: if she had known Eduardo would turn out to be so pathetic and weak, she'd never have married him. She wanted a man like her father, someone strong, with a mind of his own. A real man.

'You mean a bastard, a sadist, a murderer, a swindler, a liar and a fraud?'

This time you grab her hand in mid-air before she slaps you, and you keep on gripping it as you tell her that her father lied even to her. While she was unconscious, anaesthetised, he got hold of a baby girl for her, God knows where or who from, and passed her off as her own.

Only when Mariana collapses in an armchair and stares at him, dumbfounded, does he stop. How could you be so cruel as to tell her like this? You say you're sorry and pour out the whole story: how desperate you were when Dr Murray told you your son had died, Alfonso's threat that something might happen to her, the way you just gave in, how you hated lying to her. But even though you shouldn't have told her like this, in the middle of a fight, thank God, thank God you have. You feel an incredible relief, as if you'd just managed to root out some deep-seated pain.

'I couldn't go on loving you and sleeping with you and making love to you with that lie between us, casting a shadow over everything.'

'So it was Daddy who found her. And he never said anything to me!'

Mariana mused. The expression on her face wasn't at all what Eduardo had been expecting; in fact, it was almost the opposite.

At last she'll get angry with her father, Eduardo thinks; at last he'll fall off his damn pedestal. Mariana's idolised him all this time. But he himself has also fallen, and now he's showing his true colours – weak, desperate, and contrite.

But Mariana surprises him. 'Daddy's always tried to stop me from being hurt.'

God, this is unbelievable. He'd like to ask if she realises how serious this is, given what was going on and what her father was involved with at the time. But Luz's mother may still be alive; why should he torture Mariana by saying anything, since he doesn't really know himself whether she is or not?

Eduardo asks her if she will ever be able to forgive him for having deceived her all these years. Mariana doesn't answer. She gets up and goes to Luz's bedroom and stares at her as if she were seeing her for the first time.

What must she be feeling, knowing that Luz is not her daughter? It hurts you even to think of what she must be going through, poor thing. You follow her into the bedroom and try to hug her. You're about to beg her forgiveness from the bottom of your heart when she turns round and surprises you again. 'At least she's fair-skinned and she's got green eyes.'

What does she mean by that? You'd rather not know. So Mariana thinks that . . . Isn't she in despair? Isn't she furious with her father, or him? She just says that Luz is 'fair-skinned'.

'I mean, she's not some Indian; at least Daddy got me a baby who could be our daughter.'

Eduardo is overcome with rage. He goes to his study. He feels like ringing Dolores, but doesn't. He calls Javier instead and says he needs to talk.

At three thirty in the morning, Laura switched on her bedside lamp and resigned herself to the fact that she wasn't going to get any sleep that night. In a few hours' time she'd have to wake the kids and get them

209

dressed. She would be a zombie over breakfast. It was clear Javier couldn't sleep; he kept on tossing and turning. The tension in the room was palpable. He'd stayed up talking to Eduardo until the small hours; she had gone to bed after coffee. Something was obviously wrong with her brother-in-law; he practically never had coffee after dinner.

'You weren't dreaming after all, you were right. It's uncanny the way you worked it out, Laura. Luz isn't their daughter. That twisted old psychopath brainwashed him; he knows every trick in the book. And Eduardo is useless at standing up for himself.'

Javier was overflowing with rage, indignation and pain. Eduardo had told him the whole story, piece by piece. He could see just how easy it would have been to get dragged into it. Eduardo had been a wreck at the time; Mariana was very ill, and the colonel just kept pressuring him.

Laura couldn't believe it. She demanded the whole story. Why had Eduardo told him now? What had happened? Was it because of Dolores . . . ?

'No, it wasn't just Dolores, although she was obviously important because it was thanks to her that Eduardo started to wonder whether Luz could be a detainee's child. He just kept saying the same thing over and over again: "I had no idea, how could I possibly have imagined they could do anything so ghastly?" He felt terribly guilty and miserable at the beginning, but gradually, I don't know, time passed, and he loves Luz so much that at some level he forgot about it. But ever since he realised what had been going on, presumably through Dolores, he's been tormenting himself. This thing with Dolores means a lot to him. I think (although he hasn't actually said so) that there's something really intense between them, something that gives him another perspective on things. It's made him grow up, made a man of him; he's finally become capable of facing up to the subject, painful as it is. He and Mariana have been fighting a lot for a while, and last night, in the middle of an almighty row, he told her the truth.'

Laura asked how Mariana had reacted. 'Poor thing, after all, they've lied to her all along.' When Javier mentioned her comment about Luz being 'fair-skinned', Laura couldn't help herself. 'So she's just as much a shit as her father.'

'*Laura helped me a lot, because Javier wouldn't say anything the first couple of times I went to see him. It was Laura who convinced him he should tell me the truth, or at least as much as he knew . . .*'

She shouldn't say that; even Eduardo regretted having walked out when Mariana made the comment about Luz being fair-skinned. It doesn't necessarily mean that she knows they're stealing babies from the prisoners. It could perfectly well be just a casual comment. Laura said she didn't think so.

When Javier explained about the birth certificate, she replied that it was either a bizarre coincidence or else that it didn't mean anything. It could be just a made-up name, because they usually registered them as NN, that's what they did at the secret centres in Olmos prison and the Campo de Mayo garrison and who knows how many other places. 'Yes, but this wasn't quite the same; they made a lot of mistakes, they didn't cover their tracks. In any case, there's no point talking about it because this isn't one of those cases. The mother is alive and walking around Paraná.'

'What?' Laura didn't understand a thing; it was one shock after another that night.

'You remember what Mariana said the other day about someone trying to kidnap Luz as she came out of school? We thought she was just imagining things and making a song and dance about the fact that some woman had gone up and talked to Luz. Well, what we didn't know is that the woman told her that Mariana isn't her mother. Luz told Eduardo, and she also said that they'd built a sandcastle together in Punta del Este and that the woman's name is Miriam. That's the name on the birth certificate, you know.'

Javier had told Eduardo he should go back to the school and try to find her, even though the consequences could be painful. He offered to go with him, but Eduardo had said he could manage alone. 'If it turns out this woman gave her child up and has changed her mind, then he'll have to deal with it.'

Contrary to her expectations, Laura was not half-asleep as she dressed the children, but wide awake instead. She didn't feel at all sorry for Mariana: the way she had reacted showed what a vile person she was. A chip off the old block, after all.

'Javier was always convinced that Miriam was my mother, although the only thing he knew about her was that she was a prostitute, because Eduardo had told him. It was hard for him to tell me that. If it hadn't been for Laura . . . She was such an intuitive person that she was suspicious. If there's a sewer underneath you, you can smell it, even if you're walking on silk carpets, and Laura's very sensitive. Although all the information pointed to the fact that I'd simply been given up for adoption, Laura told me there was always a trace of doubt in her mind about where I was from.'

Miriam had swapped her hire car for one of a different make and colour so that nobody would connect her with the failed attempt a few days before. Each day, she circled the block where the school was, or parked opposite and watched from inside the car. Frank had said he would be there in two days' time, because they wouldn't have another weekend together. He had to go back to the States the following week. He'd got to work, he wasn't a sheikh. Miriam had laughed.

'I'll get you a room in another hotel.'

'Why? Aren't we going to sleep together?'

'It's just that I'm supposed to be here on business, and I'd rather do it this way. Besides, there's nothing stopping me going to sleep in your room; we can be Mr and Mrs Harrison again.'

Remembering the game she'd played that day in the hotel in Buenos Aires made her soften.

'I'll ring you tomorrow. I might be going to Buenos Aires, if I finish my work here in Entre Ríos.'

And then we'll go to Sweden, or further away, so they'll never find us, she thought. She reserved two tickets on a flight from Buenos Aires to Stockholm on Saturday, continuing on to Singapore on Sunday, using the names on the false passports made by the man in Punta del Este. It gave her a thrill to think about it. She was the superstitious type, and she thought that being able to picture the trip so clearly was a lucky sign, fate saying that it was all possible and that she would carry it off that very day – Lili was going to bring her luck.

At the beginning it would be difficult for Lili, Miriam thought. Maybe she would miss the people she thought were her parents. You don't just throw love away and forget about it, it takes time. Miriam planned to tell Lili that she'd been stolen as a baby, snatched from her mother's arms, but she also knew it would take a while for her to stop loving Mariana and Eduardo. She thought that if she lavished love on her every day, Lili would gradually start loving her back. Maybe she'd have some memory of those first few days they'd spent together. That would help.

'Of course I didn't have a conscious memory, but when I first saw Miriam, as a grown-up, I felt as if I were somehow close to her, as if she were familiar. It's possible that has something to do with those first few days, who knows. That would explain why Mum was always accusing me of going off with a stranger, a crazy woman. Perhaps I had that same sense of being close to her when I was seven, too, and that's why I wasn't afraid of her.'

Five minutes must have gone by, or maybe seven. Miriam got out of the car and walked resolutely towards the school. Luz started when she saw her. Miriam didn't like that at all: Lili's been warned – she's afraid. But it's now or never, she thought, and she went up to her.

'Hello, love.'

'Hello,' Luz murmured, looking away. Then she suddenly looked back as if in a great hurry to say something, so that no one would see her talking to the lady. 'Don't ask if you can buy me an ice-cream because I'm not allowed to.'

'No, I won't. I'll just keep you company until they come to pick you up.'

They went and stood under the tree. Miriam didn't know what to say. Lili wouldn't go with her the way she had the other day if she'd been told not to. At any moment someone would be there to fetch the child, and they'd come and arrest her and take her off to jail and kill her. Then she pictured Liliana asking her to save Lili and an enormous strength welled up inside her.

'Let's walk to the corner and back, to stretch our legs while we're waiting,' she suggested.

Luz started walking. Miriam put out her hand and when Lili took it, she knew that, whatever she might have been told, Lili wasn't afraid of her. Maybe she's just been told not to accept ice-cream from strangers, she thought, trying to bolster her nerves so that her legs wouldn't give way. Just fifty or sixty yards to go and she would have rescued Lili from her kidnappers.

'She had the crazy idea that when she got to the corner she would pick me up and run away. It was her last chance.'

Eduardo sits in the car, waiting. Five minutes go by, and then ten. It seems like eternity. He sees Miriam go up to Luz and start talking to her, and then the two of them stand under the tree without speaking. He gets out of the car when they start walking and follows them from a short distance. A few yards before the corner, he catches up with them and grabs Miriam's arm.

'And who, might I ask, are you?'

Luz lets go of Miriam's hand.

'Who am I?'

'Miriam,' says Luz. 'Her name is Miriam.'

You could ask her Miriam what, but you'd rather not know the answer, because if it's not López, the name on the birth certificate . . . Eduardo says the first thing that comes into his mind.

'What are you doing?'

'Miriam realised that Eduardo was as scared as she was; she could tell from his face. So she brazened it out; she was gutsy.'

'What do I do for a living, you mean, my job?' and she giggles hysterically. 'I'm a working girl.' She leans over and whispers in Eduardo's ear, 'A tart.'

'A tart?' stammers Eduardo, so taken aback that he loosens his hold on her arm.

'Yes, and what are you, a thief?'

They both look down at Luz, who is standing between them, looking stricken. Miriam is the first to react.

'Don't you worry, pet, we're just joking. We used to be friends when we were little and we played cops and robbers. Didn't we?'

'When Eduardo nodded, Miriam lost all her fear. She knew there was something unusual about this man; although he was so tense, he apparently

had no intention of being violent towards her. Miriam had too much experience with violence not to recognise it when she saw it.'

'Yes, we were friends,' he says. And in a low voice he adds, 'I'd like to talk to you. This obviously isn't a good time, though,' and he gestures discreetly at Luz.

Now it's Miriam's turn to be taken aback.

'Talk to me? About what?'

'About the past. I'm very interested. I want to find out about some things that happened, it could be good for . . . for everyone concerned. Will you give me your address, or a phone number where I can reach you?'

'She was on the verge of giving it to him, because the way Eduardo had reacted after she'd called him a thief, the fact that he practically begged her to meet him, made her trust him. But she said it would be better if he gave her his phone number instead, so she could call him. Eduardo gave her his card.'

'Please ring me, I need to know.' He looked down at Luz, trying to disguise things. 'Tell me what you've been up to all these years.'

'Miriam played along and kissed Eduardo goodbye as if he were an old friend. "We'll talk one of these days," she said.'

Even though he feels uncomfortable doing it, Eduardo asks Luz not to tell Mariana that she went for a walk with that lady. 'You know how upset Mummy gets.' And she wasn't to say that they'd talked either. He tells Luz that he will speak to Miriam. 'You remember I asked her to call?' And then they'd find out all about it, why she goes to see you at school, why . . .

'Why she says Mummy isn't my mummy?' interrupts Luz.

He says he's sure Luz misunderstood her the other day. He'll ask Miriam about it, and then they'll go and tell Mariana, so she can stop worrying.

They have an ice-cream before going home.

Eduardo is afraid that Mariana will pester him with questions like the last time he went to pick Luz up from school, and that he won't be able to fake it. Luz will see him lying. Now that Mariana knows Luz isn't her daughter, she'll be much more anxious about all this. But actually

Mariana is rather quiet and Eduardo notices her watching Luz as she's doing her homework. He feels griefstricken for her once again.

Dolores's mother is exultant. She says that they seem to be on to something at last, thanks to a tip-off from a while back about an army officer, a first lieutenant, who had suddenly appeared with a kid although no one had ever seen his wife pregnant. It turned out he had been stationed at El Vesubio, one of the secret centres. It might even have been him who tortured the mother. Mercedes's daughter was in El Vesubio the last time she was seen alive, and the time frame is right. That afternoon, Mercedes and Susana had gone to the district where the thief and his wife live with this child who could be Mercedes's grandson. They ran into the boy in the supermarket with the woman who's pretending to be his mother. 'Mercedes says he's got her daughter's eyes and her daughter's boyfriend's ears.' Of course they couldn't do anything more at that point, but afterwards they met up in Mercedes's house and cried their eyes out. She had wept for Pablo – so hard it did her good. 'Crying with someone else who's going through the same thing isn't the same as crying on your own, which gets you nowhere. It makes you realise that there's a time for grief and a time for action.'

Dolores is moved. She hadn't thought it possible that in just a few days her mother could have become so thoroughly involved with the Abuelas.

It's true that there are few clues about Mirta, because no one knows where she was taken after the Atlético centre. They are still missing some of the facts, but they'll put the pieces together eventually. She's very hopeful and excited.

'I'm going to call Mirta's mother right away, I'll talk her into it in the end. She's a bit like your father, the grief has been too much for her. It's understandable, she's lost two of her children.' Susana stops and hugs Dolores. 'Dolores, darling, thank goodness you're alive.'

How many of these disappeared children are out there that no one even knows exist? How many relatives have run out of strength to keep looking for them, like Mirta's mother? Dolores's mind makes the inevitable connection. Is someone looking for Eduardo's daughter? Supposing she was born in captivity, because even though he thinks she wasn't, it's quite possible. She knows that the little girl was born on 15 November 1976, but who could tell if it really was that day? She can't ask the Abuelas whether any of them are looking for a baby born around the middle of November. She's promised Eduardo she won't do anything. Maybe Luz really was put up for adoption. The business of the birth certificate would seem to point to that. But given who his father-in-law is . . .

If Eduardo doesn't manage to get in touch with that woman, what will he do? I won't let you down, he'd said, and she believes him. But it's so difficult.

It's odd the way she feels about Eduardo, the fact that she feels so sorry for him, after what he did. Why doesn't he call her? She would so much like to see him again and give him some encouragement. All of a sudden, she has a wild idea. She's still got a few days. She'll phone and offer to help him look. They can go to all the hotels one by one and find out if there is a Miriam López registered anywhere. She could go to the school gate herself, she would arouse less suspicion.

'Eduardo, I've got an idea. I'm thinking of coming to Paraná for a couple of days. I'm not going to make things complicated for you, don't worry – I just want to help. Maybe between the two of us we can find that woman.'

'I've already found her.' His voice sounds sombre. 'I've talked to her.'

'And is she the mother?'

'I couldn't ask her. Luz was there. But she said she'd ring me.'

Dolores is exasperated. 'What do you mean, she'll ring you? What did she say?'

'Something strange: that she was a prostitute. She pretended we were childhood friends, for Luz's sake. But I think I made it clear that I need to talk to her, that there are things I need to know.'

Dolores insists on coming to Entre Ríos to help him with the search. But he says he'd prefer her to stay put; he has the impression that Miriam will ring him.

'And besides, Dolores, I'd love to see you, but I've got a lot of things to sort out at the moment. I've told her.'

Dolores doesn't understand. Eduardo says he's told his wife. 'As you can imagine, I need to be here for her right now. I owe it to her.'

There's a hole in her stomach. It's great he's told her. But even though Dolores herself had pushed him to do it, she's anxious about how his wife will have reacted. She could stop him finding anything else out or reporting the case, if it turns out Luz's parents were disappeared.

Although she knows it is utterly selfish, there's a lump in her throat because she probably won't see him again, and it hurts. She can't deny that she wants to see him, not just to find out where the child came from, but also to touch and be touched by him, to make love – but she's not going to say that to him, she's not that crazy. She loves Eduardo enough not to complicate his life at this difficult juncture.

He promises that he'll ring her if he has any news; he'll tell her over the phone. He doesn't think he'll be coming to Buenos Aires. Dolores feels emptiness open up in her body. He's not coming and he'd prefer it if she didn't come and see him either.

'Of course,' she says. He's got a lot of important things to sort out. But the idea of never seeing him again makes her so wretched that she can't understand how on earth she let this happen. What a fool she is to have fallen in love with Eduardo at this point, with everything that's going on. He's got such a sinister history, that touches her own in so many ways, but as a mirror image – they're on opposite sides in this business. She can't deny the way she feels about him, but how can she have these feelings for someone who . . . But they do have one thing in common, she thinks, trying to justify herself: both of them are searching for the truth. So it's not true that Eduardo is on the other side. Even if he was once, he isn't any more, that much is clear, otherwise he wouldn't be doing what he's doing. And maybe, just maybe, this is his way of loving her. That ought to be enough.

They'll be in touch. 'Give me a ring, even if it's only to say hello, even if you don't have any news, if you just feel like talking.' She hears her voice falter and knows that she may be giving too much away about what happened between them, or maybe just to her. Eduardo promises he will call her.

When she hangs up the phone she bursts into tears. 'No, Mum, it's nothing, honestly. I'm crying about everything, and nothing at all.'

ELEVEN

E DUARDO DOESN'T KNOW how things got so hellish. He started this conversation with the best of intentions. He doesn't want to lie to Mariana any more; he wants to comfort her and ask her forgiveness, and yet here they are yelling at each other worse than ever. It doesn't really matter who started it.

The thing that set you off was when Mariana said that now she understands some things about Luz that made no sense to her before, and that used to drive her mad. 'Like why she always used to scream so much when she was little, and the nightmares she has, and the way she talks to people as if everyone were equal. Sometimes it's as if she likes being with Carmen more than with us. There are other things too, I don't know, like the way she lifts her nightie up when she dances and the way she moves, when she's only seven years old! And the way she's so forward, always smiling at people.' Mariana had always wondered where she got that behaviour from – it was so unlike a daughter of hers. 'I assume it's genetic.'

At that moment, you felt as if you were talking to an enemy, someone who couldn't possibly be your wife.

It happened again when she started talking about Luz being fair-skinned and green-eyed. 'She's a pretty girl, there's no denying that, but there are other things she could have inherited too, aren't there? That's what worries me. Goodness knows what the mother was like, a slut and a whore, probably. She must have been, to give her daughter up like that.'

By that point Eduardo's good intentions had gone out the window. 'What if she didn't give her away, what if the baby was just taken from her? Don't you know what happened to the women in those centres?'

'Look, don't start that rubbish again. I don't know who put that idea

219

into your head. If Daddy did find her for me, he would have made quite sure that she was healthy.'

Their voices clash and lacerate one another: isn't she interested in knowing who the mother was, since she's so obsessed with genetics? Why doesn't she ask her father? No, she's got no intention of upsetting him. Just because Eduardo was beastly enough to tell her doesn't mean she has to go and upset Daddy. 'He asked you never to tell me. So why did you? All you've done now is made me worry how Luz is going to turn out.'

Eduardo no longer knows what he's saying: if she won't ask him, then he will. He doesn't care how much it takes, he's going to find out if the mother is still living and who she is.

'That was the beginning of the end.'

'Why, did they split up as a result?'

'They didn't split up . . .'

Luz hesitated. She gazed off into space and there was a long silence that Carlos didn't dare interrupt. Then she looked up and stared at Carlos in a way he was beginning to recognise after hours of talking to her. Her voice, however, was calm and she spoke very clearly, as if she wanted to make sure that her words would be properly understood.

'When I told you that nobody ever looked for me, I meant like one of the Abuelas de Plaza de Mayo, or one of my parents, or an aunt or uncle; someone who was a blood relation. But some people went to a lot of trouble to find out where I was from. Eduardo for one . . .'

'Are you out of your mind? Do you want them to take Luz away from us?'

No, of course you don't. How would you live without Luz? But you just can't go on being burdened by doubt all your life. The thing is, you're frightened that . . .

'It's our duty to find out the truth, Mariana.'

'There are hundreds of couples with adopted children. I bet they're not all worrying about who the parents were.'

'Don't you realise that we didn't adopt her, your father just produced her out of a hat? Who knows where he got her? If it had been a legal adoption . . .'

'Don't you see that if that's what Daddy did, then it must have been the best thing to do at the time? And probably the quickest. I'm sure adoption is an awfully slow process, and then I would have found out.'

No, don't answer back, don't give in to your anger. It doesn't matter how late it is, Javier will understand. Eduardo leaves the room.

'Eduardo,' Mariana calls, and he turns round, a faint hope stirring. 'Where are you going?'

'I don't know, maybe I'll go and see Javier.'

'What? Are you going to tell him? Don't go, stay here with me. I've got something to say to you and I want to make myself very clear. I absolutely forbid you to try and find anything out about Luz. I trust Daddy. And it could cause problems for us.' Her voice became vaguely menacing. 'After all, it was you who registered her. I don't think it's a good idea for you to go digging things up.'

'The thing that bothers Eduardo most is that Mariana's not angry he did it, just that he told her about it. She doesn't resent her father in the least. Eduardo wanted to come over and see me last night, but he was afraid she would hit the roof, so he stayed there. I've got a feeling this isn't going to blow over. Eduardo said to me today, "I feel sorry for her, but there are moments when I really hate her." It's the first time he's ever said that and it gave me a shock. He said that if Mariana won't admit it, if she won't change, he's going to leave her.'

'He's right. Look, I know you don't like me saying this, but she's an absolute bitch. And maybe she knows a lot more than she's letting on. Didn't you say that she was worried the mother might have been a murderer or a whore? That's the sort of language *they* use, the pigs.'

'What a coincidence,' Javier mused. 'Miriam told Eduardo she was a "working girl".' Laura couldn't work out why, and neither could he. 'It must have been a very odd conversation.'

'I think she must have given the baby up for adoption and then changed her mind. Maybe she is a tart; why not? She said it defiantly, something like: "I'm a tart, and what are you, a thief?"'

Laura thought the word 'thief' was more important than 'tart'. 'If she called him a thief it must be because she knows the child was stolen.'

Javier shifted impatiently. If Laura didn't stop talking nonsense he wouldn't tell her anything else.

'The mother's name is Miriam López. It's on the birth certificate. I saw a copy of it myself; Eduardo showed it to me.'

'Does she look like Luz?'

'No. Eduardo said that she was a very attractive woman, with dark hair, but he didn't look at her too closely. He asked her to call him and told her that he needed to know more – that he's obsessed.'

'You know, your brother is really brave. I admire him. Given how much he loves Luz, this must be incredibly hard for him. Dolores must be a tremendous person, because it's thanks to her that Eduardo's so keen to make sure Luz's parents weren't disappeared. Yes, all right, I'll shut up now.'

After meeting Eduardo, Miriam locked herself in her hotel room and didn't leave, not even to eat. Frank would be arriving the next day. She'd made a reservation for them both at a hotel outside the city centre. She looked at Eduardo's card once or twice, but didn't dare dial his number.

Doubts spun around her like flies in summer. What could Eduardo possibly want to know? Why was he afraid? How could she talk to someone who was masquerading as Luz's father, and who was also Dufau's son-in-law? Still, something told her that she ought to call him, so she hadn't yet returned to Buenos Aires. After what had happened, she couldn't go back to the school or park outside his home. What was she going to do – creep into the house at night and kidnap her? There was nothing else she could do. There was only one thing left: to talk to Eduardo.

There must be some reason why he had behaved the way he did. If all he wanted was to stop her getting the kid, it would have been easy. He could have just called one of his father-in-law's thugs, or the police, and she'd be in jail or dead by now. No, there was something peculiar going on, and even though calling him was risky, it was the very last thing she could do for Lili, so she would do it.

Eduardo had spent the whole of Friday in the office. The only time he went out was to pick up Luz from school at the usual time. Miriam had not called. She said, 'We'll be in touch,' but that doesn't mean anything; maybe she only said it because Luz was there. Maybe she'll never call. If you haven't heard from her by Monday, you'll go looking for her in all the hotels. You'll ask everyone you can think of.

Frank was struck by the fact that Miriam had brought such a small bag. She told him that she was still paying for the room at the other hotel. 'But don't give me that look, of course I'll stay here with you. Seeing as I'm going back to the same hotel after you leave on Monday, I didn't want to bother moving all my stuff.'

'Right from the beginning, Frank suspected that Miriam was hiding something from him. What she'd said about staying at the other hotel for business reasons didn't ring true. Even though Miriam had quite a lively imagination, she couldn't come up with a convincing story. Maybe that was because she herself felt ambivalent; part of her didn't want Frank to know what was going on, but another part did. He pressed her to tell him the truth, but Miriam pretended to be offended. However, she made some tell-tale slips, which he spotted. At one point, she said something to him about an important phone call.'

'You mean someone's going to ring you? Is that why you've kept the room at the other hotel?'

'No, I've got to ring them.'

'He asked why. It all seemed crazy to him. He was hoping that by being persistent and affectionate, he would get through to her and persuade her to tell him what was up. So he was blunt. He told her he had to go back to the States the following Thursday and that he'd like her to go with him.'

'So, Miriam, I hope you can hurry up and finish this "work" or whatever it is you're up to. It sounds pretty fishy to me. We haven't got much longer together.'

That night, after they had made love, she told him that she loved him, but that she just wasn't sure.

All he was suggesting, he said, was that they spend some time together, to see how it worked out. It wasn't a lifetime commitment, just giving the relationship a chance to grow. He could feel the chemistry between them in everything they did. Or was he imagining that?

Miriam said there was something else holding her back, something she still had to do, which didn't concern him.

She begged him not to ask her any more questions that night, just to let her go to sleep in his arms. She needed to rest and not keep fretting over something she couldn't and wouldn't talk to him about. Frank didn't press her.

Eduardo gets home at half past nine that night, in a foul mood. Mariana is waiting for him with some good news. She has decided they should go and spend the weekend in Buenos Aires, 'to relax and help you unwind a bit'.

'I can't possibly,' said Eduardo curtly. 'I've got too much to do.'

What right have you got to treat Mariana this way? It's been a terrible week for her. Going to see her parents would be the best thing for her. But could you really sit opposite Alfonso at the table without bringing up the subject of Luz and demanding an explanation?

Eduardo has convinced himself that it would be best to talk to Miriam first. Maybe that would avoid a confrontation with his father-in-law, which would be really hard on Mariana. Why not have one peaceful night? he thinks. Just call a truce.

'All right then, maybe we will go, if I finish what I need to do at work tomorrow morning.'

He was planning to go into the office, just to wait for Miriam to call.

But that night, Eduardo loses his temper again when he finds out that Mariana has told her mother all about it and asked her not to tell Daddy because she doesn't want to hurt his feelings or make him cross with Eduardo.

In the appalling row that ensues, he throws all his jealously guarded secrets in her face: Miriam López, the birth certificate, and what Miriam said to Luz. Mariana is furious with both him and Luz for not telling her, something she will never forgive.

'How could she believe some crazy woman on the street who comes up and says I'm not her mother?'

'She didn't believe her, Mariana.'

You make one mistake after another. It's as if you can't stop yourself from provoking her, as if you wanted everything to blow sky-high.

'Don't threaten me. You can't stop me doing anything, do you understand? I'm going to do whatever it takes to find out – I'm going to talk to Miriam.'

'How? Do you know where she is?'

Mariana's expression, a mixture of amazement and hope, alerts you. How could you be so incredibly careless? Mariana could set her father on to Miriam. Who knows what you've already done to her – stolen her child probably – and now it'll be your fault if they send out some swat team. Now it really is vital to find her. After what you've said to Mariana, it's your duty to save Miriam from the claws of the Dufau family.

Mariana eggs him on: she can't believe that she's married a heartless monster who wants to take her child away from her.

'And I can't believe you can be so . . . so . . .' You can't find the right words. You can't say to her: so different from Dolores. 'So blind, so closed-minded, so immoral, so cruel, and so cavalier about the law, like your father. You're on the other side; right now, I feel as if you're my enemy.'

That's why Eduardo wants a separation. He doesn't want to go on living with someone who thinks like she does, who sees something dangerous and dirty in the fact that Luz lifts up her nightie when she dances, in the way she moves, in the fact that she talks to everybody. 'You make me sick, Mariana.'

'Is there someone else?'

Eduardo doesn't bother to answer.

'Because men never want a separation unless there's another woman involved. You're just making up any old thing to hurt me, but I'm not going to listen. I know you don't really believe what you're saying. I bet what's happened is that you've fallen for some slut, and you're just making excuses to have your little affair. But when you come back to cry on my shoulder and say you're sorry, I may not listen. Who is she? Tell me. There's another woman. Isn't there?'

Yes, there is someone else, he says wearily, but that's not the reason. 'Who is she?'

Only at six in the morning, after Eduardo has declared that there really is no one else, that he just made it up so she would be quiet, can he get to sleep. You have no idea how or why she does this, but Mariana snuggles up to you and says all you have to do is say you're sorry and that's it. Tomorrow they should all go to Buenos Aires.

She is asleep when Eduardo gets up. He leaves her a note saying he's sorry for the way he spoke to her, but not for what he said. He wants a separation and he is going to find out where Luz is from, whether she likes it or not. They should talk later on, when they've both calmed down. He needs to rest and think and be on his own. 'Don't wait for me.'

That morning, Miriam told Frank she was going back to her hotel to pick up some clothes. She intended to call Eduardo from there, although she wasn't sure if he'd be at the office on a Saturday. The night before, she had decided that she would call him. It was the only thing left she could do for Lili.

But she ended up saying yes to Frank's suggestion of a trip to the coast. She could always call that afternoon. But there was no way Eduardo would still be in the office then. Oh well, she'd call him on Monday, after Frank had left.

Mariana called Eduardo five or six times, demanding to know when he would be home. That night, was all he said. He needed to be alone, he'd already said so in the note. In desperation, Mariana called her mother and told her everything Eduardo had said.

He sees her from the car. She's with a man, sitting in a café down by the river. It's definitely Miriam. Eduardo parks the car and goes into the café. He sits down not far from their table and orders a cup of tea. Miriam hasn't seen him. She seems very happy chatting to the man. Her husband, perhaps?

Eduardo doesn't know how to catch her attention, but he can't afford to waste this opportunity. When he sees the man taking out his wallet to pay the bill, Eduardo gets up and walks over to them quickly.

Miriam gives a start when she sees him. She is clearly very embarrassed.

'Miriam, you didn't call me.'

There is such anguish in his voice that he can't continue. The two of them stare at him in consternation. Eduardo notices that Miriam is watching to see how the other man will react.

'I was going to.' And she tries to make light of it, the way she did with Luz. 'Eduardo, this is a friend of mine, Frank.'

They shake hands, unsure of what to say next. Frank gestures to a chair, inviting him to sit down, but Miriam's peremptory glance stops him.

You can't just walk away and run the risk that she'll never ring you. You must let her know precisely what you want.

'It's vital that I talk to you.' Eduardo doesn't disguise the anxiety in his voice and eyes. 'I need to know something that only you can tell me. Don't be frightened, it might be a good thing for you, because if you are who I . . .'

The man gazes at him, intrigued, and he feels awkward, he can't say it in front of him: because if you are who I think you are, if Luz is your daughter, I won't stop you seeing her or whatever. Lord knows what difficulties he might make for Miriam. Maybe she's never talked about her daughter to this bloke – if Luz is her daughter, that is.

'If you are who I think you are,' and you just hope to God that Luz is her daughter, and not someone else's, 'I won't cause any problems. I'm sure we can work something out.'

The two of them stare at him in astonishment.

'Are you sure you won't sit down, amigo?' the man says. His voice is friendly. He must feel sorry for him.

'I'll ring you on Monday. Don't worry, I promise.'

'After that meeting, Miriam couldn't keep up the pretence any longer. She told Frank the truth. He agreed that it was extremely strange, but that the man seemed truly desperate. If he hadn't seen it with his own eyes, he would have told her not to go and meet him, that it was a trap, but the way he behaved seemed to indicate that wasn't the case. Both Miriam and Frank were shaken by Eduardo's manner.'

They had to be careful. Frank said he ought to be there when she spoke to Eduardo. No way, said Miriam, she wanted to talk to Eduardo alone. Well then, said Frank, he'd keep an eye on things from near by; he didn't want her running any risks.

Of course he wouldn't leave on Sunday; he would stay with her. 'You idiot, how on earth could you think I'd go? You silly goose, I love you so much.' He was glad to know what was going on, finally. The secret between them had been getting in the way of their love.

When Amalia told her husband about this woman called Miriam López, Alfonso was extremely perturbed. Who had made up the name of the woman on the birth certificate? Animal. But there was another connection which he had just remembered. What was Animal's girlfriend called? Yes, that's right, her name was Miriam. The woman who took care of the prisoner and the baby, that gorgeous-looking woman, was called Miriam. But was that the same woman Animal had married? He wasn't sure. Alfonso hadn't been at the wedding. He seemed to recall that one day Animal had said something about having fallen out with his fiancée. But then later on he said he was getting married. How much later? Dufau told himself he just had to think hard enough and he'd remember. It took him a few phone calls before he came up with Sergeant Pitiotti's home telephone number.

'General Dufau here. Come to my house at once.'

He'd make Eduardo see sense, knock it into him if he had to. This curiosity of his was utterly out of place under the circumstances. And a divorce was out of the question. No daughter of his would get divorced.

When Alfonso telephoned Mariana at seven that evening, she relaxed somewhat. Daddy would take care of it all. He knew what to do.

'Men go through phases, you know, Mariana. They're weak. Just be patient and don't worry, you're not going to separate. Marriage is for life, and even though Eduardo's very mixed up right now, he knows that. He's from a good family. After I've had a little chat with him, he'll come begging your pardon, you'll see.'

Alfonso never mentioned the business with Luz. Mariana had talked it over with Amalia, and she knew her mother would persuade Eduardo not to do anything stupid.

'Be nice to him when he gets back,' Amalia told her. 'Even if you are furious. And don't say anything about the other woman; that's never a good idea. Just ignore it. Pretend he never said anything. Oh yes, and when he gets in, tell him Daddy wants a word with him.'

Mrs Pitiotti wanted to know why General Dufau had called. He'd given him an important assignment. He had to leave the next day for Paraná, in the province of Entre Ríos. 'That's great,' his wife said, pleased. She was tired of hearing her husband go on about the wonders of his not-too-distant past, when he was working with Dufau. She wished he could get his enthusiasm back, and lose that sour face.

Sergeant Pitiotti's golden age had come to an end. The secret detention centres had been dismantled. Things were rather dull these days, the excitement was over, and he was too well known to get anything other than a minor administrative job, nothing to write home about. So Dufau's call made him distinctly hopeful. He never imagined it could have anything to do with Miriam. That took him completely by surprise.

When he had told Dufau that he was getting married, he had hoped and prayed that the colonel would think he was marrying the woman he had met that time. It was very unlikely he would come to the wedding because it was in January, during the summer holidays, which is precisely why he had picked that date. He had contributed to the misunderstanding when his first son was born. He had told Dufau and Dufau had said, 'Oh yes, that's excellent news.' Pitiotti took that to mean that Dufau remembered him saying that his girlfriend couldn't have children.

'Luckily, the doctors are always coming up with new things and we got that problem of hers sorted out.'

But it was all an illusion. As he walked up to General Dufau's house, he was wreathed in smiles, flattered and honoured that he'd been summoned. However, the moment he walked in, he realised he had imagined the whole thing. Dufau had never stopped to think of Sergeant Pitiotti's life for an instant, apart from when he was in charge of his granddaughter. In the general's mind, Animal was merely the person who knew how to apply the most pressure in the least amount of time, the one who'd given him the maximum number of positive results.

General Dufau was the type who believed that the more subversives they liquidated, the better, and that in order to win the war, they had to eliminate the entire younger generation, since there wasn't a true patriot among them. He wasn't like the others who wanted to win the Montoneros over and form an alliance with them. For Lieutenant Colonel Dufau, as he was back then, it was simply a question of numbers, of statistics. He was proud of the fact that his detention centres had the largest percentage of 'transfers'. For him, the idea of 'rehabilitating' the terrorists was patently absurd: the only good subversive was a dead one. And Animal had been most useful in that sense.

Dufau's first question indicated that Animal had misread him not only on a personal level but also on a professional one. The reason he wanted to see him immediately had to do with a serious error he had committed in the past.

'Tell me, Pitiotti, that woman you were going out with, the one who looked after the prisoner, did you marry her? I couldn't remember.'

Animal didn't deny or confirm it, he merely asked, 'Why?', avoiding the issue.

'Was her name Miriam López?'

He couldn't deny that it was, nor could he deny the business with the birth certificate, which had been a flagrant breach of the rules. He had overstepped his authority, as Dufau is now pointing out to him, his voice shaking with rage. The sergeant himself had taken her to the hospital, so why did he put down his girlfriend's name?

'I don't know, it was the first thing that came to mind.'

'But you told me she was the right person for the job, you assured me she was.'

This time he could barely nod. Could Dufau have found out that she was Patricia, the call-girl? Or worse still, that she was working for the other side, the way Animal sometimes suspected and other times told himself no, Miriam couldn't possibly have been helping the prisoner.

'This Miriam López is sniffing around Paraná where my daughter and her husband live, and getting too close to my granddaughter. I don't want her alive and blabbing. The child wasn't even her daughter, after all.

What's she up to? I don't know and I don't care; just get rid of her as soon as possible. It has to be done in a matter of hours. And cleanly.'

Part of him feels ashamed, but another part is happy. It was deeply satisfying to be given a task that had been a burning ambition of his for years, ever since Pilón told him that story in the car. 'You can count on me, sir, to do the job properly.' His eyes must have reflected some of his wish to annihilate Miriam, because Dufau gives a satisfied smile.

Did the general know if she was using an alias at the moment, or was there any other information that might be useful? Because she tended to use aliases.

'A nom de guerre, you mean,' Dufau corrected him, surprised.

'No, an alias. When I met her, she called herself Patricia.'

Dufau couldn't believe his ears. Of course he had heard about Patricia, although he didn't go to those parties or use the agency, but his colleagues said the most . . . enthusiastic things about her. 'So you mean to say, Animal . . .' His voice was shaking with anger again. 'How dare you entrust my granddaughter to a whore?'

Pitiotti didn't know what to say. He knew he'd made a serious mistake, but he'd make up for it now. He'd need help, though.

'How about ringing the policeman who took part in the operation? What was his name?'

'Pilón.'

'Yes, he can go with you. I'll give the order.'

It is night time when Eduardo gets home. He is rather surprised when Mariana kisses him hello with a smile he's almost forgotten and says, 'Hello love, I'm glad you're back. I missed you so much.'

If Eduardo doesn't mind, she thinks they should have dinner with Luz, she can stay up late because she doesn't have school tomorrow. Afterwards they could go out for a drink and then go dancing, it's been ages since they did that. Mariana feels like having fun tonight, letting her hair down.

Eduardo doesn't know what to say. Her attempt at reconciliation touches him. Maybe she's had time to think things over too and there's still a chance try and patch things up. He smiles and tells her that he's very

231

tired but that he'll have a shower and they can have dinner together and then they'll see.

'Although I'd prefer to stay at home, Mariana, and just have a peaceful conversation.'

Mariana is determined to humour him that night, and gives him a naughty wink. She walks towards the kitchen and then turns round, absent-mindedly.

'Oh, and Daddy called, he'd like you to ring him right away.'

'Well, I'm not going to.'

The look of fury that crosses her face lasts only a second, but it's long enough for him to register just how much willpower she is exerting to smile and say gently, 'Oh, go on, love, give him a ring, otherwise he'll call us later on and maybe catch us in the middle of something.'

When the phone rings later Luz is at the table, which means Eduardo has to act normally when Mariana says it's her father, for him.

'When are you coming to Buenos Aires?'

His imperious tone of voice makes Eduardo balk. He has to fight not to hang up the receiver.

'I might come next week,' he says. 'No, the week after.'

'It will have to be this week,' the voice barks, 'Monday at the latest. We've got something to discuss that can't wait.'

'I'm sorry, I can't possibly do Monday, I've got work commitments.'

'Well, come tomorrow then. You can fly out in the morning and go back in the afternoon.'

You are sorely tempted to tell him to go to hell, but Luz and Mariana are sitting there. And maybe it would be best to get it over with once and for all; you're not afraid of him any more. If you go on Sunday, you can be there on Monday when Miriam calls. Plus it will get you out of this awkward situation with Mariana that you're not sure you can cope with, torn between not trusting her and hoping she will change. And what if you saw Dolores?

'Eduardo, answer me. What time can you get here? I've got to plan my day.'

Eduardo's got to plan his day too. And your night, you decide. Dolores, Dolores. Why forbid yourself to see her when you want her so badly?

'I'll come tomorrow. I'll confirm my arrival time when I've checked the flights. Bye.'

Mariana's smile makes you think she's in on the secret, and that the only reason she was so charming was to make sure you'd accept.

'Daddy, can we go to the country tomorrow?' asks Luz. 'And go riding, the three of us?'

'I can't tomorrow, sweetheart, Grandad needs to see me and I've got to go to Buenos Aires.'

'Tomorrow of all days, what a shame!' says Mariana.

Eduardo doesn't believe her disappointed act; she's happy. Later on, when she comes up and caresses him, he can't help feeling it's all a plan orchestrated by the Dufau clan.

'Mariana, please don't make things any more difficult than they already are. I've told you I want us to separate, and I mean it. I'm not going to talk to your father just because he's ordered me to, but because I want to ask him some questions I should have asked years ago.'

He can see her hesitating between her need to lash out at him and her parents' advice to act lovingly.

She sits down opposite him and sheds a few tears, which might not be false; don't be so hard on her.

'Why should we separate when we love each other so much?'

'Because we haven't got anything in common. We think differently, and the things you care about, like the horrible, dangerous things you think Luz might have inherited –' his voice has hardened '– and worse, what you see in her, are repugnant to me, and you think the things I care about are irrelevant.'

'And what about Luz? Don't you care about her becoming one of those poor kids from broken homes? We all know what happens to them.'

'I care about Luz, a child who was probably separated . . . or rather cruelly snatched from her parents, her real parents.'

He shouldn't have said that. He pleads for them just to leave it. He doesn't mean to say these things, which are probably unnecessary. 'We really should go to bed and get some sleep.'

Mariana runs her hand gently over your body. You would like to rediscover the pleasure you used to get from her caresses, but you can't repress an awful sense of mistrust. How can you be sure whether her hand is there because she wants you or whether it's just part of a premeditated plan?

You don't dare push her away, but you lie there motionless and inert, even when she does something uncharacteristic and reaches out and strokes your penis.

Just as Eduardo doesn't believe her, Mariana doesn't believe him when he starts breathing deeply, pretending to be asleep, although sleep is a long way off.

Mariana gave up and turned over in bed. She'd make him pay dearly for snubbing her. Once her parents got him back in line and he'd apologised, she'd make him wait years before she let him make love to her again. Although maybe she should keep up the pretence a little while longer, until the other woman disappeared from his life. The other woman she would never mention to him. Mummy was right.

Who could it possibly be? Maybe even Carola. Or was it someone from Buenos Aires? It was only after he came back from that last trip there that Eduardo started acting so strangely. It doesn't matter who it is, though, she'll vanish eventually. They always came back with their tails between their legs, according to her friend. And when he did, Mariana promised herself, she would get her own back.

Eduardo called Dolores the moment he landed, around eleven in the morning. Thank God, thank God she was in, because he wanted to see her that day.

His voice was full of excitement and happiness. Dolores could feel her heart, still as wild as it had been at fifteen, but with all that she brought to life now. So it wasn't just her, she thought; he was head over heels too.

Eduardo said he didn't know what time he'd be free; he'd try to get away as soon as possible. He had a very 'welcome and urgent' meeting, he said sarcastically. His father-in-law wanted to see him at once. When he was finished, he would call her and she could go straight to his hotel. He wouldn't be staying in the usual one; he'd let her know where to go.

'Be careful, sweetheart,' Dolores said.

It is now four o'clock in the afternoon and she has been pacing nervously near the telephone for hours, worrying about Eduardo sitting there with that murderer. Fortunately, her parents are out, because her mother would have twigged right away. She's been asking what was wrong for days; she can sense there's something Dolores is not telling her. 'It's not Eduardo, is it, Dolores?' But Dolores refuses to answer.

At last the phone rings. He sounds very agitated. Yes, she'll be there, at the Wellington in half an hour. She won't ask for him at the desk but will just go straight to his room, number 402.

On Sunday afternoon Miriam and Frank went to fetch her things from the hotel. She agreed that although Eduardo seemed OK, since he was Dufau's son-in-law, it was a good idea to play it safe.

She went in alone, as she had wanted. Frank waited for her outside on the corner so that nobody would know they were together.

Miriam asked for the bill and said that she was going to Buenos Aires.

'Will you be back?'

'Yes, of course. I really like this hotel, it's very comfortable,' she said, with a smile. 'I just don't know when exactly. I'll ring and make a reservation from Buenos Aires.'

'I only ask because there was a gentleman asking after you today. I told him you were staying here but that I hadn't seen you for a couple of days, so I thought you'd probably gone off somewhere for the weekend. He's definitely going to be back. What shall I tell him?'

'Just say I've gone to Buenos Aires,' she said, trying to sound as natural as possible. Her hands were shaking as she closed her bag, but since she had to bend over to do it the receptionist didn't see her agitation.

'Who was this man? Did he leave his name, or a message?'

'No. He had dark hair and was in his late thirties, kind of . . .' he searched for the word. 'Well, the domineering type. The sort who asks you a question and you're nervous if you don't know the answer.'

Miriam shrugged. 'I haven't the foggiest. If he returns, tell him to leave his card, and you can give it to me when I get back.'

'That was Animal, I'm positive,' Miriam said to Frank.

'Not necessarily,' he replied. 'Maybe it was someone who was working for Eduardo. But it doesn't really matter who it was; it's not a good sign. It would be best to get the hell out of Entre Ríos and forget all about the conversation with Eduardo, however nice he seems.'

'No, I'm sorry, Frank, but I'm not going anywhere before I've talked to him. My mind's made up. I've got to do it.'

She agreed to stay in the hotel room if he was worried about her. She was registered as Mrs Harrison, and they hadn't asked to see her ID at the desk, so who was to know? She'd talk to Eduardo the next day.

Frank thought it better not to argue. He said he would take the hire car back first thing in the morning, as soon as the agency opened.

TWELVE

THE MOMENT DOLORES walks into Eduardo's room, they collapse into each other's arms.

'I've been so worried about you, I was petrified. Thank God you're all right.'

She kisses your cheeks and throat. You take her head in your hands and lace your fingers in her hair, kissing her on the mouth and ears as you steer her gently towards the bed.

She lies back and giggles as you pounce on her; that pure joy of bodies in love.

But then Dolores pulls away from him. She says they'll have time to make love later – she's too wound up right now.

You tell her you're staying overnight. 'I'm planning to enjoy every minute I have with you.'

Dolores asks how the interview with Eduardo's father-in-law went, what he said.

'Did you ask him who the mother was? Did he admit that Luz's parents were disappeared?'

No, he did not, and they talked for hours.

'I don't think her mother was one of the disappeared. It's bizarre, but both Alfonso and Miriam have told me the same thing: that she was a prostitute.'

'What?' When Eduardo tells her the details of what happened at the school gate, Dolores says the most intriguing thing is that Miriam called him a thief. 'She must have meant something by that, don't you think? Perhaps that Luz was stolen; but Miriam didn't say that she was her mother. Dufau could have invented whatever he wanted. All right, all right, I won't interrupt again, I promise. Hurry up and tell me what happened.'

'All sorts of things,' says Eduardo. 'Dufau tried to talk me out of it; he lied and threatened and blustered and hedged and tried to warn me off. I ended up walking out.' Eduardo laughs happily. As he left, he had announced, 'I'll do whatever I damn well please. I'm going to find out where Luz came from, I'm going to talk to Miriam López, and I'm going to leave your daughter,' and then slammed the door. The sound must still be ringing in the Dufaus' ears.

Eduardo is elated. He chuckles and kisses Dolores.

'It felt great to speak my mind and then walk out and slam the door. I never dreamed I'd have the guts to do that. Aren't you pleased?' He hugs her again. 'If it weren't for you, I don't think I'd ever have had the nerve to face up to him finally and have the last word.'

Dolores says she's completely lost. He's going to have to start again from the beginning. Is he really thinking of leaving his wife?

'Yes.' A shadow crosses Eduardo's face. 'Mariana's just like her father, she's . . . I don't know, I loved her so much that maybe I was blind to it before, but the way she reacted when I told her about Luz made me see her in a completely different light – as a cruel person. It hurts, you know, it really hurts, that she . . .'

'Maybe you'd better not tell me this right now,' Dolores says.

But he needs to, he says. Not all of it; but there are some things Mariana's done that have cut him to the quick, like what she said about Luz, or the way she's dead set against him finding out where Luz came from.

'I'm not going to give up, though. No matter how hard it is for me, I'm not going to stop. I've told you, I won't let you down, Dolores.'

His father-in-law had started the conversation by threatening him. 'I should point out that you were the one who registered Luz; you bribed the clerk to falsify the birth certificate. Who do you think will be first to land in jail?'

Eduardo demanded to know why he'd have to go to jail, and his father-in-law gave that odious little smirk of his: apparently Eduardo wasn't aware that things had moved on in Argentina and that a lot of . . . unpleasant things could happen under a democratic government. 'Don't be a fool, my boy.' And then he started leaning on him: 'You'll lose your daughter, your wife, and your reputation. What about your family? What will your mother and brother and employees say if you're arrested?'

Although Dolores has promised herself she won't interrupt, she can't help it. 'He gave himself away right there. He as good as admitted that Luz's mother was one of the disappeared. He's threatening you by suggesting that if you say anything, or try to look into it, you'll be sent to jail. But he will too, of course.'

'What?' Does Dolores think he's going to end up in jail?

She gives Eduardo a frantic look. Of course not, it would all sort itself out, it was true what he had done was really wrong, but he was obviously doing his best to make amends. In any case, he hadn't known that they were stealing babies from the women detainees.

Eduardo shakes his head. He wouldn't normally trust his father-in-law further than he could throw him, but he could swear that Dufau had been taken by surprise when he mentioned that Luz's mother was a tart, as Miriam had called herself. Dufau actually gave him the name of a woman who ran a call-girl agency, someone called Annette, and said he would get him the phone number so he could ring and ask whether Miriam López was in fact Patricia, a well-known escort in the mid-seventies. What if Dufau was right? He'd know by tomorrow. He tells Dolores about seeing Miriam in the café and how she'd promised to ring him on Monday.

Dolores says she doesn't understand. Wasn't Dufau the one who had adamantly refused to give him any information about the mother? So why had he suddenly come up with the woman's full name and what she did for a living? Because Eduardo had told Mariana about it when they were having a fight.

Dolores is alarmed. It's very brave of him to try and find out, but he should never have given that information to his father-in-law. Eduardo doesn't know how these people operate. She has looked through the lists of the disappeared to see if there's a Miriam López and there isn't a single one, but maybe nobody's reported her missing. 'If she really is alive, she must have escaped, although it's highly unlikely she would have survived after her baby was stolen. She may very well be a tart, but why did she say you were a thief?'

239

You can't take any more. You are overwhelmed by the thought that you have put Miriam's life in danger. Dolores lies down next to you and strokes you, but even her soothing touch fails to relax you and she realises this, because she suggests that you stop talking for a bit. She'll give you a massage, she says. Just let go and concentrate on her hands. They move over your body, kneading your worries and expelling them, setting you free.

When Amalia told Alfonso that poor Mariana was worrying herself sick because it was nine o'clock and Eduardo still hadn't come home, he instantly feared the worst – that Eduardo had got in touch with Miriam the moment he arrived in Entre Ríos. Animal still hadn't rung back, damn it.

A few years earlier, when the Abuelas were first getting active and holding meetings all over the place, they published a letter in the *Buenos Aires Herald* listing all the pregnant women who had disappeared. Alfonso had checked the names, and was relieved to find that Liliana's mother wasn't a member of the organisation, and the little girl wasn't listed.

'*Nobody ever reported me missing to the Abuelas. I checked the files.*'

'*Liliana's mother, Nora, didn't know Liliana was pregnant. Liliana decided not to tell her, so as not to make it any harder on her. They met two or three times after we went underground, but Liliana wasn't showing much at that point, and she covered herself up with a coat. I respected her decision.*'

'*So you never told her mother? Does she think I don't exist? That I never existed? Not even when I was in her daughter's womb?*'

'*She did find out that Liliana was pregnant. I told her when Liliana was kidnapped. But when Dolores' mother called my father, he told her what we all thought was true: that Liliana had died in childbirth and that her baby had been stillborn. There was no reason to keep on fighting or searching. I talked to Nora in 1984, when I went back to Argentina.*' Carlos smiled sadly. '*She said, "If only I had my grandson." I think that Liliana decided not to tell her because she thought her mother wouldn't understand. Nora and her husband had a very hard time with Liliana's activism and her relationship with me. They clearly thought I was responsible for the change in her. But it wasn't true: Liliana really did believe in what she was doing. When I met her, she was already involved in grassroots organising. But as time went by, especially after that incredibly painful conversation with Nora in 1984, I realised that in her heart of hearts Nora loved Liliana deeply and that she would have understood what she was fighting for. We made some big mistakes. All of us.'*

'And what about your parents?'

'They reacted differently. They never knew all that much about what we were doing, but they approved of our idealism. They had passed it on to us themselves. They were working-class people, salt-of-the-earth types. But the things that happened during that dreadful time absolutely destroyed them. When Mum died, my sister and I weren't even there. I think she died of a broken heart.'

Alfonso would never have dreamt that Animal's girlfriend would create all these problems. Crazy bitch; what the hell did she think she was up to?

'If we can't stop Eduardo, what are we going to do?' Amalia asked, and Alfonso knew it wasn't an idle question. 'We can't let him go on digging stuff up about Luz, and he certainly can't leave Mariana. It would cause a frightful scandal: just think, him leaving her!'

Alfonso said reassuringly that she shouldn't worry too much; Eduardo would soon change his tune when he realised what the stakes were. He would talk to him again. Maybe he should have been more direct last time. Amalia agreed.

The news Alfonso received from Animal at ten o'clock that night was even more unsettling: he had managed to find the hotel where Miriam was staying, but she had unexpectedly left that afternoon. He knew the colour and the make of the car she was driving, as well as the address of the company where she'd hired it. She couldn't have returned it there, because the place was closed until Monday, and it hadn't been returned at the airport, because he'd checked. He should have good news by tomorrow morning. He knew he would find her.

'I told you, you only have a few hours left to sort this out.'

Pray God Amalia was right and Eduardo wasn't in Entre Ríos.

'The crazy way he's acting makes me think he must have found himself a mistress who's addled his brains. Maybe he's with her in a hotel somewhere. It wouldn't be that hard to find out; with a bit of luck, we could trace him,' Amalia said encouragingly.

They should wait a while, Alfonso replied. Maybe Eduardo would get home later that night.

'No, he's in Buenos Aires. My hunches are never wrong,' Amalia declared. She went running off to get the phone book.

She didn't want her husband to get upset about this; it wasn't worth it. Animal was out there looking for Miriam; presumably he was pretty keen to eliminate her, and not only because those were his orders. When Alfonso next spoke to Eduardo, he would soon put him in his place – she trusted his powers of persuasion. And if he couldn't . . . if the worst came to the worst, she had an idea. A radical one, perhaps. But if necessary . . .

What would she do after she'd talked to Eduardo? He was assuming she'd go away with him, Frank commented to Miriam over dinner. They had ordered room service in their suite.

Miriam didn't dare say no, although of course it would depend on the outcome of their conversation. Maybe she could convince Eduardo to help her tell Lili the truth. But why would he do that, if it meant he would lose the kid?

What if she told Eduardo that she was the mother and made up some story so that he would let her visit Lili from time to time? Then she could tell her that her parents were Liliana and Carlos and not those two . . .

Frank said she should stop talking nonsense, and that there were a couple of things she should bear in mind. 'What good will it do the little girl to add one set of lies to another? Or would you tell her the whole truth on your first visit, even though you wouldn't be able to do anything for her, and you'd be risking your own life into the bargain?'

Miriam realised that Frank really was her friend and that he truly loved her, because he helped her see things clearly without trying to force her into anything.

'The way Frank treated her, the fact that he was so helpful and understanding, made a big impression on Miriam and brought them a lot closer. I don't think she was in love with him; all she really wanted was protection and friendship. She told me that Frank was the only man who ever treated her like a human being, who understood her and accepted her for what she was. And it proved crucial for Miriam at that point in her life.'

'Mrs Harrison would like to go to bed with Mr Harrison now. Would that be possible?'

That was her way of telling him that even though she didn't know what would happen, she felt as if she were married to him. She preferred to say it jokingly.

Dolores is still shaken by what Dufau had said to Eduardo. 'I want you to give me your word that you won't lift a finger to investigate Luz's background, and that you'll ask Mariana's forgiveness for having said you want a separation.' Eduardo thinks it was just his father-in-law's style, a manner of speaking, but to her mind it was clearly a threat. And for Dolores, any threat from someone who deals in death, like Dufau, is a death threat. But even though Eduardo has learned such a lot in a short time, he doesn't seem to see this, and she doesn't dare spell it out. She is already upset with herself for having said too much earlier, blurting out that he'd be going to jail too.

After the massage, they let desire take over, and for a long time they managed to block out everything except the truth of their two bodies, beyond the reach of words.

Afterwards, as they were having a cold drink in the room, Eduardo started talking about Luz, saying how sweet she was, and how much he enjoyed telling her stories and going horse riding and how Luz likes talking to people and dancing, and what fun they have playing make-believe. He loves her so incredibly much. Dolores, feeling for him, said, 'But that's precisely why you have to do this, Eduardo, because you love her. You can't give up.'

Although now, as she thinks about what Dufau said, and about death, and about Eduardo not being there any more for her or anybody else either, she wonders what right she has to keep on pushing him to continue.

'Dolores, I'm going to leave Mariana. I need you. Don't go back to France. I need your support. And once I've sorted this out . . . I don't know what will happen, but all I can tell you is how I feel: I'd like us to be together. I'd like to live with you. But I can't plan anything now. Don't go, please; change your ticket.'

How can she help him? A tremor runs through her and she sees herself again, begging Pablo not to let himself get killed as she leads him right to the place where he will be kidnapped. And now she is telling Eduardo to carry on, even though he adores Luz, and it might send him to his death. In her mind's eye she sees Pablo and Mirta and the child she's never met but who she hopes is alive, the child she hopes they will find one day. She wonders whether it is really her own blood she is fighting for, whether she is just displacing her own need for reparation on to Eduardo. Please, please let Miriam be the mother, let things work out somehow, because otherwise . . .

She hugs him in desperation. Yes, of course she'll stay, as long as he wants. And she stifles the terrible thought that comes to her unbidden: or at least as long as . . .

What can she do? Tell him to stop, to give in to his father-in-law and carry on the deception? What can she do? Just love him.

She asks Eduardo to lie down and let her love him, will he? She wants to lick him and kiss him and rub his whole body with her hands and tongue and stomach and legs. She wants to brush his cheeks and eyes and ears with her clitoris and kiss the tip of him as she holds it in her hands. She opens her mouth and takes his penis very slowly inside, feeling it swell and shudder. She hears Eduardo moaning with pleasure, but she wants the pleasure to last, so she gives it a gentle goodbye lick, lays her head on his belly and stretches out. She wants to rest in this position and she wants him to rest too, to relax utterly and feel how loved he is. There is a pause. They let themselves steep in that complete peace for a long time, until Eduardo's warm hands start to explore her and she discovers the spot on her back that she didn't know existed until she felt the heat of his hands. He turns her over and kisses her on the neck and shoulders and breasts. He rolls on top of her, so full of urgency that the hairs on her skin stand on end. She feels her whole body opening up to receive him as his penis gradually slides into her, going deeper and deeper. His hands grasp at her body frantically, as if he were trying to take her from all sides at once. Wild horses are galloping over the land of her body and then comes that crazy, marvellous sensation of the self dissolving, of losing herself endlessly in his desire, becoming it, fusing with his need to possess her. She pulses open in waves like the sea and it almost happens when he groans but no, she can feel there is more and more and more and he stays with her until the end. Eventually she starts coming back into herself, exhausted and content, getting herself back whole and complete because he has taken her whole being and restored her to a self that is richer and fuller.

Mariana called her parents at two in the morning to say that Eduardo hadn't returned home. Even though they told her not to worry, he'd come to his senses and show up any minute, she was convinced that Eduardo would do as he had said that morning and get back the next day.

'Why didn't you say so before? Did he say he was going to stay in Buenos Aires?'

'Yes, if he was running late.'

There was nothing to worry about; she should go to bed. Daddy would talk to Eduardo again. He would go and find him at the airport or wherever and sort it all out.

Amalia had called the hotel where Eduardo usually stayed, but he wasn't there. However, she had a long list of hotels to go through, and all the time in the world.

She thought that perhaps, once they'd found out where he was staying, it might be better to wait until he came out. That way they would see who he was with as well.

Alfonso said his wife might be right; they had to find out who was making Eduardo act so out of character.

Even though Amalia went into the living room to use the phone, Alfonso couldn't sleep.

His insomnia irritated him. If she found out where Eduardo was, he'd have it out with him that very night.

They had been asleep for hours, worn out by the tension and their love-making, when the sound of the phone jolted them awake. Eduardo picked it up.

'I want you on the first flight to Entre Ríos. When you get there, you will ask Mariana's forgiveness. And no more digging things up about Luz, or you'll regret it. Do I make myself clear?'

Eduardo is holding the receiver away from him so that Dolores can hear. She makes out only one phrase: 'You'll regret it.' This was what she was afraid of. She shivers and tries to say something to Eduardo, but it's too late; he's already started to speak.

'I intend to talk to Miriam and whoever else it takes, whether you like it or not.'

Who does Eduardo think he is talking to? Alfonso changes his tone, from rage to a ribald laugh. 'So you're going to talk to Patricia? Well, you could have a hard time, because something might happen to that little slut and she won't have a tongue in her head. If it hasn't happened already, that is.'

It's Dolores who presses the button and cuts them off. It is five o'clock in the morning. He should go. Dufau knows where he is now. It could be dangerous. But Eduardo is too furious to comprehend the situation. 'How did he find out where I was, and how dare he ring at this time of night?' He would stay there as long as he bloody well wanted. He wasn't afraid of Dufau.

Dolores tries to reason with him: he should go now, he's got to be there so when Miriam calls he can warn her, and Dufau might be lying in wait outside the hotel.

'Let him wait, I don't care. I've had enough; I'm not taking any more orders from Alfonso. I'll catch the nine-thirty flight and I have no intention of going anywhere right now. He's not going to come here. He's already given me my orders over the phone.'

Dolores is scared. She says that she's going to leave now. 'No, don't go, who knows when we'll see each other again.' He hugs her.

'All right, I won't.' She agrees not to go, even though it's incredibly risky. She wonders when she will see Eduardo again, and is afraid that it might be never. The thought makes her give way and throw her arms around him. She starts crying and he comforts her. 'Don't worry, nothing's going to happen.' He doesn't want to see her like this, all sad.

She agrees to stay, but she won't leave the hotel with him or go to the airport, even though she'd love to be with him until the very last second. Those are the two places his father-in-law might be waiting.

At ten in the morning, when Frank went to return his friend's car, saying she had gone to Salta unexpectedly, he was told that some men had been there asking for her first thing; apparently they had something urgent to say to her. The man at the desk thought it was odd they were asking for her there, since they never gave out clients' information. 'But one of the gentlemen suggested (if you can call it that, because he sounded pretty threatening) that I'd better answer his questions. He wanted to know how long she was going to have the car for and what address she'd given. When I refused to say, the other one, who seemed a bit more reasonable, got out his police badge . . . and a gun. So I had to give them the information, although they didn't seem very pleased. I said she had hired it until Wednesday on a Uruguayan driver's licence, and I gave them the name of her hotel. Then the tough one said, "You might as well forget about the car; you should report it stolen now and save yourself some time, because she left yesterday." ' Anyhow, he was pleased to see that wasn't true. 'Thank you so much, Mr . . .'

'Rodríguez,' said Frank quickly.

'. . . for bringing it back.'

Frank glanced over the bill and said he was sure it was all fine. Miriam had left her credit-card number and signature, as usual.

'I have no idea who those men were. I'll tell my friend. It must be some sort of mistake.'

'What if they come back, though?' The car-hire man was obviously frightened.

Frank shrugged.

'You've got your car back, in perfect shape.' He smiled and turned to go.

He hired a Renault from a different company and drove back to the hotel as fast as possible.

Miriam had already called Eduardo, but he wasn't in yet. He would be there at eleven, the secretary said.

'Did you give her your name?'

'No, I said Mrs . . .'

'Harrison?' Frank's voice was loud with alarm. 'They'll track us down immediately.'

No, she had said Mrs Hernández, calm down. 'But I said I'd arranged to call Mr Iturbe today, so that he would know it was me.'

She should just forget it. What had happened at the car-hire place made it clear that they should get out of Entre Ríos at once. They could return the hire car at the airport in Rosario, or Córdoba. He'd said he was going on a trip when he hired it. Miriam told him not to make her any more nervous; she needed to think. 'How about going for a walk by the river?' No, Frank didn't want them going anywhere except away. There were two guys after her, didn't she realise how much danger she was in?

'I don't want to fight about it. Please, can't you leave me alone for a bit?'

'Only if you promise you won't call Eduardo. The phone might be tapped.'

'Eduardo isn't dangerous, I know, I can tell. The one who's after me is Animal, I'm sure of it.'

When he got to the office, he was told that Mrs Hernández had called. It's Miriam and she's alive, you think, relieved. If only she would hurry up and call back. And she does.

'Where can we meet?' Eduardo asks.

'They're looking for me everywhere.'

He had been afraid of that, but it was nothing to do with him. It was Dufau who was determined to stop them from talking at all costs. 'It's . . . because of the little girl. So please, just say a place, any place, where we can meet.' If she'd rather not do that, they could just speak over the phone.

'How do I know your phone isn't tapped?'

'Oh no, I don't think they'd go that far, we're in Entre Ríos. I don't know, though.'

Dolores had warned him it was dangerous. He doesn't know what to propose.

'I'll be in touch, at any rate,' says Miriam.

'Please do, and be quick.'

If Frank loves her, she says, if he really loves her, he'll do her this favour. 'You see, Eduardo is afraid too, and he says it's Dufau, in other words Animal, who's after me.' She hadn't wanted to say anything else over the phone, as Frank had said the line might be tapped. 'The only way I can get in touch with him is for you to go to his office and tell him to meet me here at the hotel. When he sees you, he'll realise who it's for.'

At first Frank said no, she was raving mad; but in the end he gave in, on one condition.

'When I come back I want everything ready so we can leave immediately.'

Frank left the room. Miriam didn't know what to do. She just knew that she had to speak to Eduardo.

She was overjoyed when Frank returned. She threw her arms round him when he asked her for Eduardo's card.

Mariana tells Eduardo that she is feeling miserable because he never called. He replies shortly that he told her the day before that he wouldn't be coming back until Monday, and he'd gone straight to work from the airport because he had appointments lined up.

'Are you coming home for lunch? Please do.'

'No, I don't think I'll have time. I'll go and pick Luz up from school and then we can see each other for a bit.'

Mariana starts to cry. 'Please, please come, I want to tell you something, don't leave me like this.'

You can't leave her like this. She sounds desperate. Maybe she means it.

'I'll do my best to pop in, but just for a while. I've got a very busy day.'

As Eduardo is leaving the office, he sees the man Miriam was with walking towards him, looking serious. His secretary comes out of the building at that very moment. The only thing Eduardo can think of is to walk up to him and pump his hand with great enthusiasm. He doesn't know how he did it.

'Alberto! Fancy seeing you here! What are you doing in Paraná?'

Eduardo waves at his secretary, who is watching them. Frank feigns a smile and slaps him on the back.

'Oh, fine, fine, I'm just up on business. I'm going back tonight. How's the family?'

Eduardo's secretary continues on her way, her curiosity satisfied.

'Miriam will be waiting for you at six o'clock in the bar at the Hotel de la Ribera. I trust you won't be followed. I don't like this at all. I don't know what you're after, but I don't want Miriam getting into danger.'

'Is that where you're staying?' Frank doesn't answer. 'It doesn't matter, wherever she is, just tell her not to move, stay in the room until then. Dufau is after her. He wants to stop her telling me anything, and I need to know. I'm terribly grateful for your help.'

Two things happened that led Amalia and Alfonso to acknowledge what they had both been thinking since the day before, but hadn't put into words. First, there was a desperate phone call from Mariana: Eduardo had come home at midday and told her he was going to leave her and that nothing and no one was going to stop him finding out the truth about where Luz came from. And then there was the fact that Animal hadn't managed to track Miriam down, although he did have a lead, the description of a man, presumably an accomplice of hers, who had been in Paraná that morning.

Alfonso asked him to call back at six that evening; if he hadn't managed to get rid of Miriam by that point, he would be given instructions for a new job.

When Eduardo walks into the bar, Miriam is already there at a table, pretending to read. They greet each other as if they were old friends. Frank is sitting in an armchair in the hall, where he can keep an eye on the bar as well as the hotel entrance.

'First of all, Miriam, I need to know if you are Luz's mother. If you are, we can work something out so you can see her, I promise.'

'I'm not her mother, and you're not her father either, although we've got one nasty little secret in common, because I wanted her for myself. So while you and your wife were probably getting Lili's room ready . . .'

'Lili?'

'Yes, that's what I called her. I was getting a room ready too, with baby-bear wallpaper. She'd been promised to me, you see. But she didn't belong to any of us. She was Liliana's kid. Her mother was called Liliana, I don't know her surname, and her father was called Carlos. He must have been killed. I called the baby Lili, after her mother. She was kept at my house while your wife was getting better. And that changed my life. So I . . .'

Eduardo doesn't understand any of this, he has only one question and it can't wait any longer: were Liliana and Carlos disappeared?

'Yes. But I didn't know what was going on when Animal promised me a baby.'

'I didn't either. It seems incredible, I know, but I only just found out recently, and I need all the information you can give me. Please, tell me what you know.'

'I promised Liliana that I would tell her daughter who her parents were, and that they were killed because they wanted a fairer society. I was very, very scared, so I went into hiding for years, but now I've come back to rescue her from . . . the two of you, and tell her the truth about who she is.'

'I'll tell her myself, I promise.'

Miriam tells Eduardo about Animal and how Liliana and the baby came to stay at her house, where Luz spent her first few days. She also describes what Liliana told her and their failed attempt to escape.

You find it moving that this woman, who turns out to be a prostitute, after all, has the sort of courage that you've never had. Your defences are collapsing. You feel the pain of the bullets exploding in Liliana's body and all your years of fraud and blindness and cowardice and selfishness.

'Are you going to tell Lili?'

'I'll do a lot more than that,' says Eduardo. 'I've got a friend who's got contacts with the Abuelas de Plaza de Mayo.'

He would report the case and confess his own involvement. If she wanted to, Miriam could help him. 'We've got to do it.'

All right then, she was up for it, because they'd acted like a right pair of shits so far, in different ways but . . .

'But we both love Luz.'

Miriam's eyes fill with tears and she looks out of the window. Eduardo is mystified when her expression suddenly changes to one of horror and panic. She leaps up and says, 'That's Animal! Go and tell Frank, he's sitting in one of the hall armchairs.'

She runs into the ladies'. Eduardo goes out to the hall. He sees two men striding purposefully towards the reception desk. He starts talking even before he reaches Frank, stumbling over the words.

'Animal is at the main desk and Miriam's hiding in the ladies'.'

Eduardo's hands tremble as he tries to light a cigarette.

'Would Animal recognise you? Has he ever seen you?' asks Frank.

'No. Never. I didn't even know who he was until today.'

Frank puts the room key on the chair.

'Go up to the room straight away. And don't pick up the phone, because they might be looking for me too. I'll knock three times to let you know it's me.'

Frank got up and went into the phone box, since he could watch the reception desk from there. Animal came walking towards him. Frank walked casually out, giving no sign of recognition, and went over to the bar. He saw Animal leave the phone box and wave the other man over. Then they left the hotel.

He was calling from the phone box at the hotel, he explained to General Dufau. There was a slight possibility that Miriam and her accomplice were staying there, but they weren't in the . . .

Alfonso interrupted him. 'There's no time to waste. Get out of there at once.'

He had different orders now. He passed on all the information: name, age, description, addresses for the office as well as the farm and the house (he mustn't do it there, though, of course), the brother's address, the make and colour of the car. He would know what to do. The main thing was: no witnesses and make it look like a break-in.

252

'You've only got a few hours. And this time, don't let me down, or you can say goodbye to your career.'

Sergeant Pitiotti might have noticed Eduardo's car parked just a few yards away from his, but the general had ordered him to leave at once as he hadn't found anything concrete, and he was in such a hurry to get going that he drove out of the hotel car park at top speed. Dufau had said he had only a few hours. He would check the office first.

The conversation between Miriam, Eduardo and Frank in the hotel room lasted only twenty minutes. Eduardo would talk to his friend that night or first thing the next day to see how to go about it. Would Miriam help him file the statement? They could go together.

'Miriam could testify now in the trials that are being held in Madrid. She saw them kill Liliana. And she could tell them what Liliana told her,' Carlos said. 'But anyway, go on.'

Eduardo had some errands to do; he needed to check on things at the farm and drop in at home. He would talk to his father-in-law and pretend he wasn't going to do anything, that he'd given up, that Miriam had vanished from Entre Ríos; maybe they would call off the hunt. He ought to talk to his wife, too.

Miriam and Frank flinched.

'Oh, don't worry, I won't breathe a word about what you've told me.'

Frank said there was nothing more they could do, things were getting out of hand and they would be leaving that night.

Eduardo's voice cracks. It's as if he's apologising: it wasn't only work he needed to finish; he wanted to see Luz that night, be with her, tell her a story, so he could somehow say goodbye. Tomorrow lunchtime, once he'd got all the information from his friend, he'd come to see them and they could plan their strategy. 'We can't afford a single false step.'

Judging from what Frank had told him, they weren't in any danger at the hotel. The man at the reception desk had smiled at them on the way in and hadn't mentioned anyone asking after them. Obviously Animal didn't know Frank's name. Frank agreed, but he was anxious to get away as soon as possible. He didn't see why they had to go and file the statement together.

Miriam turned to him.

'Eduardo needs a bit of time,' she said, with an imploring look. 'And he wants to spend a few hours with Lili.'

Frank didn't answer. It was clear the two of them needed one another to bolster their courage.

'I'll be here by twelve at the latest and we can work out a plan. I don't want to make any mistakes,' Eduardo said, trying to convince him.

'If we haven't heard from you by half past one, we won't wait,' Miriam added.

Either modesty or Frank's presence made Eduardo proffer a hand to Miriam as he said goodbye, but she gave him an impulsive hug instead.

Eduardo's eyes were filled with tears too as he hugged her back. They felt strong and close.

He liked Frank a lot. Frank's faint smile as they shook hands was somehow a relief.

He stops briefly at the office to call Dolores. He had rung Javier that morning to say that he would find out today, but that Alfonso had confirmed Miriam was a prostitute. He would ring back that night. No, he'd better not call from the office. He'll ring from the phone at the farm; he can be there in twenty minutes. Besides, he absolutely must see the manager to get an update and give him some instructions. Then he can close the door and talk in private.

He calls Mariana from the office to say that he'll be home in an hour or an hour and a half, and that he'd like Luz to have dinner with them.

During the drive to the farm you run through what you're going to say to Dolores. Maybe you should just stick to the essentials and let her give you advice. You will tell her, though, that you love her very much and that you need her. She rang you today but you just said that you were going to be meeting your friend and that you'd tell her about it tomorrow. Maybe she thought that was an odd, cold sort of answer, but Dolores would have understood that you were just being careful, as she asked you to.

Her love gives you incredible strength and happiness, but the thought of losing Luz is unbearably painful. You must ask Dolores if she thinks they'll let you see Luz, in spite of what you did.

The manager's van isn't there. That's too bad; you'll have to come back tomorrow. You go in to use the phone.

Dolores's mother says that her daughter is out, and she won't be back until late. 'Can I take a message?'

'Yes, just tell her I love her very much and that I'll ring her in the morning.'

It's late, but he's better off calling Javier now because it will be tricky from home. Javier isn't in, but he tells Laura that he might come round after dinner.

Eduardo walks briskly out. He is just shutting the door when someone gives him a brutal shove.

'A bullet in the head, a break-in,' said Luz, a welter of anger and pain in her voice. 'Laura never believed it. Neither did Dolores.'

'Did you?'

'Yes, I did, because that's what everybody told me my whole life. I believed it up until recently, when I finished putting the pieces of this story together, and now . . . now I think Laura was right. I'm determined to get to the bottom of this,' she says firmly. 'Javier did all he could with the police, but got nowhere. It wasn't the time of year when they had money around from the harvest, and Eduardo would never have resisted a burglar. He'd have handed over his wallet and his watch. At one point Javier thought that his brother might have committed suicide, because of how desperate he had seemed, and that maybe Mariana and the Dufaus had made up the whole business of the burglary to cover it up. A suicide would reflect badly on Mariana. But Laura always believed it wasn't a suicide or a burglary, just plain murder.'

Amalia felt a bit sad after talking to her daughter.

'She's terribly upset because Eduardo hasn't come home. It was so hard to say: "Don't worry, he'll be back soon." Do you think she'll suffer dreadfully?'

Alfonso has relaxed at last, ever since he heard Animal utter the words 'mission accomplished' over the phone. He's been under too much pressure for days. He does his best to reassure his wife that the two of them will do all they can to comfort her. 'Think how much more she would have suffered if we'd let that madman carry on any longer, Amalia. Her husband would have left her and they'd have taken away her daughter. There would have been a huge scandal and it would have been very dangerous for all of us.'

'Yes, you're right. Mariana's young and attractive, and she's such a sweet girl. She'll get her life back together.'

At that moment Amalia had an idea that made her smile. The first person she would call with the news would be Inés Ventura.

'Amalia had wanted to be connected to the Ventura family for ages. She admired them. Years ago, when Mariana's twin sisters were born, Amalia chose Inés and Daniel, who was only a boy then, as godparents. And when they killed Eduardo, Daniel had just left his wife.'

At twelve thirty their luggage was all ready to go. Miriam insisted on waiting, saying Eduardo would be there any minute. Yes, of course it would be extremely difficult for him, as Frank had pointed out, but she was sure his wife wouldn't succeed in changing his mind, and he wouldn't give way to his father-in-law's threats.

'Frank was getting more and more nervous and he went down to the hotel bar. That's where he heard on the news that Eduardo had died. Neither of them believed the story about the robbery. He asked for the bill immediately.'

He took Miriam in his arms. 'They've killed him; they killed him last night.'

'They left the hotel at once. Two days later they flew to the States, where they're still living. Miriam was very much afraid. Needless to say, there was nothing else she could do. I was really moved by the way she talked about Dad. She wept as if he'd been an old friend.'

Carlos put his hand on hers. He had finally come to accept her calling Eduardo 'Dad', something that had upset him the whole time they had been talking.

Just knowing that the baby was born healthy, even though they have no idea who's got him or where he is, is a huge step forward. Or so her mother says, and Dolores agrees. The hope of finding him suddenly seems substantial; now there's something concrete to go on. They are looking for a boy born at the end of July 1976 in the Campo de Mayo Military Hospital.

Dolores is dying to get hold of Eduardo so she can share the feeling of wrenching joy that she got when she heard the news. The Abuelas were given the tip-off over the phone. The man didn't want to give his name; he was obviously very afraid. He had seen Mirta Ballerini, Pablo's girlfriend, in the Epidemiological Unit on the men's ward at the Campo de Mayo Hospital, which was where they held prisoners whose admission wasn't registered. He knew for certain that she had had a boy, that he was healthy, and that she had named him Pablo. Mirta had asked him to tell her family. The man had said he would, but he hadn't done so. He couldn't, he said, as if trying to excuse himself. That was all he knew. Then he hung up. It matched other descriptions, the Abuelas explained. They used to take pregnant women from various different detention centres to that ward when they went into labour.

Mirta's fate wasn't hard to imagine: a transfer, death. But there's no information about what happened to the child. Dolores knows that neither she nor her family nor the Abuelas will rest until they find her nephew. She can already picture him; she imagines the colour of his eyes, his freckles, his curly hair, his smile. Yes, they'll find him, she thinks to herself. She is feeling so triumphant that she decides to tell Eduardo right away; this can't wait.

'No,' says the voice, hesitantly. 'Are you a friend of his?'

She's spoken to this particular secretary several times before. Maybe she's trying to find out who I am, Dolores worries. 'Yes, this is a friend, it's a personal call.'

'I'm terribly sorry, but Mr Eduardo Iturbe died last night.'

She can barely follow what the secretary is saying. The woman weeps as she talks about the burglary, the shot, and some sort of problem with the wake. 'The funeral is on . . .' Dolores hangs up and stands motionless and dry-eyed until her mother comes over, where she breaks down and clings to her. 'They've killed him, they've killed Eduardo.'

'Dolores told her mother everything she knew. And it was her mother, Susana Collado, who went to the Abuelas in 1983 and reported that General Dufau's

daughter, who was Eduardo Iturbe's widow, had a little girl who she had reason to believe was born in captivity, although she couldn't say so for sure. Dolores never discovered what Eduardo and Miriam had talked about. I was the one who told her. Nothing ever came of Susana Collado's statement, because there was nobody looking for me from the other side, no relatives. But the fact that Susana had discussed it with the Abuelas meant that they eventually gave in and allowed me to take the blood test, although they wouldn't at first.'

PART THREE
1995–8

THIRTEEN

I SPLASH MY FACE and head with water, trying to cool down. I'm seething with rage and desperation after the fight with Mum – I feel like smashing against something. I hurl myself down on the bed and take deep breaths.

I'm always telling myself not to listen, not to let her get under my skin, and most of all not to answer back because that only makes things worse. The thing is, she knows just how to hurt me and sometimes I can't help myself.

I don't know how these rows start. The slightest little thing can set them off. Today it was about the car, but it can be anything. One of us says something and then one thing leads to another and she gets more and more furious with me until it's become a horrendous argument and I lose track of what she's saying or why I'm trying to defend myself. She gets more and more vicious – she can run rings round me with words until I'm choking with rage and inadequacy and misery. Eventually, when I can't stand it any longer, I run and shut myself in my room, feeling as if I'm going to explode. Sometimes I walk out because I'm frightened by how much I want to hurt her. But I can't get to her the way she does to me. Although I did the other day – I blew up at her and said some horrible, mean things. Even though I felt sorry afterwards and apologised, she obviously hasn't forgotten.

I want to leave home. I can't take this any more. I can't leave, though; I've got no money and they won't give me any. I could get a job, but Mum won't let me. I wonder why? I mean, you'd think she'd want me out. She can't stand me. She says it would 'look bad'. Who cares what it looks like?

'I'll report you to the police. You're not old enough yet, and you'll just have to do what I say until you're twenty-one.'

261

Daniel was there when she said that, wearing that twisted little smirk of his, the bloody hypocrite. He loves it when Mum and I fight and she says horrible things to me. He hates me too. Things definitely got worse after I criticised his business to Mum, but it's not just that; he's never, ever loved me.

'What's wrong, Luz?' Daniel asked. 'Are you in a bad mood, or just sad?'

'That's just the way she is. She's always been like that, ever since she was little. It's genetic. She goes around looking tragic all the time, like a frightened dog.'

Mum's right, in a way. I've always had these bouts of depression and anxiety. I feel as if I don't know what to do next, as if I'm not where I belong, not at home. It's not just because of the fights with Mum and the nasty feeling I get when Daniel or his cronies stare at me. It used to happen before they got married, for no particular reason. It's like I'm afraid of something, as if I'm carrying this huge weight. As if at any moment something or someone could attack me.

When I was little and we moved to Buenos Aires, I thought it was because I missed Entre Ríos and Dad, and because I wished Mum hadn't married Daniel so quickly and we didn't have to live at his house.

'Seven months after Dad died, we went to live in Buenos Aires, in Daniel's flat. He was at the funeral, and afterwards he came to visit in Entre Ríos several times. I'm sure Amalia got together with Daniel's mother, Inés Ventura, and arranged it all. The Venturas were friends of Alfonso and Amalia, they were the ones who invited us to Punta del Este the summer that Miriam saw me on the beach. They were very rich. When Mariana was widowed, Amalia saw it as an opportunity to strengthen the alliance between the two families. Daniel was a lot older than Mariana, seventeen years older. They got married in church, even though he had been married before, to a divorcee with two kids. Amalia said they'd only lived together. I can still remember the wedding. Everyone else was happy and I was crying. Mum always held it against me that I cried that day.'

But then I started getting used to living in Buenos Aires, to my school and my new friends and my bike and the river. When we moved out to the suburbs, to Martínez, I thought I would finally get over the feeling that I wasn't living in my own home. It was our home, not Daniel's, but it still felt as if there was something missing. I wasn't missing Entre Ríos, it was something indefinable, I didn't know what. The fear was the same. I didn't know what I was afraid of – there was no actual danger, but I always had the sense that something dreadful was hanging over me. It goes back a long way; I've always had it. It must be 'genetic', as Mum says.

I asked her several times why she thought that. 'Was Dad like this too, did he get all anxious and worried like me? Because if it's genetic it must be on Dad's side.' I remember the way he used to tell me stories, and take me horse riding. I remember him smiling, not anxious. But maybe I just didn't realise, I was only seven when he died. Mum never answers. She gets that look that says, I'm not going to say anything, I can't. If I keep on at her about it, she says, 'Look, Luz, don't go making me say something I'd rather not.'

One day it occurred to me that Dad might have had the same thing I do, these sad feelings – I don't know what to call it, this illness – and that maybe he wasn't killed, he committed suicide. Maybe that's why Mum gives me that look and fobs me off whenever I ask about him.

One afternoon when I was feeling really low and she started going on about my genes again, I asked her point blank.

'No, he didn't commit suicide, he was killed during a break-in at the farm. Where do you get these ideas from? You've always had this dark, macabre side that makes you think bizarre things.'

'More than what she said, it was the way she looked at me, as if she were completely taken aback. It was as if she was wondering how her daughter could have turned out like this, as if there was something in me that frightened her. Something I thought or felt – or did. Because whenever she saw me dancing . . .'

Luz looked away, trying to conceal her feelings from Carlos, and said nothing for a long while.

Maybe she's right, because whatever it is, it's something that makes everything go black and I've had it for as long as I can remember.

'Like a blindfold. Something that makes everything go black. But you got rid of it in the end.'

'It took me twenty years!'

My best friend, Gabi, says it's all in my imagination, that I only get upset because I'm scared of Daniel, and with good reason too, because he's a nasty piece of work. Gabi told her mother she couldn't stand him, that she really didn't like him because he looked at her strangely, in a disgusting sort of way, and that she was scared of the thugs of bodyguards who were always hanging round the house. And then her mother told her things about Daniel.

'He's up to his ears in shady deals, he's in the Mafia, which is why he needs bodyguards. It's not because he's got a lot of money. Marita's father is rolling in it and he doesn't have guards at home. I shouldn't really be saying this, but I know that Daniel was horrible to his ex-wife, because Vale told me and she's a relative of hers. That's why his wife threw him out. She and the kids don't want anything more to do with him. You can sense that there's something dangerous about him, that's why he scares you. Don't go thinking strange things. Your mother's talking rubbish when she says it's genetic.'

'I never could stand Daniel. At some point in my teens I started absolutely loathing him. He used to make me horribly unsure of myself and anxious. I always wanted to run away because of him. I felt as if there was something unnatural about living with them. I used to put it down to my fights with Mum and my awkwardness around Daniel, but ever since I started trying to find out who I was, I've wondered if that feeling of unnaturalness, of not really being at home, might have been some kind of intuition. It's hard to explain, but it got a lot stronger when my son was born. That was when I started looking for something that would make sense of why I'd felt so uncomfortable until then. And I found it,' Luz smiled triumphantly. 'And here I am, in Madrid. With you.'

Gabi can't stand Mum either. She hasn't said so, but it's obvious. Especially when I told her how Mum reacted when I said I knew Daniel needed bodyguards because of the kind of work he did.

'I bet she denied it,' Gabi said. 'But it's true, I know – Mum and Dad told me. All sorts of people know. He feathered his own nest while the army was in power and now he's doing the same thing with the new government.'

Mum didn't deny it, she just said it didn't matter. I was so furious I demanded to know what Daniel did exactly, because I had no idea. She said that women don't understand business and that she keeps out of her husband's affairs, and how dare a brat like me ask questions. They gave me everything I wanted, didn't they? I should be very grateful to Daniel.

'*Mariana was always complaining about my not being grateful and not appreciating the fact that Daniel gave me so many things even though he wasn't my real father. Although it was Daniel she meant, I think she felt the same way herself, that I should be grateful to her for giving me so much even though she wasn't my real mother. And she did give me things, lots of them.*'

'There was a court case, but he's so rich he got off. He must have bribed the judges and covered everything up. Your mother can't not know what he does; after all, she is married to him,' Gabi said indignantly. 'Maybe she just doesn't want to know.'

I never asked Mum about it again, there was no point, she wouldn't tell me anything and she'd only get incensed with me for being nosy. I didn't say anything about that bodyguard of Daniel's either. The way he looked at me frightened me, so I used to avoid going out into the garden when he was there. But one afternoon I didn't see him; I was sunbathing and all of a sudden he was touching me. I jumped up and glowered at him. I was more livid than scared. 'If you ever lay a finger on me again, you'll regret it,' I told him. And he never did.

I didn't tell Daniel. What could I have said? Even he looks at me sometimes in a way that makes me wish the ground would swallow me up. He can't stand me, but all the same, sometimes he stares at me – I don't know, as if he fancied me. Twice I saw him spying on me through my bedroom door, when I was much younger. So now whenever I'm changing I lock the door. If I'd told Mum that the guard had touched me, or that I saw Daniel spying on me, I bet she'd have blamed me for it. She'd think I'd just made it up. She'd put it down to the black thing in my head or, even worse, in my body. She's thought that ever since the day she drove down by the river and caught me kissing my boyfriend Guillermo. Or even before that, when I used to dance.

In the end it was Carlos who broke the silence, because Luz seemed unable to go on, lost in memories that brought pain to her face.

'*When you danced? What do you mean?*'

'*I don't know. Mariana just couldn't stand it. I've always loved dancing. It makes me really happy and relaxed. At first she didn't say anything, she would just come in and turn the music off and give me a funny look. But then one afternoon, when I was about thirteen, I was out on the patio dancing with the music turned right up. I was having a wonderful time and it gave me an awful shock when I saw the expression on Mum's face. It was absolutely terrible. She started yelling her head off. "How can you dance that way?" and on and on like that, where had I learned to move like that, I ought to be ashamed of myself, I looked like a –'* Luz *stopped, as if reluctant to say the word or relive the scene in front of Carlos. 'Needless to say, I never let her catch me dancing in the house again. I used to dance in my room, with the door closed. Or else when they went out at night; that was great, because then I'd have the whole patio, the whole house to myself, and I could dance as much as I wanted.' She grinned. 'Oh, I had good times too.' Her eyes brightened as she looked up at Carlos. 'After all I've said, you must think that my childhood was just awful, but it wasn't. There was definitely a down side because of all the tension and clashes with Mum and the uneasy feeling I got around Daniel, but there were lots of other things too. I used to have loads of fun dancing and daydreaming and reading, enjoying the sunshine and riding my bike and swimming and going out with my friends.'*

Mum got out of the car. I didn't see her until she came running up and grabbed my arm.

'What are you doing?' she shrieked.

We were only kissing. She dragged me off to the car and told Guillermo she didn't want to see him at the house ever again. I shouted her down on the way home.

'Why did you do that? You're nuts, Guille's my boyfriend. What's the problem?'

We were both screaming at once. The problem, according to her, was that people could have seen us out on the street and then what would they think? She wasn't surprised I was behaving like a tart and a slut because it was genetic, but she'd soon sort me out.

I wasn't sleeping with Guillermo at that point, we only started afterwards. I'm not clear how much Mum influenced my decision. She was so sure that we were sleeping together, I thought we might as well be. As far as she was concerned, the shameless way I behaved in public proved I was having sex with Guillermo and God knows how many other men. She forbade me to go out with him. 'You can tell he's from a broken home.' Although she thought it was my fault anyway, and that I must have led him on. In her eyes it's always the woman's fault because 'a man never goes too far with a real lady'. That argument ended the same way as all the others, with her slapping me.

Guille and I carried on seeing each other in secret. I used to skip school and go to his house. Sometimes I would go out with a boy my mother liked and come home early. Guille would be waiting for me in his car at the corner. I used to open the garage door as if I were going into the house and as soon as the other boy had gone, I'd hop into Guille's car and we'd drive off. Until one night I ran into Mum and Daniel as I was getting out of his car. There was an unbelievable scene. Daniel actually told Guillermo he couldn't see me again.

That's not why we broke up, though. Actually the relationship probably lasted longer than it otherwise would have because we enjoyed disobeying Mum's orders not to see each other. But in the end Guille used the situation as an excuse to split up: he said he was fed up with having to jump through so many hoops, and that my parents were mad. He was interested in another girl and over the course of the summer I realised that I didn't love him any more. We ran into each other at a disco in the autumn, and told each other the truth. I said that Mum didn't act that way only with him, that there'd been scenes over another boyfriend too, she was just like that. We still see each other from time to time to catch up; we're good friends.

Guillermo says the reason I'm not interested in anybody now is because of all the hassle I get every time I go out with a bloke. But I don't think that's why; it's just that there's nobody I'm interested in, nobody I really like. Mum doesn't make scenes about everything I do, but whenever I go out with someone she wants to know what he does and where he lives, and then she seems to go slightly insane – I don't know what else to call it – and demands to know if I'm sleeping with him and stuff like that. She's called me a slut several times, not just when she caught me with Guille. Sometimes it's just because I'm wearing some-thing she thinks makes me look common. She told me I couldn't wear the green miniskirt to lectures because people would think I was trying to get off with the lecturers so I wouldn't have to work.

She went raving mad when she found out that one of them had called me; she still goes on about it. I'm petrified José will ring again and Mum will say something awful to him. There's nothing between us and there never has been. I wouldn't dream of trying anything on with him and neither would he. He's a great bloke; he must be married. He called me about my practical work. But if Mum gets an idea in her head she thinks it must be real.

'I was doing an architecture degree – I'm still working on it.'

The other day I was heading off to the university, feeling very tense because I had an exam and I hadn't slept much. I was just checking myself in the mirror when Mum came in and asked why I was looking at myself like that: there was something peculiar about me, I was behaving like a tart, a slut, and was I going to see that bloke, the lecturer. Perhaps because I was so on edge I didn't let it wash over me as usual. I challenged her. I reacted so violently I surprised myself.

'Oh yeah? So is that genetic too? What are you trying to tell me, Mum? That you used to be a tart? Did I inherit it from you?' She was so shocked she couldn't think what to say. I could see her searching for something to retaliate with, some weapon. 'If you're so worried about me being a slut it must be because you feel like one yourself. You married an older man just for his money.' Mum was coming at me with a coat-hanger she had picked up off the bed, but I couldn't stop. 'There's not much difference between you and a prostitute, except that you're more of a hypocrite.'

I ran out before she could hit me; just slammed the door and left. Later I felt bad and apologised to her. I told her I didn't mean it, I knew she loved Daniel, but that she'd struck a raw nerve and I'd said something hurtful just to get back at her. 'Please believe me, Mum, I'm sorry.' But she's still angry; she lashes out at the slightest thing. She kicked up a fuss today at the table, for no reason at all. All I did was ask if I could borrow her car because I was going to a party in the city.

'A party where? At whose house?' she said, all set to pounce and rip me to shreds.

But as it turned out, she couldn't say anything, because she happens to know Verónica's parents, they're friends with her and Daniel, she thinks they're a 'nice family'. So she started off on another tack: maybe I was only planning to be there for a while and then I'd go out flaunting myself on the streets. Driving around on my own late at night. Daniel just sat there with that little grin he gets when Mum humiliates me, enjoying himself.

Later on, she comes in to my room and puts the car keys on my bedside table.

'It's OK, I'm not going. I don't feel like it,' I say.

She pretends to be pleasant and says don't be silly, I should go, I'm bound to have a good time and meet some people, better than those I've been seeing lately.

She thinks my university friends are dangerous. She would have liked me to go to Belgrano not the University of Buenos Aires. It was hard for her to accept that it's not a hotbed of communism, until Daniel told her, 'Things have changed, Mariana. Nobody cares about communism any more.' All the same, she doesn't think it's safe.

'Luz, you really should go to this party and meet some new people.'

Now I don't know whether I want to go or not. I have this problem a lot, either because she refuses to let me go out or because she begs me to. I get cross with myself when I see I'm just reacting to her. Whether I'm going along with her or disobeying her, it all boils down to the same thing. Why doesn't she just leave me alone? I don't want to go to this party at Verónica's because of her, but I don't want to stay away because of her either. It occurs to me to go 'flaunting myself', as she puts it, but I push the idea out of my mind. What exactly is flaunting oneself anyway? I'd better not ask. I mustn't let her get to me. I don't really feel like doing anything at all.

Gabi rings to ask if I can give her a lift. She's going to the party, and she talks me into it.

'If we get bored, we can always go somewhere else.'

Go and flaunt ourselves, I think, and it almost appeals to me.

'OK,' I say. 'I'll be round at nine. We can have something to eat and then go on from there.'

Ramiro didn't feel like going anywhere. He was enjoying the conversation; why stop to go to a party with a whole lot of people he didn't know and didn't want to know either?

'I've got to go,' Rafael said. 'Verónica will be upset if I don't. It's her birthday. Oh, go on, come with me. Besides, I told her you were coming.'

Ramiro gave in. They paid the bill and left. Rafael asked him in the lift on the way up not to abandon him if he got off with someone, to at least leave with him.

'Who do you think I am, your nurse?'

He was only asking because he didn't want to get into an awkward situation with Verónica, his ex; she was still in love with him.

'Don't worry. I'm not planning to get laid. We can go whenever you want.'

They agreed that if the situation got tricky for Rafael, Ramiro would come to his rescue by saying they had another party to go to. But things didn't turn out according to plan, because Ramiro never even saw Rafael's frantic gestures. He was too engrossed dancing with Luz to notice.

'I met Ramiro on the dance floor.' Luz's expression was different now, radiant. 'We fell in love dancing.'

Rafael started dancing his way across the floor to Ramiro and Verónica followed him.

'You bloody idiot. You were supposed to come and say we were going to another party. What are you waiting for?' Rafael said in his ear.

But Ramiro was too absorbed following the turn Luz was doing as Rafael spoke; he was waiting for the moment when his arm would meet her waist: now. Rafael said nothing. Luz and Ramiro's movements meshed to the rhythm as if they were composing it themselves, inventing it. Their bodies revelled in the symmetry of the salsa, and all that followed. They never stopped dancing, although they had barely exchanged names. They danced to all the Latin rhythms, as well as rock and reggae, the whole gamut. At one point Rafael demanded, 'Look, are we going or not?' Ramiro didn't even look round; he was too enthralled by Luz's body, glued to her every move.

'You go, if you like, or stay. I'm not going to stop dancing until she does.'

That only happened a long while later. They almost gave up when the techno music came on. It sounds like the engaged signal on the phone, Ramiro said, and Luz nodded; but with Ramiro she even liked dancing techno.

In the end it was she who gave up first.

'I'm dying for a Coke.'

Ramiro said he could do with a gin and tonic, too. Only then did he remember about Rafael.

'I'll be right back. I've got to find Rafael.'

He couldn't see him anywhere. He rather hoped he had left. As he searched the living room, the balcony and the hall, he couldn't help having visions of leaving the party with Luz, getting to know her, kissing her. But he eventually found Rafael, weaving around in the hallway, having obviously had way too much to drink.

'I'm sorry,' he said.

Rafael put his hand on Ramiro's shoulder and walked back to the living room with him. There was no need to apologise; on the contrary, if it hadn't been for him and that girl – 'who's fantastic, by the way' – Rafael would have made the mistake of his life by leaving the party. He ducked his head and his eyes gleamed. 'Vero is having a shower so she'll look more presentable. She says it always shows when she's, you know, done it,' he shouted in Ramiro's ear.

'Where's your friend the dancer?' he asked. 'I want to thank her.'

Rafael kissed Luz and thanked her so enthusiastically that she got the giggles.

'That's OK. I'm glad I helped you get back together with Verónica, but you should thank your friend here too – I'm afraid I don't remember your name.'

'You don't even know his name! And look at him. I'm telling you, I've known him for years and this is the first time I've ever seen him head over heels like this.'

Verónica came over and Rafael hugged her and carried on babbling drunkenly. 'Look, Vero, these two are in love too. This is a great party! Come on, let's dance.'

'I'm Ramiro. And your name is Luz, right?'

'You got back very late last night. Did you go somewhere else afterwards?'

She was trying to get me going again, but I was in such a good mood I let it pass.

'No, I stayed at Verónica's party the whole time. It was brilliant,' I said.

I could see she was dying to snap at me – she was just getting ready to fire off one of her little barbs, but I didn't give her the chance.

'Thanks for letting me have the car, Mum.'

And I walked out before she could say anything else. This afternoon I'm going to meet Ramiro and I don't want to get dragged into a fight with her and ruin my mood. It's lucky I'd got over yesterday's row by the time Ramiro started dancing with me. Talking and joking around with Gabi and then the great music helped me get it out of my system. I started dancing almost as soon as I arrived at the party; I didn't feel like talking to anyone. He never said anything, just started dancing opposite me, and that's how it began. It was brilliant, he followed my every move like a mirror image, everything I did. He took my hand and twirled me round, and then I started following his lead. I felt as if I was flying, or swimming; it was as if we were inventing a whole new form. Even our bodies felt brand new. I'm positive he felt the same way. When he was leading me in the salsa, our feet and hips were totally in synch, as if we'd been practising together for years. Dancing with him was amazing. By the time we went to get a drink, it was as if we'd known each other for ages. Maybe that's why his friend, Vero's boyfriend, said that we were in love. God, he was pissed. It felt right when he said it, though. It was ridiculous, really, because I couldn't even remember Ramiro's name, but we danced as if we were lovers.

We didn't talk much when we went to get a drink; hardly at all, in fact. It was odd. But I liked the fact that he didn't say much, because I was thinking, 'Oh God, if he turns out to be a prat after the way he dances, it'll be such a shame.' I wanted to go on fancying him, and even though we were sitting having a drink, I felt like we were still dancing and I didn't want the spell to be broken. Neither of us asked any questions. I don't know what he does, or how old he is, I only know he's a fantastic dancer and that he's got really nice hands and expressive eyes.

It felt good just to sit there in silence. I didn't feel uncomfortable at all, even though I couldn't think of anything to say to him. We were on the same wavelength sitting there quietly as we had been when we were dancing.

After a while they put on a song by Caetano Veloso and I stood up and looked at him and he came up and put his hand on my waist and we started dancing again and didn't stop until it was very late. There was hardly anybody left at the party by the time I told him I'd got to go.

'I'll drive you,' he said laconically.

'No, thanks, I've got the car.'

'I'll go with you, then.'

I said no, because I live a long way out, in Martínez.

'Doesn't matter.'

'You won't be able to get back from there.'

'I'll manage.'

I loved the way he only said the bare minimum, and I was pleased he was coming with me. He didn't say much in the car either – just that I drove the same way I danced.

'Which is what?'

'Confidently. Everything you do is just so. It's great.'

He touched my cheek and I sensed the electricity between us.

When we got to the turn-off by the river, I told him we were almost there and he asked if he could see me again today and wrote my phone number down.

I didn't want to open the garage door because it's really noisy and if Mum was listening and decided to come down and cause a scene because of the time (it was dawn by that point) she would spoil everything. I turned off the engine and let the car roll forward just in front of the garage door on the street.

'Aren't you going to park it inside?' asked Ramiro.

'No, I can't be bothered.'

He brushed my cheek with his lips, short and sweet, the way he talks. I don't quite know what happened, whether I sat there gawking at him or whether he thought better of it, because then he gave me a long French kiss that almost blew me away.

I got out of the car and went in quickly, without looking back. I sat down in the entrance hall and waited, in a daze, staring out at the gorgeous dawn sky, until I thought he would be out of sight, and then I went out again and parked the car in the garage. Mum would have hit the roof otherwise.

'Luz, it's for you.'

We're going to meet at the Plaza de San Isidro, at seven. He offered to come and pick me up, but I said no. Mum and Daniel aren't going out tonight and I don't want any problems. I don't want Mum asking who he is; I don't have the foggiest idea what his surname is or what he does or where he lives or any of the things she always wants to know. She's bound to disapprove of him for some reason or other.

Luz carried on lying about Ramiro to Mariana for three months after she started going out with him, without really knowing why. She didn't know for sure what Mariana would think of him. The prospect of listing all the things she would approve or disapprove of sickened her, but she couldn't help doing it anyway. Her mother would approve of the fact that he lived in Palermo. Luz had seen his house and met his parents, and she hadn't noticed anything that Mariana wouldn't like. But she would never tell her that she'd slept with Ramiro and that the next morning, when his mother found them in the kitchen, she'd said hello as if it was the most natural thing in the world. Mariana couldn't object to the fact that Ramiro's father was dead and that his mother had remarried, because she had done the same thing herself. Ramiro's father had been killed too, but not in a robbery: by the army. Ramiro was five years old at the time. How could she say to him, 'When you meet Mum, you'd better not tell her about that, she's a general's daughter'? A general who was 'saved by the Law of Due Obedience', according to her friend Natalia.

'I didn't even know what that was. I was eleven when the Law of Due Obedience was passed. As you can imagine, it was never discussed at home. Or maybe it was, but I just wasn't paying attention. They must have talked about it a lot at my friend Natalia's house, though, because one day we got into a fight for some reason and she said to me, "You can just shut up, because your granddad is one of those bastards who got off because of Due Obedience." When I asked Mariana what Due Obedience was, she asked me why I wanted to know. She practically interrogated me, and I ended up defending Natalia, even though we

274

were furious with one another. Natalia's parents had met Mum and Alfonso and
Amalia at the school sports day.

'So your school had a sports day?' Carlos interrupted. 'Sounds like you went to
a posh school then.'

'Yes, it was an English school, Saint Catherine's.'

'And what did Mariana say about Due Obedience? What was her version?'

'She didn't explain anything. She said that the only people who talked like that
were riff-raff and subversives and she absolutely forbade me to speak to Natalia. It
was outrageous that a girl like that was allowed in my school. In the end it was
Natalia who explained it to me. She felt sorry for what she'd said and apologised.
She said it was something she had heard about at home. Her mother had told her
she wasn't keen on her being friends with me either, but she didn't tell her she
couldn't, like mine did. I begged her to explain it to me because I didn't know
what it was. She gave me the version of a thirteen year old who'd been brought up
in a family with very different politics from my own. I was kind of confused about
the whole thing afterwards; I didn't understand properly what Natalia said, but
from then on, I felt uncomfortable whenever I saw Alfonso, although he was always
very sweet to me. I couldn't possibly ask Mariana and I didn't dare talk to Alfonso
or Amalia. So I didn't work it out until much later, and then it was thanks to
Ramiro. He became one more link in the chain that made me start trying to find
out who I was.'

It was very painful for Ramiro to talk about his father's disappearance,
but he did. His parents had separated two years beforehand, but his
father, who he called a 'brilliant, fantastic person', always came to fetch
him for visits and once or twice his mother had taken Ramiro to see him.
The last time, they had gone to a house in El Tigre where his father was
in hiding.

'I remember Mum and Dad hugging each other goodbye. And I
remember when Mum told me. She didn't say he was dead; she said he
had fallen, and that we'd probably never see him again. They were
separated, but they still loved one another.'

After his father disappeared, Ramiro and his mother went into
exile in Mexico, where they lived until 1984. Marta, Ramiro's
mother, got remarried while she was there, to Antonio, another
Argentinian exile.

'The things Ramiro told me about his life gave me a different perspective on Argentinian history. Even though he was surprised when I started obsessing about where I'd come from,' Luz smiled, 'he had a lot to do with getting me started. Not consciously, just by what he took for granted. When he talked about what he had heard at home ever since he was a boy, I realised there was a different history, a different way of talking, a different way of seeing the world. Above all, he'd had much more freedom and access to information than me.'

They were at Ramiro's home when he told her how he had sat in on parts of the trial of the Juntas in 1985, when he was fourteen, and how he had read or rather devoured the newspaper reports of it as it was going on, as if he might find his father or avenge him in some way.

Luz listened and watched in rapt attention. She burst into tears as she relived with him the afternoon when the worst bastards of all, Admiral Massera and General Videla, were sentenced to life imprisonment. Ramiro had drunk a toast to the sentence with his mother and Antonio.

'But Alfonsín passed the Laws of Due Obedience and Punto Final, which stopped people pressing any more charges related to the dirty war. And then came the pardon. Menem pardoned them after they had been tried and condemned, do you realise that? God, that man is so fucking despicable. This country's got amnesia.'

Due Obedience; her friend Natalia. Luz jumped off Ramiro's bed, as if ejected by those two words. She sat down on the floor opposite him.

'What was the Law of Due Obedience?'

'God, Luz, what planet are you on?'

'I want you to explain it to me properly. I was only little when it happened.'

'The Law of Due Obedience was passed in 1987, and it meant that hundreds of lower-ranking torturers and murderers were set free, that they can't be held responsible, because they were simply following orders. As if anyone could make you do the kinds of horrific things they did.'

Luz said something, but so slowly that he had to ask her to repeat herself because he couldn't hear. Something about the expression on her face made him pull her closer and hug her.

'What's wrong, love, what are you looking like that for?'

Luz turned her head and looked the other way as she spoke.

'My grandfather, Mum's father, is one of them. He got off because of the Law of Due Obedience.'

I felt ashamed as I told him, dreadfully ashamed, but it was a huge relief too. I couldn't carry on listening to the things he was telling me and feeling so close to him, and loving him so much, and go on hiding the fact that my grandfather is one of those 'fucking officers', as he calls them. I'm glad I've told him, even though at first he took it badly. He took his arm off my shoulder and stood up with his back to me, and then turned round and stared at me for a long time, looking extremely serious. I just held his stare and didn't say anything. Now at last I don't have to feel like a fraud, which is how I've been feeling when he told me things and I tried to avoid giving away what I'd heard at home, or rather what I hadn't heard. Ramiro knew practically nothing about me or my life until yesterday – just that I live in Martínez and that I don't get on with Mum and that she makes a fuss about the blokes I like, so I'd rather Ramiro doesn't meet her. When I told him about Granddad I felt as if I were finally being myself, come what may. I've owned up to being their daughter and granddaughter; I'm me, the real me. I felt free, the way I feel when I dance or when we make love.

'Look, Luz, the fact that you're Dufau's granddaughter makes me sick,' Ramiro said. 'Can you understand that?', and I shrugged. I didn't know what to say. What was I supposed to do? I didn't know if I understood, but it hurt to hear that I made him sick. I'm not my grandfather, I'm me.

I just sat there on the carpet and didn't say anything. Ramiro suddenly slammed his fist down on the desk as if he were furious.

'I'm such an idiot, I shouldn't have said that. It's just that this has never happened before, I've never had anything to do with anyone who was connected to the military. Luz, your grandfather was . . . You do know, don't you?'

I shook my head, hating myself for never having asked before. After what Natalia said, I think I'd avoided the subject. Ramiro started asking me all sorts of things I didn't know the answers to. I got really upset and he hugged me. I could tell he loved me but he thought it wouldn't work out, and I said so.

As I said it I kept kissing him and he kissed me back, but all of a sudden he drew away. He said he didn't feel well, he needed to think, on his own, and that maybe he'd better take me home.

'No, there's no need, I can go by myself.'

I picked up my bag and my books and walked out. I could hear him calling while I was going down in the lift, but I just carried on. He caught up with me at the corner and asked me not to leave like that. He hadn't meant to upset me, it was just it had been a big shock for him and he'd taken it the wrong way. We went for a drink and somehow I started telling him things about my life, about Mum and Daniel. Things I'd have been ashamed to say before but which kept coming out anyway, as if I'd been carrying a great weight for years and the only way to get rid of it was by talking to Ramiro. Part of me needed just to say whatever I felt like, and if he didn't like it, too bad.

But he loves me, he really does. We stayed up until four in the morning and made love. It was fantastic, amazing, incredible, much better than ever before. I'm sure it's because I'd taken off my mask and was just being myself, my real self. Now I can tell him all that stuff I was bottling up without even knowing. When we made love this time I felt new things, things I'd never felt before – it was incredibly powerful. Maybe it's because of everything that had happened between us. It's as if it made us more naked and needy.

When he took me home, he said that he's going to come and pick me up today and that he wants me to introduce him. He thinks it's absolutely ridiculous to go on lying, and he's right. Why should I have to hide this relationship, when it's so wonderful? Last night all that sounded well and good, but now I'm scared to death.

Mum did ask about him once, when he rang to speak to me. I told her that he was a friend of Verónica's, as if I had nothing to do with him. I've lied to her systematically. Every time I'm with him, I tell her I'm somewhere else.

Contrary to all expectations, Mariana behaved graciously when she was introduced to Ramiro. The next day she asked the usual questions and

Luz told her the bare minimum so she wouldn't get annoyed. Although she had promised Ramiro not to go on lying to her mother, Luz omitted some things, skipping the parts she thought Mariana might not approve of and stressing those she knew would reassure her: that he was a friend of Verónica, that he was a designer at an advertising agency and that she really liked him.

Fortunately for Luz, Mariana was very preoccupied at the time planning a long holiday in the Caribbean and she left her pretty much to her own devices. Luz was particularly nice to her and even smiled a lot.

'You seem happy, Luz. What's wrong, are you ill?' Daniel joked over lunch one day.

Mariana gave her an inquisitive glance, scanning her face for something to object to. Luz tried to look as blank as possible.

'What? What's wrong?'

The telephone rang, breaking the silence between them. Luz was afraid Mariana would send her to stay with Alfonso and Amalia while she was away, or with one of her twin aunts. There was no way she'd let them do that, because it would mean she wouldn't be able to see Ramiro. But Mariana came back exultant from her phone call.

'Something had just come through, you know, like managing to hire the best boat for the Caribbean cruise or getting a reservation at a posh hotel, the sort of thing that makes her happy. Luckily whatever it was was important enough for her to forget about me, so I was let off the hook. Otherwise I'd be at my grandparents' for sure by now.'

'Well, you wouldn't catch me going to see you there,' said Ramiro.

FOURTEEN

M UM RANG TODAY to say that she won't be coming back for another two weeks. Brilliant. I wish it was two years; I could never have spent all this time with Ramiro if the two of them were here. I'm basically living at his place – I work, eat, dance, talk, make love, and sleep there. I don't know what I'm going to do when they come back, it'll be really hard.

Ramiro left home and rented a flat in Belgrano: Luz helped him move. They spent hours together; often Luz would stay until dawn and then rush home because she felt she ought to be there before the maids woke up. Ramiro thought it was absurd to be living a lie – it was bad for her.

'Luz, stop playing these silly games and grow up. If your parents won't let you do that, then leave. Actually, leaving home would be the best thing for you.'

'I can't just leave – where would I get the money? There's no way they'd let me have any.'

'Well, come and live with me, then.'

'No. I don't want to move in with you just to get away from home.'

'Why? Don't you want to live with me? Wouldn't you like to fall asleep and wake up in bed together and share everything?'

Luz's face lit up, but her smile quickly faded.

'You're only saying that because you want to get me away from my family.'

'That too, but that's not the only reason. I don't care if it's mad for us to live together, that's the way I feel and that's what I want.'

Luz did too, but she knew it was impossible. Mariana would go to any lengths to stop them – she'd even take them to court.

Ramiro didn't believe it. 'She's just saying that to scare you. It's all talk.'

Luz was well aware that it wasn't, but she decided it was worth the risk. She asked Ramiro if he could handle the scenes Mariana was sure to make. He shouldn't be surprised if she turned up at his flat or his parents' house and raised hell. Luz didn't want their magical time together to be spoilt by the horrible, loaded atmosphere her mother generated.

'Can you hear what you're saying, Luz? You just called it a "horrible, loaded atmosphere" and yet you want to go on living there?'

All the same, she was exaggerating, thought Ramiro. Mariana was her mother, after all; there was no way she would take Luz to court, as if she were a criminal.

When Ramiro told his mother, Marta, about their decision, she looked worried.

'Be careful, Ramiro. Luz's mother is Dufau's daughter. You're lucky you don't know those people.'

Marta approved, though. 'I think it's wonderful the two of you are in love. Who cares that you haven't been going out for very long? If you love each other and you want to be together, why not? It's just the other part that worries me, that dreadful family of hers. It might catch up with you.'

Luz still had doubts, but Ramiro gradually persuaded her that it wouldn't be the huge drama she imagined; they'd be so happy together that it wouldn't matter if they had to put up with some hassle at the beginning. They would throw a birthday party for Luz and invite all their friends and dance until dawn. Living together would be fun.

Luz took her bag over to Ramiro's the day before Mariana got back. She had decided not to leave before Mariana's return; she wanted to tell her the truth and give her a chance to show if she cared at all, if she was capable of empathising. Luz had it all planned out. The first thing she would mention would be love. She would tell Mariana how happy she was because she'd fallen in love. Her mother must have been in love with her father once. Had Mariana and Eduardo loved one another? Mariana had never talked about it. In the name of love and truthfulness, Luz didn't want to lie to her: she and Ramiro had decided to move in together, right away.

After seeing Mum's reaction to the first few things I said, I gave up any hope of ever getting close to her or having the kind of conversation where I could ask if she'd ever been in love with Dad.

'Yes, Eduardo married Mariana, but so what? What's wrong with that? It doesn't mean he was like them. He must have been very much in love,' said Luz.

'I could never have fallen in love with the daughter of some army brute.'

'Ramiro fell in love with someone he thought was Dufau's granddaughter, and he knew who Dufau was.'

'He's from a different generation – or maybe you were different. But Eduardo married Mariana.'

Luz looked away impatiently. Carlos made an effort to let go of his irritation, resentment and jealousy. Yes, jealousy. Even though it was difficult for him to admit it, Carlos was jealous of Eduardo. It bothered him that Luz loved and defended him.

'Listen, the man who married Mariana lost his life finding out who I was. Maybe you would never have married into an army family. But you're my own flesh and blood, and what did you do for me?'

Carlos bowed his head. He didn't try to justify himself, but simply laid his hand timidly on top of hers. He would have to give it time, he told himself, but this feeling of Luz's would eventually wear off and be replaced with something else. At that moment, Carlos felt for the first time like her father.

No, it's impossible to ask this woman anything. I've just told her I'm head over heels in love, and all she can do is point out that there's a dreadful stain on the sofa. She calls angrily for the maid to demand an explanation. I've been listening to them talk for fifteen minutes about the stain and the stain remover and how careless it was of the maid to drop that tray on the sofa. I decide to cut down what I was going to say.

'What were you saying, Luz? Oh yes. And who are you in love with?'

'Ramiro,' I say, as she tries to remove the stain. 'Do you remember him? The bloke I introduced you to before you went on holiday.'

'Oh yes.' She doesn't even look at me. 'You see? It's not coming out.

And I'll never be able to replace the fabric. It's English and they've stopped importing English cloth.'

Why wait?

'Mum, I'm going to live with Ramiro, today.'

I've got her attention at last. She jumps up and faces me, eyes blazing.

'Are you out of your mind? What are you talking about?'

'You heard. I'm going to live with Ramiro. I didn't move out before because I was waiting to tell you. I wanted to leave, not run away,' I say from the doorway.

I don't make it through the door because she grabs my arm. I can feel her nails digging into my flesh. She drags me back into the living room. I lose track of what she's saying; it's all accusations and threats, an angry drone that I can't shut off or bear to listen to a moment longer. She calls after me as I run down the stairs and before the front door closes I hear her shout, 'You'll never set foot in this house again.'

If only that were true, I thought to myself, but by the evening I was crying too much to sleep. Ramiro told me not to worry, it was to be expected, we both knew it wasn't going to be easy. He didn't want me to pretend; I didn't have to put on a happy face if I didn't feel happy. But I couldn't stop wondering what she'd do to get back at me. How would she go about it? She didn't have Ramiro's address or even a phone number. I would rather not have left like that, but she didn't give me any option. It drove me mad that she cared more about the stain on the sofa than what I was telling her. And when I said I was moving in with Ramiro, she just yelled and started saying all those stupid things.

The first sign came the next day when they had a call from Mariana's friend, Verónica's mother. She had got the number from Rafael.

She asked Ramiro why they were doing this. They should try and put themselves in Luz's mother's place; she didn't know him or where he lived. She knew nothing about him.

'And besides, Luz is only eighteen.'

'You let Verónica go and stay with Rafael at the weekends,' Ramiro argued. 'Luz isn't allowed any leeway, she had no choice but to do this.'

She said she would like to talk to his mother, if he didn't mind.

'Not at all.'

Ramiro was furious. He told Luz he was sure his mother would soon deal with that stupid bloody cow.

However, it wasn't Verónica's mother who rang Marta, but Mariana herself.

'I beg your pardon, Mrs . . . I don't know your name. It just shows how ridiculous all this is. I'm Luz's mother. Did you know that Luz is living with your son?'

'Yes, I did.'

Both of them were trying to stay calm. For Mariana, it was vital to get this woman to co-operate. Her friend, Verónica's mother, had said that Marta was a good person and that she was bound to behave decently and help her out. Marta, meanwhile, knew that she needed to resist the overpowering urge to tell Mariana to go to hell, as if doing that to Dufau's daughter were somehow doing it to all of them. If only she could, just once. But she couldn't let her feelings get the better of her, for Ramiro's sake. She didn't want to cause problems for her son.

Mariana suggested that Marta come and see her before she called the magistrate. She would prefer to sort this out privately, amongst them-selves.

'Why would you go to a magistrate?'

'Luz is still under age. I imagine your son is not. He must be twenty-something.'

'Twenty-four. Why?'

The question irritated Mariana and she was about to snap back, but then it occurred to her that actually, even if this woman disapproved of what was going on, it was different for her, because it was her son who was involved. The one who would look like a slut was her own daughter.

'I didn't bring her up to do this sort of thing, believe me,' she explained. Marta, who had been getting more and more indignant, was on the verge of exploding.

'This isn't my problem, it's yours. I've no intention of meeting you, either at your house or mine.' She wasn't going to let Dufau's daughter anywhere near. 'I think this is Luz and Ramiro's business. It's their decision.'

Marta was torn between the urge to get at Mariana and her wish to protect her son as much as possible; now she changed tack and softened her voice.

'Listen, what's your name?'

'Mariana.'

'Mariana, just relax. It's not as bad as all that. They've rushed into this, I know, but they'll soon change their minds if it turns out they made a mistake. They're young. You'll only make it worse by fighting it.'

'So you think it's all right? You think I should just accept it? Look, I don't know how you brought up your son but Luz isn't the type of girl he must have gone out with before.'

'Oh, for goodness' sake.' Marta's patience was running out, one more comment like that and she was going to say something really rude. 'Do what you want. I'm not going to interfere. Goodbye.'

The moment she hung up, Marta rang Ramiro at work and told him what had happened.

'Be careful, love. This could be really nasty for Luz. Why don't you wait a bit? She's still quite young.'

Ramiro was furious. He couldn't believe it. What could that bitch have said to his mother to make her think it was better for Luz to go back home, after everything he'd told her about the family?

'Haven't you just said that woman is awful? What am I supposed to do? Simply abandon Luz?'

'You're right, Ramiro, but be careful. That woman frightened me.'

Marta's heart was in her mouth the rest of the day. She rang Ramiro again and asked if she could come and see them. Once there, she suggested they come and hide at her house for a few days, until things blew over. Luz thought it was a good idea; knowing Mariana, there was no way she'd ever suspect they were at Ramiro's mother's.

'No, I refuse to leave the flat. Why should we have to hide?' Ramiro said indignantly. 'Are you both off your heads? Mum, what year are we in? What's going on?'

'I don't know, it's like a shadow from the past. I have this panicky feeling, the way we used to during those awful years. Luz's mother made me very scared . . . like back then.'

I felt awful when Marta said that the conversation with my mum had brought back the bad old days. I didn't know what she meant, since I was too young at the time. She tried to explain, but the only thing that made sense to me was her fear of Mum, because I'm afraid of her too. I've just thought of something else that's made me feel even worse. What does Mum do when she's in trouble? Call her parents. What if Alfonso decides to intervene? What if Granddad goes to see Ramiro's mother?

'Rami, I'd better go home. I want to live with you, but I can't mess up so many people's lives. Look at the state your mother's in. I wanted it to be fun, the way we envisaged, not like this. I'd better go.'

He said he wasn't going to let me, no way. He was angry at his mother for making me more scared. Poor thing, she didn't do it on purpose – he knew she was just trying to help. 'But honestly, the way she's reacting is ridiculous. This is 1995, not 1976. She's only made you more anxious by coming over. You're not leaving. Don't be scared, sweetheart, nothing's going to happen. I'll protect you.'

But I'm leaving anyway. I can't take another night like this. I don't dare tell Ramiro my fear about Alfonso. I'll just write him a letter and go.

Mariana gave Amalia a blow-by-blow account of her conversation with Marta. Something would have to be done, but she'd rather not invite the scandal of going to a magistrate. Amalia said she would ring her back in a little while; she shouldn't rush into anything.

Alfonso agreed to take care of things himself. That was best. They couldn't leave such a disagreeable task up to Daniel – after all, Luz wasn't his daughter. What an embarrassing situation.

He would go and see the boy's mother himself and make sure she understood the sort of problems her son would encounter if he carried on living with Luz. He thought it would be best to deal with the mother directly. He knew exactly what to say to make her persuade her son to break up with Luz and throw her out.

Amalia said it would be a good lesson for that rebellious girl. 'That way she'll find out what men do when you give them everything for free. Poor little Mariana; look at all the trouble that child creates.' But they'd soon sort her out. 'Do you think it could be . . . genetic? I just can't see why else a nicely brought-up girl like Luz would do something like this. Mariana told me that Luz had already slept with someone by the time she was sixteen. That child's got a devil in her.'

Marta was still shaking when she got to her husband Antonio's surgery.

'Why on earth did you agree to see Dufau? Are you out of your mind, Marta?'

She'd only said yes to stop Dufau going to see Ramiro. She hadn't wanted to give him Ramiro's address or phone number. She had been very frightened and thought it best to deal with him face to face. 'Heaven only knows how far that dreadful man is prepared to go.' But now the mere thought of meeting him was giving her the shivers. 'Antonio, can you come with me? It's tomorrow, at eleven.'

Antonio told her to calm down; he thought she was getting muddled. He understood that Dufau's name brought back hellish memories, but she shouldn't let that colour her opinion.

'Things have moved on, Marta; times have changed. Ramiro's not a child. If anyone has to talk to Dufau it's him.'

There is panic on Marta's face. No, she'd prefer to go herself; she'll put a stop to this if only Antonio will help her. He will, but he wants to make sure she's thought things through.

'Why didn't you tell Ramiro?'

'Dufau asked me not to.'

That was too much; she shouldn't give way to intimidation. They needed to calm down a bit and then talk to Ramiro and Luz that night. They would go home and work out what was best. He didn't want her to go through the agony of sitting down with that murderer; there was no reason for that. Of course he would help her, but not the way she wanted, he didn't think it was right.

The only thing he could do, and the best thing, was to hug and reassure her. 'It will all work out, love; don't be frightened.'

When Marta rang Ramiro to tell him she was coming to visit, he had just read the letter Luz had left him.

'I'm not feeling too good, Mum, I'm sorry. Can we leave it till another day?'

Antonio took the receiver away from her. 'I'm sorry, but we're going to have to see you tonight. Dufau has demanded that Marta meet him. Things are getting out of hand, Ramiro; we need to talk this over. It's not fair to your mother to . . .'

'Don't worry, Luz isn't here any more. She's left me.'

I told her I didn't want to discuss it. I was home to stay and would she please not say a single word, because right then I couldn't face talking.

'Don't think things are going to go back the way they were, as if nothing had ever happened,' she yelled.

'Please, Mum, can we just leave it for today, I've had enough. We can talk some other time. Don't make me go again. Can't you see I'm too sad to talk?'

Fortunately I managed to shut her up. She knows I'm not kidding. She locked herself in her room and I overheard her speaking to Amalia. She must have been telling her that I've come home.

If Luz had left Ramiro, that meant Marta wouldn't have to go and meet Dufau. She was relieved but worried about her heartbroken son.

'Luz is very young. If this thing between you is really as good as you think, you needn't worry, you'll get back together again. She just needs to grow up. Sometimes, Ramiro, you just can't rush things.'

Ramiro and I had been thinking of throwing a party for my nineteenth birthday. I loved the idea of inviting all our friends over to dance. Some birthday it'll be now: I'm going out to dinner with Mum and Daniel. I couldn't say no. She's making a huge effort to keep her mouth shut. When I asked her please not to invite Amalia and Alfonso, she started to get angry.

'Why not? They're your grandparents.'

'Because I'd just rather not, Mum, that's all.'

She didn't say anything else, just walked off wiping her eyes. She's determined to make me feel guilty. But at least one good thing came out of my running away: she doesn't lose her temper with me any more. She starts on at me sometimes, but I look at her and she shuts up. She must be afraid I'll run off again. She's always going on about how embarrassing it was for her.

Ramiro is very upset with me. The other day he came to pick me up from university. He said I was a coward for breaking up with him by letter. I could say whatever I felt like in a letter, but what about him, what about his feelings? He's right. I listened to him. But we can't get back together. I told him our relationship is impossible because I don't want to mess up everybody's lives, but he's too angry to understand. I asked him to stop coming to meet me and ringing me, and he went off believing I don't love him, which isn't true. I do – I just can't be with him. Not now.

There are all sorts of things I need to know. I meant to find something out about Alfonso, but I can't possibly get Mum to tell me. I asked her how involved Alfonso was in the repression and what he did, and all she said was, what kind of a question is that? I told her I just wanted to know, because I'd been hearing things about what went on back then and I knew that since he was in the army, he . . . Then she started going on about the university and how she wanted me to go to Belgrano instead, because the state university is crawling with communists, and that's why I'm against the army.

'It was that pathetic man Alfonsín who started this whole campaign to stigmatise the army, and now look at the state the country's in. Inflation has sky-rocketed, thanks to him.'

She and Daniel were always complaining about how disastrous Alfonsín's government was. I asked her to please answer my question.

'There was a period when this country was being overrun by subversives and the army stepped in and saved the day. It was a war, a dreadful war. Daddy fought in it and I'm proud of him. You should be too, Luz, he's your grandfather.'

Then she started rambling on about how so many people seem to have lost their memory and are going around slandering the army.

She demanded to know why I was so curious all of a sudden. No doubt I'd fallen into bad company. When she gets like that, it's better just to give up because we end up going round and round in circles and I never get a concrete answer. I don't want to start one of those awful rows with her; I don't want to make her angry. Or myself, because I know it's her fault that I split up with Ramiro, although I don't want to say so.

In any case, I'm not prepared to live with Ramiro with all this going on. I don't know if I'll actually be able to stick to my decision. I'm dying to ring him up and tell him I miss him, but there's no point, if I can't be with him. I've got to get down to work; I want to do well in my exams. I've just got to work and not think about anything else, so it won't hurt so much, so I'll get over this empty feeling of wanting Ramiro so much I could die.

Luz did her best to forget Ramiro, but she couldn't. She revised and went to the beach and out with friends, but memories of him kept resurfacing no matter what.

For a while, Mariana and Luz managed to avoid the kinds of arguments they used to have. Mariana was afraid that Luz would run away from home again and that made her more careful. But in January, while they were at Punta del Este, they had a major row. Mariana completely lost her temper and said all the things she'd been bottling up for months.

Luz wanted to go back to Buenos Aires but she knew Mariana would stop her. So she decided to take up the invitation Laura and Javier had extended over the phone at Christmas.

They had not seen much of the Iturbes for several years; they met once or twice a year at most. Laura was the one who stayed in touch; she never lost contact with Luz. Mariana had only allowed her to go and visit them once, when Luz was thirteen. Daniel and Mariana had been going on a trip to Europe for some reason and the Dufaus weren't in Buenos Aires either. Luz had spent a fortnight at the farm and she had good memories of that time.

When she told Mariana of her decision, she avoided making it sound as if it had anything to do with their fight. She simply said that she needed to revise for her exams in March and that she thought it would be a good idea to spend a few days on the farm with her aunt and uncle, because it was difficult to concentrate in Punta del Este. Mariana was obviously suspicious.

'To Entre Ríos? What a ridiculous idea. The heat will be atrocious and you'll be bored to death. If you're lying to me, Luz, you needn't bother; I can ring Laura and Javier and check.'

'Go ahead and ring them, if you want. I've already told Laura I'll be coming on Monday or Tuesday.'

When I came back from my ride, Laura was alone in the house. She told me that my mother had called and that they'd had a little talk. Something in her eyes gave away her long-standing dislike of Mum.

It's obvious to me that they can't bear each other, although neither of them has ever said so. Once in a while Mum would pass some stupid comment, such as Laura is rather loud and uncouth and she gets on her nerves. That must be why whenever Laura's been to visit us in Buenos Aires, Mum always makes up some excuse to be out or to stay only a few minutes.

'What did she say? That I should ring back?'

Laura looked at me and paused before replying.

'She asked me to keep a close eye on you because you're going through a difficult phase. What's happened, Luz? Do you want to tell me about it?'

I was almost sure that Mum hadn't told Laura I'd gone to live with Ramiro. That would be far too close to the bone, as she puts it. She must be really afraid of what I might do to tell Laura anything at all.

I'm really envious of the relationship my cousins Claudia and Facundo have with their parents. Maybe that's why I started talking to Laura about Ramiro and how much I loved him. I wanted to bring him back for a while, if I possibly could. Laura and I had the conversation I'd wanted to have with Mum, the one that didn't work out. Just as I thought, Mum hadn't told her about it. Laura was shocked.

'So you moved in with him? Mariana must have been livid.'

She smiled, as if enjoying picturing Mum's reaction.

'Yes, and I didn't give her the address or the phone number or anything.'

'What happened then? How did it end? Because you went back home.'

I told her everything. She kept encouraging me to go on. What struck me most was the way she reacted when I told her about Ramiro's mother and how terrified she was after talking to Mum.

'Of course,' she said.

'Why of course?'

Laura seemed uncomfortable, as if she wanted to tell me something but knew she couldn't. She didn't come right out with it, but when she started talking about the way things had been under the military, I understood why she'd said 'of course'. There was something else, too, that got me thinking, something to do with Dad's death.

'A while ago, before I really suspected anything, I was given a clue. It was Laura who gave it to me. We were talking about something else, about a problem I was having at the time, and we started discussing Alfonso. She said that Dad hadn't realised for a long while, but that when he did, he refused to toe the line and that . . . She didn't say that's why he was killed or anything like that, but she stammered something that made me sense she was hiding something about his death. I asked her about it, but she wouldn't say anything more until much later, when I was a lot further on with my search.'

She told me a lot of things about the military dictatorship. She said that she had suspected for a long time that Alfonso was involved, but that she never knew exactly what he did. But when she started reading statements from the trial of the Juntas and found out just how savage and brutal the dirty war had been, she realised that my grandfather was 'an absolute bastard, I'm sorry to say, Luz'.

'Why?'

She told me about the secret detention centres and some of the horrific things they did back then. She gave me the newspaper reports of the trial that Ramiro had told me about, as well as the book *Nunca más*.*

---

* *Never Again*. Report by the Argentine National Commission on the Disappeared.

Javier couldn't believe it when Laura said she had given Luz the reports of the trial which she had kept ever since they first came out.

'Why did you do that? I know you loathe Mariana, but you mustn't forget Luz is her daughter, and she'll see . . .'

'Her daughter?' Laura interrupted. 'What do you mean? Have you forgotten that she isn't Eduardo and Mariana's daughter? You should never, ever forget that, even if only for Eduardo's sake.'

Laura never let go of the idea that Eduardo had been assassinated because he was trying to find out about something that might reflect badly on his father-in-law. She never believed the story of the break-in.

Neither did Javier, but he was never certain that what he'd been told wasn't true. He tried to find out more at the time of Eduardo's death, but got nowhere. He suggested a few lines of approach to Mariana and was very hurt by his sister-in-law's attitude. All she said was that she was confident the police would do a good job, and then a few months later she moved to Buenos Aires. One thing was certain: Eduardo's killers had never been found and Mariana had not lifted a finger to keep the investigation alive. But Javier never went beyond feeling hurt that Mariana didn't seem to care. He didn't really believe that Alfonso could have had Eduardo killed, or that Mariana could possibly have been involved.

A few days after the funeral, Mariana was talking to Javier and Laura and some friends and told them how well she and Eduardo got on and how much they loved each other. She claimed that a few days before he died, Eduardo had told her how happy he was that he'd found someone so right for him. She went on in that vein, giving the impression that she was his ideal woman.

Javier tried to swallow this lie as Mariana's way of dealing with the pain. Laura, on the other hand, was so angry that she had to leave so as not to say something unforgivable.

'She's a bloody liar. Eduardo wanted a separation. Why on earth would he say a thing like that? I can't stand her; I hate her guts. The only thing she cares about is what people think.'

'Everyone has their own way of dealing with grief. You've no right to be so judgmental,' Javier had answered. 'They weren't getting on, but they did love each other very much; that's why Mariana felt the need to say that.'

'You think she loved him?' Laura retorted. 'Then why did she never do a thing to find out why he'd been murdered? Because even if she didn't know for sure, she should have suspected that Eduardo's death might have had something to do with her father.'

They hadn't talked about it for years. At some point Laura realised it was too painful for Javier and started avoiding the subject. Why were they arguing about this again? Javier demanded.

'Because of Luz.' Because Luz had told her some things about her life that had revived her suspicions. 'Can you understand that, Javier?'

'You've no idea how much harm you could do if you tell Luz what's on your mind. After all, he is her grandfather.'

'He's a bastard, and he isn't her grandfather.'

'So what are you going to do? Tell Luz that she's not her parents' daughter? Some favour you'll be doing her. Her real mother never showed up again.'

'Maybe they killed her, like Eduardo.'

'Why didn't Miriam ever look for you again?'

'Miriam?' Luz couldn't help herself. 'And what about you? Why did you just give in and accept that you'd had a stillborn boy? Look how wrong you were: here I am. Alive.'

Carlos didn't answer. He simply held her gaze, mutely begging for mercy.

'I'm sorry. I shouldn't say that sort of thing; but I just get so angry. I can't help it.'

'Don't worry, we'll have plenty of time to work through your anger. It's hard to keep all this straight. Put yourself in my place for a minute. You find out at forty-nine that you've got a grown-up daughter with a child and that you're a grandfather.' Carlos laughed nervously. 'It's incredible – you told me you'd got a son, but it hadn't clicked: I'm a grandfather. It usually takes years to get used to the idea, whereas I've found out in a matter of hours. And then there's Liliana, Liliana . . . Luz, of course I understand why you're angry, but I've got enough on my plate trying to deal with my feelings about Liliana and everything that happened, the horrific things they did to her. I thought I'd anaesthetised my grief, but you being here, telling me your story, has opened up the wound again. It's as if

295

she was murdered only a few hours ago, when you told me about how she was mown down . . .'

He faltered and couldn't go on. Luz reached for his hand, sharing his grief for Liliana's death, although in a different way. It's hard to grieve for a mother you never knew. It hurt, of course, but it was not that raw, piercing pain that she could feel in Carlos. When she spoke, it wasn't a question but a statement. 'You loved her very much.'

'I can't tell you how much. We were incredibly close. That's why . . . I couldn't explain it earlier when you asked, but that was our only reason – and I don't care whether it was a good one or not – for wanting you to be born. Everything you've accused me of – that we were irresponsible, that it was our fault you were disappeared, and so on . . . I don't know what to tell you. I've got to rethink all this . . . The only thing I can say is that we wanted you to be born because we loved one another.'

'I'm really glad. It's nice to know I was a wanted child and that you were looking forward to having me. I've spent all my life thinking that wasn't the case. I thought Dad did, but Mum . . . It was hard to feel as if she loved me, even though she probably did, in her own way. But I never knew whether they loved one another; so it's nice to know that you two really did.'

Laura explained to Javier that she'd been very moved by her conversation with Luz. 'Especially when she asked me about it; you know, I felt like hugging her. I told her a lie . . . or maybe not.'

'When she asked what?'

'Whether Mariana and Eduardo loved one another. Whether they wanted her to be born or if Mariana just got pregnant by mistake. I said they did want her and that they loved one another. I told her a lie.'

'No, it wasn't a lie. They did love each other. Not at the end, of course, but I'm glad you didn't tell her that. What's the point?'

Laura had told her they loved each other but that they were very different and that towards the end they argued a lot about politics and about Dufau, because Eduardo hated him. 'I told her he loathed him, and her mother adored him.'

'Why did you have to say that?' Javier didn't approve, although he agreed with Laura that Eduardo had risked a lot and that Luz deserved to know how brave he'd been, how he'd stood up to those bastards instead of going along with them. He simply ran out of time, because they killed him before he found out just how horrific things were during the dirty war.

'Luz was very happy – I swear, when she found out that Eduardo was against military rule, she really cheered up. I think that somebody needed to tell her, for Eduardo's sake. But don't worry, I didn't say anything about where she came from. I don't know myself anyway – I mean whether she's Mariana's daughter or not.'

Laura still suspected that Luz's parents were disappeared prisoners, although she never said so to Javier.

'So you still think the same thing?'

Laura nodded, and said, half-apologetically, 'Maybe because Miriam never showed up again.'

'I tried to find her.'

'Really?' Laura said, shocked. 'You never told me.'

'No, but I did look for her.'

Javier decided after all these years to tell Laura something he had chosen to keep to himself at the time. He had gone to Coronel Pringles and looked for Miriam López. He had even talked to an aunt of hers, because the locals at the bar knew Miriam well and gave him the aunt's address. 'Miriam was one of the small-town local beauty queens who started working as a model in Buenos Aires, and then as . . . something else, I assume, although they all talked about her as if she were a famous international model.'

Javier had gone to Miriam's aunt's house pretending to be a sales rep for an Italian fashion designer who was looking for Miriam to make her a great offer.

'When did you do all this?' There was pride as well as surprise in Laura's voice.

It had been two years after Eduardo's death, after Mariana and Luz had been living in Buenos Aires for some time. He hadn't been trying to find the mother to get her to reclaim Luz; it was nothing like that. He had just gone to make sure that Laura's fears weren't true. 'Because even though I told you I didn't share your suspicion, you went on about it so often and Eduardo was so desperate to find out the truth that I wanted to know for

297

sure that what he feared didn't happen. I wanted to take up where Eduardo left off, draw a line under it, so I could accept that he'd been killed by ordinary burglars. I just wanted to breathe freely, Laura.'

'And what did you find out? Was she Luz's mother or not?'

'I suppose so. They said she'd given up modelling and gone to live in the States. Apparently she got married and was very happy.'

That had been enough for Javier. He could imagine what Miriam's life must have been like, an ordinary one that, because of what had happened, had been filled with ghosts.

'I hope you can understand this, but I didn't tell you because I couldn't accept that I too suspected that Luz was – or that she could have been . . .'

Laura hugged him. Of course she understood. She was happy it wasn't true.

'Yes, Miriam stayed in the States with Frank. I don't think she forgot about me; she just gave up. She left things where they were at that point; she decided not to tell me. She didn't come back to Argentina for ten or eleven years. She built another life for herself. But she told me that when she went to Argentina for Frank's mother's funeral she was tempted to come and look for me again. She called the Dufaus and got Mariana's home number, but she couldn't pluck up the courage to call me. I'm sure Frank advised against it.'

Laura promised Javier that she would be more careful about what she said to Luz in future. She would just listen to Luz's stories about her boyfriend. 'You have no idea, Javier, how much she needs someone to listen to her. She can't possibly confide in Mariana. I'm going to keep talking to her and encourage her to carry on seeing that boy, if she loves him so much. It's so ironic that Luz should have fallen in love with the son of one of the disappeared.'

FIFTEEN

I SHUT THE BOOK and hide it behind some others on the shelf in my room. I'm still shaking after that last testimony, as if it was my own flesh in agony, seared raw. Imagine that woman carrying a life inside her, surrounded by death day after day. I couldn't bear to read any more. That disgusting guard raped her in the room where they'd taken her to do a Caesarean! How can there be so much cruelty in the world? They put that filthy sadist in custody for ten days and then he carried on working at the Campo de Mayo as if nothing had happened, according to one of the survivors. Who knows where the baby is now, or who it's with. Nothing was ever heard of the mother again; presumably she was killed. Being sent to your death after you've given birth must be the worst thing of all, worse than all the degradation and the beatings.

I push my course books to one side. My light stays on until dawn these days; I can't stop reading the testimonies, even though they leave me so shaken. It's like an encyclopedia of perversion: secret detention centres where men, women, children and old people were tortured with electric shocks, hung, burnt with cigarette lighters, spread-eagled, blindfolded, chained and flayed; all of them filthy, crawling with lice, and completely at the killers' mercy.

I could never have dreamt that human beings could be so evil.

What did evil mean to me, until now? Not much – the way Mum treats me; Daniel and his cronies, and what they stand for; the odd betrayal by a friend. I never dreamed that people could hate like this or be so sick and cruel.

Ghosts are rising from these yellow newspapers and taking over my life. I see that girl Beatriz going to the toilet at the detention centre with a broken leg and finding her mother's letters and diary there for her to wipe herself with. I imagine her trying to hide the pages under her clothes, because they belonged to her mother who had recently committed suicide after going mad with horror at what would happen to her daughter. They'd put them there on purpose so she would see them, as if physically torturing her wasn't enough. I see the man who never cracked or gave anything away, despite being tortured with electric shocks on his gums and nipples and everywhere else and being regularly and methodically beaten with wooden clubs and having his testicles twisted and being hung and having the skin flayed from his feet with a razor. Until he saw the blood-stained rag, that is. 'It's your daughter's,' they told him. His daughter was twelve years old. Now maybe he'd co-operate and talk to them.

And those mock executions, and the sinister mind-games the torturers played, and the screams of agony that pierced the walls of the tiny, kennel-like cells.

What I've just read is merely one more case, but it's as if I can't take any more, as if my own body were a mass of bruises.

I think of Ramiro and what he must have felt when he read these reports of the trial, imagining that something like this might have happened to his father.

Alfonso was involved in the dirty war. He knew what he was doing, he gave the orders himself. Mum must not know, she can't, otherwise she wouldn't love him the way she does. She may be neurotic and unfair and mad, but she's not evil. She can't know. I'd been wondering about that a lot recently, so it was a relief when I came across the statement by that NCO, Urien, yesterday. He said their orders were that everything to do with the subversives was now top secret – everything that had been done and everything that was known. So of course Alfonso wouldn't have told anybody. Maybe not even Amalia. And definitely not Mum.

I wonder, though, what she was doing during the trial of the Juntas. As far as I can remember, I never heard anyone mention it at home. It was public, though. I wonder if Mum ever went to one of the sessions?

She is in her room. I go in and ask her. She stares at me in astonishment.

'What do you mean, Luz? You must be out of your mind. Why on earth would I go and listen to a bunch of thankless, unpatriotic good-for-nothings who had the gall to attack the people who saved them from the threat of subversion?' I've never seen her like this, so vehement, so convinced.

'But you must have read things at the time of the trial.'

'Trial, my foot! What right did they have to try them? Who do they think they are?'

'There was a trial with judges and a prosecution and a defence. They were sentenced.'

'And what happened in the end? Nothing. They let them all go, except for the commanders who gave the orders. If anyone made a mistake it was them. The others were just following orders. But you needn't think I agree they should have sentenced the commanders. It wasn't a conventional war and they saved the country in the end.'

'What do you mean, it wasn't a conventional war?' I try to stay calm so I can find out what she thinks. She couldn't possibly defend them if she knew all the horrific, degrading things they did to people.

'It wasn't conventional because the enemy wasn't on the outside – they had infiltrated the country, which is why the armed forces had to take a different tack. They may have gone too far occasionally, but it was a war and the main thing in a war is to win, by whatever means possible.'

I'd like to ask her if she thinks that masked gangs kidnapping people in the middle of the night is war; or supposed shoot-outs between decaying corpses and ghosts, as that girl put it in her statement; or torture and robbery. But I hold my tongue and let her go on. 'They saved the day, and what did that idiot Alfonsín do besides destroying their reputations? I'm telling you, Luz, he brought the most terrible chaos to this country. There was rampant inflation. Of course you would never have noticed, because fortunately you've never wanted for anything. But since you're so concerned about the poor,' – she's trying to insult me by being sarcastic – 'well, he made things even worse for them. They must have had a hard time even putting food on the table, although of course they're used to that.' She lights a cigarette and her voice goes back to normal, as if talking about the president and the problem of inflation had jolted her out of her burst of patriotic zeal and brought her down to earth, back to her usual snobbish, self-satisfied stupidity. 'Of course, they're used to not having anything; it was much worse for those of us who actually had something to lose, seeing our property and our lifestyle under threat.'

'You're changing the subject, Mum. I asked if you'd ever read a summary of the trial in the papers; if you ever had the slightest suspicion that things weren't the way your father said.' Now I'm going to say it, she's got to wake up. 'He can't have told you they used to torture people with cattle prods or that they'd let women give birth and then steal the child and kill the mother.'

Now I've sent her off the deep end. She's screaming at me.

'Where did you get all that rubbish from, Luz? It's a pack of lies, just like that business about the twins. Do you remember them?' She's lowered her voice. She's trying to convince me. 'Didn't you see that boy on television saying that he just wanted to be with his mother and instead he was being forced to live with some wretched man who wouldn't even let the twins carry on going to Catholic school? They loved their mother, they preferred her. Why were they sent to live with some uncle they'd never even met and who was awful? They were nice, well-brought-up boys, do you remember?'

It's useless. I'd rather not listen to her any more.

'No, I can hardly remember any of it. It doesn't matter, Mum. I get the message. I'll leave you alone.'

'Luz.' She is standing in front of the window and the light filtering through the curtains gives her a tragic air. She's searching for the right words. 'Why did you ask me that?'

'Because you never talked to me about it. It happened when I was very young and I didn't find out until much later, and I've been wondering, I don't know, if there were things you didn't know about . . . But it doesn't matter, let's just leave it.'

Her face relaxes, as if she's relieved by my reply. Alfonso can't have told her anything, and she didn't want to know because she worships her father.

One thing I do understand, though, is Ramiro's reaction – the way it made him sick when I told him I was Alfonso Dufau's granddaughter. How would I feel if I met someone from the other side, someone who was a relative of one of the killers, if my mother or father had gone through what his father did? I've got to tell Ramiro that now I really do understand.

Luz listened to Ramiro's voice on the answering machine twice, but didn't leave a message. Even though her friend Gabi agreed with Laura that it was stupid to be this crazy about a bloke and not ring him, it was hard to do.

'I don't know if he still loves me,' she told Gabi. 'Maybe he's forgotten me. He's never rung. Anyway, Valeria told me he's going out with an older woman.'

'What do you expect him to do, silly, hang around waiting for you to call? How's he supposed to know you're still in love with him? Tell him. So what if he's got another girlfriend? If he likes you more, he'll get rid of her.'

'Ramiro had a lot to do with getting me started. He was the one who opened my eyes and then I began making connections to the things Laura told me afterwards, and the stuff I read, and the protest demonstration on the twentieth anniversary of the coup. That was a very important day for me.' Luz's face lit up. *'In a lot of ways.'*

Luz kept remembering what Laura had said: 'You have to fight for love.' But the more she immersed herself in horror stories, the more convinced she became that her relationship with Ramiro wouldn't work out. It was impossible.

Ramiro was planning to go and meet Mónica and the others in a café near Congreso and then head out to the demonstration from there. The phone rang, but nobody picked it up. Ramiro wondered if it might have been Luz and hated himself for doing so. He'd already spent far too much time hoping it would be her whenever the phone rang and getting disappointed when it wasn't. He was over her. Things were fine with Mónica, but nevertheless here he was missing Luz again.

'Luz dumped you,' Rafael said. 'She's gone. Mónica's bloody gorgeous, Ramiro. Why are you still thinking about that silly little cow?'

'I'm not thinking about her. Well, actually, I am. Too much, perhaps.'

'Because she was the one who left you. That's always the way. If you'd stayed together, you'd have broken up with her within a month and you'd never have given her another thought,' Rafael declared, knowingly.

Ramiro knew Rafael was wrong. He still felt a great deal for Luz. He wished her well, whether or not she was with him. The main thing was for her to get away from that damn family, to break free and live the way she deserved. He would tell her that, he promised himself, as soon as this wound healed. The raw spot inside was almost palpable during those random moments when he found himself missing Luz – at work, or dropping off to sleep, at home or out dancing. But she hadn't called once in all these months. She was at the mercy of her family, whom he equated with the lowest of the low. She was Dufau's granddaughter. That meant it just wasn't going to work out. It was impossible.

'That day, as Ramiro and I were making our separate ways to the Plaza de Mayo with our friends, we were both thinking the same thing: that our relationship was doomed.'

Nunca más, never again. It's a unanimous cry and I feel a new emotion welling up in me at the sound of all those thousands of voices. Now they're chanting, 'Skip or you're a squaddie,' and I chant and skip with my university friends and all the other people here who are gravitating towards the Plaza de Mayo. I can feel the power surging in the voices I've joined in with, become one with. These people feel like my brothers and sisters, which is odd, because I've never had any. Our voices ring out, chanting in unison, as if we were flesh and blood. One group is chanting, 'We'll never forget the blood that's been shed.'

How can I live with the daughter of a murderer who has so much blood on his hands? But she's my mother, my own flesh and blood. I chant loudly, as if I can overcome that. I leave my friends and carry on alone, threading my way through the crowd. I feel so close to them all, each and every one of them. I walk alongside a group called HIJOS, the children of the disappeared. Then I get an image of Alfonso. What would these people say if they knew that someone in my family was responsible for the death of their parents? I feel ashamed and break away from them,

304

trying to hide my feelings and lose myself in the throng. I walk on, not knowing what I'm looking for. It's as if I couldn't stay in any one place, as if I had to see it all and be with each of them, although at the same time I feel I've got no right to be here. I'm struck by the look on the face of that woman wearing a photo of her disappeared children round her neck. I look at her companions, with their white headscarves and their wrinkles. They're so courageous. Maybe that one over there is the mother of those three brothers who vanished one after another, without her ever knowing where they were, or of that fifteen-year-old girl. She and her schoolmates were only campaigning for a cut in the school bus fare – they took her life for that.

There's a lump in my throat. I feel as if I'm going to cry. I head off in another direction. That man over there who's chanting so furiously has sombre eyes. Maybe he's the one who somehow survived listening to his wife scream as she was tortured and raped in front of him day after day. I just don't want anyone to know who I am or who my mother and grandfather are. Suddenly a strong hand grabs my arm and I start: it's Ramiro. He knows. He stares at me and I'm ashamed to be here. His father, his own flesh and blood, was murdered by my grandfather. How can our blood ever come together? He doesn't say anything, just looks at me, without letting go. He seems very surprised. I glance at the girl beside him, who is watching us, and smile faintly. Hello, I say, and turn away, but Ramiro stops me.

'I'm so glad to see you here,' he says.

I whisper in his ear, 'Now I understand why you felt sick when you found out I was . . .' I can't even finish the sentence. I turn round and continue wandering through the crowd. I wanted to tell Ramiro that – I needed to. I feel sick about it myself. It makes me want to run away and bury myself. My heart is beating fast. I stop for a moment. Never again, never again. Suddenly two hands are wrapping themselves around my waist – his hands – and we hop in time, his body against mine. Never again, never again.

'Luz, Luz.'

Ramiro knows about my grandfather and he's hugging me anyway. It's as if all of them were letting me in and hugging me and telling me that it's OK, it's right for me to be with them if that's the way I feel. 'We will never forget the blood that's been shed.' Forgive or forget. My body, my skin, my head and my heart have decided for me. I will never forgive.

They spent hours and hours at the Plaza de Mayo. They listened to all the famous singers who were there – Fito Páez and Teresa Parodi and León Gieco. Later, in a café, they started talking hesitantly and not entirely truthfully, both claiming they'd lost track of their friends in the crowd, until they went to Ramiro's flat and cast off their misunderstandings and fears along with their clothes. There was nothing left but the wisdom and warmth of their skin and hands and mouths. What they had both sensed in the plaza was true: everything they had thought about it being impossible for them to be together was wrong. There they were, making love hungrily, making up for lost time in a story that was as natural as their own bodies. Maybe because they were afraid of losing sight of that certainty, Ramiro and Luz didn't say anything else that night until she left and they said goodbye with a long kiss. Neither of them said, 'I'll ring you,' or 'See you soon,' or 'Goodbye, then.'

Ramiro didn't ask me to stay and I didn't ask him what happened to that girl he was going out with. We just carried on seeing each other every day, without trying to define what was going on. We let ourselves float along on a cloud of happiness. But last night I finally explained every-thing I had felt during the demonstration: how excited I was and how different people's faces kept bringing back all those stories I'd read, and how ashamed I felt when we ran into each other because he's the son of one of the disappeared and I'm the granddaughter of an officer. I told him about feeling as if his hands were accepting me on behalf of all of them, and promising myself never to forgive or forget what happened.

'But you're still living at home.'

I agreed it was absurd, ridiculous and illogical to be saying these things and yet sleeping at home.

'I'll stay here with you then,' I said, feeling scared. 'Tonight, if you like.'

'What did you tell your mother today?'

I couldn't defend myself. All I could do was show him I meant it. I picked up the phone and dialled. Mum answered. I just said, 'I won't be coming home tonight,' and hung up. Ramiro hugged me. He was delighted. I made up my mind that very moment.

'Do you still want me to come and live with you?'

'Of course I do.'

'No matter what Mum does?'

'Yes.'

So now I'm on my way home to get my things and give Mum the news. I'm very frightened, but I really want to do this. It doesn't matter what she says or does. I'm going to live with Ramiro.

My hand is shaking as I open the front door. I get a physical shock all over my body at the mere thought of how she will react. I'll go up to my room first and pack my bag and then I'll go and tell her. No, it would be better to leave her a note. What's the point of talking? But I can't possibly avoid talking to her, because if she's at home I'll never hear the end of what I did last night. She's not in the living room. I run into Claudia, the maid.

'Your mother's in her room, go and see her, quick,' she says, in a worried voice. 'She's in a terrible state.'

I can only imagine the scene she must have created if even Claudia is almost in tears. Oh God, this is going to be worse than I thought. We can't go on living like this. She shouldn't be going round the bend just because I told her I wasn't coming home for a night. I can hear her sobbing now as I walk through the hallway to the bedrooms, and it shocks me. It's insane. How can she be this upset? I walk towards her room. I can make out Daniel's voice. I'd prefer it if he wasn't here, but it doesn't matter. I look at her, collapsed on the bed, and for a moment I feel moved by her pain.

'Your grandfather's died,' Daniel says laconically.

She sits up, throws her arms around me and sobs inconsolably on my shoulder. She doesn't shout at me; in fact, she doesn't say anything at all about last night. Her grief has blotted out everything else. Maybe that's why we can have this contact, this strange situation of being so close and hugging each other. I feel guilty I'm this happy when she's in so much pain, but I can't help loving her in a confused sort of way. This unexpected intimacy makes me oddly emotional; we hug each other while she weeps on my shoulder. I'm crying too because at last I can hug my mother.

'What happened? When was it?'

'A stroke. Amalia rang to tell us. He died right away.'

They've draped a flag over his coffin. I've no idea who that stooge in uniform is who's speaking right now. I'd rather not listen. Mum's hand is gripping mine and I don't want to get angry at what that bastard is saying and spoil this bond between us. Mum must love me, otherwise she wouldn't need to hold my hand like this. She lets go and walks up to the coffin with her mother and sisters. She is sobbing as if her heart would break. I look at the four of them standing at the foot of the coffin. At least they know that the body inside is their husband or father. How many people in this country never had the opportunity to pay their last farewell to their loved ones because of that bastard in there, draped in the national flag? I look at the soldiers, standing proudly to attention in full regalia. How dare they show themselves in uniform after what they've done? Why doesn't someone shoot them? Why aren't people screaming at them?

They're lowering the coffin into the grave on chains. I wonder if the prisoners' chains clanked like that? Alfonso, I'm glad you're dead and that I'll never have to see you again. You swine, you murderer, you bastard. I mentally insult him for the last time as the rest of the family weeps. I feel a sort of giddy nausea. Now the coffin has disappeared from view. Mum comes up and hugs me. I stop thinking about who Alfonso was. My mother's father has died. She's in pain and she needs her daughter.

It was hard for Ramiro to understand what Luz was saying about how much closer she felt to her mother now.

'You see, I've never felt this way before. How can I tell her I'm leaving when she's only just found out that her father's died? I know he was a bastard, but he was her father. And she's . . . I don't know how to say this; she is who she is, but she's my mother. This is the first time she's ever needed me. I don't know, maybe you'll think this is stupid, but I like bringing her cups of tea or just sitting next to her in an armchair as she stares out the window, and being able to put my hand on her arm and even give her a hug. It's not just for her sake, it's for mine too. I've never had this before. You and I can wait for a while. Just a little while. As soon as she's feeling better, I'll tell her I'm moving in with you.'

I keep checking. I go to the bathroom fifty times a day to see if there's any trace yet, but there never is. I should have started ten days ago. Even though Ramiro hasn't said anything, I know it bothers him that I'm still living at home. Maybe that's why I didn't tell him I was late until last night.

I don't know what I was expecting, but he took me totally by surprise – he grinned and then burst out laughing. What was he laughing about? I asked. Didn't he realise what this meant?

'Yes, of course I do. It's a real mess, but it makes me happy, Luz. What can I say?'

I feel so safe in his arms. How could I ever be afraid of anything with Ramiro hugging me like this?

Now that I'm home again I keep checking, but still nothing. I'm going to do the test later on, when I go to Ramiro's. Mum calls me in and asks me to stay with her. I say I can only hang on for a while because I have to go over to Gabi's to work on a project. How much longer do I have to carry on lying like this? I touch my stomach, instinctively.

Her voice is dull with grief.

'Oh well,' she says tamely. 'I just wanted to tell you about when Daddy used to take us to see the parades with him. We used to sit in the car and . . .'

I try not to follow what she's saying, just to listen as if this were a prayer she needs to recite, a prayer that has no meaning. I've managed to block out everything that might spoil this soft voice I'm so unused to. As she goes on, telling some story that drifts over me, I think how sad I'll be to have to break this wonderful truce with Mum, but also that it's inevitable, which is too bad, because we've only just learned how to hug one another.

They planned it all very quickly. Luz took a couple of days to think it over, but they made up their minds the moment they saw the little line on the tube that meant positive. They hugged each other excitedly.

Marta was the first to know.

'Yes, maybe it's crazy, Mum, but we both want it.'

Marta looks in the mirror instead of replying. 'You know, Ramiro, I've started to look like a grandmother. Don't I look lovely?'

They laughed for a long while. At first it seemed mad to her, but they were so happy and so convinced that it was what they wanted. She herself was so delighted by the news that it couldn't be all that mad.

'Mum, I'm pregnant.'

Mariana said she had done it on purpose to hurt her. Why couldn't she have thought of her, why was she telling her this, couldn't that stupid boy go with her? He was twenty-five, wasn't he?

'What do you mean? Are you saying I should have had an abortion without telling you?'

Mariana didn't even answer.

Of course Ramiro was going to take responsibility, but not by taking her to have an abortion. He was going to be a father.

'You're out of your mind.' Mariana wasn't going to allow it.

She couldn't do that. Now it was Luz's turn to threaten to go to a magistrate if her mother wouldn't let them. They had decided to get married – mainly for her sake, so that she'd have one less thing to worry about. They really didn't care one way or the other.

How could she get married when they were still in mourning? Or had she forgotten that she'd only buried her father two months ago?

'Well, what would you rather I do? Wait until I'm huge?'

Mariana sobbed furiously. It sounded completely different from the way she cried when her father died, Luz thought. She listened to her weeping for a very long time. There was no way she could make her mother understand how happy she was, so the least she could do was to let her cry.

'When is it due?' Mariana said at last.

'In January.'

That was one good thing, at least. There would be nobody around in Buenos Aires in January because of the summer holidays. But they'd have to say something to justify why they were getting married now. Couldn't they go to the States? She would be willing to pay their way for a year or two. It would be best if they just disappeared for a long time, otherwise people would find out. Oh, Lord, what was she going to do?

That night Ramiro went to talk to Daniel and Mariana. They repeated their offer to pay for the two of them to go abroad. As for the wedding, Mariana had thought that . . .

Luz couldn't believe that Mariana had hatched so many insane plans in one afternoon.

She felt sorry for her mother as she listened to her telling her friends over the next few days that Luz's boyfriend had been offered a fantastic contract in the States with one of the top publicity agencies and that he wanted Luz to go with him. Yes, she'd suggested they wait too, but they'd been going out together for a while, you know what kids are like these days, and after all it was such a good opportunity for him.

This enterprising young man from a good family was the same person who'd been a dastardly corruptor of under-age girls a few months ago. Luz felt sorry for the way Mariana was such a slave to other people's opinions.

Mariana made them promise they wouldn't breathe a single word. Although neither Luz nor Ramiro would submit to going to the States, they did agree to play along with her fiction if they ran into one of her friends. Fortunately there wouldn't be a reception, since they were in mourning.

'Let's just have a toast,' Mariana begged.

Thank goodness Alfonso was dead and buried. Marta and Antonio wouldn't have to go through the humiliation of shaking his hand.

'All right, Mum, we'll just have a toast.'

Luz and Ramiro celebrated privately by dancing until dawn.

SIXTEEN

I PUSH DOWN AGAIN and again through my open legs. He's coming – he's almost out. He's pushing too. It's not just me, he's pushing too. I hoist myself up and see his little head emerging, smeared red with my blood. He is still connected to me by the cord which Ramiro is cutting right now with the doctor.

They lay him on my stomach. He feels warm and his head is turned towards me. Yes, I'm your mother. This feeling is so powerful it's incredible. A savage joy.

Ramiro kisses me and someone's hands lift Juan off my stomach. I tell Ramiro I don't want them to take him away. He's explaining something but I don't understand. I'm in a lot of pain: the placenta is coming out and the midwife is pressing on my belly, but I don't want to lose track of Juan even for a second. He isn't inside me any more; that means they can take him away. I have this crazy feeling that I want him to go on being part of me. A giant wave of anguish breaks over my body. I want them to give Juan back and let me move.

'Ramiro, Ramiro,' I call out. 'Where's Juan?'

'They're just doing a check-up, Luz. He's doing fine. He's perfect.'

'I want them to bring him back.'

'Don't worry, they'll move you to your room in a little while.' He gives me a kiss and turns away.

'Ramiro, Ramiro. Are you going with Juan? Don't leave him on his own!'

Ramiro gives me a surprised look, but he doesn't want to lose track of him either. He walks out. That's better. I don't want him leaving Juan alone with strangers.

'When am I going to get my son back?' I ask the nurse who's wheeling my bed.

She laughs. 'In a little while.'

I'm sure I could get up and stay there while they examine him. But they won't let me.

Luz spent the whole of that first day rollercoasting between absolute joy and terrible dread. At one point, a nurse came to take the baby away while she was asleep, but the moment the cot moved, she woke with a start.

'What are you doing? Where are you taking him?'

She had to do a check-up and change him, the nurse explained, amused at first.

'Can't you do that here?'

No, she couldn't. The nurse looked at Ramiro as if appealing for help. But Luz didn't want Ramiro to explain to her; she just wanted him to follow the nurse, go with her and not let Juan out of his sight.

Ramiro only left the room to humour her. He asked himself what on earth he was doing, trotting down the hallway after the nurse, whose irritated glance indicated that he wasn't welcome.

Luz was in tears when he returned. She couldn't bear it when they took Juan away like that. There was nothing Ramiro could say or do to relieve her pain.

Although Ramiro didn't understand what was going on, the next time the nurse came in, he asked if it would be possible not to take the baby out of the room because it upset his wife so. Yes, of course he knew there was a reason for it, but he was asking as a special favour if she could avoid taking him away if at all possible. He didn't want to see Luz suffering like this. It made no sense, because at the same time she was so happy. It had been the same on the labour ward. Her eyes shone with joy when they laid the baby on her stomach, yet she looked panic-stricken when they took him away.

His uncle Marcelo, a psychoanalyst, tried to reassure him. 'It's quite normal. Don't worry. Women often get postpartum depression.'

But Ramiro didn't think it was normal. It frightened him. It didn't seem to matter what he or Luz said, or how hard he hugged her. His embrace always used to melt away her fears, but now he could do nothing to defuse her terror. He could feel it snaking through her body; it radiated through her pores. Maybe he would come to understand her reasons, in time. For now, he just wished they would let them all go home as soon as possible.

Those rhythmic little sucking sounds calm me down and a sense of wellbeing floods through me. I'm still shaken by how angry I got with Mum just now. Thank goodness I told her to go. 'What are you doing?' she asked. There was something in her voice and eyes that I'd almost forgotten about lately: a sort of repugnance and rejection. All the cutting looks she used to give me for the way I danced came back and I could feel a surge of uncontrollable rage. Why was she asking what I was doing, she could see, couldn't she? I was holding Juan and trying to get him to latch on. I tried to stay calm and made some comment about colostrum and the milk letting down.

'Are you going to breastfeed him? What for? There are plenty of perfectly good products out there these days. It's such a shame – you'll lose your figure.'

I asked her to leave because I wanted to be alone with Juan. I refuse to miss out on this wonderful experience because of her. I hope she's not waiting outside. I hope she's still as offended as when she left and that she'll go as far away as possible.

When the nurse asks me if my mother can come in, I can't help feeling furious, the way I used to. I look at Juan. Not now, not any more, Luz: things are different now.

'Yes, of course.'

I ignore what she's saying about how she's lied and hushed up the birth and how she'll tell people once they get back from holiday. She says that right now, only her sisters and Amalia know, although of course they haven't been to visit because I asked them not to, even though Ramiro's uncle is allowed in. I let it roll over me. It's just an irritating noise, a squeaky wheel. But then she gets a little package out of her bag and hands it to me. I open it happily because her visit's come to an end and she's leaving, but when I see what's inside, I have to make a real effort not to throw it at her.

'I'm planning to breastfeed him, Mum.'

She acts as if she hadn't heard. 'But you'll give him a bottle too,' she replies, and starts explaining something or other about the teat. She takes my hand and puts it on the teat and the touch of the rubber makes me start. I pull away so sharply that my hand flies upwards, as if the rubber were burning hot.

I put the bottle down on the bedside table so as not to throw it on the floor. I don't want to fight with her. I don't want to tell her that I'm outraged by her gift, just a little something, as she puts it; she wants his first bottle to be from her.

Ramiro is woken by the sound of glass shattering against the wall or the floor. Luz is crying desperately but there is Juan in his cot. 'What's happened?' She had smashed the bottle Mariana gave her.

He didn't understand. Hadn't she agreed there was no reason to get so angry with her mother? She'd gone to sleep so happy. Why was she going on about Mariana in the middle of the night in this stupid way?

'No, it's not Mum. It's . . . I don't know.'

Luz had woken when she accidentally touched the teat of the bottle. Just as the previous afternoon, it had given her the most terrible feeling.

'As if I'd touched a spider or a scorpion. I hate bottles. Juan is never going to have one.'

It was no good trying to work out what was going on. He had to get her to calm down. He lay down next to her and put his arms around her. This wasn't like the terror she felt when they took Juan away. It was a deep anguish, a bottomless sadness, which Ramiro found as inexplicable as her panic. He could feel how overwhelming it was for her, but he could do nothing to alleviate it. What was wrong, how could this have happened, at this point in their lives, when they were together with their son? Where did all this sadness come from?

Luz didn't know. Maybe it had something to do with her mother.

'That memory did have to do with my mother, with the day they took me away from her. My real mother, not the person I thought was my mother.'

She herself was never breastfed. Mariana was very ill when she was born. 'Maybe something happened to me when I was a baby. Something to do with a bottle and that's why . . . I don't understand.'

Ramiro let her talk for a long time. She rambled on, reliving old memories, but they seemed to lead nowhere.

The best thing would be to go back to sleep. They could talk at home; they were due to leave the next day. Ramiro was tired too; he needed to rest.

Luz woke him with a kiss. She was perched on the edge of the bed.

'Is it time to go already? What time is it?'

She said she had woken him up because she'd been looking at Juan and thinking hard. She spoke very slowly, as if she were afraid that someone might overhear them. It had occurred to her that there was something that might explain what was happening to her, and she needed to talk to him about it right away. Ramiro looked at his watch. It was six o'clock. The gleam in Luz's eyes frightened him. Now what? He hugged her to find out more quickly. But Luz pulled away. She wanted him to look at her.

'Ramiro, I was born on 15 November 1976. Do you realise what that means? 1976.'

No, he had no idea. What was so special about that? What did she mean, 1976?

'It wasn't just any old year, as you very well know. Your father disappeared that year, and so did a lot of other people, including pregnant women. I've read about it and I know what they did to them.'

Ramiro sat up. Somehow he had to stop her, but she obviously needed to talk. Luz said she had known at some level before this, but somehow it had never clicked. She reminds him of that television show about the twin boys. 'Remember that? It was before I met you.'

'I don't know if you remember the case of the twins who lived with Miara, the police officer. He had tortured their mother himself. Years went by before they were returned to the family; the judges kept creating obstacles. And then, when they were finally returned, the kids said they missed their "mother", in other words the killer's wife.'

'Yes, it all happened while I was visiting Buenos Aires. I saw one of the boys on TV. I could see how the media were manipulating the whole thing. And I heard the way people talked, people with no memory, who were never called to account. That was my last trip. I haven't set foot in Argentina since then.'

'Mariana followed the case as if it were a soap opera. She was furious with the people who wanted to give the boys back to their real family. One day I mentioned something about it, although I didn't know much. I'd only seen bits of it on TV, but anyway I commented that they should give them back to the family or some such thing and Mariana hit the roof. I didn't pay much attention at the time. It was just one more thing we disagreed about. It wasn't until I was in the clinic that I remembered and started to connect it with other incidents in my life.'

Luz laid out the chain of events that had happened to her, over the course of her life. There was what Natalia had said about Due Obedience, and that business of the woman who came to fetch her from school – did she ever tell him about that? – and the way she suspected she was adopted whenever she fought with Mariana, and her mother's fear that she would get involved with communists at university. She joined up the dots in such a way that Ramiro could not help asking the inevitable question: 'You think you could be a child of the disappeared? Why?'

'Well, Mum couldn't have children after me and if in fact I wasn't born . . . I mean, maybe she lost the child and I'm not who I think I am.' She was racing, out of control. 'And maybe Alfonso got her another baby from somewhere. Given who he was, where do you think he would have got one from? Maybe I'm that baby.'

'You're getting carried away, Luz. You've got no proof whatsoever.'

'Haven't I?' She is agitated but firm. 'Then why do you think Mum used to talk about my genes every time she got angry with me? I used to assume it was because of Dad, but think about it – she could perfectly well have been talking about the genes I got from someone else.'

'Luz, I understand why you're angry with your mother, but she does love you, in her own way.'

'No, she's never loved me,' she said categorically.

Juan started crying just then and succeeded in doing what Ramiro could not – stopping this delirium that had started with the touch of a rubber teat. Luz picked Juan up, propped herself up on the bed, undid her nightgown and started feeding him.

She was calm and smiling. She seemed to have recovered her equilibrium. Ramiro looked at the two of them tenderly. Maybe it would be a good idea if Luz started therapy, he thought. He would suggest it later on. Right now he didn't want anything to intrude on their peace and happiness. He wanted to hold on to that sensation and forget about everything Luz had told him. Nevertheless, he remembered that when he was first going out with her and she told him some of the things Mariana had said and done, he had found it hard to believe that a woman who could behave like that could actually have given birth to Luz herself, carried her in her own body. But naturally he had put it down to his mother-in-law's ghastly politics and her horrendous personality.

After they got married, Mariana had behaved reasonably well. They hadn't seen much of her in any case. To be fair, she had opted to stay at home instead of going on holiday in order to be there when Luz's baby was born, which for her was quite something. Even Luz had been surprised.

Ramiro had been there when Mariana walked out of the room that afternoon, looking distraught. She told him that Luz had thrown her out, and he felt then that Mariana loved Luz, despite herself. That's why he had convinced her to stay at the clinic, telling her it was all a misunderstanding, that Luz simply liked to be alone when she was breast-feeding the baby, that was all. Ramiro was so happy that he even felt generous towards his mother-in-law.

He had to talk to Luz and ask her not to spoil this wonderful time by fighting with her mother. After all, Mariana had been quite good recently, Luz had said so herself. None of them needed what Luz called that 'nasty, loaded atmosphere' taking over their little kingdom.

I wanted to talk it over with Ramiro, but today was hard. Juan kept crying and we didn't know what to do, whether to feed him or change him or pick him up or put him down in his cot. We were scared there might be something wrong with him.

'It's always this way,' Marta said reassuringly. 'The first few days, you don't understand anything. You get scared about everything, until eventually you get used to it.'

'You used to scream a lot harder than that,' my mother said. 'Goodness, how you screamed! It was incredible.'

'I screamed?'

I looked for any excuse to get her to talk about when I was born. Although she had already told me that she hardly saw me during the first month.

'So who looked after me?'

'The clinic at first, and then I took over. Where did you buy the cot? It's gorgeous.'

When Mum was out of earshot, I said to Ramiro, 'Didn't you think she was changing the subject? As if she didn't want to talk about my first few days?'

No, he didn't. He hadn't noticed anything. 'Please,' he begged, 'for goodness' sake don't say anything to your mother about what you told me today in the clinic. Promise.'

I promised. We couldn't talk any more because Juan started to cry.

Now Ramiro and Juan are fast asleep. What did she mean by saying I screamed a lot? It's half past eleven. She goes to bed late.

'Hi, Mum. No, nothing, everything's fine. I was just wondering about what you said about me screaming a lot. When did I scream like that?'

I feel as if the question bothered her. There's tension in her voice. I can sense her trying to be nice to me, the way she has since I moved out. She says I used to have nightmares, that the paediatrician said they were nightmares. 'Nightmares? When I was a baby?'

'Yes, you used to wake up very frightened,' she says. I can tell what an effort she's making from the sarcastic edge in her voice that I had begun to forget about. She gave a dismissive snort. 'You were always that way. Remember how I used to say you always wore a hangdog look? It's just that at some point you stopped screaming.'

'No, I'm not asking you because I think Juan looks frightened. I'm just asking out of curiosity. It must be that when you have a child it makes you want to remember what it was like when you were a baby, the first few days.'

I can't help interpreting her silence as being laden since, of course, she didn't see my first few days because she was very ill at the time. 'Well, Mum, I'm off to bed.'

If I was having nightmares when I was only a month old . . . I have to stop thinking about it and go to sleep. Juan will be awake again in a little while. I'll find out somehow.

What did Ramiro mean she wasn't happy? Luz asked. How could he say that? She was very hurt by his comment. Didn't he realise it was the first time in her life that she had woken up thinking how lucky she was to be alive and wondering what wonderful thing Juan would do next? She appreciated Ramiro's warmth so much, and being able to talk to him and sleeping with him and watching him bath Juan and rock him to sleep on his shoulder. Didn't he realise that she had never ever been this happy before? Why was he saying that he was upset because she wasn't happy at a time like this?

Yes, of course Ramiro could see what she was saying. Her smile was so generous and there was a glow in her eyes – in fact her whole body glowed. She looked lovely and round these days. Her breasts were bigger and her face had become incredibly beautiful. There was something softer, more womanly, more wifely about her. But there was this other side too, the way this obsession of hers cut into their happiness because she was so preoccupied with finding something that might confirm her theory. Maybe she was right about some things, but others, like the fact that Javier had snorted . . . She'd found endless interpretations just for someone having snorted, a sound that doesn't mean anything. 'You don't think you might be blowing this up too much, Luz?'

Maybe I am blowing it all up too much. I'm looking so hard for anything that might confirm my suspicions, and sometimes I wonder why. I brought the subject up with Javier on purpose and when I saw how uncomfortable it made him, I went on.

I told him that Mum was still terribly upset about Alfonso's death. And there was a slight curl in his lip, a shadow in his eyes. I wanted to make sure. 'My grandfather, Alfonso Dufau,' I repeated. I could see the distaste on his face again, as if he couldn't stop himself.

'You couldn't stand Alfonso, could you?' Javier shrugs. 'Laura told me. You don't have to hide it from me. I hate him. I'm ashamed to be his granddaughter. I don't dare tell Mum that, and not just because he's died. I couldn't before either.'

Javier gives a slight smile. It's clear he's pleased I'm saying this.

'It's not because of the way he treated me when I was little. He was . . . normal, even affectionate with me; I've hated him ever since I found out that he was actively involved in that shit with the military regime. Did you know about that back then?'

Javier gives a one-word assent. But I don't give him a chance to catch his breath and change the subject.

'Did Dad know? I'm asking because he died before all this came out. Did Dad hate him?'

'What are you asking me for now, Luz? That's morbid stuff to be dwelling on after you've just married the man of your dreams. I've heard all about your Romeo.' Javier was desperately trying to distract my attention. 'And you've got such a lovely baby.'

'Just tell me,' I interrupted. I needed to know, it was very important to me. And then he told me that Dad couldn't stand him either but that he didn't talk much about his father-in-law. He didn't say anything else for a while, as if he were lost in his reminiscences. That's when he let slip that thing about the clinic. 'I remember that when you were born . . .' He gave a dismissive snort. 'When they were in the clinic, your mother was in intensive care and your father was very upset and he kept saying that Alfonso and Amalia were driving him mad.'

'You said "when you were born", then you snorted and said "when they were in the clinic". What did you mean by that snort?'

Javier, looking extremely perturbed, said he had done no such thing, or that if he had, it had been involuntary. He glanced at his watch in desperation. Where on earth was Laura, she was supposed to be there by now. 'Every time she comes to Buenos Aires the kids ask her to . . .'

'Why was Dad so upset in the clinic?'

'Because your mother had been extremely ill for many days and your grandparents wouldn't leave him alone, they kept meddling all the time.' He seemed to forget about being careful. An old hatred resurfaced in his voice. 'They wouldn't even let him grieve in peace. I was there, I saw it.'

'Did you see me in the clinic?'

I don't know whether he said yes or no. He made an odd sound, as if my question had forced him to the edge of an abyss he didn't want to fall into. Then the doorbell rang. It was Laura. He got up to answer the door himself and Juan woke up. I breastfed him and told Laura about the labour and Juan's first few days, and the sound of that snort started fading in my mind.

But that night, as I talked to Ramiro, it grew and grew until it became the irrefutable proof that I wasn't born in the clinic and that Javier knows it and won't tell me. And he hates Alfonso, he really does. It all fits together, doesn't it?

Why was she so desperate to prove all this? Ramiro asked. It wasn't as if she was open-minded about the answer to her questions – all this obsessing night and day was only about confirming one thing. How could she be so sure? 'How can you want to know that, Luz? How can you be so set on finding out that you were born in captivity? Why does something so sinister have to happen just when everything is going so well in our lives?'

'I *am* sure, you're right. I don't exactly know why. Maybe it's just a way of making sense of all these things that don't add up. I know it's terrible, but I've got to find out the truth. The more I search, the better I feel. I've stopped feeling that dread I had in the clinic that somebody was going to steal Juan; I no longer have that feeling of anxiety.

'It may be hard to understand, but this process of looking for myself and where I came from and who I am doesn't stem from pain but from happiness. If I wasn't so happy I wouldn't have the strength to go into these dark places. It's got a lot to do with you, Ramiro. If it hadn't been for you, I wouldn't be looking. It's not just because of what you told me, it's everything we have together: your love, your unconditional friendship, the way you always help me to think things through, the way you understand me and accept me without judging, and the way you hug me.

When we make love, God, I feel so wonderful when we make love. That's what all this is based on, Ramiro: from love and happiness. That's what's making me look for the truth. It's because I feel truly loved for the first time ever, because I'm with you and Juan that I'm not afraid and I want to know.'

It was difficult for Ramiro to understand, but if Luz was doing this because of love, it couldn't be so bad. He was the one who suggested making an appointment to see the Abuelas de Plaza de Mayo. He would look after Juan.

Marta got there just as Luz was getting ready to leave. Ramiro was happy to see her. He needed to talk to someone, either to confirm that Luz was on the right track, or else to stop her, because ultimately it was her life, not his, and maybe he was getting too involved.

It was hard for him to bring up the subject. It was lucky he'd been able to get a month off to be with Juan and Luz, not just for Juan's sake, for hers too. Ever since Juan was born she'd become obsessed with an idea that at the beginning he thought was ridiculous but now he was starting to believe. But since he spent all his time with Luz, he was afraid he was getting dragged into the web she'd been weaving day after day. Without meaning to, he was encouraging her in this crazy scheme of hers.

Marta says she doesn't understand; Ramiro replies that he simply needs her help and advice.

'What is this idea of hers? I don't follow, Ramiro.'

So he told her. 'Luz suspects that she is not her parents' daughter, that they swapped her and that her real parents were disappeared.'

Marta's first reaction was enthusiasm verging on delight, even though what her son was saying was so horrific. She was very fond of Luz and had never been able to work out how she managed to come from that family. Nevertheless, she knew she ought to exercise caution.

'What makes her think that? Or do you think she's inventing it?'

He didn't know. Ramiro sketched out the connections as well as Luz had done for him. He also told Marta how much Luz had matured recently. She had become aware of all sorts of things they had hidden from her for years.

'While she was pregnant we talked a lot about Dad. She was the one who kept asking. She got stuck on the idea that her grandfather might have had something to do with his disappearance. I said I knew he didn't, because Dad was kidnapped by the navy, even though it didn't make any difference who it was, they were all just as guilty. I said that for her sake, because I didn't want to see her suffer.'

Marta was on the verge of tears. 'Luz is a wonderful girl, Ramiro, and I find it really moving that you love her enough to support her in this and not tell her that she's mad, that the pregnancy has pushed her over the edge or something like that. Luz must know what's driving her to this. Give her all the support you can.'

He shouldn't have told his mother. He had promised Luz that nobody but the two of them would know. But he needed to confide in somebody. It was too much responsibility to bear.

'Hasn't she asked Mariana?'

'No, I asked her not to. Because if she's wrong, it's a terribly damning accusation. But I've got the feeling she might say it at any point. The other day, before Mariana left for Punta del Este, Luz lost her temper with her because she couldn't remember the name of the clinic Luz was born in. Luz really shouted at her. She thinks Mariana does it on purpose, that she won't tell her things so she can't go and find anything out.'

It was he who had come up with the idea of going to the Abuelas as a way of uncovering the truth without having to ask Mariana. Had he done something crazy?

No, of course not, his mother said reassuringly. He was doing everything a husband should.

No, it didn't go well. I got the sense the woman I talked to, Delia, thought I was mad. The first thing I asked her was whether there was any way of finding out whether a baby born in 1976 was a child of the disappeared. She wanted to know why I was asking, and I asked her to please answer my question first because I didn't have much time. She described the database they have with blood samples of relatives of the disappeared. I simply had to take a blood test and I would know. 'When can I do it and where do I have to go?' But it wasn't as easy as I'd thought. She asked all sorts of questions that I didn't want to answer.

'Why didn't they let you take the blood test?'

'Because they didn't believe me. The things I said in that first meeting – I was so stupid. They got the impression I was crazy.'

I had to say that it was me who was interested in getting the test done. But I wouldn't tell her that I was Dufau's granddaughter. When she insisted, I told her I was suspicious because my mother had never loved me and we fought a lot, and I had often suspected that I was adopted. I listened to her go on about how that's very common amongst teenage girls when they fight with their mothers, but that I was taking it too far. It was the same thing Ramiro said. The fact that I didn't get on with my mother didn't mean that . . . What could I do? Tell her about the rubber teat, and Javier snorting, and the business about my personality being 'genetic'? No, that would be ridiculous. I said that I used to suspect that she wasn't my mother but that now I was almost positive, since I'd had a baby myself a month and a half ago. Then I looked at my watch and said I had to go. She went with me to the door. I asked her if I could come back, if they had any documentation on babies who disappeared in mid-November 1976, possibly earlier or later. They told me I was born on 15 November, but I can't be sure.

Delia humoured me. She laid her hand on my shoulder and suggested that I talk it over with my mother first. How can I talk it over with her? If she did steal me, she's hardly likely to say so.

'Are you going to let me see the documents or not?' I said, raising my voice.

Yes, of course I could see then, although I couldn't take the blood test. But I should feel free to come and talk to her whenever I wanted.

Marta was moved when Ramiro told her what Luz was up to. 'It doesn't matter if she's just imagining it, the main thing is that she trusted a stranger enough to tell her that her mother didn't love her, simply because that person was a grandmother and a mother. That's a huge step, Ramiro. I wouldn't interfere, if I were you. Luz needed to do that. I'm sure she'll keep going. Eventually she'll tell them who her grandfather was and how her mother had problems in labour.'

Ramiro suggested to Luz that he go there himself and tell the Abuelas about the peculiar circumstances surrounding her delivery, and who her grandfather was, so they would let her take the blood test.

'No, please don't, otherwise they won't let me look at anything. They'll hate me. I'd rather go alone.'

The other day, as I was working in the archives, making notes, Delia kept staring at me. She didn't say anything. As I was getting ready to go she asked if I'd had a talk with my mother, and I just scowled at her and left. So I'm surprised to see her coming towards me now with a smile. She looks at Juan (I brought him so I could stay longer) and sits down opposite me.

'What an adorable baby!'

I smile back. She says that she'd like to have a chat. She wants to hear more about my life. I tell her I don't have anything else to say. I don't know why I'm being so rude. I know what these women do and I really admire them for it. I'm afraid they'll find out who I am, or who I'm supposed to be. Because if I'm wrong – if I really am Alfonso's grandchild – then she'd be perfectly within her rights to throw me out.

I carry on writing things down, as if she weren't there.

'Look, Luz, since you're so pig-headed we're going to let you take the blood test.'

'Something had happened that changed Delia's mind. She told me later on because we became good friends. In some ways I feel as if she's more like my grandmother than a friend. Apparently when she mentioned my visit to the Abuelas, she gave my name and surname, and another woman remembered what Susana Collado had said . . .'

'Dolores's mother?'

'Yes. She told them that Dufau's daughter had a little girl who wasn't her own. That's why they let me take the test, even though I still hadn't let on who I was.'

I'm so overwhelmed I'm speechless. Right then Juan starts crying and I breastfeed him. I'm touched by the way she looks at us: there are tears in her eyes.

'You look just like my daughter the last time I saw her. My little grandson, Martín, was two months old when he disappeared.'

327

She gets up, pats my head, and leaves before she breaks down altogether.

She's recovered by the time I go into her office. I thank her and ask when and where I should go for the test.

'But it was useless. There was nothing to link my blood to anybody else's. For a while I thought I'd been wrong, that I'd imagined the whole thing because I was so angry with Mum and I needed to distance myself from the Dufaus and my grandfather's sadistic behaviour. But it didn't set me back for long. When I went to stay with Laura and Javier a few months later, I decided to go there a few days before Ramiro, so I could carry on asking around.'

'Why not tell Luz the truth?' Laura didn't understand. She would honour Javier's decision, of course, because he had asked her to, but she thought it was terribly unfair. The other day she had gone with Luz to the clinic where she'd supposedly been born, and it had been awful to have to bite her tongue and not say anything. 'If you'd only seen her, Javier. She insisted on getting the names of the people who worked in the records department, the ones who kept the registry of births.' Laura could tell by watching her that Luz was determined to get her own way and that she would just keep on trying until she found out the truth. 'Why not save her some time? Now she's desperately looking for a farmhand's daughter who gave birth at sixteen and decided to give her daughter up for adoption. Since we know that woman doesn't exist, why not tell her?'

'What do you want me to do, tell her she's a prostitute's daughter? A prostitute who never showed up again, besides.' They couldn't be so sure of that, Laura said; it wasn't certain. 'Let's not go through all that again.' How long were they going to live not knowing? Wasn't Eduardo's death enough?

Luz had asked her about that, too, and Laura had told her she had never believed the story about the burglary. 'You've got to talk to Luz, Javier. She knows you're hiding something.'

When Ramiro arrived, Luz was euphoric. So much had happened. She told him everything; she'd been to the clinic and interviewed the woman who used to work there and found out about the farmhand's daughter and met Dr Murray. 'You see, Ramiro, I wasn't mad. Mariana isn't my mother. When I told Laura, she didn't seem surprised. I'm sure Javier knows more than he's letting on about my real mother and he's stopping Laura from telling me. I was waiting for you to get here so I could confront him.'

If he hadn't gone through the whole thing from the start with her, Ramiro would have been baffled by her joy at discovering that she was not her parents' daughter. But this meant things weren't as they'd thought. What a relief.

'So your parents weren't disappeared, Luz.'

But the idea that she was born in captivity was like a huge, heavy boulder: nothing could shift it. Whenever she came across something that didn't fit, like the blood test, or what they'd just told her about the farmhand's daughter, she discounted it. In her eyes, only the things that supported her theory were relevant. Ramiro said he was going to raise it with Javier himself and tell him the truth about her suspicion. 'Why wait any longer?'

'No, wait. We're having dinner with him and Laura and the kids tonight. Laura said she would talk to Javier. It sounded like a promise. She will know when the moment is right.'

When Luz's cousins had left, the four of them sat down for a drink in the living room. It was Javier himself who brought the subject up. It was obviously hard for him; the words seemed to come from a long way away, loaded with immense shame and sadness.

There was no sixteen-year-old farmhand's daughter. He was going to tell her everything he knew about the circumstances that had led Eduardo to register her as his daughter and the pressure he was under from his in-laws. It was clear Eduardo had had the same concerns as Luz, because of the year she was born and everything that was going on at the time. That's why Javier had done his best to find out. But it turned out it wasn't true. The birth certificate said Miriam López, he'd seen it himself. Did Luz remember the woman who tried to pick her up from school?

Eduardo had met her at one point. But after that, they never heard anything more of her, and he died shortly afterwards.

329

Javier is embarrassed to answer Luz's question: 'How do you know it's not true? Why? It would be unusual for her still to be alive if I was born in captivity, but maybe she escaped.' Hope blazes in her eyes. 'Maybe my mother is still alive.'

'I know you definitely weren't born in captivity, because I went to look for Miriam López and I found out a few things about her life.'

'Did you see her? Do you know her? Do I look like her?'

Laura interrupted, saying that she had suspected the same thing as Luz and Eduardo, but that what they knew about Miriam López seemed to rule it out.

Laura took over from Javier, who could not go on. She told them about Miriam and Dolores, avoiding the things that might be hard for Luz to hear. She told them that Mariana did find out, though not what she said about Luz being fair-skinned and sexually precocious. It was Luz herself who said that she now understood so many things about Mariana and her own life.

Javier was hunched over on the sofa, crushed by the weight of all the things they had talked about.

Luz went over and gave him a hug. In a low voice, she said, 'Don't ever regret telling me. You did me a huge favour. I knew anyway, I think I've always known, and it's a relief. I'm happy I'm on the right track.'

Luz gave him a kiss and went off to bed and Javier broke down and wept for his brother as if he had only just died. Did he have the right to tell Luz what Eduardo had chosen to hide? he asked Laura. It was not only his right but his duty, she replied. Eduardo wasn't able to do it himself, because they stopped him by cutting his life short.

But it wasn't until several months later that Luz's letter convinced Javier he hadn't made a mistake, that his brother could rest in peace at last. *I'm saying this to you, Javier, because I can't say it to him — I forgive you, I love you.*

SEVENTEEN

AFTER WHAT LAURA and Javier told us, Ramiro doesn't believe my adoption has anything to do with the repression. There are various things that don't fit my theory, such as what Javier knows about Miriam and the fact that the hospital issued a birth certificate and that it lists a first and last name for my mother.

But then again, what Javier heard about Miriam in Coronel Pringles is probably not true. Maybe they only said she was a model because they were afraid to say she was an activist. A lot of people were afraid to mention it. If one of your relatives disappeared, you had to face not only the grief but also being ostracised. If she was one of the disappeared, though, how come she showed up in Entre Ríos seven years later?

It's odd that the hospital issued a birth certificate. In the cases that Delia and the Abuelas have described, the birth was never documented. It's also unusual that they listed the mother's name but not her address or ID number. There must be some explanation, and I'm determined to find out what it is.

It would be easier to ask Mum all this . . . or rather, Mariana. She must know. But I don't feel like discussing it with her right now. I can't, I'm not up to it. She rang me today to say that she was coming over for a while this afternoon, but I told her I had to take Juan to the doctor and that we'd talk some other time.

I have to tell Delia this right away.

'We became very good friends around then. I was a little ashamed the first time I went back to the Abuelas' office after the blood test, because they couldn't find a match in the database. But after Delia told me that they knew who my grandfather was, I felt much more comfortable. I didn't have to be afraid of being found out or treated as if I were crazy. I carried on going there, not to work in the archives but to

talk to her. I took Juan along. Delia watched him grow up. Juan used to give her the most gorgeous smiles.' Luz smiled. 'I had a very special relationship with Delia, which was good for all of us. She told me so many terrible and at the same time moving stories. Like the one about Susana, Dolores's mother. She did everything possible to find her grandson: talked to magistrates at juvenile courts, bishops, orphanages, army officers, priests, politicians, you name it. She tried every avenue she could think of, always seesawing between hope and disappointment.'

'And did she find him?'

'No, she died without ever having traced him. At one point they followed up a lead they had been given and Susana got very excited. She tracked down a man she thought had stolen her grandchild and fought tooth and nail for him with the judges, who were reluctant to do anything, and in the end he turned out not to be her grandson after all. But at least she had proved that he didn't belong to his fake parents. He carried on living with them, though, because nobody was looking for him either.'

Delia will be so surprised when I tell her that Susana Collado's daughter, Dolores, was friends with my father. Not with my father, I think, and then change my mind. Yes, he was my father too.

I ring her and ask if she's got time to meet me and Juan at the plaza. 'It's a lovely, sunny day and the trees are out,' I say, to tempt her. 'And Juan is adorable these days. He missed you a lot in Entre Ríos. Shall I come and pick you up?'

'You look so happy!' she says, when she sees me.

'You won't believe what I'm going to tell you, Delia.' I begin with what happened at the clinic; all the obstacles they put in my way and the lies they told and everything I did and said. How in the end I got to see the registry of births and the paediatrician's notes. 'They had a stillborn son.'

Delia's face lights up. 'So it's definite! You've got proof!'

Yes, and it was she who taught me not to take no for an answer, thanks to all the stories she told me about the Abuelas. I even got the names of the administrative staff who were working at that time, as well as the doctor who delivered the baby. In ten days. And I managed to see them. It's easier in Paraná, there are fewer people. You talk to one person after another and in the end, if you're pig-headed enough like me, you find the one you're looking for. I tracked the doctor down in Rosario. Someone in his family gave me the address.

We reach the plaza. I lift Juan up and spin him round in the air before putting him down in the sandpit. I'm so happy. Every day I get closer to my mother and father. Maybe my dad's still alive.

Delia and I sit down on the edge of the sandpit and I carry on telling her what I found out over the last few days. Her expression changes as I talk.

'So it's not what you thought, Luz. You're not the daughter of . . .'

'We don't know that,' I interrupt. 'They could have said anything. I checked the lists I have at home and there's no Miriam López anywhere. Maybe you could help me look into it some more.'

Like Ramiro, Delia doesn't believe my theory is true. But I still feel it is. Maybe just because of who my grandfather was, or my supposed grandfather. 'That bastard wasn't my grandfather after all,' I say joyfully.

'That's what I always used to say to the Abuelas,' Delia said, with a smile. 'She's so pretty and sensitive, she can't be from the same family as that brute.'

'You can't say that. Mum . . . I mean Mariana is very pretty. Although she's about as sensitive as a block of marble.'

Delia gives me a worried look and says, very gently, as if she were afraid the words might hurt, 'Have you talked it over with her?'

'No, I haven't said anything to her yet. I don't know what to do. She didn't know about me, they fooled her too. Dad didn't tell her until I was seven years old. That's when he started trying to find out where I was from. I believe – I sometimes think that maybe it wasn't a break-in – that maybe he was murdered.'

'You're going too far, my dear.'

'That's what you told me the day we first met, and now look, I wasn't wrong after all.'

Delia thinks that maybe the things I've read and heard about from the Abuelas have affected me so much that I've internalised them and come to believe they actually happened to me. She says she can understand it, because the Abuelas feel as if each of the children they've found is a member of their own family. She remembers the day when Paula was due to be returned to her grandmother after endless disappointments and delays. Delia was there in the court room when the judge said he needed to think it over, even though he had all the evidence, including the blood tests proving the little girl's identity beyond any shred of doubt. 'You bastard, you pig,' Delia shouted at him. She used to be incapable of ever raising her voice to anyone. She felt as if Paula were her own grandchild, like Beto and Tamara and all the others. The Abuelas were over the moon when Sacha got Carlita back.

'You feel as if it happened to you because you identify so strongly with everything you hear about. But you don't have to have gone through it in person, in your own body, to support our work. Don't make that mistake, Luz.'

I'm scared, I'm so scared because Delia and Ramiro keep insisting that this didn't happen to me. I know it did, I'm positive. I take her hands and ask her not to give up on me, not now, after all I've managed to find out. Her eyes fill with tears. 'Why are you crying?' I ask.

It's stupid and selfish, but she'd just wondered if something like this was happening to her daughter's little boy, Martín. If he had this same intuition, and the strength to do all that I've done, my stubbornness, maybe he too would re-emerge from the shadows.

Tears are rolling down her cheeks. It's the first time I've ever seen her cry. I put my arm around her shoulder.

'Oh, Delia, do you know how many times I've thought the same thing, only in reverse? How come I haven't got a Delia, a grandmother who's looking for me the way you are looking for your grandson? I would have found out much sooner.'

'She never got any leads about where her grandson is. He disappeared during the raid when they seized his parents. Delia's daughter thought they had dropped him at a neighbour's house – she told someone in the detention centre so. But it wasn't true. They killed his parents a few months later. Someone testified that they saw them putting the baby in a car. And that's where all the clues stop. The soldiers who took part in the raid always denied there was a baby in the house.'

I take the sandy spade out of Juan's mouth. I don't want to start crying. I've got to cheer Delia up. She seems so fragile now. I tell her I'm not her little grandson, but that since I haven't got a grandmother, or rather I don't know if I have, I'm choosing her. I tell her we're going to play make-believe, like when I was a child.

'Let's pretend that I am your grandchild and this adorable baby is your great-grandson.' I pick up Juan and put him in her lap. 'Ooh, you're so old, Great-Grandma.'

We laugh and Juan smiles his marvellous smile, as if he understood. She promises not to tell me I'm wrong again, until we've got proof.

I've got to go to Coronel Pringles right away. Ramiro will come and join me this weekend. I've got to find Miriam López.

It was the first thing that went through my head when they gave me the diagnosis. Well, not the first, the second. The first was, I'm dying, and then immediately afterwards came a flashback of Liliana in the plaza, and I haven't done anything.

'What do you mean, you haven't done anything? Miriam, please. You couldn't have done anything more,' Frank said that night, when I told him.

Three years ago, when we were in Buenos Aires, it occurred to me to go and look for Lili again.

'So Miriam called the Dufaus' house. They were in Buenos Aires for Frank's mother's funeral. She made up a story to explain why she wanted Mariana's number. She faked an American accent (she had been speaking English all day long for many years) but it was much easier than she expected. The cleaning lady answered. The Dufaus weren't in Buenos Aires. "Yes, just a minute, Mrs Dufau left me her daughter's number just in case." And she gave it to her. But Miriam's plans stopped there. She didn't have a clear idea of what to do next. It was her illness, three years later, that gave her the impetus to carry out the promise she had made Liliana twenty years earlier.'

I wanted to call Lili, but what was I going to say? What if someone suspected I was the woman who had tried to kidnap her in Entre Ríos, and had me killed? I felt a stab of fear, opening up the wound that had healed in all these years of cosy torpor with Frank, helping with the hotel and seeing his friends. If I owe anything to this city it's the fact that I don't feel that bubble of terror dancing madly round my body any more. I'd reached my limit. I'd gone through as much fear as one human being can handle, though Liliana and all of the others must have gone through a lot worse than me. But they were stronger and they had ideals to fight for. I'm just a wimp. There's no way I could try and save Lili now. I just couldn't. Anyway, I don't know if it would be a good idea. Both times I tried to help, they killed someone: first Liliana, then Eduardo. I think it was just pure chance I got away.

The first few years in the States I used to shiver whenever I thought of who Lili was with. But the pain wore off with time. It got easier, overlaid by everyday things. Every once in a while, though, I'd get this sudden rush of anguish about Lili's future and I'd say to myself, well, maybe I'll tell her when she's grown up.

Lili, Lili. I wonder what's become of her, brought up by that delightful creature. She must be a teenager by now.

'Frank convinced her it was pointless because it was too late to tell me the secret at my age.'

'I don't agree. No matter what age you are, it's always good to know the truth about your roots.'

'I don't agree either, obviously, given everything I've done. But I can sort of understand Frank's thinking. I was grown up, and if these other people had brought me up, there was nothing much that could be done for me. But he was wrong about that, too, because finding out who you really are can change you a lot.'

But now I've got cancer, I thought. What if there is no later on? What if this story disappears with me? The idea of it gave me a nasty jolt. So I decided to write to Lili. I wrote and rewrote the letter, over and over again. It always seemed too strongly worded, too raw.

Will Lili believe me? I may never know. Tomorrow I'm going in for the operation and I don't know if I'll come out alive.

I'll put it in an envelope and address it to Luz Iturbe.

It would be easier if I write the address, that way someone will post it for me after I die.

'The day before her operation, she called Mariana's house from the States and asked for the address on some pretext or other. But they wouldn't give it to her.'

I wonder if it's for security reasons? Is she afraid of some kind of revenge because she's the daughter of a man who murdered so many?

How come they don't get killed? How can they walk the streets and sit in cafés alongside the relatives of their victims? That's what I thought the night I saw that naval officer, Scilingo, on TV when he talked about giving them injections and throwing them into the sea. I didn't know about that. The things those people did are beyond belief.

I was with my friends Sally and Berenice when the programme came on, and I started crying my eyes out. In between hiccups and sobs, I told them everything Liliana had said. She was a friend of mine, I explained, the only real friend I had there, and they killed her. The moment I talked about it, that agonising pain and fear came back, right there in Sally's living room, where we used to get together to chat and have a laugh. That's why I'm living here, so I don't have to be afraid. I'm never going back, even if those things have stopped happening.

It was Sally who reacted. 'How come nobody kills them if they're just walking around on the streets?' I couldn't explain it. Although the fact is, I thought, I didn't kill them either. I wasn't even capable of rescuing a child from their clutches and, what's even worse, I never reported it. No, I just lay low here, lulled into a sense of wellbeing.

I wasn't just a coward, I was a collaborator. I can't stand it. This letter has to get there. Lili must know her parents were killed, and who did it and why. Those bloody murderers. I see Liliana, smiling, breastfeeding her baby, and then lying there riddled with bullets in the plaza, and I feel this rage that's been bottled up so long it smells musty. I can't believe that Lili may never find out.

What if I ring and ask for Luz and tell her a lie so I can get her address? That way I'll hear her voice and I can try and picture what she's like. The doorbell rings. It's Berenice; that's perfect.

'*A good friend of hers, a Brazilian woman, came round just then, and Miriam asked her if she wouldn't mind ringing and asking for me. She needed another voice, another accent, so nobody would suspect, because she had called half an hour earlier.*'

Berenice's Spanish is terrible, although she thinks she speaks it perfectly and tries to sound cool by using Argentinian slang.

'*Miriam's plan was to pick up the phone when I came on. That's how she found out that I'd stopped living with Mariana.*'

She's left home. Can she have escaped on her own? Lili, love, maybe you turned out as brave as your mum and dad, and ran away.

'Would you mind giving me her phone number, please?'

'Who is this speaking?'

It's Mariana, it's got to be. I can just imagine her from this voice over the phone, a throaty voice with a nasty hint of shrillness. Who knows, maybe it was Mariana herself who ordered Eduardo's death so he wouldn't go ahead and report Dufau. Which I didn't do either.

'*But now she could,*' Carlos said. '*She could report Animal here in Madrid. And we can report Dufau in Argentina too. It doesn't matter that he's dead.*'

'This is Berenice. We met *numa viagem,*' Berenice improvises.

'Oh, on Luz's trip to Europe?'

Berenice goes on making things up in her funny broken Spanish until she gets Lili's phone number.

I call her. A man's voice answers – her boyfriend?

'*But I wasn't there.*'

'Could you give me her address? I'd like to send her an invitation,' I say. I pretend that I'm a childhood friend. How on earth is he going to believe me, with this old-lady voice? But luckily he doesn't ask, he just gives it to me. I tell him my name is Silvia.

At the end of the letter I write: 'PS. The Silvia who called one afternoon was me.'

I put the envelope inside a bigger one and write on the front: 'To be opened after my death.'

Frank sees it and picks it up.

'You're not going to die, Miriam. They're going to operate and it'll all work out, I promise.'

I think he's going to open the envelope and I shout so loudly that he jumps.

'Don't open that! I've spent days writing it, mulling over every word.'

'What is it? Your will?' he says, trying to make a joke out of it.

'It's a letter for Lili. Frank, love, promise me you'll give it to her.'

'*No, I never read that letter. Because Miriam didn't die during the operation, as she was afraid she would.*'

Who should I ask? Javier mentioned a bar, just round the corner from the aunt's house, a few blocks away. He said he didn't know the name, it had been so many years.

There are various bars. We go into the first one we come across. I tell Ramiro he'd better order, I'm too nervous. The bloke behind the bar is very young. 'Do you know Miriam López? Have you ever heard of her?' He gives no sign of having heard and carries on working.

'A girl who was a beauty queen, some years ago.'

'Nope,' he says sullenly.

The man at the bar opposite is not so young but he doesn't know who Miriam López is either.

I'm sitting with Juan on my shoulder. He's very fretful. I think he senses how tense I am.

'Don't say anything about the beauty-queen thing, it's stupid. I bet the aunt just made it up.'

This week has completely convinced me that the aunt really did make that part up, but Ramiro remembers that Javier heard it in a bar.

I call Javier from a phone box. Yes, that's how he managed to find the aunt, Nuncia her name was. He doesn't remember anything else, he's already said so. I can sense he is ill at ease at all my questions. I try to stay calm and friendly. 'When I find her, I'll give you a call,' I say cheerfully.

Juan is in the pushchair, bawling his head off, and I can't get him to stop. We go to the plaza to see if he will calm down. I point out the trees to him. He loves staring at leaves.

'I think we should just ask elderly people.'

I go up to two women who are sitting on a bench. I don't have time to beat around the bush. The aunt must have told everybody the same story, I imagine.

'I'm looking for a lady who used to be a model, called Miriam. You don't happen to know her, do you?'

They look at me, startled. I feel obliged to say something. 'I'm writing an article on Argentinian women who were top models, and this Miriam used to live in Coronel Pringles, but I don't have her current address.'

Perhaps I meant Alejandra, so-and-so's daughter? She was a model. 'No, it doesn't matter, I'll just keep asking.'

Juan's crying is unmistakable: he is tired. I get him out of the pushchair and try and calm him down. 'We'd be better off putting him in his carseat and driving around.'

I get in the back seat with him. Ramiro looks at me in the mirror. I admit I'm practically hysterical. I thought it was going to be easier than this. Juan is terribly upset. He's picking up on my anxiety, I can't help it. I sing to him to soothe us both and gradually he settles down and goes to sleep. I clamber over the seat and sit in the front. 'All right then, let's carry on,' I say to Ramiro who is driving in circles around Coronel Pringles, totally lost.

He smiles at me. The shops haven't shut yet and he suggests we look for a chemist's. 'The one over there looks pretty old.' He gets out of the car. But he comes back because they don't know anything at the chemist's, or the supermarket. He spends a little longer in the haberdashery but they don't know either. 'I bet someone will know something at this little grocer's,' he says before going in. He's being so helpful; he's my best friend, the love of my life.

After an encouragingly long time, he gets back into the car, smiling. 'Doña Nuncia died two years ago. Don't look like that; your husband is quite the detective. The woman in the grocer's almost didn't remember Miriam's name, she said it had been years since she'd seen that lovely niece of Doña Nuncia's. Apparently Miriam really was a beauty queen, but now she lives abroad. And that's not all: Nuncia's daughter is called Noemí, and – da dah! – I've got her husband's name and surname.'

I hug him ecstatically. 'You're a genius.'

'The not-so-good news is that she doesn't know if they're still living in Coronel Pringles; she thinks they moved to Buenos Aires. She suggested I try their old house. Maybe the phone is still in their name.'

We check with the phone company and then go straight to Miriam's cousins' house. We cross a small garden, go up some stairs and ring the doorbell several times.

'They're not there.' A well-meaning neighbour has come over. 'They're usually away on Saturdays, and sometimes for the whole weekend.'

'We're looking for the Vignoletos.'

'Oh, no, they don't live here any more.' The neighbour doesn't have the phone number. 'Noemí and I didn't get along.'

I can see she wants to tell us something but I get impatient and turn to go. Just then Ramiro remarks, 'That Noemí; she's got quite a temper!' I'm amazed how well he improvises. 'She got into a row with my mother too.'

'Oh, yes?' said the neighbour, leaning forward eagerly.

'I'm going to check on Juan,' I say, so I don't get the giggles.

I watch Ramiro chatting to the neighbour for a long time. Finally he shakes her hand, a big smile on his face.

He gets back in the car, very pleased with himself. 'I'm going to give up advertising and set up a detective agency. The tenants have got Noemí's number. Apparently Miriam lives in the States. She remembers Miriam as being really stunning and says that Noemí detests her, she's incredibly jealous. She's going to tell her neighbour when she gets back that she should give us Noemí's number when we call.'

Ramiro's already got their phone number from directory enquiries. He wrote it down, otherwise we wouldn't have been able to find the house. They never changed the name on the account.

Ramiro's so good at taking this weight off my shoulders. It's incredible the way he can get me to relax and let go of this driven, frenzied feeling. With his support I know I'll reach the truth.

The operation went well. The treatment now is just to be on the safe side, they said. But how do I know it won't come back? These gringos are so cold, but they tell you the truth, which I like. He gave me the statistics: it recurs in 46 per cent of cases, but in the other 54 per cent it clears up with treatment.

So I've got a fifty-fifty chance of living or dying. Not bad. I always had a fifty-fifty life – until I came here it was a disaster. There were a few good moments, but not many. The time I spent with Liliana and Lili was happy, even though what was happening was so horrific. And if I die, someone will send my letter to Lili. I left it just as it was, the way I wrote it, unopened.

The tenant gave me Noemí's phone number no problem. I rang several times but nobody answered until just now, at five. I spoke to a bloke who told me to ring back after nine thirty. That's so long to wait!

I don't know what to tell Mum so I don't have to see her. I don't want to. It's going to be horrible when I tell her. I'd prefer to do it after I've seen Miriam. Is she my mother? It's weird to think someone I don't know is my mother. Ever since people have described Miriam to me I've been trying to recall what the woman who offered me an ice-cream looked like, but I can't. She's just 'that crazy woman who said I wasn't your mummy'.

How could Mariana keep on reminding me about that? This afternoon I told her she'd better not come round because I have to revise. I'm doing some courses on my own and sitting two exams this December. But I can't carry on making up excuses for ever. At some point I'm going to have to face up to things. Once I find out the truth from Miriam, I'll be able to deal with Mum better. It's my birthday next week and she's bound to want to come over. But is that my real birthday? Was I really born on 15 November? Or was the date concocted, like everything else on my birth certificate?

Delia asked me which hospital issued the birth certificate Javier talked about. But he couldn't remember, and the document must have disappeared along with Dad. According to Delia, they sometimes took the women to hospital to give birth. A girl who'd been admitted to Quilmes hospital in labour was registered under her own name in the paediatrics file, but the ink had been erased and 'NN' was scrawled over the top. However, her real name was still listed on the registry of births. 'They made mistakes,' Delia said. 'That's why sometimes we can follow the trail.' Maybe they took Miriam there. But it's odd that her name has never come up in any of the files.

She told me over the phone that she didn't have Miriam's address because they hadn't seen each other for years, but I kept pressing her. Couldn't we meet up and talk for a bit? She must have known her well, they were cousins.

'I told her I was researching a piece for a magazine, which would probably go into a book. I promised her that if she could tell me anything about Miriam she would be listed in the acknowledgments, and that someone from the magazine would come to take her picture. That got her interest, and she agreed to meet the

342

next day. I took a camera along myself. I had learned to use whatever worked.
Talking to Delia and the other Abuelas had given me some idea of the lengths you
had to go to. Apparently, while Noemí's mother was still alive Noemí used to hear
a bit about Miriam's life, but that stopped when Nuncia died. I asked her to tell me
about her childhood and adolescence.'

That woman Noemí is a real cow. Not only did she refuse to give
me Miriam's address, she badmouthed her. At first she tried to seem
nice, but as time went on and she started reminiscing, she couldn't help
showing how much she resents Miriam. Maybe she's been jealous for
years. I told her a barefaced lie: I said I had some really gorgeous photos
of Miriam and asked if she had any of her when she was a kid? I was
trembling at the prospect of seeing them because of all the tense,
desperate moments I'd spent scanning pictures for likenesses in the
Abuelas' office.

'Ramiro told me that when he was fifteen, Marta took him to see an exhibition
on children who were disappeared or born in captivity. There were photos of the
missing parents and children, and birth certificates and letters, souvenirs of those
mutilated lives. The thing that made the biggest impression on him, which he could
still remember quite clearly, were the unisex child-size silhouettes in black
cardboard with a question mark next to them, which stood for the babies born
in captivity. I asked the Abuelas if they still had the photos from that exhibition
and I spent hours looking for family resemblances to me. They were incredibly
patient. I would point out a girl and they would say, "No, it can't be her, she
disappeared in 78," or, "We know she had a boy."'

'Miriam wasn't all that pretty,' she said crossly. 'She was just photo-
genic.'

She said she didn't have any photos, but I wouldn't give up. I kept
asking her questions, greedy for any scrap of information that might lead
me to Miriam. She reluctantly told me a few things – that she left
Coronel Pringles when she got married and she'd seen her on TV a few
times when she was a model, because her mother always told her when
Miriam was going to be appearing. Nuncia was really fond of Miriam,
although she didn't deserve it.

'Really? Why not?'

She stood up, obviously irritated, and said, 'Why don't you find someone else for this piece of yours? She's not a nice person, she's a selfish, two-faced show-off.'

Noemí knew her well because they had grown up together. Her mother had brought them up as sisters because Miriam's had abandoned her. She was a fast one too, like Miriam.

'A "fast one". I couldn't help making a connection with what Laura had said. I'd often heard Mum use the word "fast", in that way, to mean a loose woman. Someone who wasn't a prostitute but who enjoyed sex would have been a "fast one", according to Mariana.' Luz laughed, rather bitterly.

'Yes, that's the way people used to use it,' Carlos commented.

I asked her right out. 'Do you mean a prostitute?'

'I don't know, I couldn't say so categorically, but she was quite a flirt. And I think she got mixed up in some strange things after she left home. That I'm sure of.'

'At that point she went into great detail about how her and her mother's house had been smashed up by some men she was sure were from the police, although they weren't in uniform. They were looking for Miriam.'

My heart does a somersault. A swat team. So the armed forces were after Miriam, then. I wasn't wrong.

'I think she got away. Maybe she was mixed up in drugs. I always thought she was,' she went on. Old sourpuss. 'But Mum liked to think she had left because she'd fallen in love with an American.'

'So that wasn't true?'

She shrugged. Apparently it was, because Nuncia had been to visit once. Miriam had sent her a plane ticket and she'd stayed with them for a few days.

I could have slapped her. How could she not have the address if her mother had been there? She had lost it. She couldn't even remember which city it was in the States. I listed a few. Cleveland sounded familiar, but so did Chicago and she didn't know if it was because of Miriam or because of the films she'd seen on TV.

'They're rolling in money,' she said, her voice hollow with envy.

They had told her mother that their money came from a hotel the husband owned. But her mother was so naïve! Noemí couldn't get it out of her head that it came from drug trafficking or something like that. As

344

far as she knew, Miriam had never been back to Argentina, so she must have had a reason for staying away.

As I was leaving, she asked about the photos. I got out the camera and took a few shots. 'It'll be such a pity if I can't get in touch with Miriam, because the article might not come out,' I said, trying to put pressure on her. If she remembered anything else, she should call. I gave her my card.

'Now where do I look?' I ask Delia. I'm at the Abuelas' office. They're no longer surprised to see me here. Juan is crawling around the room at top speed, picking up everything he finds and sticking it in his mouth.

Just then it occurs to me that I should get in touch with Dolores. Could they give me her address? Maybe she'll know something more. Delia says that she will write to her personally, explaining the situation, and that she'll let me know how Dolores responds.

'The trail seemed to come to a dead end with Noemí, Miriam's cousin. There were no other leads left. A few months went by, but I never stopped looking for a single day. I would scour the testimonies, comparing dates. Delia and Julia, another of the Abuelas, agreed with me that the business of the swat team was a sign that Miriam could have been a victim of the regime. But since it took place at the beginning of '77, after I was born, it was hard to work out what had happened. We checked the archives again. We tried to piece the story together like a puzzle.'

'Didn't you talk to Mariana about it?'

Luz turned and looked the other way. The memory was obviously a painful one.

'I put the conversation off as long as possible. I couldn't bear the thought of it. In the end, it happened almost by accident, the day Juan started walking.'

I reach out to him, and he toddles two or three steps towards me, chuckles and falls over. We start again. I stand him back up and let go and he takes a few steps on his own. He thinks it's hilarious. We're both laughing. I'm so proud of him. The doorbell rings and I run to answer it. Delia said that if she had time she would come round.

'Surprise, surprise,' Mum says with a smile. We're supposed to be pleased to see her.

She has come back from Punta del Este to Buenos Aires to keep Daniel company. He has to host some Americans for a few days, so she's taking the opportunity to visit her daughter and grandson.

It bothers me that she's here at all, and the fact that she calls us her daughter and grandson, without batting an eyelid, enrages me. I wonder if she actually believes it, after lying for so many years? But I give none of this away, merely saying accusingly, 'Don't talk about your grandson, you hardly know him. He's walking already and you had no idea.'

I'll make up anything to avoid saying it. Am I afraid? Yes. I prefer complaining like this, even though I have no justification – I'm the one who's spent months coming up with reasons to keep her away, and if I do see her it's only when there are a lot of people around, to avoid a situation in which we could talk.

'Show Mariana how you walk,' she says to Juan, as if she hadn't heard me. 'Come on, sweetheart, show her.'

'Why do you call yourself Mariana and not Granny?' I challenge her.

What a stupid thing to say. I barely ever called Amalia 'Granny'; you're clutching at straws, Luz. But I carry on regardless. I tell her the usual thing would be for her to call herself 'Granny'. And then she says something that really gets me: that the word Granny is so vulgar.

'You call yourself Mariana, as if you weren't his grandmother.' I'm going to say it; I'm actually going to say it. 'Because you aren't. You aren't his grandmother.'

She gives me a frightened look. 'What do you mean?' She's pretending to be offended, but she's scared.

I accuse her of never having told me, of deceiving me all my life, and she stares at me wide-eyed and says nothing. I take Juan to his room and put him in his playpen. He knows already, because I've told him, but I don't want him to witness this conversation. When I get back to the living room she has regrouped and goes on the attack.

'Luz, I don't believe in psychologists, but maybe you ought to see one. Saying such awful things – I just have to assume that you're unbalanced because of your hormones.'

'How can you carry on lying, Mum? I saw your child's birth certificate. It was a boy and he was stillborn.'

Her face crumples and her beautiful, smooth skin is suddenly covered in wrinkles. I feel a moment's pity. She didn't know herself at the time, I remember.

'They deceived you, too, didn't they?' I say, trying to be conciliatory. 'But in the end you found out.'

Who told me, she wants to know, who could have been so incredibly evil and cruel? 'That dreadful woman Laura, it must be.' She falls into a rage. Both of us are shouting and demanding things. She wants me to say whether or not Laura told me and I want to know what she found out about my real mother. Juan is screaming in the other room. I go and pick him up and try to quiet him. I see her weeping bitterly on the sofa, her rage spent. I don't want to give in to pity. I ask her to calm down, making a huge effort to speak gently, although everything inside me is on fire. 'For Juan's sake, it's better if we talk this over calmly, not with both of us in a state.'

'What do you expect, after what you've said? You still hold it against me, after I devoted years of my life to you. I gave you everything, I had to put up with your damn sulky faces all the time and your disobedience and your bizarre behaviour – and that's putting it mildly – and now when you find out, instead of saying thank you, you act as if I'd done something wrong.'

'I just think you should have told me.'

She gets to her feet and picks up her handbag as I'm about to fetch some water for Juan.

'Wait,' I order. 'I'll be back in a second.'

I put Juan back in his playpen and go to meet her. Her martyred air makes me indignant. She'd better go, she announces, before she says something awful.

'Like what?' I snap back. 'That I was stolen from a defenceless woman? Tell me,' and I grab hold of her dress as she moves forward. I get a painful flashback of myself as a little girl, hanging on to her dress. I don't want to have this feeling, just when I've dared to tell her, so I shout at her instead. 'Your father must have stolen me, and you know perfectly well what your father was.'

'Although, I tell you, I'm still not sure if she knows. I think she never wanted to know what her father did or where I really came from. In any case, she never said.'

'Don't you dare make insinuations about my father. He was so fond of you. You should be endlessly grateful to him. Thanks to him, you had a mother and a family.'

'Oh, yeah? Who asked him to do that? Did he do it for my sake? Or so that his little girl wouldn't have to suffer?'

She stalks off in the direction of the hall, and turns to look at me one last time. There's a mixture of pity and rage on her face, and her voice is tremulous.

'Luz, I feel sorry for you. You are very sick. When you come to your senses, call me.'

'Yes, I did ring. I asked her about my real mother. She said she didn't know who she was. Someone who didn't want me, that's all she knew.'

'Did you ask her about Miriam?'

'Yes. One day I went to her house to save Juan being upset. She said she didn't know who Miriam was, but I thought she started when she heard the name. I couldn't be sure, though. Just about everything I said to Mariana put her on edge. After a few pointless arguments, I avoided seeing her altogether. It didn't help me with my search and the conversations with her were killing me. I had . . . I still have very mixed feelings about Mariana. Sometimes I feel sorry for her. And she feels sorry for me. Sometimes I miss her.' Luz's voice faded, as if she were talking to herself. 'I wonder if she misses me? I don't know . . . maybe. It's strange, the way our affections work.'

I don't move, I just stand there paralysed for a long time until eventually I manage to walk to Juan's room. His smile calms me down. Yes, sweetheart, we'll practise again. One step, and another and another. I love you so much. We're going to show Daddy how well you can walk. He's going to be thrilled to bits.

I've got to go back for more treatment: just a few sessions, they said. Why do I need them? They said that I'd already had enough and the danger had passed. Here I am looking death in the face again and the same old anxiety returns. What if Lili doesn't believe the letter I wrote her? I have to go and see her so I can convince her in person.

Why has this thought come back now so strongly? Because if I die, I'll never know if Liliana's message ever reached her daughter. I feel fairly fit at the moment, I can travel. Later on, who knows? I can't tell her over the phone.

How old is Lili now? She must be twenty-one.

'It's pointless now,' Frank said last night. 'Her parents are dead. And so is the bastard who kidnapped her. He can't be sent to jail any more, which would be the main reason to tell her.'

'How do you know?'

'I didn't tell you because I didn't want to stir up bad memories. When I went to Aerolíneas to buy our plane tickets over a year ago, I read about it by chance in an Argentinian newspaper. They even did an obituary for him! For that murderer! I wasn't sure I wanted to go to Argentina, and you didn't seem too keen either, in fact you weren't keen at all.' It's funny how well Frank knows me. 'And then, as I was waiting, I came across that article. It was the last straw. I vowed never to set foot in the country again. I'd rather keep my fond memories. So I gave my brother power of attorney and insisted that they come and see us instead.'

I explained that I was afraid if I didn't talk to Lili now, I wasn't sure if I'd be able to later on. 'I could put off starting the treatment for ten days, the doctor has agreed.'

Frank thinks I'm overreacting; the treatment is just a precaution, I'm not seriously ill. He doesn't think I'm going to die soon. But I do. And I don't want to die without seeing Lili. 'Please understand. I want to meet her now she's grown up. And I'll only tell her the truth if it seems right, if there's a good reason to do so.'

Frank doesn't understand or agree with me.

I'm revising as hard as I can. I'm studying for these two exams by myself, and then in April I'll register as a normal student again. Marta has offered to look after Juan for a few hours when I have to go in to the university. And Delia and the Abuelas have said that I can leave him there for a while too. Everybody seems to agree that I should go back to my degree. They don't say so, but it's clear they'd be relieved if I stopped constantly chasing ghosts. But I carry on. It's as if giving up would mean losing myself for ever, never knowing who I am. I've still got one hope left. Dolores is coming to Buenos Aires in a few days. Maybe I'll be able to find out something more from her.

I am on my way. Fortunately Frank didn't get cross with me. 'You never change, do you?' he said with a smile. 'Take care, you nutcase, and make sure you ring me.'

I promised to come back in a week. I've got to restart the treatment.

I'm trying to work out how to see her. Since I've got the address, I just need an excuse to go to the house. I could say I was a friend of her father's. Yes, that would be the best thing. No, I'd better ring first. But what if she tells Mariana? She knows that Miriam López was the person who tried to kidnap Lili, because Eduardo told her. All right then, I'll say I'm Miriam Harrison. What will Lili be like now? Will she believe me? Will I have the guts to tell her?

I've got to revise, I've got to. The exam is tomorrow, and it's not helping that my chest is constricted and I'm so tense. I know it would be good for me to finish my degree and carry on with my life. Juan, the university, Ramiro. What room does that leave for my search? It's like throwing in the towel, giving up.

The search has taken up a huge part of my life for over a year now. What am I looking for? My mother and father. But why am I looking for them in the testimonies? Maybe it wasn't like that, after all; maybe Delia and Ramiro are right, and my mother's just some girl who got pregnant by accident and gave me up.

I'm feeling low. It makes me sad to think about her, for both our sakes. If she is alive, why didn't she ever come and see me? And if she's not, what happened to her? Did she die? Was she killed?

I ring Delia and tell her I'm upset. 'How can I be sad because someone I don't even know might be dead?' She tells me to study and be patient. I may get a surprise some day.

'Some of those women are incredibly patient, you know. They can spend years searching and never give up.'

'What about Dolores?' I ask anxiously. She knows that Dolores is due to arrive in Buenos Aires any day now.

'You just concentrate on studying, Luz, and take care of Juan. That's the best you can do.'

Luckily I'm feeling less down now. Juan staggers drunkenly towards me. He's such a sweet little boy. 'Come with me, I'm going to answer the door.'

It's a dark-haired woman, gorgeous-looking and very elegantly dressed, who says nothing. She looks at me and Juan and smiles shyly. I stare at her questioningly.

'Luz? Luz Iturbe?'

I nod. She looks at Juan.

'And this is . . . ?'

'Juan, my son.'

I wonder who this woman can be. She's staring at us with such a peculiar look on her face.

'You don't know me.' I can barely hear her. 'I am . . . or was . . . a friend of your father's.'

Dolores! I think at once and open the door. Delia must have wanted to give me a surprise. I tell her to come in and sit down.

'Who gave you my address? Delia?'

'No. I think it must have been your husband. A few months ago.'

'I didn't know.'

Ramiro must have got in touch with Dolores and asked her to visit. He probably didn't say anything to me so I wouldn't build my hopes up.

'I . . . rang a few months ago and he gave me the address.'

She rang me? I don't understand at all. Isn't she Dolores Collado? No, she says, she's Mrs Harrison. She hasn't been in Buenos Aires for a long time. 'I left more or less at the same time that your father died. Round about then.'

'She made a few incoherent comments. That she had seen him the day he passed away, and then she snorted. She shrugged, and I remembered the time I'd heard Javier do exactly the same thing. She said they had talked a long time that day and that he had told her a lot of things. But she didn't tell me who she was. Her surname didn't mean anything to me. She broke off to pat Juan on the head. Then he tripped over and bumped himself and started crying.'

351

'It's OK, sweetheart, let me kiss it better, there you go, all gone.' But Juan goes on crying. Then the woman who's done nothing but stammer so far does something unexpected: she starts to sing a nursery rhyme. '*Manuelita vivía en Pehuajó, pero un día se marchó.*' The sound of her voice has a strange effect on me. I can't tell if I'm moved or surprised. I look at her and she stops suddenly. Juan does too.

'Then she started talking and I couldn't stop to analyse what was happening to me; she went on about how sweet Juan was and what lovely eyes he had, just like me and Liliana.'

'The same eyes as who?' said Lili, visibly shaken. Now I'm scared. I've got to slow down. I was doing well talking about Eduardo, her father, or at least the one she knows, and all of a sudden I launched into that. Lili repeats her question. I quickly invent something. 'Oh, just a friend of mine, one I was very fond of. She had eyes like you, sparkly, as if they were full of fireflies. It just reminded me of her, that's all.'

Lili gives me a strange look. She is very tense. Her voice has turned sharp, the same as Liliana's.

'Who the hell are you? I don't understand. A friend of my father's, you said. Do you mean Eduardo Iturbe?'

'Of course.'

'And what's your name? You only gave your surname.'

If I say Miriam, she'll know I'm the person who tried to kidnap her and she'll get upset. I look down and don't answer.

'Are you going to answer me or not?'

'Miriam Harrison.'

'Miriam,' Lili repeats in a dazed voice, 'Miriam. You mean to say you're Miriam?' She paces round the room and then sits down opposite me and stares. I assume somebody must have told her all about me, or maybe she remembers the time when I said her mother wasn't her mother.

'Miriam López?' She's almost screaming.

I nod and ask her to listen to me, please, yes, it's me, the person who met her at the school gate a couple of times, but I want to explain why I did that, will she please listen. Lili's eyes are shining and she sits down on the floor in front of me, on the carpet.

'Are you my mother?'

I can't believe my ears.

Miriam bursts into tears. I feel tremendous compassion towards this woman. Maybe it's not like I thought at all, maybe she just gave me up and that's why she can't tell me about it. I start crying myself. 'It doesn't matter, really, don't feel guilty. I'm happy you've come. I just need to know, I need you to tell me. Are you my mother?'

'No, I'm not. Your mother was Liliana something, I never knew her surname, and your father's name was Carlos Squirru and they were killed because they wanted a fairer society.'

'Ever since that day I've been checking the testimonies of every Carlos and Liliana I could find. We went off on the wrong track several times. I rang all the Squirrus in the phone book. In the end, a distant cousin of yours confirmed that you had been living in Spain for years. And here I am. Or rather, here we are.' Luz grinned, triumphantly.

EPILOGUE
1998

O N 3 AUGUST 1998, Nora Mendilarzu de Ortiz stepped
hesitatingly into the Abuelas' office. She didn't know where to
start. She would have liked to take Carlos at his word, but the whole
thing seemed so bizarre that she didn't want to raise her hopes in vain.
She gave her name and asked if she could talk to someone. Delia invited
her in.

She was there, she explained, because . . . she had received a peculiar
phone call from the man who had been her daughter's husband. 'My
daughter disappeared during the military dictatorship. She was pregnant,
but her baby boy was stillborn.' She had found this out many years ago.
Her son-in-law had suggested that she go and see the Abuelas because
. . . 'He said the strangest thing – apparently some girl went to see him in
Madrid, where he lives now.'

Delia's face lit up. Nora tried to carry on, but Delia was so excited she
cut her off.

'What is your son-in-law's name?'

'Carlos Squirru.'

Nora couldn't understand the other woman's reaction: she stood up
with tears in her eyes and embraced her.

'Then you must be Liliana's mother . . . How wonderful!'

'So you know who my daughter was?'

'I don't know her surname but we've been trying to trace her for a
long time.'

'Her name was Liliana Ortiz.'

Nora had spent ages trying to work out how to explain the phone call from Carlos and now this woman was talking non-stop. She seemed to know much more about the situation than Nora herself. She knew Luz, the girl Carlos had mentioned, very well. Stumbling over her words, Delia explained what a wonderful person Luz was, how determined she'd been and how desperately she had wanted to find out where she came from. She told Nora a stream of unrelated anecdotes. Nora listened in silence.

Suddenly Delia looked at her. She realised that she hadn't given her time to recover from the shock.

'I'm sorry, I'm a bit shaken up. The proper thing to do now would be for you to take a blood test to check for compatibility. They already have Luz's data at the lab.'

As she spoke, Delia rummaged through her desk drawer. Yes, there it was. She passed the photo to Nora. 'This is Luz, with her son, Juan. This is incredible. You're so young to be a great-grandmother. How old are you, if you don't mind my asking?'

'Sixty-five.'

'Luz had the test done, but needless to say there was no match for her family's blood in the genetic databank. There are so many questions I'd love to ask you. But it would be better for you to get the test done first. It would be a huge relief for Luz.'

Nora looked at the photo without uttering a sound.

'No,' she said at last. Her words were almost inaudible, choked by emotion. She didn't think it was necessary, she went on, staring at the image in her hand. Not after what Delia had said and now this. She touched Luz's face in the picture with her finger. 'It's Liliana. She's got the same eyes, the same way of holding herself.'

Finally Nora was able to put the photograph down and look at Delia. Her voice was firmer. 'I can't tell you how happy I am to get this news, out of the blue. I don't need proof. I believe that Luz is my granddaughter. I'm absolutely positive. But if you think it's important to her, I've no objection to taking the blood test.'

'Can I hug you?' asked Delia. 'I'm so thrilled. This is the first time we've found a grandmother.'

A NOTE ON THE AUTHOR

Born in Buenos Aires, Elsa Osorio is an award-winning writer and teacher. Winner of the Premio Nacional de Literatura in Argentina for this novel, she now lives in Madrid.

A NOTE ON THE TYPE

The text of this book is set in Bembo. This type was first used in 1495 by the Venetian printer Aldus Manutius for Cardinal Bembo's *De Aetna*, and was cut for Manutius by Francesco Griffo. It was one of the types used by Claude Garamond (1480–1561) as a model for his Romain de L'Université, and so it was the forerunner of what became standard European type for the following two centuries. Its modern form follows the original types and was designed for Monotype in 1929.